# A PATRIOTIC NIGHTMARE

# A PATRIOTIC NIGHTMARE

## A Tale of Domestic Terrorism

by Don E. Post

SANTA FE

*The events, people, and incidents in this story are the sole product of the author's imagination. The story is fictional and any resemblance to individuals living or dead is purely coincidental.*



Sunstone books may be purchased for educational, business, or sales promotional use. For information please write: Special Markets Department, Sunstone Press, P.O. Box 2321, Santa Fe, New Mexico 87504-2321.

---

Library of Congress Cataloging-in-Publication Data:

Post, Don E.
A patriotic nightmare : a tale of domestic terrorism / by Don E. Post.
p. cm.
ISBN 0-86534-464-7 (hardcover : alk. paper)
1. Terrorism—Fiction. I. Title.
PS3616.O838P38 2005
813'.6—dc22

2005007669

---

**WWW.SUNSTONEPRESS.COM**
SUNSTONE PRESS / POST OFFICE BOX 2321 / SANTA FE, NM 87504-2321 /USA
(505) 988-4418 / *ORDERS ONLY* (800) 243-5644 / FAX (505) 988-1025

# A PATRIOTIC NIGHTMARE

# 1

**PORT EL KANTAOUI, TUNISIA**
Monday, February 3

Sunday night Yuri Tavanovich received an urgent call from a man in Rome urging him to meet a client in Tunisia to discuss a new construction project—the code for an arms purchase. He grabbed the earliest flight he could using a forged French passport to move rapidly through passport control. He then rented a car and enjoyed the three-hour drive from Nabeul to Port El Kantaoui along the eastern Mediterranean coast of Tunisia.

The day was beginning to fade as the former Russian KGB agent settled into his room at the El Hana Palace Hotel and anxiously awaited his meeting. His room provided an unfettered view over the yacht basin. He walked onto his balcony and gazed out across the blue Mediterranean to the east and watched, transfixed, as a deep, rich, burnt orange sky seemed to explode across the heavens as the sun sank in the west. The azure sea responded surrealistically to the sun's display, and he felt his tensions melt away.

As he watched boats enter the harbor after a day of sailing or fishing, his gaze fell on a group of children sitting on the wall that edged the cliff north of the hotel. They all wore short, faded pants, tee shirts with holes, and no shoes and were pointing to various boats in the harbor, imagining owning a boat when they grew up. Their giggles and excited talk echoed across the basin and mixed with distant calls of fishermen and boaters in the marina below.

Yuri turned to observe sea gulls gliding blissfully across the orange Mediterranean sky. As he absorbed the scene, he kept looking for the arrival of his Arab buyers who were supposed to arrive aboard a two hundred-forty-five-foot motor yacht named The Medallion flying a Turkish flag. Giving up, he went inside.

The sharp ring of the phone startled Yuri. He had fallen asleep. Picking up the phone, he heard a deep baritone voice softly ask, "Yurgi Tavanbich?"

"Nyet, no, no. Name is Yuri Tavanovich," he said, slowly emphasizing the correct pronunciation.

"Okay, okay. Yurgi Tabanobisch," the speaker replied, still mispronouncing his name.

Stupid camel herder, Yuri thought. No wonder they can't do anything but kill each other off. As soon as all that oil's gone, they'll be back herding camels and goats.

The speaker on the line continued in a monotone, staccato voice. "I glad you speak English. We don't speak French or Russian. We arrive and moor at northern edge of marina, near end of jetty. Why don't you come dinner with us nine o'clock? We have powerboat pick up you. Pilot of boat is young man, Ali Ashwari."

"First, I must tell you that I will not come if any member of the Al-Qaida is present. We just can't take the chance."

"There is no Al-Qaida present. We understand that issue."

"Okay. Spahsseebah. Thank you, that will be fine." For a split second Yuri's native language showed itself. The Soviet government had all KGB agents learn English and he had found it a valuable tool on many occasions. French, however, gave him a tough time. All the French people he knew laughed at his pronunciation, which didn't encourage him to learn the language. He cursed them in Russian to their faces while smiling apologetically. "The French are stupid idiots," he muttered aloud.

He glanced at his wristwatch. An hour and a half to wait. He walked over to his valise on the bed and took out his binoculars. Then he turned off the lamp for total darkness and went out on the balcony to see if he could spot the yacht. He scanned the darkening marina. The ship was easily identified. It dwarfed the other boats. The yacht's lights lit up the area for a hundred yards. What a beauty, he thought. But it was so large it drew attention to itself, which seemed to Yuri like a stupid thing to do when one is trying to buy arms on the black market. Four men with guns guarded the decks, nicely dressed in white slacks and navy blazers. They would just have to put up with this old KGB agent in blue jeans.

Yuri grabbed his light briefcase, stuffed pictures of the weapons he hawked into a side pocket and walked leisurely down to the marina. He arrived at the jetty's small dock a few minutes before nine. A young Tunisian couple kissed and fondled each other in the dark. Yuri walked as far away from the couple as he could, leaned against the rail and waited. The couple, chagrined that their private space had been invaded, soon departed to find another sanctuary for their passion. Yuri leaned over the guardrail. Intermittent laughter from a nearby yacht and water lapping against the rocks of the jetty were the only sounds that broke the silence.

Finally, at nine-twenty, a motorboat approached and a young man shot a broad spotlight beam along the platform until he found Yuri. "Mister Tabanobich?"

"Yes, I am here." He quickly climbed aboard and settled into a seat. There seemed little sense trying to correct the young man's pronunciation of his name. "I assume you are Ali."

"Yes," the young man answered as he slowly moved away from the small dock, turned and piloted the small craft out to The Medallion without saying another word.

As Yuri stepped aboard the yacht, a man who introduced himself as Mr. Ghaleb stuck out his hand in greeting. Yuri recognized the voice as that on the phone from Rome. Ghaleb led him up a set of stairs to the second deck and a large dining room where nine other men sat. They all rose when Yuri entered. Ghaleb turned and said, "Mr. Yurgi, not necessary for you to know our names, yeah? Only matter important is we are not of Al-Qaida and we will put U.S. dollars in your company account before you ship merchandise. Okay? If you have what we need and price is right. You understand the reason for secrecy, yeah? Okay for you?"

"Yeah. Okay." Yuri glanced around at the others, who all nodded and grinned. He doubted any of them understood much English.

"We eat, and then talk business, yeah?" Ghaleb said. The men seated themselves and a young man in a white, v-necked, loose-fitting cotton tunic, asked Yuri what drink he would like. Yuri asked for vodka.

While waiting to eat, Yuri and Ghaleb carried on a polite conversation about the yacht. Ghaleb said that he and his Arab associates liked to meet in Tunisia because they could come and go without government interference. Although a Muslim, the country's president, Ben Ali, head of the Constitutional Democratic Rally Party, had insisted that fundamental Islamic groups not use his country to foster their terrorist aims. He feared American retaliation. In return for being left alone to run his own country, he tried to provide funds and cover for various Muslim groups, but had found that increasingly difficult since September 11th, 2001. And the borders with Libya stayed open and uncontrolled. Yet, Ghaleb explained, they tried to meet at a different place each time to keep their enemies confused.

"Mr. Yurgi, why did you and Russian friends start business in France?" Ghaleb asked.

Amazed by Ghaleb's butchering his name again, Yuri let out a sigh and said slowly, "We are all former KGB colleagues and selling arms after the fall of the Soviet Union was all we knew to do. Our founder, General Vladimir Chekhov, got contracts from a number of Russian and Ukrainian arms manufacturers to handle foreign sales, so we went to work."

"But France?" Ghaleb asked with a quizzical look.

"Yes, France. General Chekhov said we needed to keep our assets in a more stable economy and he had a lot of experience and friends in France. So, we moved the business to Marseille. There are a lot of foreigners there, so we can go and come as needed."

"Don't the French know what you are doing?" Ghaleb continued.

"No, not to our knowledge. As you know, we are registered as a construction company and have French engineers that do legitimate projects."

"Ah, since the America's World Trade Center was destroyed and the Americans removed Saddam from office we must all be very careful," Ghaleb whispered.

"True," Yuri said, whispering back and nodding assent.

This seemed to satisfy Mr. Ghaleb. He looked around, shouted some orders in Arabic and immediately the food started arriving.

Yuri had thought they would never eat. Yuri looked at his watch and saw it was almost midnight. Might as well be having breakfast!

"Mr. Yogi," Ghaleb said, arms flying in different directions for emphasis, "We hired Tunisia's finest chef to prepare food. You will like food, yeah? We love to meet here. Food is very good!" Ghaleb and several of his partners laughed boisterously.

Yuri had trouble with the spicy food. He wondered how these people's stomachs could digest the stuff. He ate enough to be polite. After dinner the group moved to the aft deck. Yuri's chair faced the shoreline whose rocky cliffs, subtly lit by the soft glow of lights from homes and buildings, created an enchanting backdrop. The nervous bark of a dog pierced the hypnotic silence of the cool Mediterranean night from time to time.

As silence descended on the small group gathered on deck, Ghaleb turned toward Yuri, "How big order can your company handle now?"

"We have one hundred million U.S. dollars worth of stock. Most is surplus materials."

"What condition is surplus?" Ghaleb asked.

"Forty percent is new. The remainder is used, but totally reconditioned. We had each military depot clean, repair and pack each item for storage. They are in excellent shape and we will guarantee each weapon with money back," Yuri answered.

A long silence ensued as the men contemplated Yuri's comments. A discussion in Arabic broke out. Finally, Ghaleb asked, "Give us run down of what you have now, yeah?"

Yuri thought about the best way to do this, and then pulled pictures out of his briefcase, placing each on the deck in front of Ghaleb as he talked. In Arabic, Ghaleb asked for more light.

Yuri said cautiously, "To start, we have many, many AKM-7.62-mm assault rifles. You know this is newest replacement for the AK-47s. The weapon weighs less than old AK-47s and is from new lightweight aluminum and plastic mags." Yuri pointed at the pictures with his right index finger as he spoke and then looked up at the men to see if they had understood.

He continued, "The stock is straighter, which gives the shooter better control. The gas cylinder is better; there is rate-of-fire control alongside the trigger, a rear sight increased to one thousand meters rather than the former eight hundred and a better, detachable bayonet." Again Yuri looked at the men and waited. Then he stood, stretched and said, "We have folding-stock version, the AKMS. Their range is three hundred meters."

He paused to let Ghaleb translate and once each nodded understanding, he continued his presentation, showing more pictures of the armaments, including tanks, armored vehicles and air-defense systems.

The men passed the pictures around and talked in Arabic for fifteen to twenty minutes. Periodically they had Ghaleb ask Yuri a question in English. Finally, Yuri handed each a price list. The unit price had been listed for each weapon, followed by a ten percent reduction in cost per twenty-five AKMs and machine guns, a ten percent reduction per ten support weapons and so forth.

After the men discussed the prices, Yuri added, "You may inspect these weapons before taking possession. Your money will be returned on any item not same as my representation. Our prices are below what can be purchased through the Chinese, the Germans or any other dealers. I am sure you know about price of armaments very well. We will deal honestly with you because we want more of your business." Again, there was a period of silence.

Finally, at around two o'clock in the morning, Ghaleb stood, came over to

Yuri, stuck out his hand and said, "Thanks you for coming to meet us. Let us talk and get back tomorrow for lunch, yeah? Okay?"

"Da. Yes, fine," stammered a bleary-eyed Yuri. Ghaleb put his arm around Yuri's shoulder and ushered him to the stairs where the boat waited to take him to shore.

Back in his hotel room Yuri fell asleep fully clothed as soon as he hit the bed.

Yuri awakened to the sun streaming through the French doors to the balcony. His watch showed eight-thirty. Rarely did he sleep so late. Voices and motors could be heard coming from the marina. He called room service and ordered coffee and toast and then took a shower. The waiter arrived just as he finished shaving. He tipped the young boy and then carried his coffee and toast onto the balcony to enjoy the morning. After a few sips he suddenly noticed that The Medallion had disappeared. "That's strange," he muttered in disbelief. He jumped up and got his binoculars. Scanning the Mediterranean from north to south it seemed evident that the buyers had left.

Puzzled, he hastily finished dressing and then went out on the balcony and stood for a few moments trying to collect his thoughts. He decided to take a walk through the village and wait until noon for Ghaleb and his friends to show up. If they didn't, he would leave. He felt a strange discomfort. Something was wrong. As he carefully studied the room, it hit him. He had not left the binoculars on the dressing table with the lens-caps off last night. He always put everything back in place. He knew that for sure. He looked in his valise to see if he could detect any other disturbance. He kept traveler's checques strapped to his body and never left anything of value in his room. Maybe some of the hotel staff tried to find something valuable. Maybe they used the binoculars for their own pleasure. Ahh, maybe the Arabs had searched his stuff.

His plane tickets seemed undisturbed. Yet, his KGB instincts registered alarm. He felt a chill. He strapped his plane ticket to his body with his traveler's checques, stashed everything else neatly in his valise, then rigged the rest so he could tell if they had been tampered with and left for a walk through the village.

Returning to his room at eleven-thirty, he checked the valise and found that all the traps seemed intact. Maybe I'm too cautious, he thought. He took his binoculars, stepped out on the balcony and scanned the Marina. He found the yacht anchored closer to shore. The moment he spotted her, the phone rang. Ghaleb's cheerful voice asked, "How are you this morning?"

"Fine. You?"

"Oh, we are fine. We motor down coast and moor in secluded bay. One can't be too cautious."

"Yes, I wondered where you had gone."

"Can I come your room and maybe we come to agreement, yeah? Maybe we order something to eat there, yeah?"

"Yes. You know I'm in room three-forty-eight." A slight laugh could be heard, then Ghaleb hung up. Yuri realized that he should have brought a de-bugging device. "Stupid," he said aloud, as he swung his fist in the air. He quickly searched the phone, lamps, table, bed and all other nooks and crannies that make nice homes for bugs. Nothing.

Twenty minutes later Ghaleb knocked on the door. Yuri ordered a light lunch for the two as they settled down to talk business at the small corner table. In a quiet whisper Ghaleb said, "Yuri, we want first order for fifty million U.S. dollars in arms. Give banking information and we can put one million in advance." Yuri pulled out a piece of paper with the company letterhead, indicating the Swiss bank, banker, account number and information for wire transfers. Ghaleb slid the paper into a manila folder and stuffed it into his briefcase, then added, "If this shipment goes well, we will buy about one hundred million dollars more over the next few months."

Yuri nodded. "Good, we will be happy to help you."

"In addition to arms you show us, we want three-thousand blast and three-thousand fragmentation land-mines," Ghaleb said. "The frags can be variety of regular trip-wire, above ground, and boundary and directional type. Let us know what you have. And can you get us Italian plastic mines?"

"I'll send you list of what we have. I don't know if we can get Italian mines, but I'll let you know. Since the Americans went to war against you people it is difficult to get armaments like we use to. Send the rest of the order to me in Marseille," Yuri said matter-of-factly. "We will confirm receipt of funds. You must arrange to have someone inspect the cargo at the warehouse in Odessa. They can watch them loaded. We will pay the expenses of four of your inspectors while in Odessa. We can also arrange someone with us who speaks Arabic, if you need. Upon loading, but before the ship leaves the harbor, we will expect notice that the rest of the funds have been sent to our Swiss account. Is all acceptable?"

"Yes, agreeable," Ghaleb said with a nod of his head. Then he rose and shook Yuri's hand. "We look forward to business with you. Good-bye."

Yuri, relieved that the Arab had left and elated over the deal, walked to the balcony and watched as Ghaleb, joined by two of the bodyguards from the boat, walked down to the marina, climbed into the small motorboat and sped toward The Medallion. Why are the Mideasterners always looking back at the terrible times? he wondered. They take revenge, then those people take revenge and the killing never ends. He remembered how relieved he had been when his country pulled out of Afghanistan. What a nightmare. And now he's selling arms to those he once fought against and whose aim is to bring down the West. The Americans hadn't helped themselves by getting impatient with the diplomatic path. I guess it's their instant gratification culture. Now every Arab is a potential killer. Ah well, this is a dirty business, but someone has to provide the weapons. Screw them all!

Yuri grabbed his valise, checked out and headed back to Tunis to catch his flight home. As he flew out over the blue Mediterranean for the short hop to Marseille, he gazed out at the beauty of the area and thought how easily arms sold in this world. But he couldn't shake the uncomfortable feeling that something seemed amiss.

In a modest room on the third floor of the U.S. Embassy at 144 Avenue de la Liberte, in Tunis, CIA agent and Paris station chief, Mark Easton, encrypted a message about Yuri Tavanovich's arms sale for his colleagues in Langley, Virginia. The CIA's French counterpart had been monitoring Yuri's construction firm and Russian staff in Marseille since opening day. The French and the CIA knew Yuri's group was selling Russian arms to terrorist organizations, but neither the arms nor the funds ended up in France so the French had not been able to take legal action. The French did the surveillance and the CIA chased the guns and money. Yuri's group had been strangely silent since the World Trade Center bombing. The Americans were persuaded that their demonstration of power in Iraq had silenced them for good. The French had notified the U.S. Embassy in Paris the night Ghaleb called Yuri Tavanovich's home and asked to meet in Tunisia. Alarmed, Mark had immediately hopped a French military flight to Tunis and picked up Yuri's trail as he left the airport terminal the next morning.

Mark had observed Yuri checking in at the El Hana Palace Hotel and he had checked in at the nearby Diar El Andaloui hotel, and then driven to Yuri's hotel.

He had a cup of coffee in the main dining room, and then roamed the hotel grounds to gain familiarity with the environment. He noticed the hotel manager eyeing him suspiciously. Finally the manager approached him to see if he could help with anything. Mark explained that he needed a site for a small convention of his company's salesmen and was deeply enchanted with his fine hotel. Mark handed the man a business card presenting himself as a marketing consultant to a leading French cosmetics firm.

At this point, the manager lost his suspicious edge and became eager to go over every detail of his hotel's design, pointing out all the nooks and crannies of the property. Mark took detailed notes. During the course of the conversation Mark mentioned that he had planned to meet a colleague there, but he hadn't shown up. Had any European types checked in lately? The manager walked back to the front desk and asked the clerk the name of the European who had checked in earlier. The clerk looked at his computer screen and said, "The man is Russian because his name is "Ta-van-o-veetch."

"No, that's not my friend. But is that man middle age, thinning black hair, about five feet ten inches?"

The clerk and manager looked at each other, shrugged their shoulders, held out their arms, palms up and with a tilt of the head to one side said, "No, sorry, this man did not look like that."

"He seemed a strong and stout man, the manager said. "He had reddish cheeks like the people in Scandinavia or Russia. His brown hair had fallen out a lot. How do you say...uhh."

"Balding?"

"Yes, yes, balding,"

"How old is he?"

The two hotel men looked at each other intently, wrinkled their brows, pulling their necks down into their shoulders as they shrugged again. Then the manager said, "Maybe middle age. We don't know for sure."

"That's strange. That same guy seems to show up wherever I go. He must represent a competitor." He slipped the manager some dollars and asked, "Would you let me know when this guy comes and goes?"

"Oh, happy to."

"But keep this between us. Okay?"

"Yes, of course, monsieur. Yes, yes," replied the manger, smiling excitedly.

"What room is this Russian fellow staying in?"

The manager excused himself, stepped over to the clerk, then returned to whisper to Mark, "He's in three-forty-eight. But he just left."

"Okay. Merci."

Mark registered under a fake name as he slipped the manager more dollars. He was given room 326. He took the elevator to his room, then walked down to Yuri's room, where he picked the lock. Noting Yuri's small briefcase he carefully planted a small listening device in the seam of one flap without disturbing the bag in any manner. Then he left.

Yuri had returned not long after Mark had done his work. Then, a few minutes before nine, the manager called Mark and alerted him to Yuri's departure. Mark thanked him profusely, hung up and stepped out on his balcony. Using night-vision binoculars, he spotted Yuri on the small dock at the north end of the marina and watched as the small motorboat picked him up and delivered him to the yacht. Mark now had time to search Yuri's room more thoroughly. He carefully re-entered the room and went through all of the arms merchant's belongings. A few brochures of MIG fighters and missiles and price lists of the company's weapons Yuri had left behind interested Mark. After taking pictures of the materials, he put everything back in place and quietly left.

The next morning Mark noticed a well-dressed man coming to shore in a small motor launch and managed to get pictures. He watched as Ghaleb climbed the steps and followed the flowery walkways through the hotel's gardens to the lobby. Mark went back into his room, then cautiously opened his door and walked down the hallway to the ice machine. He pretended to get ice as he kept an eye on Yuri's door. He ducked from sight as Ghaleb came off the elevator onto the third floor. He heard Ghaleb gently tap on room three-forty-eight and then enter. Mark hurried back to his room to record the conversation.

He heard the arms transaction clearly. As soon as Ghaleb left Yuri's room, Mark slipped down the south-side emergency stairs, out the door and through the garden to his own hotel. He went to his room, took a shower, shaved, checked out, and waited in his car until Yuri drove away. He followed Yuri to the airport and watched him board a non-stop flight to Marseille.

Mark then returned to the U.S. Embassy, called his Paris office and made his report. He requested a check on The Medallion through Istanbul. He hoped that other agents could identify the men aboard the yacht. He sat back and took a slow deep breath.

Two hours later Agent Andrew McCall called from Langley. "Mark, you landed at the right place at the right time. One of our agents in Istanbul has had several of these guys under surveillance for months and they've been pretty quiet. We think they are part of a new group that has splintered off from Al-Qaida in an attempt to reinvent themselves. But we don't know for sure. He thought their joining a yacht party significant and sent in a report. Two of the yahoos are Saudi agents, two are Libyan and the others are from various Arab countries. Anyway, a big arms shipment seems to be their goal. Did you find anything to indicate the ultimate destination of these arms?"

"None," Mark answered. "They'll be picked up in Odessa, Ukraine, so we need to be present. I suspect the arms are headed to Arab countries, don't you?"

"Well, let's see. We need to know when this shipment's taking place, so stay on your toes in Marseille. We've got the yacht under surveillance."

"Fine. The French have the construction firm bugged so we'll know when a large sum of money arrives at the Swiss bank. McCall, do you think those Russian guys have fifty million dollars worth of small arms left to sell?"

"If they don't we'll hear soon enough. The Mideasterners will be furious. The Arab fundamentalists do their homework well. If they didn't think they could buy that amount of material cheaply, they wouldn't have proceeded. I don't think it's a fishing expedition. Do you?"

"No, sir," Mark responded.

McCall continued, "The Director and I have been discussing this for the last hour or so. We think the order will be processed within a week and that the Mideasterners will want those weapons shipped immediately. We'll set up surveillance in the Ukraine, but you need to get over to Istanbul and stay on top of things. Oh, wait."

Mark could hear the rustling of paper and a muffled voice. In a few minutes McCall continued. "I've just been handed a memo that the yacht belongs to the Sarioglu ShippingCompany. We will try to find out who leased it. Agent Angela Miller will meet you when you arrive in Istanbul and have things arranged."

"Okay," Mark said.

"We need to stay with the two main guys in this deal. We don't think they'll go back to their home country until they arrange the order and movement of funds and prepare for picking up the arms. There's no doubt where the money's coming from, but we need to document that anyway. Our biggest interest, as you know, is finding out the destinations of those arms."

Mark got up from his desk chair and, stretching the phone's cord, walked over to a window looking out on a busy street. "Are our relations with the Turkish military any better since the Iraqi war?"

"We just agreed to give them more F-Sixteens so they better be! We also must remember that they backed us in Afghanistan. The Islamist Welfare Party's involvement in government is always going to be a problem. Libya's Quaddafi has been courting the guy that's head of it. And, of course, all the Muslim countries are wired in there. One way or another. That's why these buyers are working out of Istanbul. They've got protection and help. But Agent Miller will fill you in on that. She's been there for three years and knows the back alleys pretty well. She has also developed some fine sources within the government and industry. Have you had a chance to meet her yet?"

"No, I haven't." He paused to think a moment, then continued. "I find the fact that no one from the PLO office here in Tunis attended the meeting on the yacht very interesting. Why didn't they attend?"

"Ummm. We have to assume that this particular arms purchase is run by the guys aboard the yacht. Besides, doesn't the staff of that PLO Tunisian office maintain a low profile there?"

"According to the Embassy staff they do. They've had no problems here for the last several years."

"Keep your head down anyway. There is no substitute for caution. I'll be in touch when you get back to Paris. Let's see what develops in the next few days."

Mark caught a flight to Paris in late afternoon. He reached his office to find a report from McCall saying that The Medallion had dropped two men off in Tripoli. So, Mark thought, our intelligence has been right. The Libyans are involved. The last satellite report has The Medallion on a heading toward the Aegean Sea, so it's probably heading back to Istanbul through the Dardanelles.

Mark called Agent Miller in Istanbul and found she had received orders from McCall to put The Medallion's remaining passengers under surveillance when they docked. Several additional agents in the Ukraine had been called in to keep a twenty four-hour surveillance on the six Odessa warehouses used by Yuri's group for storing arms. Mark kept close contact with the French as they continued monitoring Yuri's construction company.

# 2

**WASHINGTON, D.C.**
Monday, February 3

While an arms transaction was taking place in Tunisia, 36-year-old Darren Hopkins slowly trudged up the stairs of the west entrance to the old executive office building in Washington, D.C. It was a few minutes after seven in the morning, and the worst snowstorm of the season ravaged the nation's capitol. Old timers bitterly complained, and everyone admitted tiring of the dark, cold winter days.

The icy wind whipped the wet snow down Seventeenth Street, penetrating Darren's bones in spite of his new coat. "Why don't they shut down this whole city until this storm blows over? It takes a moron to be out in weather like this!"

He quickly looked around to make sure no one heard him. "No one's dumb enough to be out this early on such an atrocious day but me," he said aloud. At last he reached the sanctity of the foyer. He stomped snow off his shoes and then made his way to the elevator and the second-floor cubbyhole he called an office. The room, adjacent to the suite occupied by his boss, General George Burcks, a retired Marine, had grown cramped, but Darren managed. Burcks, chairman of President Carl Evans' National Security Council (NSC), wore four stars, was in his mid-sixties, stood a trim, athletic, six feet three inches tall, and sported silky white hair. His decorations reflected major roles in every war and skirmish since Korea.

As he entered the elevator, Darren reflected on the weird process that brought him to Washington a year ago, which now seemed like decades. Many of the factors still eluded him. He did not know Burcks nor had he ever worked in government. And he had never worked in D.C. Never wanted to. He grew up in Texas but spent some of his childhood in Latin America and Asia. His parents, both medical doctors, spent a great deal of time assisting international health organizations. Two sisters practiced law in Houston and Austin. Darren landed a job with Global Analysis, a California international think-tank, after graduating from the University of Texas in nineteen eighty-five with a degree in international relations. Political risk analysis, business development tasks, and marketing research had kept him in Asia and the Mideast over the years. The move to the National Security Council began in Singapore, and he vividly remembers Ms. Clark's phone call.

He had just pulled himself out of bed that fateful Wednesday morning at Singapore's Hyatt Regency Hotel and sat on the edge of the bed worrying about losing some of his 240 pounds, when the phone rang.

"Mr. Hopkins, I'm Jo Clark, administrative assistant to General George Burcks who chairs the President's National Security Council. The general would like to talk to you about a senior research analyst's job."

"Well," he stammered in his sleepy condition, "you caught me on my blindside." He could hear her laugh.

"I understand," she said. "There's a high degree of urgency in getting this position filled, so he hopes you'll at least be willing to come to Washington at our expense to discuss it."

"Uh, gosh," he replied as he fought to shake the fog out of his head. "I've got a number of appointments set up over here, and I'd have to talk to my boss before I could agree to do that."

"The President of Global Analysis has already given General Burcks permission to bring you to Washington. And, if things work out and you join us, your Global Analysis job will be waiting for you when you decide to return. You can't top that can you?

"Wow. I'm impressed!"

"Can you postpone your meetings?"

"I suppose so," Darren said slowly. His mind tried to process what had happened as rapidly as possible.

"Good. You need to catch an immediate flight to Washington. Can you arrange those flights or shall we?"

"Wait, let's back up one step. How much time do I have to consider this?"

"The general wants an answer by noon our time. Again, remember, this is just an interview."

"Well, I need to get the cobwebs out of my head before I answer."

"Of course," Ms. Clark said softly. "I'll call you back in two hours. Is that okay?"

"I guess so." He stared at the Singapore skyline from his twelfth floor window for several minutes after Ms. Clark hung up. Wow, he thought. The National Security Council? I don't even know what the hell it does. His curiosity got the upper hand. He wanted to talk to General Burcks.

Whoops! The elevator opened on the second floor and Darren, so engrossed in the trip down memory lane, almost missed his floor. He headed down the musty corridor to his office, hung up his coat, and went to the kitchen off Ms. Clark's office to prepare a pot of coffee. Letting the coffee perk, he returned to his office. At least the office is warm and cozy, he thought. The fierce wind rattled the old windows. He walked over and stood watching the snow pile up in Lafayette Park. His mind returned to that initial trip from Singapore to Burcks' office.

The Singapore Airlines 747 taxied to the gate at Dulles International Airport at around ten a.m., Thursday, thirty hours after Ms. Clark's phone call. Two Marines met Darren as he came down the ramp and entered the airport lounge. He still remembered his disbelief. The encounter went something like this:

"Sir, General Burcks sent us to pick you up. Come with us."

Before Darren could get a response out of his mouth, they whisked him through a nearby door, down two flights of stairs, out another door and into a gray Mercury Marquis. One man loaded Darren's suitcase in the trunk, jumped into the driver's seat and shot off the tarmac so fast Darren grabbed for something to hang on to. As they sped through airport security gates and east on the Dulles Toll Road, the other marine, a major, asked, "Sir, may I have your passport?

"I guess," Darren said , as he handed it over.

The major handed the passport to a young lieutenant, and then turned to Darren and said, "Sir, your passport will be processed and delivered to your hotel room later this evening."

"Well, thanks, that's great service." Darren began to feel a mounting apprehension, much like that experienced by pets owned by taxidermists!

The car finally entered an unmarked drive at the old executive office building next to the White House and parked in an underground garage with a musty odor. The major escorted him to the elevator and General Burcks' office on the second floor. Washington's cold but sunny weather invigorated him after the humid ambience of Southeast Asia. Thankfully he brought a light coat.

Ms. Clark greeted him warmly, took his coat and asked that he be seated while the general finished his phone conversation with the President. Wow, heady stuff, Darren recalled thinking. A few minutes later Ms. Clark escorted Darren into the office, introduced him and stood by for further orders.

"Darren, glad to finally meet you. I hope you had a pleasant trip," Burcks said, rising to shake Darren's hand.

"I slept most of the way. Thanks for asking."

"Let's get our luncheon order in before we start." As the General relayed their request to Ms. Clark, Darren scanned Burcks' office, noting pictures of several U.S. presidents and numerous notables as well as an unimpeded view of the White House and Lafayette Square.

Burcks wasted no time on pleasantries. Darren could feel his heart racing lickity-split. Sweat built up in his armpits.

"Darren, your boss at Global Analysis, Faulk Landrum, is an old friend of mine. Your name came up in a recent conversation as one whom we'd like to have working with us."

"Ahhh, so he triggered this?" Darren said with a slight smile and a nod of his head.

"He and another friend of mine at Pentagon named Al Olsen. I've known Olsen for years and also value his counsel. And we've talked with dozens of people who have known you over the years. I think our research has been pretty thorough."

Caught off guard, blushing slightly, Darren sputtered, "Really?

"Really." Burcks got out of his chair, stared at Darren with fire in his narrowed eyes. Then, in a voice that would have made Moses proud, he said, "Since September eleventh, two-thousand-two, times have been tough. We are scouring the landscape to find the best talent. To date I've found nothing in your background that would be either a security risk or embarrass the present administration, but is there anything in your background that our investigation did not find that could prove to be embarrassing to you, me or the administration? If there is, tell me now and we won't waste each other's time. If you don't tell me and the issue crops up to bloody my nose, I will be very unhappy. Am I clear?"

"General, my life has been embarrassingly plain vanilla! Anyone looking at my life would be bored to tears. And," he emphasized, shaking his head back and forth as he said, "there's not a thing in my background to embarrass anyone. Well, maybe a bad grade in high school English, but nothing more profound than that."

"Are you sure?"

"Yes, Sir, I am sure." Darren shifted the focus as he leaned forward and asked, "But what do you think I can do for you? Washington is awash with talented Wannabies. I've never worked in government and may end up being a square peg in a round hole. If I am, that will be embarrassing to both of us."

Burcks Leaned back in his chair and said, "Yes, there is a lot of talent in D.C. I've talked to many. Wannabies are a dime a dozen here. But, frankly, I don't want a wannabies. I want a ratherbie, as in 'I'd rather be somewhere else.' Someone untainted by government service, a self-starter, a doer and most important, someone with international experience beyond just tourist crap. This person has got to be smart enough to know a problem when hit in the face with it and guts enough to pursue the fixes. Above all, I've gotta have loyalty. One hundred ten-percent loyalty."

Silence descended. Burcks stared at Darren with an intensity that made Darren uncomfortable.

Burcks continued, "I like the fact that you don't have an ego that needs the limelight. We've got too many of those in government now. Also this is a fairly hectic place. We spend most of our time reacting to fires around the world. The White House pressures me, I pressure my staff and" after a slight pause, Burcks said, "Well, I suggest you get a punching bag you can whup-up on. If we can reach an agreement, that is." Burcks again leaned back in his chair, waiting for Darren's response.

Darren's lips curled slightly and he let the silence linger. He raised his head and let each word trickle out, "General Burcks, someone may outthink me from time to time, but no one outworks me." Burcks nodded, but said nothing. Darren continued, "Could you be more specific? What would I be doing?"

"Whatever task I assign you."

"You must have something in mind for a starter," Darren said.

"Yes, in fact I do. I'll want you to help analyze our international reports. We need a new perspective. And you've not only got the international academic studies, but you also have years of work experience in dozens of countries. I also like that you can speak several languages."

"My language skills are only as good as the amount of time I've been in that country. In other words, I'm not that fluent."

Burcks nodded understanding, pushed his chair back, and said, "I get worried. The CIA and embassy staff around the world feed off each other. Hell, with all our intelligence gathering around the world, we didn't know that the Shah of Iran had lost all chances of holding on, that the Soviet Union and East Germany had called it quits, that the students in the People's Republic of China planned a revolution, and we sure didn't have a clue that some Arab terrorists were planning to fly our own commercial aircraft into the World Trade Center. Since nine-eleven things seem to have improved in that area, but I still worry."

"Yeah, that all looked pretty bad," Darren said.

Burcks shook his head from side to side as he said, "By and large our agents are good people. And it's true that budget cuts during the nineties left us wanting in our espionage efforts. But I also suspect many are afraid to pass bad news to their superiors. Or they've gotten too cozy with their foreign contacts and have been compromised. Good lord, we've even found agents sleeping with the enemy."

"Yeah, I guess it's easy to get comfortable and careless," added Darren.

"I don't want to be too harsh here," Burcks said, as his voice softened and he threw his arms up and locked his hands behind his head. "Some congressional hearings suggest that correct information is often sent up the line, but the reports get trashed by some senior level analyst because they don't support his or her views."

"Okay. What else would I be doing?" Darren asked.

Both men sat quietly for a few moments. Burcks started drumming the desk with the eraser end of a pencil as he pondered how to answer Darren.

Darren broke the silence, "I have a suspicion there's something lurking in the bushes. Or another shoe to fall, as they say." Burcks smiled as he glanced up.

"You have good instincts. Yeah, we've got a major problem emerging. In addition to the Osama and a lot of angry Arabs, we've an increasing number of new American super patriots who may want to use the current state of fear and instability to establish their own political agenda. State militias have been cropping up like Johnson grass. Extremism seems to spread like a virus. Some of these nuts may eventually connect with foreign terrorists, if they haven't already. We have to contain this thing before it gets out of hand."

"Yeah, unfortunately Ruby Ridge and Waco created waves," Darren recalled stating.

"Yeah. Well, whatever. Darren, I don't know if this is as serious as some think. America has always had a fringe bunch like the John Birchers or the KKK. But we can't take chances. There are reports that there are sleeper cells out there composed of domestic and foreign terrorists. I would like you to quietly focus on these kooky people. We want to know who the leaders are, what they're thinking and planning. And, most important, if they've had any contact with Arab terrorists."

"I understand. But I'll need some time to think about all this."

"You've got two hours. Use the office across the hall from Ms. Clark. Use the phone. Call anyone you need to. Let me have your decision at once. I have a narrow window of time to act on this."

Stunned, Darren got up to leave, then turned and asked, "General, do you think some of our domestic terrorists were responsible for the outbreak of anthrax after the World Trade Center catastrophe?"

"We don't know." Then, as an aside he added, "But I wouldn't be surprised."

Darren turned and exited as ordered. He pondered his situation as he stood at the window watching the heavy traffic on Pennsylvania Avenue.

Finally, Ms. Clark stuck her head in and beckoned him. "Ready?"

"Shocked that his time was up, Darren's eyes widened. He sucked in his breath, exhaled, then whispered, "Yes."

"Go on into the General's office. He's waiting."

The wood floor squeaked slightly as Darren strode across the wide hall, through Ms. Clark's office and into Burcks'. He knocked on the doorjamb at the open doorway and peeked inside. Burcks motioned him in as he finished signing some papers and stacked them in an out-basket.

Leaning back in his chair, he asked, "Well, did you decide?"

Quietly, Darren said, "I'll take a shot."

"Well, don't look so forlorn! We're not going to put you against a wall and shoot you," laughed Burcks. "At least not now!"

"I know. Sorry about that. A change of this magnitude is always difficult."

Burcks rose from his desk, came around and shook Darren's hand as he said with a serious frown, "Sure it is. Welcome aboard!" He took Darren's right elbow and gently ushered him toward the door as he continued, "The security check is done, so you can start immediately. Ms. Clark has arranged a car to take you to your hotel. Let her know your transition travel plans and she'll arrange the tickets and have them delivered to your hotel tonight. She'll fill you in. Again, good to have you aboard."

The smell of freshly brewed coffee brought Darren back to the present. He poured a cup and returned to his office. He sat at the round table next to the windows. The snowstorm mesmerized him as he waited for Ms. Clark and Burcks. He reflected on his recent experiences at the NSC. After almost a year in the belly of the whale, as Darren dubbed the federal bureaucracy, he learned that one's Washington career does, in fact, revolve around who you know and not what you know. He tired of the phonies and psychos seeking positions of power to placate their weak egos. The frantic bureaucratic activity over the months changed him, made him heartless and angry. If not for his affection for his boss and a growing concern over the increasing terrorist activities, he would prefer to return to Global Analysis.

While the Arab terrorists had been pretty quiet since the Afghan and Iraqi wars, the number of criminal acts committed by domestic super patriots had steadily increased. They seem to have taken some pages from Al-Qaida's playbook. Indiscriminate bombings, assassinations, young men flying private planes into tall buildings, counterfeiting, bank robberies and hooliganism in general had become weekly events.

Darren had followed the tragic events at Ruby Ridge, Waco, Oklahoma City, the burning of Afro-American churches, the attempted killing of children at a Jewish daycare facility in Los Angeles, the refusal of many people to pay income taxes, register their cars, or see themselves as citizens of the United States. Frighteningly, militia groups began conducting their own "Peoples' Courts." Using these contrived courts, the patriots threatened to execute U.S. congressmen, judges and law enforcement officials.

That so many marginalized or disenfranchised citizens viewed government employees as pawns in the hands of either a universal conspiracy by a few elite Jewish families or some insidious power clique within the United Nations seemed incredulous to Darren. Many believed these sinister forces resulted in The Brady Bill, the assault weapons ban, and the heightened security since nine-eleven. Especially disturbing was the movement from within the conservative evangelical wing of Christianity who believed their faith to be the national religion. Many Christian fundamentalists viewed Ruby Ridge, Waco, the World Trade Center destruction, and war in the Middle East as apocalyptic signs. Some even believed that the World Trade Center tragedy was a Jewish conspiracy to force the U.S. into a war with the Arab states. Christian fundamentalists had become as big a threat as Muslim extremists. The more he had heard from fundamentalists, the more Darren saw their kinship with the Osama bin Ladens of the world. All were constipated in faith and theology.

"Ahhh," he sighed. So much for the trip down memory lane. I better get ready to see Burcks. He carried his files into Jo Clark's office. Jo, an attractive woman, had lost her husband in Vietnam. She raised their two boys with help from her parents who lived on a farm near Shelton, Nebraska. A quiet and efficient person, Jo became Burcks' administrative assistant four years ago. She took care of the general from the time he stepped out his front door until his driver dropped him off again at night. He never went anywhere without Jo's direction. Since coming to NSC from the Pentagon, she had reviewed all the files and knew all the processes and key issues.

Burcks would certainly be concerned with his new findings. Bombs exploded in towns and cities across America on a weekly basis, killing innocent people. An internal FBI report linked ninety-six bank robberies over the last twelve months to these new super patriots. Many state and local governmental officials seem afraid to act. Some enforcement officers and judges sympathized with the movement, a few others had joined the patriot organizations, and the rest didn't have sufficient evidence to arrest and convict.

Darren opened a large manila folder and pulled out some high altitude pictures of what the FBI had labeled extremist settlements. He had studied them carefully. Ten people in the picture clearly carried rifles. The agency said that many of the groups maintained warehouse facilities loaded with arms and ammunition. A few sites even had tanks. Now Darren had to tell Burcks that some of the patriots had met with Mideast terrorists in Thailand.

Darren had recorded last night's phone call from Vasin Boonchanta, a Thai friend from the University of Texas days. He replayed the tape.

Darren, given your new position with the U.S. government, I thought you might want to know about a strange group of guys who took over the Chaing Mai Sports Club back in early January."

"Of course. Where's the Sports Club?"

"The club is in an isolated valley about seven kilometers from the city of Chaing Mai."

"Does your family still have the computer store up there?"

"Yes. In Chaing Mai. And it's making good money."

"Great. Send me some!" Both laughed. "I assume you went to the Sports Club to play golf. Correct?"

"Right as usual. They wouldn't let us play. In fact, we had a difficult time getting in to see the manager, who's a friend of my dad."

"Wow, they really had it shut down. Your country's overrun with tourists, so what's the big deal?"

"This group stood out from all the others. They had men from Mideast countries, Australia, United States, Canada, England, Germany, Russia and even Japan. The hotel staff figured another sex tour had taken over the hotel. But they never even asked about women. They never went out. Just stayed in the hotel the entire week."

"Maybe they tried to work out some business deals. Did they represent one company?

"No. Not at all. According to the hotel staff, they acted very secretive, but no company connection existed as far as any staff member I talked to could find. Some identified their nationality to staff and taxi drivers through brief conversations that always turned to politics. They made critical remarks about our king to staff members. They said the Thai should rise up and take control of their own lives. The Thai were unnerved by this rudeness."

"Yeah," Darren said. "That didn't show good taste. But that's not unusual for Americans or Europeans, is it?"

"Let me finish."

"Sorry."

"We're used to tourists asking about shopping, local foods, and similar subjects. And, as you know, big men's groups are generally tours. These guys didn't care about that stuff."

"Okay."

"Not only did they seem preoccupied with government, but rarely strayed from their private conference rooms. Staff left food on serving carts in the hall adjacent to the elevator. The staff had never encountered anything as crazy as that."

"Yeah, I'll bet that got their attention. What happened when they went to clean the dishes off the tables?"

"They couldn't," Vasin said laughingly. "Someone would call from the conference hall and inform the kitchen staff that the dirty dishes and remaining food could be picked up."

Uhmmm," groaned Darren as he wandered where all this would lead.

"Big guys guarded the outside doors to the conference and dining rooms, according to one of the Thai waiters I talked with. They said some of these guys searched all the rooms two or three times a day using hand-held devices."

"Well, makes sense to me," Darren said.

"But some of the other bellhops chimed in and said that other conferees said they didn't have any products and didn't come on any kind of company business. There was one American man registered as Reverend John Chudders from Fort Davis, Texas."

"I'd say you just got my undivided attention!" Darren said." Go on."

"The staff said that all the men seemed odd."

"And what does that mean?"

"They had never seen people dress so funny. They're used to the Arab abas. Many had shaved heads, tattoos and layers of gold earrings and necklaces. All dressed shabbily, even the older guys.

"That's terrible. I'm afraid shabby dress has become an American tradition."

Vasin continued, "One of the bellhops met several of the bald, tattooed young men in the lobby when they checked out. He asked them if they planned to be Buddhist monks. The young guys smirked and skulked off."

"The group certainly does sound strange. What do you think they were doing?"

"Oh, I think they're bad guys. The manager of the club told us they acted like thugs."

"And how did he define a thug?"

"As a terrorist. His fear prevented him from saying too much, but he did finally whisper to my dad that they talked about getting millions of U.S. dollars worth of guns."

"And John Chudders attended!" Darren said aloud.

Darren couldn't sleep after Vasin's call. The more he thought about the meeting, the more it seemed that the patriots were, in fact, setting up a support network among the world's politically disgruntled. In his seventies, John Chudders had become a key spokesman for America's Christian identity movement, a loose-knit organization of right-wing extremist groups. Darren wanted to know who else attended that meeting. At 11:00 p.m. he grabbed the phone and called a friend in U.S. Immigration Services.

"Bob? Darren Hopkins here. Sorry to bother you so late. I need help. Can you go into your database and find some folks traveling to Thailand back in January? Probably left around January third."

"Sure. How soon do you need it?"

"Well, can you get me something by eight in the morning?"

"I assume this is really important."

"I promise you it is," Darren said.

"Okay. But you owe me big time."

"Okay. Anytime. Send me the info by email." Darren gave him Chudder's name and a list of another twenty-five key patriots that came off the top of his head. The FBI had aerial photos of Chudders' community, hidden away and heavily fortified in the Davis Mountains of West Texas. Some photos showed armaments being unloaded over many months. And Darren's reporter friend in Austin hinted that Chudders' group derailed Amtrak's Sunset Limited in the early morning of October 9, 1995. The wreck claimed the life of one Amtrak employee and injured hundreds of passengers. The reporter refused to share his source.

The FBI also had photos, phone messages and other evidence showing religious zealots traveling between Chudders' Davis Mountain enclave and other extremists' encampments, such as the Aryan Nation's hide-away in Idaho and groups in Washington, Montana, Pennsylvania, Michigan and Arizona, to name a few of the most infamous.

The skinheads probably came from Germany, he mused. Darren had a New York Times article from April, 1995, in which a former German neo-Nazi leader with strong skinhead affiliations, stated that their racist propaganda and military training manuals came from right-wing groups in the United States.

A noise in the hall roused Darren from his memories. He looked up to see Jo racing into the office dusting the snow off her hat, scarf and coat as she hung them in the closet.

"Darren, you're here earlier than usual."

"I really need to see Burcks before he gets tied up," Darren answered.

Just as Darren finished that statement, Burcks entered the office. He said, "You two seem to be in a good mood this morning." Burcks put his hand on the doorjamb, turned back to Darren and said, "Let's talk!"

"Of course, I've been waiting to catch you." Darren grimaced, grabbing his coffee cup and following the general to his office. He whispered to Jo, "I hope he's not in a bad mood!"

Burcks watched silently as Darren seated himself to the right of his desk. This morning Burcks seemed soft and extremely thoughtful. He almost whispered, and the usual hard look had disappeared. Darren had rarely seen him in such a relaxed mood. As Darren sat down, Burcks smiled slightly, and then said, "I went over that lengthy report you laid on my desk a few days ago. Seems like the crazies are up to something."

"General, I have a chilling update. We have evidence that our super patriots are getting outside help."

Burcks said, "How so?"

"A Thai friend called last night. Some of our domestic dissenters have had a meeting with Islamic fundamentalists in northern Thailand in early January. Maybe they only shared strategies. But they may be setting up arms purchases. Maybe even coordinating terrorist acts on a global scale."

Burcks' soft demeanor vanished. As he spoke, Darren noted the hard set jaw, the furrowed brow and narrowed eyelids. Burcks said, "That earlier report gave me heart burn." He sighed, and in a more relaxed tone, said, "Okay, give me the whole story."

Darren reported his conversation with Vasin and the U.S. immigration report that twelve key super patriots left the country on January second and third. Reading from the email his friend in Immigration sent, Darren said, "They departed L.A. International en route to Hong Kong in teams of two over a two-day period. They spent one night at the Holiday Inn Harbor View in Kowloon. Then they vanished. I have yet to trace their travel from Hong Kong to Chiang Mai." Darren shifted in his chair, looked up to make sure he had Burcks' full attention. He continued, "They show back up in Hong Kong on January eleventh. This time they checked into the Holiday Inn. Again, they split into pairs and returned via Los Angeles airport on different flights."

"Let's not waste time worrying about how these misfits got from Hong Kong to Chiang Mai," the General said. "We need to know the results of the meeting. Let's see if any of the other agencies have anything. We must be very, very careful how we proceed. Although this is certainly a national security issue, it has now taken an international tinge. As you know, these extremists have friends in high places. While not all are disloyal Americans, too many harbor hatreds and heretical religious views that often lead to a host of unnecessary deaths. There'll probably be more federal building bombings. More day-care centers and churches blown up. God help us."

"Yeah," Darren echoed.

General Burcks continued, "We can't gather up everyone we define as troublemakers, nuts and wackos, and put them in prison. Everyone's waiting for us to make the slightest mistake. We look like a bunch of gutless, whimpering dummies right now. But we've got to follow the law to the letter."

"Yes, sir. It's a difficult situation."

"What I wouldn't give for an old fashion foreign conflict. Those were easier to deal with, at least in hindsight. See if you can find out the details of that meeting in Thailand?" softly asked the General.

"Yes sir."

"And, by the way, you need to be sitting in on sessions of the new inter-agency domestic counter-terrorism task force run by F.B.I. Agents Wade and Carlson. We'll share some of our data, but not all until we see how trustworthy the group is."

"Yes sir."

After a few moments Burcks softly asked, "How about that reporter friend of yours in Austin? He seems to have an interest in these crazies. Is he any help?"

"He seems to keep up with a lot of these people, but I've promised him anonymity."

"That's not a problem. Don't forget to use the special phone number I gave you months ago to call me. It's totally secure. A news media leak is the last thing we need."

"Yes sir."

"Uh, Darren, I think you ought to know that your friend Ann Jones is missing."

A knot developed in the pit of Darren's stomach as Burcks' words sank in. "What do you mean?"

"I got a call from the Thailand CIA Station Chief last night. He informed me that they've lost touch with her. They're concerned that she is not communicating through agreed upon channels. They know of your relationship and wanted to know if you've heard from her lately?"

"Yes. She left a message on my answering machine last night."

"What did she say?"

"She said she missed me, but couldn't be in touch with me for an indeterminate time. She said some strange things were happening and she hoped my work was challenging."

Burcks said, "She didn't say where she was calling from?"

"No sir."

"How long has she been with Army intelligence?" Burcks asked.

"About ten years."

"Can you tell me about the relationship?" Burcks asked.

"Of course. We've seen each other as work permitted over the last five years. I guess if I had to get married right now it would be to Ann." Then, as an after thought he smiled and added, "If she'd have me."

Burcks cracked a brief smile, and then said, "Well, the problem is probably not as bad as it may seem. Let's give her time to surface. Let me know when you hear from her again. Okay?"

"Yes sir."

Darren left Burcks' office that cold wintry day feeling like he had been hit with a sledgehammer. Before he shut the General's office door, he glanced back to see Burcks rubbing his forehead with both hands, eyes closed. Darren went to his office, feeling guilty for not telling Burcks of his relationship with Ann. But he had only taken a few steps when Burcks' voice stopped him dead in his tracks.

"Darren!"

Darren turned and walked back to the door of Burcks' office. Yes sir?"

"I almost forgot. There's one of those super patriots meetings out in Bellingham next Monday night. The Bureau is sending an agent to the meeting, but I'd like you to be there."

"Yes sir." At that, Burcks returned to his desk, and Darren shut the door and headed back to his office to prepare for the Bellingham meeting. Ann was still on his mind.

# 3

**BELLINGHAM, WASHINGTON**
Monday, February 10

Darren's taxi dropped him at the entrance to Bellingham's Northwood Hall off North Interstate 5 just a few minutes before the program began. As he entered, his heart sank at the sight of a packed room. Not a jovial looking bunch, he mused, then quickly noted that he was the only one wearing a business suit. He felt as if six hundred pairs of eyes were staring at him, their faces reflecting suspicion and tenseness. He started sweating. Once seated, Darren pulled his return plane ticket from his coat pocket and pretended to read in hopes he could fade from sight. After a few minutes he glanced up to find others chatting with their neighbors or staring straight at the front. He wiped sweat from his forehead, face and neck.

Whew, he thought, what a crew. Most needed to go on a diet. Balloon-like stomachs and sagging jowls adorned the large frames of most. Men sat quietly, arms crossed and resting on their bulging stomachs, eyes fixed straight ahead and squinting threateningly, while their women chatted noisily with each other and tried to control the kids. Most of the men wore suspenders to keep their blue jeans or khaki pants from falling. Darren thought the women had bought their clothes at rummage sales. A fiftyish looking couple sat at the far end of the row in front of him. The woman's broom-skinny frame, which Darren judged to be about five foot eleven, stood out in the obese crowd. A faded scarf covered her light brown hair in an attempt to hide rollers. A short, bald and pudgy guy, wearing a gray sweatshirt and overalls sat next to her. Darren assumed he was her husband. Right arm encircling his neck, she patted and stroked his bald head and fondled his right ear. She whispered to him as he sat stoically, eyes transfixed on something at the front of the hall. Her eyes kept glancing down Darren's row as she whispered. She had a number of teeth missing. A good old snaggle-toothed mountain gal. All solid working class Americans.

Children of all ages abounded. A runny- nosed toddler occupied the seat in front of him and kept turning around to stare. The middle-aged mother, sans make-up and hair in a bun, scolded the tyke and made her turn around. The girl kept ignoring her mother's warnings, so she finally got smacked pretty hard. The ensuing screaming almost gave Darren a headache.

Then he noticed Agent Fred Blaylock enter and cautiously survey the crowd. "Oh, crap," Darren said under his breath. "The guy looks like an FBI agent right out of the catalog," Darren gasped silently. He reached down to re-lace his shoes in hopes Blaylock would sit somewhere else.

No such luck. Blaylock found him. As he entered the back row to sit with Darren, he boomed in a voice loud enough to be heard in Seattle, "Hi! You must be Darren Hopkins. Didn't know if you made the trip." Darren hit his head on the back of the seat in front of him as his head jerked up in shock. As he raised his hand in greeting, he noticed people staring at them. Oh, boy, the fat's in the fire now.

Blaylock sat down and turned to Darren. "Sorry I'm late. Planes aren't running on time."

"Glad to meet you," replied Darren in a pronounced hush tone as he furtively eyed the crowd around them. The little girl in front, now with tear-stained cheeks, stared up at Darren once again, her mouth firmly clamped to the back of her seat as she chewed away. He heard a loud slap as the mother administered another dose of love to the child's backside. Again the screams pealed forth. Thank goodness for the distraction.

He leaned toward Blaylock, cupped his hand over his mouth so others wouldn't hear and asked, "Are we in trouble here?"

"I hope not! This is a public gathering, right? And we're part of that public."

"Yeah, true."

"My only task is to report on what takes place. I suspect there'll be some in attendance that have outstanding warrants, but I'm not going to pursue 'em in this crowd." Blaylock couldn't have been more relaxed. His calm manner stunned Darren. The people in the rows ahead could clearly hear everything the man said. Hell, doesn't this guy understand what this crowd could do to us? Nonchalantly, Blaylock asked, "Have you been to many of these shindigs?"

"Nope," he replied. "I've read reports about them, but I'm just now getting my feet wet in the field, as they say."

Ole Reverend Jim Petsch took the microphone and quieted the crowd, much to Darren's relief. Petsch's white suit, red carnation in the lapel, set off by a black shirt and bright red tie, got Darren and Agent Blaylock's attention. Darren craned his neck to see Petsch's black and white wing tipped shoes over the edge of the rostrum. Petsch then led the group in singing "God Bless America" and offered up a prayer. Blaylock whispered to Darren, "Who's this nut?"

Keeping his head down and cupping his mouth to prevent others from hearing, Darren said, "I'm told he has some little off-beat church in Pennsylvania. At least he says he does. To my knowledge no one's checked. The national Christian patriotic bunch sucked him up when he helped organize the Pennsylvania state militia. He's all showman! Makes up his theology as he goes along. Like Jim Jones and all these other TV evangelists."

When Petsch finished, James Robert Earl, a local Whatcom county deputy sheriff, took the mike and set the stage for the night's program.

"Ladies and gentlemen, let me thank ya'll for coming. I know you'll not regret bein' here. All of us know somethin's bad wrong in our country. They can't protect us from those stinkin' Arabs, and they keep gettin' more and more of our money, and if yer a white male yer mak'in less and less. Things in this country are gradually being taken over by foreign types and minorities who can't do things the way they should be done. They've taken over our schools and 'bout everthin' else, and now we oughta do somethin' to take the thing back 'fore we 'come another one'a them banana republics. Pretty soon our children won't be prayin' to Jesus Christ but to some foreign God."

A few amen's echoed throughout the hall. Earl acknowledged these with a nod of his head and continued.

"Weaver's family's dead because of them government people. And they killed all those God-fearing folks down in Waco. And the killin's continued, but you won't read about it. The little people across this country are startin' to get together and armin' themselves to keep from bein' wiped out. Tonight we're fortunate to have us several who have helped others organize and they'll tell us why and how to do this."

Earl then introduced Ron Chapmann, a lean, wiry man in his late fifties.

And who's this guy?" asked Blaylock, in a louder than necessary voice.

Darren, wishing Blaylock would shut up, whispered irritably, "He's a fairly successful business man from Georgia that moved his family to a remote area of Washington fifteen years ago. His brother and brother-in-law followed with their families. Reportedly they dusted off an old eighteen fifty-four state law regarding squatter's rights to build on fifty acres inside the Okanogan National Forest. They supported Randy Weaver during the siege at Ruby Ridge, then created their own state militia, and they did such a good job that other states asked for help. Ron and his brother reportedly spend their time raising funds for all these groups. Militias are now active in at least twenty states and membership is around five thousand. And growing fast."

"Ummm," murmured Stevens. "I thought the movement was larger."

"Could be," Darren responded. "There's a lot of secrecy among these people."

Ron Chapmann's speech mesmerized the Bellingham crowd as he told about his family's experiences fighting the federal government and his vision of an international Zionist conspiracy. He warned of black helicopters cruising the skies preparing the way for an invasion of UN forces that would enslave all true patriots and turn the country over to foreign rabble. A lengthy diatribe against NAFTA, GATT, World Affairs Council, Trilateral Commission, the Atlantic Council and the lack of resolve to annihilate all the Arabs in the Mideast during the Iraqi war comprised the rest of his speech. He concluded with an evangelistic fervor that would have made Billy Graham envious. He walked from behind the lectern to the edge of the dais, leaned over slightly and in a slow, steely and mono-toned voice said, "I want you to know I'm not the head of any organization. My family is one of many who have decided the existing government is treasonous, and therefore not the legally valid representative of the people. We do not recognize any state or national authority as presently constituted. We do not pay any taxes, do not register any of our vehicles or property deeds with the State, and do not recognize the legitimacy of any state or federal laws to govern or control any portion of our lives. We live quietly on our own sovereign land, bother no one, and view the encroachment of our domain by anyone not personally invited to be an act of war."

He paused, took a deep breath and straightened his small frame. Whoops, hollers and applause echoed across the hall. He wiped his sweaty brow with his handkerchief as he waited for the crowd to calm down, and then continued in the same passionate manner.

"As patriots there's a great diversity of opinion among us, which is okay. We do agree on some things. First, the existing government has betrayed the founding fathers and, therefore, is illegitimate. Second, the nation has lost the historic Christian foundation. Third, the white race is targeted for extinction."

Again, he paused and the crowd applauded. Shouts of "amen" echoed throughout the hall. Someone yelled, "You tell'um, Ron!" Laughter rippled through the crowd. Ron motioned for quiet, and then continued.

"If you share these beliefs, we want you to join us in returnin' to the America as originally conceived by our founding fathers. The state militia has a network to help you fulfill your patriotism. Thanks for invitin' us. We look forward to having many of you join us in our crusade to restore America!"

The crowd jumped up clapping, screaming and shouting "amen" and "hallelujah." Blaylock nudged Darren as they stood and said, "Guess we better clap too!"

"Yeah, guess so." The snaggle-toothed woman in the next row joined those jumping for joy. Her husband continued to sit quietly. Darren thought the guy might drop off to sleep.

Although relatively new to the national patriotic scene, the next speaker, Colonel Arlo White, U.S. Army (Ret.), age 64, had amassed a great following since joining the movement. His six foot two, two hundred and thirty pounds seemed all muscle. His silver hair, in traditional military crew-cut fashion, and bulldog face communicated authority. His experiences in Vietnam and Desert Storm made him a highly decorated war hero. He reportedly led several private missions to Southeast Asia to search for U.S. POWs. He now trained state militia across the nation.

The crowd, already on an emotional high, cheered the introduction. Meanwhile, Darren realized that he and Stevens could easily be beaten to death by this crowd if someone just pointed a finger in their direction and said, "There's some feds folks. Sic'um!" He shook his head in disgust at the thought. His stomach began hurting, a sure sign of stress.

As the crowd gradually took their seats, White stood, unleashing his huge frame, then strode with regal authority to the lectern. Blaylock turned to Darren and whispered, "There's a man bloated with his own importance!"

"Yeah, seems to be."

White stared at the crowd for eight to ten seconds. Deathly silence saturated the hall. Afraid to shift in his seat for fear the noise would echo throughout the hall, Darren remained immobile. His sore rear end would have to suffer. Then, in a deep baritone voice that boomed across the hall, White gave the crowd a vision of the movement's growth across the nation. Complementing Chapmann's sinister forces idea, he emphasized corruption and abuse of power in state and federal governments. He named politicians who had been convicted and sent to prison for abuse of power. (In truth none of the politicos mentioned had been indicted, but truth was a scarce commodity at such meetings.) He used the Brady Bill, NAFTA, financial support of Israel, unwillingness to carry the Vietnam War to its ''just conclusion," and inability to wipe out Al-Qaida and find Saddam Hussein as tools to paint the government illegitimate. The Constitution, he assured them, gave them the right to bear arms and overthrow the government.

People loved the show. Many jumped to their feet cheering and clapping. Hopkins applauded meekly for fear of attracting attention. Blaylock sat with his arms crossed and looked bored. Arlo White beamed down upon the crowd, then lifted his two arms over his head and waved like an Olympian who had just won the one hundred yard dash.

Meanwhile, Darren noticed that James Robert Earl had moved into White's chair next to Ron Chapmann. He saw Earl lean over and whisper to Chapmann, then point toward Darren and his colleague. Darren suspected they had been identified. He tensed in his seat as he noticed that the only exit was toward the front. Then Earl, still whispering to White, motioned toward the exit door. Darren then saw a large man leaning against the wall by the exit motion for White and Earl's attention. The man must weigh three hundred pounds, Darren thought.

Petsch concluded the speeches as he bounced around the podium shouting and exhorting a message filled with fear and hate. Words and phrases often disappeared when Petsch screamed, so Hopkins and Blaylock couldn't hear the whole message. They did hear him say,

"God created the Aryan race to establish a Christian world. Them that get in the way are instruments of Satan. This Godly group has been sifted and winnowed and now is the Anglo-Saxon Protestants, Hallelujah, Amen!"

Blaylock elbowed Darren and said, "What a bunch of ignorant crap!"

"Boy, you can say amen to that." Again, the snaggle-tooth lady eyed them. He didn't care any more. The hate in the room disgusted him. He smiled at her. She turned away.

Petsch also said that Cain satanically spawned the other religions and racial groups and they should be ignored or eliminated. "There would eventually be," he shouted, "an Armageddon and God will strike down all non-whites and non-Christians." An international satanic cartel of rich Jewish families, he explained, had taken control of the main line protestant groups. "God," he continued, "will eliminate most people in the coming great war of liberation."

Someone in the audience yelled, "Send 'em back to Israel and let the A-rabs kill 'em!"

While some people clapped, others intoned amens while waving their arms to the ceiling, others quietly nodded approval. He certainly had the group in the palm of his hand thought Darren.

Petsch continued, "Can't ya see the signs and smell the scent of Satan in America today? The number of the anti-Christ system is six-six-six, a six within a six within a six. Six sides, six angles, six points. And what is that? The Magen David, the six-pointed star of Jud'ism. Jew families control the Federal Reserve, and only three of them are American. Satan's weav'n his web and tryin' to kill God's creation. Never before have we been so threatened. Satan's tryin' to change the America, a nation created by God, into USA, incorporated, ruled by Zionists. The scent of Satan is all around. He's disarming us. He's tak'n God from the center of our national life. He's trying to rid white Christians of responsible positions to give them to foreign, evil forces who'll enslave us."

The roar of the crowd forced Petsch to stop. He used the time to sip some water from a glass, then returned to the task. He renewed his message in a soft voice as the audience quieted.

"Some patriots among us say we not only gotta be ready to defend ourselves, but we gotta rise up against our tormenters, these disciples of Satan, with great fury or we will be eaten up by'um. Let everyone unnerstand that we don't hate these people as individuals, but we can't live together in peace. The massacres at Ruby Ridge, Waco and the World Trade Center show what these people of Satan can and will do. This is only the beginning, for Satan has been preparing for these last days for decades, and unless we take heroic measures there will be no future for our children or us."

Now, noted Darren, Petsch started screaming again.

"Unless you're brain dead you can see that the government's now the enemy of God and of our white race. The government has fallen treasonous and the penalty for treason has always been death."

The crowd went wild. People stood, clapped, and jumped in the air shouting "amen, hallelujah" and "give'm hell preacher." The snaggled-toothed lady joined the hallelujah choir. She stared down at Darren as she clapped and screamed as if to say, "Take that you son-of-a-bitch heathen!" He felt sad that so many felt so disconnected from their nation's political processes and thought in such simplistic terms. He didn't have much time to grieve as the crowd quieted and Petsch began again.

"The founders of our nation understood all this. In the Declaration of

Independence they stated that the people had the 'right and duty' to throw off a treasonous government." Petsch paused, walked back and forth on the rostrum as though trying to think of the next point, stopped, stared hard at those in the front rows, then began again in a soft, pleading tone. "I know these are hard words. This has not been easy for those of us who have been the solidest of citizens, whose ancestors founded and shaped this nation, who've lost loved ones defending it or have shed blood ourselves in those wars, to come now where we have to take up arms to defend the nation against our own. Patrick Henry once asked, 'Is peace so dear that it should be bought with the chains of slavery?' Slavery, some will argue, is preferable to death. Others will say that Christians should never take up arms. I think killing is only justified when one is convinced that Satan needs killing. Satan has taken our government and is gradually killing us off. The time has come when we can do no other under God. In Hebrews chapter nine, twenty-second verse, we read: 'Without the shedding of blood, is no remission of sins.' Amen.

Another round of applause, cheers, and amens followed Petsch as he returned to his seat. Earl looked at Ron Chapmann, nodded his head slightly and Chapmann and White quickly left the rostrum. They followed the large bearded man waiting at the doorway, through a bunch of supporters that had crowded around the edge of the rostrum, out a side door and, Darren later learned, into a waiting car.

Earl gave up trying to get the crowd settled back down for a formal closing. People wandered around. Kids ran amuck. He approached the mike and shouted, "Goodnight!" Few even heard the announcement.

Hopkins and Blaylock had a problem. They had seen White and Chapmann disappear but couldn't follow. The word had silently spread and a number of the muscular and obese patriots, including the stringy, snaggle-toothed gal at the end of the next row and her pudgy little man, blocked the aisles. The two men gave up and waited for the crowd to disperse. They slowly edged down the row to their right where a dozen or so clustered in twos and threes discussing the speeches. They smiled and cordially joined the discussion of one small group after another until they reached the rear exit.

As they climbed into Blaylock's rented Ford Taurus to leave the meeting, Darren said, "Man let's get out of here."

"Yeah, you seemed uncomfortable. You'll get used to that."

"Maybe. They certainly got our number tonight. Besides the speakers we wore the only business suits."

"Ah hell, even if we'd worn some old work clothes they would've spotted us. They can spot us feds a mile off. I've come to think we must develop a certain smell!"

"Where do you think Chapmann and White disappeared to?" Darren asked.

"Don't know, but don't worry. We've got 'em covered," Blaylock said.

"What do you mean?" Darren asked.

"Some of our boys in a new surveillance helicopter followed White in here and they are waiting for him at the airport to take off. They can listen in on every conversation."

"Wow," Darren exclaimed.

Blaylock dropped Darren off at the Airport Holiday Inn on his way to catch a night flight back to Chicago.

Meanwhile, Chapmann and White flew out of the Bellingham Municipal airport into a clear night sky aboard White's Cessna 210. They climbed to fifteen thousand feet on a southeast heading through the valley south of Mount Baker for the little airport in Amak. They landed a few minutes before ten p.m. Chapmann thanked White for the ride and jumped out and scrambled into the waiting car. White taxied for takeoff as Ron Chapmann's wife, Jill, drove off. Grass and gravel flew as her tires spun. She turned south on highway 215 to pick up the highway to Conconully and home.

"How'd the meeting go?" Jill asked.

"Great. But I suspect we had a couple of feds there. Earl and his men snuck us out a side door and we must have driven down every back alley in town before getting to the airport."

"You know the feds monitor every move we make," Jill said.

"Yeah. On the way back I could swear I saw one of those black helicopters off to our right. I had an edgy feeling during the whole trip. Spooky."

"Ummmm," she said. "Well, I guess I should break some bad news to you."

"Oh God, what now!"

"I returned yesterday afternoon to find paper and stuff all over the house."

# 4

**ISTANBUL, TURKEY**
Monday, February 10

While Darren attended the Bellingham meeting, Mideast terrorists prepared to ship the first load of Russian arms to the super patriots in the United States. Mr. Ghaleb, a.k.a. Mohammed Javad, a former colonel in Iran's army and now advisor to several Arab leaders, returned The Medallion to its owner in Istanbul. His colleagues scattered to report to their respective organizations.

Ghaleb returned to his sixth floor apartment and office in Istanbul's oldest district of Stamboul. He felt ecstatic after dropping by the Iranian Embassy and reporting his progress. Iranian officials seemed delighted with his achievement. He hummed the Iranian national anthem as he returned to his apartment.

His wife looked up from her sewing and with a furrowed brow asked, "What are you so happy about?"

"Ah, woman, my president thinks I will be a national hero if I can get these arms to the Americans!"

"Really?"

"Yes, yes," he said, as his head nodded rhythmically. He sauntered into the room overlooking the street that served as his office and sat at the ornate mahogany desk. Putting down her sewing, his wife followed and moved quickly to close the louvered windows to shut out the noise from the narrow, cobbled street below. Family pictures decorated the otherwise bare walls. A hand-made rug covered most of the wooden floor.

"Maybe you are just being used by the right-wing religious fanatics," she said.

"Ahhh, woman," he said, with a wave of his hand and a sneer on his face.

Ghaleb's wife picked up another sewing task she had left earlier and after a period of silence and without looking up, asked, "When are we going to move to America or England?"

"Now, now. I wish you would not talk like that. Some day we will."

"I want to be near our children in Detroit or London. I don't even like these Turkish people!"

"I know you don't, but my work is important. Please. In time."

"Yieee. In time, in time. Always it's in time."

Ghaleb stared at papers on his desk while trying to fend off his wife's needling. Ahh, these women, he thought. What a burden they are. Allah has not been merciful to me.

His wife interrupted his thoughts to ask, head tilted to the side and eyes squinting questioningly, "Where do you meet all these characters? You're not a practicing Muslim. And the radicals, like Osama bin Laden, scare you. So why are you getting involved?"

He looked over at his wife. After a few moments, he said, "Well, some important people in the Arab world believe I can help. Besides, they pay me well."

"Well, I am just wondering why you keep trying to help them attack the Israelis," she said, as she looked down and continued to sew.

"I hate them. Don't you?"

"Yes and no."

"And what is this yes and no?" he asked, wide-eyed and arms extended as a gesture of bewilderment.

"Yes, the Israelis have done some wicked things. But so have the Palestinians. And no, because we will never have peace as long as people are unable to forget the past and work out their differences in a peaceful means. I'm tired of all the killing."

"Shuuuu," he sighed. Here we go again.

Thursday, February 13

Ghaleb's group went to work on shipping strategies. The president of Iran's aide called to say that a Maersk Line freighter Sea Novia would dock in Odessa to pick up the valued cargo. Stopping at Istanbul, it would transfer one half the cargo to a ship from the fleet of an Algerian company, Compagnie Nationale Algerienne De Navigation (CNAN), and dock at Vera Cruz, Mexico. The aide also said that the Algerians had agreed to arrange Mexican trucking for the cargo from Vera Cruz to the border town of Ojinaga, a small village across the border from the U.S. town of Presidio. The Iranian President planned to ask the Libyan President to call Castro and see if he would pay off Mexican immigration officials. They would notify Ghaleb of their success. The remaining weapons would be transferred to a Turkish freight company, D.B. Turkish Cargo, which had recently established a new lane to Vancouver.

ESTES PARK, COLORADO
Friday, February 14

While Arab terrorists prepared the arms shipment and U.S. federal law enforcement officials scurried to put the pieces together, the patriot movement faced some rapid and momentous changes. In order to further unite the many disparate patriotic groups into a more cohesive organization White, Chapmann, and other key elites brought major leaders together at the secluded Aspen Lodge Ranch Resort and Conference Center near Estes Park. Those in attendance included: Reverend Chudders, from Texas; the newest president of the Republic of Texas, Reginald Herring; Reverend Petsch; Colonel Arlo White; and representatives from the KKK, Christian Identity Group, The Order, State Citizenship Sovereignty, Gun Owners of America, Police Against the New World Order, along with numerous state militia groups and interested parties. Thirty invitations had been extended. Forty-two showed up, not counting ten heavily armed security guards. White dubbed it the second Unified Patriot's Council meeting.

Colonel White introduced Chapmann to his friend and colleague, Retired General Ernst Boorgers. Boorgers had been running the Universal Anti-Communist League of America. His name had also surfaced in the Iran-Contra congressional hearings for supplying weapons to counter-subversives during the Nicaraguan revolution.

The meeting took place in wood paneled, Long's Peak conference room at the main lodge.

"Gentlemen, let me have your attention, please," Chapmann announced. The group quieted. "Welcome to this get-together of true American patriots. None of us has a great deal of appreciation for bureaucracies, especially when they deny our individual rights and freedoms to think and act as God has so ordered us."

A number of private conversations erupted at the rear of the room, disrupting Chapmann's introductory speech. He stopped for a moment, then shouted, "Quiet back there!" Finally, he continued. "Our purpose here is not to create another bureaucratic monster, but to provide enough information to keep us from stepping on one another's toes. There's not goin' to be any long-winded speeches here."

A ripple of applause ran through the group, and then White said, "For those of you who don't know it, we have arms stored in a number of warehouses around the country. In a few weeks those facilities will bulge at the seams, so we need to get them distributed." He turned, pointed at Boorgers, and said, "My good friend, General Boorgers, will arrange distribution. He'll say a word about this process."

Five or so minutes of chaos ensued while it seemed that everyone tried to talk at the same time. Finally, Colonel White shouted as only a career military officer can: "Hey, let's come to order here! The general has the floor."

White sat down as Boorgers stretched his two-hundred-sixty-pound, six foot, five inch frame out of his chair, walked to the front and said, "Gentlemen, we are increasingly in need of coordinating activities nationally. Keep in communication with White or myself. But maintain your phantom cells. If no one knows the details of a cell's activity, there will be no leaks. Got it?"

Most quietly clapped their approval. Some whistled and yelled. Again, numerous conversations broke out. White, miffed by the group's lack of decorum, whispered to Boorgers, "Jeeesus Christ, we've raised a population of savages in this country!"

"Yeah, and we've got some who are just inherently nasty and others that were never house broken," Boorgers responded. White snickered quietly as Boorgers smirked.

Then several individuals took the floor, pushing their own agenda or, as Chapmann whispered to White, "Some of these guys like to hear themselves talk. I can't make any sense out of most of it. This meeting may not have been a good idea." White nodded his agreement, folded his arms, leaned back and stared off across the room as people ranted and raved. Two or three often spoke at the same time.

Reverend Chudders finally took the floor and asked for all to stand for prayer. However, the noise from private conversations, significantly abated, continued. Chudders had to pause. The group quieted after a few moments, and Chudders finished his prayer.

Arlo White took the floor to close the session, saying in a voice loud, "It's important that you know we've been unable to get the United Nations and the Red Cross to recognize that our people should be treated as prisoners of war in case war breaks out." The crowd responded with hoots, cat calls, and cursing.

White, Boorgers, and Chapmann stood, watched and listened to the fracas for a few minutes, and then left the room shaking their heads in disbelief and laughing. Chudders, left alone in front of the group, looked bewildered and forlorn. He finally got up and wandered out of the room.

The afternoon session was canceled and participants were left to find their own diversions. By breakfast time the next morning most had drifted out of Estes Park, disenchanted with the proceedings.

Chapmann, Chudders and White stayed to meet with General Boorgers and a few other national-level leaders. As the men stood to depart, White stunned Chapmann and Chudders by saying, "Gentlemen, let's prepare for war with an evil empire!"

Chapmann walked up to Chudders. "Did I hear White call for a war with America or did I imagine it?"

"Yep, yes, sir, you shore did."

"How did we get to this point?" Chapmann asked.

PORT OF ODESSA, UKRAINE
Saturday, February 15

While the super patriots tried to organize themselves in Colorado, agents Easton and Miller stood under a Roman colonnade at the top of the Petemkenksi Steps trying to view the loading docks. Though midnight, the docks were lit with floodlights as if it were high noon.

The agents took turns observing and photographing the loading of the Sea Novia through high-powered binoculars and the other watching for anyone coming up the steps behind them. Several couples huddled in the darker corners of the colonnade, so Easton and Miller hoped their rapt focus on the port facility would not seem unusual.

Easton spotted Yuri Tavanovich on the docks through his binoculars, clipboard in hand, counting off the crates marked construction materials, as each pallet was loaded by mechanical lifts. At every lull in the loading process, Yuri roamed the docks, checking nooks and crannies.

The American agents photographically captured close shots of each pallet and everyone associated with the loading. The loading finished at 3:20 a.m., the ship pulled away from port at 5:30 a.m., and the two exhausted agents returned to the Passage Hotel to clean up, eat some breakfast and grab some sleep. Agent Miller took the film to a lab run by the CIA and then arranged to get a copy of the ship's manifest from a friend of a friend who worked the Port Authority.

Sunday, February 16

Agent Miller met her friend Andri Gudunov by the Atlantis statues on Golgol Street at twelve noon. She handed him a shopping bag in which she had placed a nicely wrapped gift, saying, "Please, take this to your wife and give her my best regards." He thanked her profusely as they stood and chatted about their families. As they started to part Gudunov said, "You may want to take the latest edition of the English language paper from Kiev with you. I finished it." Agent Miller thanked him and they went their separate ways.

Gudunov had taped the ship's manifest to the sports page of the newspaper he had handed Miller. According to the documents, the construction materials were to be shipped to Istanbul, reloaded aboard another ship enroute to Vera Cruz, Mexico. Agent Miller immediately sent copies of the translated documents to CIA Langley.

# 5

## WASHINGTON, D.C.

Friday, February 14

FBI Agent Carlson prepared for the morning's domestic terrorism meeting unaware that Russian arms were headed for the U.S. Although the unit had been set up prior to the World Trade Center destruction, after that date the group found itself the centerpiece of the new Homeland Security Agency. More money had been allocated and it had become an elite task force with a primary goal of sniffing out and eliminating all terrorists. The unit regularly met on Fridays to review the week's activities and revise its strategy for the ensuing week. Members represented the various law enforcement agencies and coordinated agency efforts. The FBI's Lenora Carlson reviewed and organized the incoming surveillance reports from agents across the nation and around the world each morning.

An attorney and twelve-year veteran with the Bureau, Agent Carlson served as the director of the agency's counter-Intelligence unit under the administrative hand of Deputy-Director of the FBI, Sam Wade. Wade had been with the bureau thirty-eight years.

On this particular Friday morning Carlson prepared for the meeting by working through the field reports that arrived during the night and adding news that enhanced the composite. History had often punished the bureau's failure to identify the fine nuances that often clarify complex social issues. Once the command group studied her summary and made amendments, the results were transmitted to all field agents as a public strategy called ANSIR (Awareness of National Security Issues).

Carlson had worked out of the Sacramento field office for eight years before being transferred to the newly created terrorism task force. She assumed task force command when Deputy-Director Wade was absent. In California she had managed the bureau's western surveillance of domestic extremists and led the investigation of the Amtrak derailment case (code name, Splitrail) in Arizona.

The task force met in a subterranean conference room. Each of the nine agents—excluding Wade and Carlson—in addition to monitoring foreign terrorist activity had recently been assigned responsibility for observing segments of the growing extremist movement within the U.S. One agent had the task of monitoring the groups under the Christian Identity umbrella, another the separatist groups, another the KKK, the U.S. Taxpayers League, the skinheads and other less visible groups. Each of these organizations used strident, anti-government rhetoric and had members with violent records.

Agent Carlson opened the morning meeting by noting that a staff member from the National Security Council (NSC) had been assigned to work with the task force.

"Must be the guy who attended that meeting of super kooks with Blaylock at Bellingham," an agent said.

"Yep, I'll bet he's the one," Sam Lockney added, one of the bureau's most experienced field agents. "He seems to be an all right guy." Lockney, seated at the far end of the oval table, then turned to an agent on his right and asked, "What'd you do to get this assignment?"

"Wha'd' ya mean?"

Smiling, Lockney said, "Oh, I figured each agency assigned their worst nightmare!" Both men laughed quietly.

"Naw, maybe not. Sam, one of the things that bother me is that there are some well meaning souls among all those super patriots. This could end up being a real tar baby."

"Maybe, but shit, we ought to round the son-of-a-bitches up and ship them over to Afghanistan, Iraq, Somalia or wherever the Al-Qaida bunch is holed up now. They deserve each other!"

Then, from the head of the table they heard Carlson say, "Okay, let's listen up. What's your reaction to these reports?"

"Well, I've got to admit that the activity between these groups does seem to be intensifying," ATF's Carrasco said softly. "The hardcore, covert movement is in the West, especially centered in the activities of Chapmann up in Washington, the Montana militia, the folks holed up in the Davis Mountains, old Reverend Chubby down in Texas, and that TV preacher, Petz."

"Petsch," Carlson corrected, with a slight grin.

"Whatever," Carrasco said, with a smirk and a nonchalant wave of his right hand. Everyone smiled. He continued, "How do we know this isn't some political posturing?"

"Yeah, my thoughts as well," another offered.

"Well, there may be some of that," Christine Wheeler responded. Wheeler, an Afro-American ATF agent, continued. "But there's some serious stuff going on out there. A Colonel Arlo White, retired Army, has been in Texas training folks to set up the New Texas Republic and dozens of other wild-eyed groups who claim to have no interest in the separatist movement, but hate the government."

"Ah, those are guys who love to play cowboys and Indians," Lockney said. "There have always been those type of guys. I think every macho male in the West mouths anti-government stuff. They think it's manly. But there's no reason to take 'em seriously."

"This is different, Sam," Wheeler replied, as she leaned forward and stared down the table toward Sam. "We suspect White and Chapmann are directly linked to dozens of armored car robberies, the printing of counterfeit money, bank robberies and much, much more."

"You really believe these so-called patriots actually pose a serious threat to America, as opposed to the Muslim fundamentalists?" Lockney countered in a tone of disbelief.

"Now I do," Wheeler said, staring Lockney down. Lockney shook his head and rolled his eyes to underscore his chagrin.

"Christine," interrupted Wade, "Why can't we get our hands on some of these guys?"

"They protect each other," Christine said.

"Rumors are floating around Aryan Nation's groups that we tore up Chapmann's home," Lockney offered with a smile.

"Aw baloney!" Carlson exclaimed agitatedly. "State and local officials have jumped us about that incident. It's just not true. Sam, you were busy with Chapmann and White the night that raid supposedly took place. And two others agents were monitoring his brother and brother-in-law's homes farther down the mountain. No one else was in the area, and our guys didn't go near his place."

"It was probably disgruntled members of his own bunch, a related extremist group, or some of the local law enforcement that had an axe to grind or wanted to add to the myth that we're a bunch of Gestapos," clicked off Christine. "That whole ranch is booby-trapped. So whoever trashed his place had to know the layout."

"I agree," another agent said. "Whoever laid out Chapmann's security system did a very professional job. We fixed one spot so we could come and go without attracting attention, but that took real labor."

"Hell, I'd have trashed the place if it had been me!" Lockney smirked. Laughter rippled around the table." As the laughter ebbed, Lockney added, "Jeez, if they're a threat, then we ought'a take'em out and worry about the consequences later, just like in Afghanistan."

"Lockney, thank God we know you better," Christine said.

"It seems to me that the state should accept responsibility for the Chapmanns. If they let'em get away with such acts, then let them suffer the consequence," Carrasco said. "Why should they eat up our time and budget?"

A silence fell over the group. Finally, Wade looked up and said, "Okay people, let's stay with this for a little longer. Good points have been made by all. If all this patriotic activity is no more than innocent posturing by a bunch of testosterone-loaded nuts, then let's find out. But this administration wants action."

A U.S. Marshall broke in to say, "I must admit that in the light of the foreign terrorist threats, I haven't taken all these people very seriously, but I'm changing my mind. Our people have picked up rumors from local law enforcement that some of these people are storing caches of weapons. Even surface to air missiles. We've done some checking and believe there's a flow of arms from National Guard units to these various groups. My agents would like to coordinate efforts with FBI and DOD to confirm the size of this loss and take these back. While we've been focusing on foreign terrorists, a homegrown brood seems to have hatched in our own backyard."

"Good, let's try to get an inventory of what weaponry they have on hand," Wade said. "Agent Carlson, arrange to pool resources on that issue. Anyone else getting reports of arms build up?"

Carlson replied, "Yes, Darren Hopkins of the National Security Council, received a report from friends in Thailand that some of our super patriots met with Mideast terrorists and evidently arranged to buy some weapons. I put his report in the stack of material in front of each of you. Study it carefully. Share any additional information your agency receives with the rest of us."

"Agents Lockney and Wheeler, anything further to add?" Wade asked.

"Sir, we're getting increased covert movement among core members of the Christian Identity groups, but we've heard nothing about a weapons build up," Christine offered. "The leaders, including a number of these TV media preachers, have been seen in coffee clutches with key members of the KKK and various militia leaders around the country." She went on to explain how the super patriots had organized into two-person units called phantom cells. Each cell decides its own activity so others cannot be named as accomplices."

"They learned that from the Al-Qaida terrorists," Lockney said.

Wheeler looked at Lockney and nodded, then continued, saying, "And, by the way, their main targets are federal law enforcement employees."

Carlson broke in to say, "And blacks, Jews, Asians, gays and anyone else that's different. The real kooky wing of the extremists is getting more coordinated, and we better get a lid on that or we're all in deep trouble. Isn't it interesting how some of our national religious TV personalities sound like Muslim clerics?"

"Yeah," Wheeler nodded, "Extreme fundamentalists of any religion believe their world view should be imposed on everyone else. They all believe their way is God's way."

"Yeah, and if others won't accept my religious vision, then let's kill the sons-a-bitches," Lockney said, as he raised his right fist and slammed it down on the table.

The others laughed, shook their heads in wonder at Lockney's brashness, and then started leaving the meeting. Agent Carrasco almost reached the door when he turned, cocked a puzzled look at Carlson and Wade, and asked, "By the way, why is it that we plant bugs and see them disappear overnight?" The others stopped dead in their tracks at this observation. Carrasco continued, "Or, we can set a trap to serve an arrest warrant to some turkey who's been printing bogus money, sending out bogus liens or who hasn't filed an income tax for ten years, and we find the guy has flown the coop. And he hadn't changed his daily living pattern for months."

Lockney, sauntering by, said, "Someone's leaking information!"

"I don't know," Wade sighed, as he shrugged his shoulders. Then he yelled, "Meetings adjourned." Agent Wade caught Lockney outside the meeting room. "Sam, got a minute?"

"Sure, what's up?" Lockney moved to the side of the hall so others could pass, set his briefcase down and leaned against the wall.

In a whispered voice Wade said, "I heard you previewed those new stealth helicopters. What's your impression?"

"Whew, they're awesome!" Lockney said, as his eyes lit up and a big smile erupted across his face.

"No one seems to want to talk about them," Wade said. "What can you tell me?"

"I'll tell you what I've learned, but you better not tell anyone that you got this from me. Promise?"

"Promise."

"Well, it's amazing that no one on the ground can see or hear that bird."

"How so?" Wade asked.

"I mean you can hover fifty feet above someone, and they can't hear you or see you," Lockney explained, as he quickly lowered his voice and glanced up and down the hallway.

"Really?"

"True. Real stealth. I saw one guy we flew past look up and around trying to figure out where the sudden winds came from. He sensed something but never saw us. And we could hear and see everything White and Chapmann said and did in their plane."

"That's amazing. How fast will it go?"

"I don't know, but the night we tailed White and Chapmann we flew around their Cessna Two-Ten like it stood still. And I am convinced that the pilot didn't have it opened up," Lockney said.

"I didn't know they had solved the problem of speed on helicopters," Wade said. "Heretofore one-hundred-fifty knots was tops."

"Oh, this baby far exceeded that. I don't know how it works. The crew wouldn't tell me. But it seemed to be using jet propulsion somehow. It sure puts the Longbow Apache in the shade."

"Is it like the new Osprey?" asked Wade.

"No. I couldn't even tell if there were blades moving. In fact, when it was over I couldn't remember seeing any blades. The body looked like a 'copter and that's what I assumed we were in, so I didn't look too hard upon entering the craft. But when we took off we just quietly went swoosh," said Lockney, as his right hand rose and cut through the air. "I never heard any of the sounds we're used to hearing when flying. It felt like we had just cut gravity and were floating."

"God, I can't imagine," Wade exclaimed. "Do you think the Russians can keep up with it?" Wade asked, as the two men walked to the building's entrance deeply engrossed in their discussion unaware that, once again, the life of every American was about to be radically altered once again.

# 6

**DAVIS MOUNTAINS, WEST TEXAS**

Sunday, February 16

*Onward Christian Soldiers. Marching as to war,*
*With the cross of Jesus going on before!*
*Christ, the royal Master, Leads against the foe; forward into battle, See His banner go!*

The hymn faintly echoed from the little pre-fab church nestled against the mountainside, thirty or so yards off a narrow, rocky road in the Davis Mountains of West Texas. At 7:00 a.m. on this cold still dark Sunday morning in February, events transpiring in Odessa and Washington D.C. were light years away. Snow fell softly, adding to the four to five inches that had fallen during the night. The faint singing broke the quiet of the mountains. The little Davis Mountain church had a simple, glossy black cross nailed over the entrance. If not for that cross the church would have been lost among the jumble of other khaki colored prefab structures scattered indiscriminately over some twenty acres. Each had been etched into the Davis Mountains at six thousand feet. Some housed the fifty families comprising John Chudders' little band. Others served as meeting halls or work areas.

The little community nestled precariously into the sides of two large V-shaped canyons. Visitors feared to stay overnight in case a small earthquake or strong wind would send the whole community to the bottom of the canyon. The sides of each canyon had been terraced for five or six hundred feet in order to make room for the various buildings. Rock-layered paths and well-engineered gravel-covered roads provided access to the buildings. Revetments prevented landslides by buttressing the embankments along each terrace. Four ponds maintained a water supply for the compound.

A complex of rooms, chiseled into the mountains over the last twenty-five years, provided the most notable, but disguised, feature of the compound. This included living accommodations for all families, well-stocked medical and dining facilities, and workrooms and storage facilities sufficient to maintain the community in case of an emergency. The new five-thousand-square-foot weapons storage facility, located several hundred yards west of the caverns main entrance, currently stored about $3.2 million in weapons. Only family members were aware of its presence.

Reverend Chudders, a self-styled minister of an off-shoot variety brought his little band from Michigan to Fort Davis County, Texas, twenty-five years ago. He called his hideaway Yahweh City, or City of God.

In addition, Chudders' group housed ten to fifteen illegal Mexican workers a mile down the canyon. Chudders paid the workers an adequate wage and had even converted some to his fundamentalist Christian views over the years. The laborers worked a month or more and then returned to Mexico to be replaced by close friends or family members. They had early learned to keep the mountain compound a secret. The U.S. Border Patrol knew of the illegal immigrant workers, but they had their hands full. The illegal aliens working for Chudders were effectively out-of-sight and out-of-mind. Rumors did abound among West Texas law enforcement officers that Chudders had spawned a revolutionary group in Mexico, but no one could prove it. The state's attorney general laid recent conflicts in the southern Mexican State of Chiapas at Chudders' feet on several public occasions, but he couldn't prove it either.

Only about five miles of FM Road 17 between Yahweh City and the nearby town of Toyahvale had a hard-topped surface. Toyahvale lies within the southern boundary of Reeves County on West Texas's high desert plateau at approximately 3,000 feet above sea level.

The whole region is lucky to see eighteen inches of rain during any given year. The county seat is Pecos, located forty miles north of Toyahvale.

The mayor of Toyahvale claimed Yahweh City as part of the DeLaney Ranch, while other town people insisted Chudders squatted on government land. A few miles south of Toyahvale, on FM Road 17, one turned right onto a gravel road numbered 1832. It ended in eleven miles. Six strands of barbed wire protected the land on either side. Locked gates guarded the numerous roads leading off into the vast prairie. An unmarked gate on the right, located one hundred yards beyond the Stevenson Ranch gate led to Yahweh City. The road's sign kept disappearing, making the gate difficult to find. People in Toyahvale believed Chudders group kept taking it off so outsiders couldn't find them. It was true.

If one managed to find the road to Yahweh City there followed a rugged, tortuous and mountainous drive, which took almost two hours to drive in good weather. Only 4-wheeled vehicles could make it on rainy or snowy days so all Yahweh City families had 4-wheelers.

Toyahvale claimed a population of sixty. It was supported by one gas pump at a new mini mart out on U.S. 290 east, one IGA grocery, a post office, one mechanic and a dozen or so abandoned old buildings, all reminiscent of more prosperous days. One ancient amber blinking light hung as a lone vigil at the intersection of FM Road 17 and U.S. 290, which in turn looped down from Interstate 10. In addition to the ranching economy, the town drew some sportsmen and sportswomen who came to fish and boat on Lake Balmorhea, five miles northeast of town.

People of Toyahvale toiled hard to wrest a living from the West Texas environment. They talked little and were suspicious of strangers asking questions about "those folks up in the mountains." When asked about the Chudders group, people generally begged off by insisting "we don't want no trouble 'round here."

The First National Bank stood forlornly at the southwest corner of Main Street. The bank's old sign hung at an angle so traffic coming from the south and traffic going east and west on Main Street could see it. Martinez's IGA store abutted the bank's west side and faced Main Street.

The IGA store lacked air-conditioning, so two heavy glass-paned double doors always stood open, and people came and went through beat-up screen doors. The metal plates on the screen doors had originally advertised Rainbow bread, but now shone brightly from the touch of thousands of hands over the decades.

The green, wooden-slated bench to the left of the worn screen doors stretched twelve feet to the edge of the bank building. The town's old timers had hung out on this bench for as long as anyone could remember. One or two could be found there drinking coffee at the break of day, coffee freely provided by the store. And someone would be keeping watch on the bench late into the night—weather permitting. Some said Grandpa Martinez had the bench built right after World War I so returning vets would have a place to gather. He instituted the "free coffee to old timers" policy.

In the late nineteen forties the old timers' bench was bolted to the cement so pranksters couldn't move it. Some of the young men had hauled it to the top of the water tower on one occasion. It still received a new coat of paint each spring, but if you looked closely you could still see old timers' initials carved into the slats.

In recent times, J.D. Boerne, Bob Smith and Delbert Robbins manned the bench by mid-morning. They admitted to swapping lies and watching traffic zoom through town. They seemed to be the only people willing to talk to strangers about John Chudders' group. But they did that cautiously. "You better not mess with them folks, and git out'a here whil' ya can," J.D. warned.

When asked if they ever saw John Chudders, J.D. looked cautiously around to see who might be eves-dropping, then said, head shaking for emphasis, "Yeah, but he pretty much stays holed up out thar with his folks and as far as we know, he and his folks don't bother nobody 'roun here."

If pressured to give directions, they would do so reluctantly with a further warning. "You jest head off down highway seventeen here til you come to a gravel road 'bout four or five miles out and take a right. That's eighteen thirty-two. Ya go on down there 'til ya get to the Stevenson's place," Robbins said, in a tone of voice that suggested that he didn't think you could find it.

Bob Smith, pointing in the direction of the mountains as he raised his right foot to rest it on the bench, said, "The road that goes up to them folks place is about a hundred yards beyond the Stevensons, but sometimes the sign's tore down. That's what we hear anyway." His gaze turned to watch a cockroach scavenging for food on the curb.

Robbins, elbows on his legs as he leaned forward, walking cane in hand that he used to nervously tap the sidewalk, would chime in, "That's true. And if ya find it, ya probably won't make it on that road less ya' got one a them four-wheel jobbies. Ya probably shouldn't go up there in the first place. No one 'round here thinks 'bout going hunting anywhere nears them folks. We don't want no trouble." Then, he would casually gaze up and down the sidewalk to see who might be approaching.

J.D., taking his foot down off the bench as he stretched out and leaned back on the bench, said, "That's true, sure 'nuf." But if ya go you'll know you're agit'n close when ya start seein' them big 'No Trespass'n' signs. Ya better keep an eye out careful like from thar on. All them folks carry high-powered army guns and you may not see 'em, but they's a watchin' ya from behin' the cover of rocks. They's liable to shoot ya! Yeah, they sure as hell will!"

"And don't tell nobody we told ya how to get out there. We don't want no trouble," Robbins said. Both men eyed each other, and then gazed down the street in hopes the stranger would go away.

The family filled the church this frigid Sunday morning to hear John Chudders' report on his trip to Thailand. A virus caught in Asia had kept him abed since returning, so all were eager to hear about the trip.

The males wore a mixture of military camouflage khaki-colored clothes and military-style combat boots. The women sported denim jeans with heavy wool-plaid shirts, while others wore pants or old-style men's bib-overalls. All wore fleece-lined, military jackets and coats.

Sara Chudders, John's senior wife, led the singing this snowy morning, as usual. One of Chudders' daughters played the piano. Son-in-law, Jeb Harris, read the scriptures. Everyone present was related either by blood or marriage. When asked how many wives and children Chudders had, members of the group laughed saying, "Oh, dozens." Or, "It's nobody's business."

Chudders asked Jeb to read from the Book of Revelation, chapter 11:15-19:

Then the seventh angel blew his trumpet, and there were
loud voices in heaven, saying,
'The Kingdom of the world has become
the kingdom of our Lord and of his
Messiah, and he will reign forever and ever.
Then the twenty-four elders who sit on their thrones before
God fell on their faces and worshipped God, singing
We give you thanks, Lord God Almighty,
who are and who were,
for you have taken your great power and
begun to reign.
The nations raged, but your wrath has come,
and the time for judging the dead,
for rewarding your servants, the prophets
and saints and all who fear your name
both small and great,
and for destroying those who destroy
the earth.

Chudders' sermon lasted for almost three hours and seemed to excite everyone except the children. The network of kindred revolutionary spirits had been established worldwide, and they looked forward to the second coming of Jesus Christ. Finally, about the Thailand meeting, Chudders, looking exhausted as he leaned on the pulpit, said, "The time is a comin' my family, when this nation will be cleansed of its sin and the wicked punished. I went with some other dedicated Christian men last month to meet some folks from other countries who might wanna help us in this fight." He stepped back, took his handkerchief from his left rear pocket and wiped the sweat from his face.

After a few seconds, he leaned back on the pulpit and continued, "We had men from the Aryan Nations, Jubilee, Scriptures for America, The Order, KKK, Police Against the New World Order, and a lots a others. We share many things. We believe our White race is in critical danger, and we need to cleanse our nation of all them inferior races by whatever means. Second, we agreed there is a plot by big international companies and Jew families to create a single world government."

Chudders paused for emphasis. After a few seconds he used his right finger in a stabbing motion, as he said menacingly, "Which they'll control. Third, we agreed that our own gover'ment is the enemy of our race and is guilty of treason." Again he paused for emphasis, then leaned over the pulpit and yelled, "And the penalty for treason has always been death!"

He straightened up, wiped the sweat from his increasingly red face, then continued, "Our foundin' fathers unnerstood this, for they wrote the Declaration of Independence, saying it's the 'right' and 'duty' of the people to throw off a wicked and ungodly gover'ment."

Chudders motioned to one of his sons to bring him a chair, which he placed on the edge of the dais. He continued, "The A-rabs seem to wanna help us with arms and money. We told them we didn't want them meddl'in in our cause in any other way. We can share information and resources, but we told 'em that when we succeed we don't want no meddling in our business. We hope they'll eventually kill each other off over there."

At that moment, a sudden wind hit the building. It whipped the church with such force that windows shook and the little church rattled. While mothers calmed their children and the teens and older youth looked at each other for reassurance, John Chudders railed on.

"When the arms start comin', we'll be only one of many hiding places. They ought a start showin' up here on a regular basis in March. They be packed in from Mexico." He wiped his face, scratched vigorously behind his left ear, stared off to his right for a moment, as if trying to remember what he had to say, and then continued.

"Them Germans skin-heads wuz gangsters, in my opinion. I wuz ag'inst havin' em there, but they wuz invited anyhow." He shook his head in disbelief, then said, "Some a our people believed they could be put to good use. They wanted to help, which is no problem to us as long as they kill off the sick elements of their country and leave us alone."

The storm intensified outside. Chudders continued to sweat as he ranted on. "Some a our group believed we may have problems with them skinheads in the future, I don'no."

Then, he stood up and paced back and forth on the dais, hands clasped behind his back and head down. "As we've discussed so often, that stuff at Ruby Ridge, Waco and the daily abuse by the government against ordinary, good Christian folk, have showed us that the gover'ment's working as fast as it can to destroy us." He jerked his right arm from behind his back and shook his fist in the air to emphasize his point.

Then, he stopped, looked directly at his little congregation and said, "We are told by good sources that they's buildin' prison camps to put us in. We also know the gover'ment's supporting city gangs, like them Bloods and Crips, so they'll kill whites and create. . . " Here he paused and stammered as he searched for the right words, then said, "terror in the cities."

He stopped, wiped more sweat from his face, rubbed his eyes and started pacing the dais again. After a few strides he said, "This gives the gover'ment the excuse to do martial law. They's tryin' to disarm us, so they can slaughter us like innocent lambs." At this point he sounded like he would cry, but after a few seconds of silence he composed himself, and with a fist flailing the air, screamed, "But we're Yahweh's loyal disciples, and we'll join with others of his children to make a new creation where all will live by Yahweh's laws."

The storm continued to rage and Chudders' voice continued to rise as he attempted to shout over the storm's frenzy. Children huddled close to their mothers or older women. Some cried softly as their mothers tried to comfort them. Chudders' ranting could hardly be heard over the storm.

Finally, Chudders' senior wife went up, put her arm around him and said softly, "John, dear, we can't hear you anymore. Let's get everyone to safety. The wind is rattling the building and scaring the children."

# 7

## AUSTIN, TEXAS

Tuesday, February 18

Chudders' family seemed primed for the second coming of Jesus Christ as they awaited the Russian arms shipment. But, in Austin prowled a reporter for the Austin American-Statesman named Mo Childs. Mo had staked out the rise of the Texas militia and the extremist movement as his personal turf. He had developed many friends within the extremist groups "cuz he was just a good ole Texas boy," as they say in the Lone Star State. This particular Sunday evening he tried desperately to reach his childhood chum, Darren Hopkins. John Chudders had finally agreed to an interview, and Mo thought Darren might want to be there.

Mo, legally named Morris-Allen-Hopkins-Lillijedahl-Landrum-Crawford-Wagner-Childs. Everyone who knew him referred to him as a piece of work. When introduced to anyone, Mo rattled off his whole legal name, then added, "My friends jes' call me Mo." Mo acquired his long name by legally adding the surname of anyone who became significant in his life. This habit started when he graduated from high school in Austin.

Though only five feet eight or nine at age thirty-four, Mo had a lean build. His excellent gymnastics ability often proved a source of embarrassment to others because he didn't care where he chose to exhibit it. On one occasion he did a handstand on Darren's shopping cart in a local grocery.

When Darren went to work for Burcks, Mo called to announce that he had become a reporter. "But you never liked writing!" Darren declared.

"Yeah, but this is different. I love pokin' around and gettin' into things."

Same ole' Mo, thought Darren. Mo marched to the tune of a drum no one on this earth had heard before. And he always would. Astonishingly, he became a good newshound. The growing super patriot movement fascinated him. He even used his vacation time to visit militia and the many Christian identity groups throughout the nation. He'd leave his old Ford Explorer in the garage, crank up his Harley and take to the highways. Mo became a critical source of Darren's information about the super patriot movement.

Even before Darren went to work for the NSC Mo had told him that the patriots' network teemed with hints that federal agents would be killed by a big explosion around the nineteenth of April, as a memorial to the Branch-Davidians who died in nineteen ninety three. He did not know the details of this bombing, so he could not alert authorities. He also had a suspicion that they would try to blow up the FBI Building in Washington. A few weeks later Oklahoma City's Murrah Building exploded. While the Muslim attack on the World Trade Center and the subsequent war against the terrorists preoccupied the super patriots, it unintentionally forged a greater unity among the various parties. In their opinion, the government's failure to prosecute the war more militantly reminded them of Vietnam and added another nail in the coffin of America's demise.

Mo's information proved to be more detailed and reliable than the FBI's. Darren needed to know when meetings had been held, by whom and for what purpose, and the plans to establish state militia throughout all fifty states. In the early months of research, Mo treated the super patriot activity humorously. Laughingly, he told Darren on one early occasion, "Man, these militia are a bunch of macho, social misfits, who love playing soldier." But since the bombing of the World Trade Center and the war against Mideast terrorists, Mo's attitude had changed. He now found a new sense of militancy among the extremists. "Darren, these guys want to take over the government and nuke all the people in the axis of evil."

"What do you mean?" Darren asked.

"Since the war on Mideast terrorists they seemed to have become more strident and more sophisticated. But I can't tell where this is coming from as yet."

Darren noticed that Mo's voice became increasingly tinged with fear. Mo called several times a week to report on events. Darren passed his notes on to General Burcks. He has only revealed the source of his information to Burcks, who agreed to protect Darren's source.

Darren found a call from Mo waiting when he got to his office this Tuesday morning. He called Mo, and after listening to his invitation to meet John Chudders, asked, "What's our risk?"

"Aw, there ain't any risks going out there. I'll introduce you as an old friend. In fact, we'll plan a float trip down the Rio Grande River through the Big Bend canyons. That'll satisfy the old guy's suspicions about you."

"When is he expecting you?"

"I've got to be up there sometime Saturday. Can you make it?"

"I guess so. I'd like another trip out to the Big Bend country. Let me clear this with General Burcks. I'll try to come in Thursday. Okay?"

"Sure. Just let me know as quick as you can."

"I will. Let's eat at the County Line Thursday night, okay?"

"Okay. But you're buying."

Same old Mo.

Thursday, February 20

Darren exited the Austin airport terminal to a temperature in the mid-sixties and a clear blue sky. Flowers bloomed and birds sang. "How sweet it is!" he sighed, as he inhaled deeply. Every return to Austin felt like stepping into the past. Same streets, same scenes, same smells.

He picked up a rental car, then dropped off his suitcase at his parents' home. He donned some leisure clothes before Mo picked him up and they hit the County Line restaurant. After exchanging information on old friends, Mo asked the inevitable. "Heard anything from Ann?"

"We've talked off and on. Right now she's on some kind of hush-hush assignment. I worry a lot, but there doesn't seem to be anything I can do."

"Well, ya could marry the gal," replied Mo.

"That's true," Darren responded. "But neither one of us seems to be willing to settle down. She loves her job." After a few moments of silence, Darren asked, "Why don't you bring me up-to-date on the extremist movement." Then, looking around he asked impatiently, "Where the hell's the waiter? I'm thirsty." He caught a young woman's eye, and she came over and took their drink orders.

"You can't imagine what these guys are trying to do!" Mo said.

"Wait," Darren said as he reached into his briefcase for a tape recorder. "I need to get this on tape." Mo scanned the menu as Darren got his recorder ready. "Okay. Shoot."

"Well," Mo said as he tried to pick up his thought pattern, "the most public group established a secessionist Republic of Texas, complete with a president, vice-president, secretary-of-state and all the rest. They've even set up their own defense force in each county and have their own version of the Texas Rangers."

"Yeah, so you've been telling me."

"The state's attorney general became concerned, but only after government officials all over the state started receiving warrants issued by the new Texas Republic which said they had been acting illegally."

"Oh you've got'a be kiddin'!"

"Not at all. Last year they tried to arrest a U.S. district judge in San Antonio. Then they sent out thousands of official lookin' indictments, arrest warrants and liens, that still clog court dockets throughout the state of Texas." The waitress arrived with their steaks and Darren put away his tape recorder.

After they had eaten, Darren restarted his recorder and asked, "Go ahead, what else happened?"

"Well, after this crap hit the fan, the state's attorney general filed a motion for civil contempt against all the officials of the new Republic of Texas." Both laughed.

"It's hard to believe what goes on in the heads of people," Darren said.

"Yeah, and this would be comical, but the movement seems to be growing."

"How committed is the leadership?" Darren asked.

"Last month the fellow they elected an ambassador looked me in the eye with a steely glare and said, 'We have a chance to have a bloodless coup. But we won't wait forever." Mo tried to look authoritative as he deepened his voice, squinted his eyes and put on a mean look.

"You're kidding!" Darren said.

"Not at all. He told me last week that the state and federal governments had to vacate their offices and turn control of Texas over to the Republic."

"These people have been eating loco weed," Darren said.

"Nope. They are dead serious. I've been told July fourth is the deadline for compliance, which is also when they plan to have their Constitutional Convention."

Darren asked, "And what if the state and federal governments don't respond to the new republic's threat?"

"They threaten to go to war."

Mo, stared into space, leaned across the table and continued. "These guys think all Texas lands, funds and securities belong to their republic. Using some kind of mental mumbo-jumbo, they've convinced themselves the state's original ratification is illegal and that Texas is an independent nation."

At this point Mo shook his head, took another drink, and said, "One of the guys they appointed as judge went and notified the Internal Revenue Service in Washington to cease all operations in Texas. He gave 'em ten days to vacate their Texas offices."

"Well, that's the sanest thing I've heard them do!" Darren said. Both men laughed. "But given the total picture of what we know nationally, it doesn't seem out of the ordinary for a segment of these so-called patriots."

"Maybe not, but there's more fun stuff. They wear uniforms with special militia symbols and train with live ammunition."

"Where's the ammo coming from?" Darren asked, as he eyed a couple across the dining room. They looked familiar. Then he realized how tired he felt.

Mo said, "I'm told that sympathetic members of the Texas National Guard steal the stuff."

Darren brought his attention back to Mo's narrative, took a deep breath and asked, "How does it get in the right hands?"

"It's stored in hidden warehouses. And to make matters worse, the crazy governing council authorized militia members to execute their laws whenever a county, municipal or Texas peace officer failed to do so. They've set up their own damn court system across the state."

"Unbelievable. Wait, let's get some more drinks." He motioned for the waitress, who came immediately. "Bring us some more ice tea," Darren asked. "Okay, Mo, go ahead."

"Well, let's see."

"You mentioned the governing council."

"Oh yeah. Well, the governing council also issued a resolution urging militia members to defend Texans against covert or overt action by the United Nations, North Atlantic Treaty Organization, the United States of America or the state of Texas. Ain't that a kicker?" Mo said with a laugh.

"I'll say."

"Furthermore, they've taken the flag designed by the first Texas Congress in eighteen thirty-six as their own. It has a yellow star against a blue background."

"That's interesting. I wonder what members of the Christian Identity movement think about that? They rail about the Jewish conspiracy, yet accept a flag with a yellow star, reminiscent of the Star of David."

"Yeah. Crazy logic."

The popular dining facility had filled while they talked and, as they looked around, Mo said, "Good thing we came early."

"Yeah," Darren agreed. "For a minute I didn't think they'd let us in when they saw your dirty ole cut off pants."

"Ah, hell with 'em. This is Austin, for cryin' out loud. We wear anything, and nothing." Both chuckled at the thought of Austin's laid-back atmosphere.

Mo stared out the large window at nothing in particular. His mind seemed locked on something far away. Finally, he said quietly, "Did I tell you that the Republic's governing council also filed a ninety-three-trillion-dollar claim against the U.S. federal government, the international monetary fund and the Holy See of the Roman Catholic Church?"

"What?" Darren said, almost dropping his tea. "That's hilarious. But why the Catholic Church?"

"They claim it's payback for one-hundred-fifty years of plundering. Then, before the latest UN General Secretary left office they petitioned his office for acceptance of the new Republic of Texas. I've been told that the cover letter ended with a paragraph stating something like, 'thousands of Texians are prepared to defend their nation by force of arms if invaded by United States or United Nations troops.'"

"Wow," Darren said as he shook his head in disbelief. "Did they get a response?"

"Nah. At least none that I'm aware of."

"Mo, what legal action has been taken to rein in this separatist's movement?"

"Oh, they pick up a few people now and then driving without license plates. They haul 'em in and fine 'em, but they're out'a court quick as a wink," Mo said with a snap of his fingers.

"They must have plenty of financial backing."

"Yep, an attorney pops up when needed. Last year San Antonio's Federal Judge Floyd Berry convicted some guys of mail fraud. One disappeared during the trial, and they haven't found him yet."

"He's probably still running!" Darren laughed. "What happened to the others?"

"Oh, they got some jail time and fines. I think they're out now. A number of others have been charged and jailed for filing hundreds of bogus liens. Most of the time these guys don't show up in court. They've got an extensive network of hideaways. Besides, most local lawmen are either members or sympathizers."

"I'm not surprised. There's a lot of anger toward the federal and state governments today. This morning a federal judge gave an old gal in California sixteen years for running a phony check scam. She said she picked it up from the Montana groups."

Just then a couple of old acquaintances dropped by the table and visited with Darren and Mo for a few minutes.

"Mo, let's get out'a here. I think they want our table. The waitress keeps staring at us." Darren put his tape recorder away as the cashier took his credit card.

As they walked across the parking lot, Mo said, "I didn't watch the news this morning, but I've been hearin' about that phony check scam for some time now. A guy in New Braunfels named Billy Bob Horton told me some gal in California also sold eight hundred million dollars worth of phony warrants." Both grinned.

Darren said, "Yep, sadly, the folks who bought 'em tried to pay off mortgages and debts with the junk."

"That's sad," Mo said .

"Yeah. Before the judge sentenced her he reportedly told her that she had done more damage to the banking system than most bank robbers. He said she dropped an atomic bomb on the system."

"I'm sure that made her happy!" Mo exclaimed.

"Oh, you can bet on that. She'll be a new martyr to the separatist cause."

They drove over to take in the sights on east Sixth Street, a popular hangout for University of Texas students, visitors and the rest of Austin's denizens. The crowds made conversation difficult. They paused at the corner of San Jacinto Street to watch a longhaired, tattooed old hippie painting a girl's face. A line had formed. They threaded their way through the crowd as they walked on toward Congress.

Darren moved close to Mo's left ear as they walked and said, "I'd like to get a list of the super patriots across this country if possible. We know some of the key leaders, but we need as complete a list as possible. Can you help me?"

Pausing to think about Darren's proposal, Mo turned to look him square in the eye and said, "Yeah, as long as you swear on your mother's grave that you'll never tell where ya got it."

"I promise."

"And, in return you got'a promise me that I'll get inside information from your office before other reporters do."

"I'll agree to that generally. And you must promise on your mother's grave never to tell where you got that information either!" Both laughed.

"Checkmate!" Mo yelled.

Finally, Darren said, "Mo, I'm pooped. Let's call it a night."

As Darren crawled into bed, the phone rang. "Who in the hell would that be," he muttered.

"Hopkins, you still awake?" General Burcks asks.

"Barely. I've been out with my reporter friend. We're heading to West Texas in a few hours."

"Fine," Burcks said. "I wanted you to know that I've been in a fairly lengthy NSC meeting and that a huge Russian arms shipment seems to be moving. CIA doesn't know where the stuff is headed, but when the discussion reviewed all the possibilities I couldn't help but think of our super patriots."

"There's no doubt in my mind where it's headed," Darren said softly. His tired eyelids refused to open. Aware that Burcks often experienced trouble sleeping and that misery loves company, he hoped this would not be a lengthy discussion.

George Burcks finally signed off, "Just be careful out there. I'd hate to have to find and train another aide."

Darren and Mo left Austin early the next morning, headed southwest on IH-35 in Mo's old Bronco, and then picked up IH-10 out of San Antonio. They took turns driving and dozing as Mo's old beat-up 1978 Ford Bronco hummed along. They found the road just beyond the old Stevenson's place out on FM Road 1832 south of Toyahvale by mid-afternoon. They maneuvered the rocky rutted road that threaded its way up and down the canyons of the rugged Davis Mountains. They covered the thirty-five miles in two hours.

They knew they had arrived when they rounded a bend and found the road blocked by two surplus army trucks. Behind each truck stood four unsmiling men pointing rifles at them.

"Mo, you better do something quick. This is your party!" Darren said.

Mo, who had been driving, got out, raised his hands and yelled, "Hey, I'm Mo Childs from the Austin American-Statesman in Austin. I have an appointment with Reverend Chudders."

One of the men approached and asked to see some identification. Mo and Darren handed him their business cards. He glared at Mo and Darren. Finally, he said, "Follow us."

"Thank God you didn't rattle off all your surnames or we both would've been shot!" Darren said.

They drove for several miles along a smooth, well-maintained graveled road. The climb got sharper and the canyons more rugged as they climbed. Finally, they emerged to see a fairly substantial complex of buildings covering both sides of a steep canyon. They followed the two vehicles into a parking area next to a modest sized Quonset type structure, evidently used as a church. Mo parked between the two trucks. As they stepped from the Bronco four men surrounded Darren and Mo and ushered them along a path to a room attached to the rear of the church. They waited while one man disappeared into an office. Three or four minutes passed while the other three men stared at Mo and Darren. Mo tried to engage the men in conversation, but no one responded. Darren, getting a bit irked, said, "Mo, they're obviously not supposed to speak to us."

"Guess not. Boy, sure hurts my feelings."

Finally the fourth man reappeared and motioned for Mo and Darren. As they entered they came face to face with John Chudders. They gazed upon an old man, probably in his mid-seventies. (Mo and Darren would argue about his age for a long time). Chudders, smaller than expected, had thick flowing gray hair and a white beard highlighted by a ruddy face and bulbous nose. Later Mo remarked that he looked like a miniature Santa Claus. He wore a red-flannel shirt under a pair of dark blue, old-fashioned farmer's coveralls and sported a well-developed stomach bulge.

Contrary to expectations, Chudders exuded a warm and charming personality. After shaking hands and patting Mo and Darren on the back in a friendly fashion, he said, "Boys, so good of ya'll to come all this way jest to visit this ole man." As he moved to sit at his desk, he pointed to two worn out padded chairs and said, "Have a seat thar." Darren and Mo sat. "I bet you fellas are thirsty. Luke, get these boys somethin' cold to drink." He turned and asked Mo and Darren, "Coke, tea or plain mountain water?"

"Water would be fine," Mo said, as Darren nodded his assent. Within a few minutes a middle-aged woman arrived with a pitcher of iced water and three glasses.

"Want'cha boys to meet my old lady. Sara, this here's Mo Childs, that reporter I wuz tellin' ya about, and his friend. What'cha say your name wuz young fella?"

"Darren Hopkins."

"Oh yeah."

Mo nodded politely. Darren smiled broadly and emitted a somewhat lame, "Howdy." Sara bowed her head gracefully, but didn't say a word. She left quietly and quickly.

Chudders looked at Darren and asked, "Are you with the newspaper?"

"No sir. I do some overseas consulting for a company out of California."

"Mr. Chudders," Mo said, "he came along to keep me company. We thought we might have time after the interview to float down Mariscal or Boquillas canyons "

"Aw, shucks, I don't mind him bein' here. I ain't got nuthin' to hide, for goodness sake. Jest cuz we choose to live out in the mountains away from other people don't mean I'm not sociable or doin' somethin' wrong, like crankin' out moonshine or somethin'." Everyone laughed politely.

"May I tape this interview so I can keep my mind on our conversation?" Mo asked.

After a few moments of silence, John Chudders said, "Sure. Like I said, I got nothin' to hide." Mo sat the tape machine on the desk in front of Chudders.

Mo, never one to dilly-dally, went right to the heart of the issue. "Let me start by asking why you came out here."

Somewhat taken aback by Mo's directness, Chudder's eyes widened, and then he smiled knowingly. He began a lengthy historical sketch of the community's history, the gist being that he moved his religious family to West Texas so they could practice their Christian faith without being polluted by the mainline churches, all of which Satan had taken over. "The time is near when God is going to purify this nation and my little flock will be ready to join a few other groups around the nation and institute the real Church of Jesus Christ," Chudders stated calmly.

"Why do you think you are the only true believers?" Mo asked.

"Well, first of all, God spoke to me in a special way and told me that hisself."

Chudders leaned back in his chair and hooked his thumbs the bib of his coveralls. Then, with a slight smile he said, "Now, ain't no one goin' to believe me." Then, fanning the air with his arms, said, "But he told me to leave Sodom and Gamorra, which is all them cities and towns out there 'cross this country, and go into a far country."

His voice gradually got louder. "I figured after lookin' at the map and talkin' to people that these West Texas mountains seemed as far a country as we could find."

Chudders rose from his chair and walked to a window where he pointed to the mountains and his community. "My people study the Bible daily, we pray daily, and we take care of each other, and we don't bother nobody. We jes' wanna be left alone."

"Do you own this property?" Mo asked.

Chudders walked back to his chair in deep thought, sat down, relaxed somewhat, took a deep breath, cocked his head to the side and narrowly eyed Mo. Then, in a soft and steely voice he said, "Yes, little man, we do. God gave it to us. It wuz untamed wilderness, good-fer-nothin' and we paid the price to carve our home into the sides of these mountains, jest like they did in Jesus' day. Yep, this is ours."

Chudders abruptly leaned across his desk, shoved his index finger at Mo, grimaced, and said, "Better no gover'ment come in here and try to take it away either."

"I assume you don't pay state or federal taxes of any kind, Mo said. "And we noticed that you don't have license plates and inspection stickers on your trucks."

Darren found himself wincing at Mo's directness. Trying to pretend disinterested in the interview, Darren looked around the room, stared at his hands and glanced at Mo, then John Chudders. He had never seen this facet of Mo's personality.

"Boy, you're somethin," Chudders said with a tight grin. "You're right. We don't pay nobody nothin'. We don't belong to the United States of 'merica anymore. We don't belong to the State of Texas neither. Yahweh City is God's, and only God's."

"Well, how do you pay for groceries, clothes and other materials you need from that outside world?" Mo asked.

In a soft voice, Chudders replied, "We're pretty self-sufficient here. We trade some things we make here for other goods from time to time. But we brought a lot of things we already owned with us when we came. And as others join from time to time, they donate their stuff. Then we have a whole bunch of people who send us things."

Darren made mental notes of the office's furnishings. A used four-drawer file cabinet occupied one corner, a scratched up oak desk faced one wall, and two stuffed chairs stood against a second wall. A small lamp table, with peeling paint stood against a third wall. A path had been worn into the plain wooden floor from the outside door to what they later decided was a church sanctuary's entrance. Pictures of Jesus adorned the walls. The furnishings may be plain, but the place is clean, Darren thought.

"I've heard you've joined some militia groups in the northwest to print your money. Is that true?" Mo asked.

"Wellllll," he drawled, pausing to consider his response. "Let me jes' say this 'bout that. Yep, there's folks who think a lot like we do that have banded together and are gettin' ready for the cleansing fires. Some printed money and, yes, we used it. But ya gotta understan' that we used that money within the new nation that's emergin'. We don't go down here to no store and buy their goods with it. No sir. That ain't right."

"You mentioned cleansing fires, and I noticed when we drove in that your men are armed," Mo said. "Is a war coming and are you stockpiling weapons like the militia and other so-called patriot's groups are doing?"

"Have you seen any stockpiles?"

"No sir, sure haven't."

Chudders spread his arms out to either side. "Well, there ya go. See?" Then, shaking his head from side to side and waggling his right index finger in the air in a no-no sign, said, "Rumors. Evil rumors."

He relaxed and took a sip of water. "Satan works that way, don't ya see. The devil starts these rumors to get God's people killed and imprisoned. Right now the gov'ment of the United States is preparing prison compounds to put us away. As to cleanin' fires, well, the final judgment day is coming soon! Satan's people are fightin' it. A lot' a good people are gonna git killed."

"When's this killing going to start?" Mo asked.

Chudders, disbelief flowing from widened eyes, extended his arms once again, "It's already started! Don't you keep up with your own papers and that television stuff."

Chudders pointed north. "Where ya been lately? All the killin' that's been goin' on in those Arab countries. And then, that fella's wife and kid got killed by government men up there in Idaho and all those people in Waco." He let that sink in, then continued. "Many others been killed but the government has kept it from the people or there'd be an uprising ag'in the government." He shook his head vigorously. "Lordy, man. Lordy, Lordy. It's comin'. But this time God's children ain't goin'a be slaughtered like lambs. No sir. Uh-huh. Not this time!" He slammed his right fist on the table and then sat back with his arms folded across his chest.

Darren broke in. "You mentioned the Muslim terrorists. Did you agree with what they did to the World Trade Center?"

"No, sir. But it's like them TV preachers said, you folks brought that on yurselves. God was punishing ya'll."

"Do you really believe that?" Darren asked.

"Yes, sir. I do. It's in the Bible."

As Chudders took a deep breath and prepared to answer, Mo spoke up. "Sounds like you and others are preparing for a war with your own countrymen!"

Eyes widening in alarm, Chudders replied, "Now, I didn't say that." Again, he waggled his right index finger in the air to make his point. "What I said wuz we'll not be slaughtered like lambs. We'll protect ourselves if they try to take us off to them prisons."

Darren changed the subject. "How many people live up here?" he asked, as he stood, stretched and poured himself another glass of water.

"Oh, 'tween two to three hunnert," Chudders replied, as he seemed to relax in his chair.

"All blood relations?" Darren asked.

"Oh, I see," Chudders said, smiling and throwing his head back slightly. "Ya heard I got a bunch a wives. Well, let me say this about that. Yes, I do have a few wives. Four to be exact. But that's nobody's business."

"I didn't mean to get into your personal life, I'm wondering about your community's diversity," Darren said. Chudders looked blank. "Do you have any Hispanics, Afro-Americans or other non-Anglo races among your group?" Darren continued.

Chudders leaned out of his seat and, as he fixed Darren with a steely gaze, the right elbow resting on his knee, his right index finger stabbed the air menacingly, punctuating each word for emphasis, as he said in a high pitched voice, "No, son, we don't. The Bible don't go for mixin' races." He stopped stabbing the air with his finger and leaned back in his chair as he continued. "I got nuthin' against blacks, browns, pinks or purples. But God called the white race together to be the new tribe of Israel and that's all I'm gonna say 'bout that. No sense arguing with you boys cuz you don't understan'."

Chudders leaned back in his chair as he eyed Darren and Mo. Chudders broke the silence. "Tell me somethin' now. You boys got any religion?"

Mo shrugged and said he believed in God if that's what Chudders meant. Chudders then looked at Darren and waited for a response. "I'm not religious." Darren said. I consider myself a Christian and there's a world of difference between being religious and being Christian."

Chudders' eyes widened.

"What'd ya mean?" he asked.

"Christianity's a celebration of God's redemptive act in human history on behalf of all humankind," Darren started. Chudders squinted his eyes as he tried to get his mental arms around the thought. Darren continued, "Religion, on the other hand, is the stuff people do to either manipulate God or create our own righteousness. Man's religious exercises have led to more deaths than any other human motive, political or economic."

"Ummm," Chudders replied. "I hadn't thought 'bout that. But I can see I rang your bell." Darren grinned. Chudders slapped his knees in merriment. "I don't see the difference you're makin' though."

Mo jumped in. "Is it possible that we can get a tour of Yahweh City?"

Chudders pulled a handkerchief from his left rear pocket and wiped his eyes. "Boys, I can take ya'll outside and point out houses, but you can stand there in the parking lot and see all our little village. We don't like outsiders wander'n around like we're a zoo or somthin'. Uh-uh, that's no good. Sorry."

"That's okay," Mo said. "We noticed you have some huge iron doors on the side of the mountain up there. Have you dug some caves?"

Chudders' eyes narrowed and his voice took on an irritated tinge. "Naw, we've gouged out a little bit'a dirt to give us a few places to keep some food. The women do some cannin'. That's all."

"Well, let me get back to these other groups you've often mentioned. Are you in contact with the Christian Identity, state militia and men like Petsch and others?"

"Oh, we know some fellas out there. Yes, indeedy. But like I said earlier, we jes' wanna be left alone."

"Some patriots in the San Antonio-Austin area say you're one of the key leaders of this new movement across the country."

"Oh, I don't know 'bout that," Chudders shrugged, blushing.

"And I hear there's to be a national level meeting of some of the main shakers and movers soon. Do you know where it'll be?"

"Wow, hold on!" Chudders exclaimed. He started to get out of his chair but sat back down, shook his head and took a deep breath. "I don't know nuthin' about no meetin'."

The three men bantered back and forth a few minutes, then Chudders stood and Mo and Darren followed suit. Chudders put his hand on Mo's left shoulder and pushed him gently toward the door, "That's all the time I got. You boys come back agin' some time."

Darren and Mo drove out of the compound area in silence. The two military trucks led them back down the mountain. When they waved them on, Mo looked out the rear-view mirror and noticed that the men were watching them with binoculars.

Five miles down the road, Mo said, "I'll bet they're still watching us from somewhere."

"I suppose," Darren replied. "That was an interesting session. I appreciate coming along. Those buildings they've built up there don't look strong enough to stand up to a real storm. I'd be afraid to live up there for very long."

"You may be right. I thought you got his blood boiling when you denied being a religious man!" They both laughed.

"Sorry. I couldn't help it. I get irritated with religious fundamentalists. They're always trouble. And it doesn't matter whether they're Christian or Muslim. They use the Divine to impose their will and destroy others."

They drove on to the Big Bend's Panther Junction in silence. They had reserved a cabin and planned to rise early to run the Rio Grande River's Mariscal and Boquillas Canyon rapids.

After checking in, Darren called General Burcks' secure line and left a message:

"Met Chudders. Interesting man, he's hiding a lot of arms in those mountains. A veritable fortress up in those canyons. I left a bug in his office, so alert military intelligence surveillance. More later." Darren.

John and Sara Chudders stood in the office doorway and watched the two strangers leave. Several others joined them. "Well, I think that went all right. That reporter fella knows a lot about what's goin' on. Makes me nervous!"

One of the men standing nearby asked, "Why'd ya let'em come up? Ya never let strangers come."

"Yep, but Chapmann and the rest'a those fellas that went to Asia with me said it'd be better ta let a reporter come up once awhile. They said it'd help stop all them lies they say 'bout us."

"Who were those guys?"

"Oh, that little one's Mo Childs with that Austin paper. Some say he writes fair. We want them state official's ta let up on us some. One'a you boys take that other fella's business card and check up on him. I got a funny feeling about that one."

"By the way," Sara said, "We got a message on the short-wave that said we should expect a shipment of arms from Mexico shortly."

"Wow! Things is movin'!" Chudders exclaimed. "Them camel jockeys are serious."

# 8

**WASHINGTON D.C.**
Monday, February 24

Darren had lunch with General Burcks at the Willard Hotel and reported the results of his meeting with Chudders.

"Could you tell what the man's got hidden in those mountains?" Burcks asked.

"All we know for sure is that he has a large group of women, some couples and a lot of children. He calls the whole gaggle his family."

"And are they?" Burcks asked.

"Very doubtful. We didn't get to visit with any of them, but other members of the super patriotic movement say there are a number of outside couples and their children who have joined the group over the years. They view the United States as an evil empire. I suspect they would be happy to see the Islamic fundamentalists destroy us."

Burcks smiled and nodded. "That's pretty grim."

"His followers believe Chudder's claim to be some kind of special messenger from God," Darren said.

"Yes, those types crop up around this world in every age," Burcks said , as he shook his head in disgust. "They'll always pop up because many people can't cope with life in the real world. Others are so theologically ignorant they fall for anyone who is passionate about his beliefs. Hell, he could believe in the alligator god and people would follow him. Shades of Osama bin Laden!"

"There are historians who see such religious behavior as a sign of growing decadence."

"How so?" Burcks asked.

"Supposedly people lose the sense of a future or of the possible, so they retreat into some simplified version of the past. A simpler time. The present is sinful. It's controlled by demons."

"We certainly seem to have an increasing number of those," Burcks said.

"Yeah, so do the Mideast folks. Osama bin Laden and his associates are expressions of societal decadence in the Arab societies."

"As is old Jim Jones, Dr. Moon, and all the other cultic groups we've seen lately," Burcks said.

"Yeah, and a lot of these TV preachers find this fertile ground for riches." After a few seconds of silence, Darren said, "Chudders has a formidable fortress up there."

"Well, we may have to go in there one of these days and pry him out of it," Burcks said . "For the present, I think you ought to get a set of pictures of our most notorious super patriot leaders and go to Thailand and see if anyone at that resort can identify those who attended that meeting. I probably should have had you do that when we first heard about that party. We need evidence that will put them away."

"That's fine with me, sir."

After a few moments of silence, Burcks asked, "Any news from Ann?"

"No sir. Have you heard any more?"

"Nothing. I know you're worried. Maybe you can find out something helpful during your trip. She has a first rate reputation, so it may be that we are receiving some disinformation to harass you."

"Do you think so?"

"I thought that from the beginning. So did her station chief in Bangkok."

Burcks picked up the check. "If we can get enough evidence to identify each of those guys beyond a shadow of a doubt, we can bring charges against them and put them away for a long time." Burcks continued talking as he walked toward the cashier. "I'm anxious to know how they got from Hong Kong to Changmai without being noticed."

"I'll work on that. The CIA promised to supply me with pictures of those on that yacht with Yuri Tavanovich and Agent Carlson, the FBI's representative on the domestic task force staff, said they would install pictures of super patriot suspects on a lap top computer I could carry. By the way, how'd you know I was planning to ask permission to go over and do this research?" Both men laughed.

"I've come to know you pretty well. There's been an increase in the number of times you've raised the question as to those guy's identity. And it's increasingly clear that we need this information, and I knew you would want to chase it. But I also know you wanted a chance to find out about Ann."

"I appreciate that."

"I hate to see you moping around like a sick puppy. But, better watch your rear. We can't protect you from here."

YAHWEH CITY, TEXAS
Monday, February 24

While Darren and Burcks were meeting, the leaders of the new super patriot movement were gathering at Chudders' West Texas fortress. Colonel Arlo White, General Ernst Boorgers, Ron Chapmann, and the Reverends Petsch and Chudders met around a large circular table in a cavernous room deep in the bowels of the mountain of Yahweh City. Stacks of military armaments surrounded the men. "John," an astonished Ron Chapmann asked, "did all this come out of that Louisiana depot?"

"Naw, we got three truckloads up here night 'fore last from there, but the rest come from Lubbock, El Paso, Tucson and Amarillo. And, if memory serves me right, some come down from Denver last year."

"How much have you issued?" White asked.

"We ain't kept no records," Chudders said. "We don't think that's wise. But 'bout once a week, a few guys notify us they're comin' by to get some guns. So, we dole 'em out some."

"Do you let people come up here and pick through the inventory?" Petsch asked.

"Oh, no, sir. Nooooo, sireee. We meet 'em at a spot down the mountain that you might'a seen a comin' up." Then drawing a circle in the air with his right index finger, he said, "That large turnaround down there we carved into the canyon 'bout two miles back. Took a bit of dynamite to do that," he said, with a slight smile. "But once someone calls and lets us know they's comin', what they'll be drivin', their identity so we can verify'em, and what weapons they'd like to have, we load up what they think they ought 'a get and haul it down there."

"How much more space have you been able to carve out in the last few months?" Chapmann asked.

"Le'me show ya." Chudders led the group down a large tunnel into a newly cut room of about four thousand square feet. "We got all the wetbacks we could out 'a Mexico and worked 'em 'round the clock. Two of my folks is engineers. They know their stuff. U.S. Army taught 'em 'bout explosives. Yep, taught 'em good." Then Chudders led the men into another room of about fifty-six hundred square feet. "I should fess up, and tell ya'll we been a work'n on these extra rooms for months. We just had a feelin' they'd come in handy, and my boys told me that this area of the mountain wuz the easiest to excavate."

"Wow," Chapmann said. "General, don't you think this is a nice addition to our stockpiling needs?"

"It's fine," barked an emotionless Boorgers. "We're going to need a lot of storage when all those arms hit our borders in the next few weeks."

The men then returned to the conference room.

Chapmann, mouth ajar in surprise, looked questioningly at White as Boorgers took charge. White ignored Chapmann's gaze and kept his eyes on Boorgers.

Boorgers leaned against some of the weapon's crates. "Let's review where we are in our preparation for receiving the shipment. Approximately half is being shipped through the Panama Canal to Vancouver." He looked at White. "I don't have the name of the vessel yet, but I've lined up enough small boats so we can unload the freighter off the coast at Ladner."

Boorgers stepped away from the crates and thrust a finger in the air. "Each man will take his load up the Fraser River to his own vehicle. Each is responsible for getting his load to the right storage facility." He stopped to let that sink in, and then added, "The equipment will be doled out as equitably as possible to the caches we've been constructing in the north and northeast part of the country. What's coming in through Mexico will be spread through the south and southwest. Understood?" Everyone nodded agreement.

"Have you guys lined up volunteers to haul the arms coming in from Mexico?" White asked, turning to Chudders and Chapmann.

"More than we need," Chapmann answered, hat in hand, as he sat on one of the crates. "Thanks to Petsch's recruiting. We even got enough good ole Texas boys to offer their four wheelers, pick-ups and horses to haul crates out of Mexico to all the new facilities in the south and southwest. We've paid off key Mexican officials along the border and have plenty of wetbacks lined up to haul the stuff across. But the longer it takes for those arms to show, the greater the possibility that our plans will leak"

As Boorgers walked back to the conference table, he said, "The key to safety is in having troops who are disciplined and obedient." He stopped, stared at the men, thrust his right fist in the air and waved it in a hammer-like motion. "We must make sure every person hauling is a hard core patriot! Each must know what is expected. They can't drive fast or crazy or drink or do anything stupid that might get them stopped by the law. If that happens, we don't know them." He paused. "They're on their own."

"I believe we can all buy that," Petsch said. Boorgers glanced at him and then continued walking.

"How many more shipments of arms can we expect from overseas?" White asked.

"They put no limit on it," Chapmann replied. "I suspect they'll ship all we want, but we need to be prudent."

They reached the cave's first room. White said, "It's important to get rid of the weapons quickly. It won't play well in Peoria if the Feds uncover one of our facilities full of Russian weapons!"

"That's sure true!" Chapmann said. "We've got to get this stuff to the people. We don't want a conventional war. We only want a solid defensive operation. The American people won't understand anything else. If some of these guys bomb and kill indiscriminately, they ought to take the punishment alone. The rest of us have to keep training the troops, educating people and expanding our resources. Time's on our side."

As Chapmann spoke, Chudders left the cave for a few moments and returned with two young people carrying soft drinks and chocolates.

"What are some of our people going to think when they pick up a weapon and discover it's Russian?" Petsch asked.

"We'll, some are going to be angry," Chapmann replied. "Maybe a lot!"

White said, "Put the word out that these are confiscated weapons from our own arsenals. If that doesn't shut'em up, tell them we want it to look like a foreign terrorist act or don't let'em have any. Tell them to go get their own weapons." Everyone nodded.

"I hope all those Skinheads get out there on the front line," Petsch said under his breath with a smirk. The others laughed.

"Yeah, they's as full of plain ole hate as I ever seen!" Chudders said. "You guys ever see one of them tattoos they get when they go out and kill a black? It's a black spider web. The first time I saw it I couldn't believe it."

"Yeah, a few German Skinheads showed up at our meeting in Thailand," Chapmann said. "Javad said they wanted to get arms for their revolution in Europe. We made sure the Skinheads were not in our meetings with the Arabs. And those

German guys smelled better than our Skinheads. I hope they all get out there and get killed."

"Kill'em all and let God straighten it out," Petsch said.

"How have you guys been funding your activities?" Boorgers asked, trying to get the group back on track.

"Each person or phantom cell is responsible for its own financial support," Chapmann said. "Yet, we've helped some groups that seemed to have their heads screwed on straight."

Pushing for information, Boorgers asked, "Chapmann, are you giving funds out of your own pocket?"

Chapmann looked around at the group as he thought for a moment. "I don't want what I am about to say to be repeated outside this room. I will never admit to saying it anyway." The others nodded in agreement. He continued, "A number of us have printed counterfeit dollars and other documents. Some groups have taken money from banks and other financial institutions. While we've never encouraged that, we haven't discouraged it, either. We take in an average of a million dollars a year from that activity. They just bring it in."

"That's true," Chudders said. "I ask them who wants me to come speak to pay the expenses and donate to Yahweh City."

Boorgers listened carefully, then, when a lull set in, added, "We have a lot of Washington bureaucrats that need to be removed. We have to put such a fear in that crowd that they stop fighting us. Especially that domestic terrorist bunch with Homeland Security."

"I suspect one of those agents came up here a few weeks ago," Chudders said. "He and his reporter friend plan a'goin' rafting down the Rio Gran'."

"What'd you tell them?" White asked.

"Oh, the usual. We're jest a Christian family wantin' to be left alone. Nothin' more."

"If anyone hears from him again, let the rest of us know," Boorgers said. All nodded in agreement. "As you all know by now, the CIA has been tracking the ships. So the shipping arrangements were changed."

"Mr. Javad has matters under control," Chapmann said.

The next morning, the group flew out using the old ranch airstrip. White flew Petsch, Boorgers and Chapmann to Denver. Before leaving, they agreed to meet at a ranch near Reserve, New Mexico, after the weapons arrived.

CIA HQ, LANGLEY, VA
Monday, February 24

Lights burned in Agent McCall's office until well after midnight. Agent Easton had arrived from Europe with a copy of the arms manifest. Agent Carlson and other federal agents joined the late night conference to discuss the arms shipment.

"How much time do we have?" McCall asked.

"That ship should have docked in Istanbul by now," Easton replied. "They may not get the load transferred immediately, but we need to assume they will. Turkish contacts tell us that the ship is a special consign and will depart when the captain feels he's ready."

"Let's look at our options," McCall suggested. "First, we can have the ship blown up at sea and have done with it. But this'll trigger an investigation we don't need. Second, we can intercept the shipment as soon as it's unloaded. I don't have to tell any of you the dangers we face in doing that. Third, we can maintain surveillance and wait for the arms to cross the Texas border and hope we catch everything."

Silence descended on the room. McCall got up from his chair and started pacing the floor. Finally, he said, "Or, fourth, we can let the stuff get to their ultimate destinations and try to confiscate them all at those points. If we do that," McCall paused, stopped pacing, then said, "we'll probably have a small war on our hands. Most of it is undoubtedly going to Chudders or Chapmann. Women and children will be killed and we'll be the bad guys again. Just like Waco. Any other suggestions?"

Finally, Carlson said, "Whatever we do, we can't allow these weapons to end up on the streets in the hands of extremists."

"I think we ought'a blow up that ship in the Vera Cruz harbor before it can unload and have it done by Mexican nationals so we have creditable denial," Agent Carassco suggested.

Several groaned. "Wait a minute. Let me finish, damn it. Weigh the alternatives and you'll see it has the least problems. If those boxes hit the Mexican wharf, they'll probably be packed out of there by all sorts of means—from mules to trucks. If they're smart, and I believe they are, they'll want to land-haul that stuff in the most inconspicuous ways possible. By breaking the materials up into small shipments, they reduce their risk of losing it all. You know they're going to spread plenty of money around Mexico to get the job done. If we try to set something up to catch every single small carrier, we'll be facing an organizational nightmare. And we don't have much time. What? Ten days before it reaches Vera Cruz?" he looked at each of the others for a moment and continued, "Okay, then, you say, let's set up interdiction at the border. Where? Sure, we can guess, but what if we're wrong? We don't have the manpower to staff the whole damn border!"

Silence again fell over the group as they contemplated Carrasco's logic. Lenora Carlson rubbed her tired eyes, closed them and reclined back in the big chair. Lockney stood up, refilled his coffee mug, then softly said, "You know, he's right."

"Has there been any thought of asking the Mexican government to confiscate the weapons when the ship enters their waters? Wheeler said. "We could suggest that the arms might be destined for their guerrillas!"

"Yeah, the director and I thought about that," McCall said. "We suspect they've already been bought off. All we would do is alert them to the fact that we know about the shipment." Again silence settled over the anguished group.

"It seems to me we face the least liabilities by blowing the ship up somewhere, preferably in the harbor after most of the crew has gone ashore," Lockney said. "We don't want to kill innocent people."

After discussing the issue for several more hours, they opted for destroying the ship in the Vera Cruz harbor. Taking a chance on the goods coming across the border somewhere between Del Rio and Presidio, Texas, came in second.

CIA's Easton accepted responsibility for forming a team to blow the ship in the Vera Cruz harbor. The Bureau's explosive expert, Agent Morgan, agreed to assist. All were warned not to act until notified that all agency heads had signed off on the plans. The meeting adjourned around 4 a.m.

ISTANBUL, TURKEY
Tuesday, February 25

While America's intelligence experts mulled over various interdiction strategies, Ghaleb dispatched a coded report on the arms shipment to his boss in Tehran. Alerted that the CIA had discovered the shipment, he had quickly changed the shipping strategies. Friends in the Turkish security force suggested he create a dummy cargo, even though it would cost more money.

After a matter of days the Sea Novia pulled into Istanbul and unloaded the real cargo next to a dummy shipment. The Russians had their men reload the arms aboard the Sea Novia and the dummy crates onto a CNAN ship named The Golden Vessel bound for Vera Cruz. The Sea Novia scheduled its arrival in Dublin a few days before The Golden Vessel arrived in Vera Cruz, giving Ghaleb's people time to off-load the arms onto yet another North America bound vessel. The process went smoothly. The Sea Novia departed at dawn, with The Golden Vessel prepared to leave at sunset. Ghaleb now waited to see if his president's staff had been able to work a contract with a Panamanian flag carrier out of Nicaragua named the Viva Libertad.

Ghaleb knew the American patriots would not be happy with any delays, but he felt it wise to be safe. He also knew that he would be severely punished if he allowed the arms to end up in the hands of the American CIA.

# 9

**HONG KONG**

Friday, February 28

Darren arrived in Hong Kong at 8:30 p.m. and found the new Lantau Island airport far more expansive than the old Kai Tak airport. As he walked through the lobby on his way to customs he couldn't help but think of an old Brit friend, who had recently died. After accepting the Japanese surrender on the runway at the old Kai Tak airport in nineteen forty five he had stayed in Asia to fly for Cathy Pacific Airways. Too much booze led to his death.

Darren headed immediately to the Shangri-La Hotel on Mody Road in Kowloon, checked in, then wandered down to the coffee shop for something to eat. He had been staying at the Shangri-La for many years and was disappointed when they had built several new hotels across the street that blocked some of the harbor view.

After a good night's sleep he met his old friend Paul Yee for breakfast. "Gosh," Paul exclaimed, "You Americans and your breakfast meetings!" Both men laughed. Darren always kidded Paul about his penchant for late night hours.

"Well, where have you been?" Paul asked. "I haven't seen you in months. I thought terrorist and SARS had scared you off the international circuit."

"Well, since our last visit I took a job with the government."

"Are you helping find another banana republic to bomb?"

"Darren smiled. "Be nice. I have joined the National Security Council."

"What do you do?"

"Whatever my boss, General Burcks, tells me."

"And?"

"Well, right now I'm trying to solve a puzzle."

"What? Finding more evil guys to blow away?"

Darren ignored Paul's dig. "It looks like some of our citizens landed in Hong Kong back in early January, then just disappeared. They showed up in Chaing Mai, Thailand, a few days later, then, puff, they disappeared. And ten days later they show up at Kai Tak climbing on planes for their return to the U.S. Their passports were only stamped with the Hong Kong immigration imprint. We need to find out how they got to Chaing Mai and who helped them, if possible."

Darren then briefly explained about the fringe of patriots that had arisen that seemed bent on bringing down the United States government.

"Well, first of all, you've been over here enough to know that with money anything's possible in Asia," said Paul. "But we Chinese have never understood you Americans. I don't mean to be rude, but so many Americans act like spoiled children. They've got the most democratically just system in the world, all that wealth and freedom and still too many whine. In any other society the people you mention would be picked up and shot in some remote place and no one would ever hear of them again."

"True. Many people have difficulty being content."

"And," Paul continued, "you people use more of the world's resources than anyone else in the world. Still you complain. In the midst of all your riches, your youth seem to be the most screwed up bunch in the whole world. Because of all this, Asians are quick to see that your cultural permissiveness and extreme tolerance for the rights of the individual is utterly absurd! You've shown the rest of us what the radicalization of the individual ultimately means. And, if that's not enough, if anyone disagrees with your government, they get blown away. You've all gone berserk!"

Darren laughed at Paul's outburst. "Well, not all. But you certainly have a point. Meanwhile, my job is to help stop the berserk ones. Do you know anyone you can trust in the Chinese government security service that might be able to find out something about our guy's movements?"

"Let me think about that." The two men then turned their attention to their breakfast and chatted about the new Chinese administration of Hong Kong.

"Darren, getting back to your question, an old childhood friend, named Aung Ming Yok, came up through the police department and is supposed to be high up in the new administration. Let me check with him and see if he will help."

"My flight to Bangkok leaves Monday afternoon. Is that too soon?"

"Let me call him when I get back to my office."

Paul left for his office and Darren returned to his room to read the morning newspaper. He found it as expected, totally cleaned while he had been at breakfast. His pajamas wee neatly folded at the foot of the bed. His extra pair of shoes was stored in the closet and had been shined. A book he had been reading and had left open on the floor next to the bed, had been placed next to the phone. A note marked his reading spot, "Mr. Hopkins, you read to this page. Sincerely, your maid."

Ahhh, such wonderful service! he thought.

Darren had just finished the crossword puzzle when the phone rang. "Darren, Mr. Aung will meet us for lunch at the Polo Club at twelve thirty. Is that okay?" Paul Yee asked. "I'll meet you in your hotel lobby."

A few minutes after Darren and Paul had arrived and were standing in the lobby of the club, Aung Ming Yok came off the elevator.

He was a large, muscular man whose five foot ten inch frame carried about two hundred and ten lean, mean pounds. Darren guessed he was in his late fifties and did not possess a bubbly personality. He rarely smiled. When he did it had a tight-lipped expression that snapped back tautly, like a new rubber band. After introductory pleasantries Paul briefly sketched his family's historical relations with the Aung family and the men placed their orders with the waiter. Then Aung turned to Darren and, with a soft but steely voice, asked, "What do you want from me?"

Darren offered Aung his NSC credentials. Aung looked at the NSC photo badge carefully, handed it back to Darren and waited patiently for an answer to his question. Darren then explained his situation.

"Why didn't your government just contact our government about this?" Aung asked.

"First, for a variety of reasons my boss doesn't want my visit known," Darren explained. "I've been ordered to make an inquiry as quietly as possible. Second, yes, the CIA has been notified but haven't come up with anything. At least we've not been told anything. My boss, General Burcks, thought while I passed through Hong Kong on my way to Thailand that I might be able to get some further information. Maybe I can't," he added as an afterthought with the shrug of his shoulders.

After lunch the men moved to the more relaxing atmosphere of the clubroom, which maintained its old English touch. Huge leather-bound chairs and sofas were scattered about, framed with heavy ebony furniture throughout the dimly lit room. It reeked of British titled-culture. Tea was served.

"Mr. Hopkins," Aung said, returning to the issue. "I don't know if I can help you. As you know, things have changed since the mainland took control of Hong Kong. Quite honestly, I can't find out anything in one day. When are you coming back through from Thailand?"

"I'm not sure. It depends on what you find. I need to be back in Washington in nine days for a critical meeting."

"Well then," Aung said, "It's safer for us to maintain contact through Paul. Calls coming into my office are monitored and I do not know if my home phone is tapped or not. Or my car or office. It will be better if Paul and I get together on the street to exchange information. I want to keep this out of my official business channels. I also think that your people arranged to be smuggled in and out of Thailand by one of the many gangs that ply the South China Sea. They smuggle cigarettes and whiskey to the mainland. These guys claim to be fishermen, but they fish in one hundred twenty-foot corvettes powered by five hundred horsepower Chrysler engines. They have the latest radar equipment and are armed to the teeth, as you say in America. I need time to check this out."

"I will be most appreciative," Darren said. "Thank you very much." The men chatted until about two o'clock. Mr. Aung returned to his office and Paul had his driver take them to the Shangri-La Hotel. As they drove Darren asked , "What precisely does Aung do? His card stated that he is a senior management secretary to the Hong Kong Council. What does that mean in the new regime?"

"He's head of the regional secret service for the Chinese. They were evidently very pleased with the professional manner in which he carried out his police work."

"Somehow that went over my head," Darren muttered. Paul laughed. "I still have a difficult time now and then decoding the subtle ways you Chinese wear and wield power. In the West we flaunt it, like big silver-backed gorillas tearing through the underbrush slamming big sticks to the ground, making all the racket we can in order to say, 'Hey, look at me. I'm a big shot!'"

Paul laughed again. "Yes, there is a big difference between us. Our cultural tradition frowns on flaunting one's power. It is more desirable to act humbly, to be gentle and to speak softly. Americans pompous displays are barbaric to us."

"I can understand that," Darren replied. After a pause, he continued, "Paul,

In response to your comments earlier today, it's important that the rest of the world understand that many Americans have fought and died so people can whine, bitch and moan about anything and everything under the sun. We idealize a person's freedom to disagree on anything. They can even hold weird opinions. It makes for a strange polyglot of people."

A long pause ensued as both men seemed lost in thought. Then Paul said, "Yes, that is easy to forget. But you're still too permissive. Too nice."

"There are a lot of Americans who agree with you," responded Darren. "And I'm sure that from time to time we overlook irresponsible behavior in the name of personal freedom."

"You know, one of my friends suggested that you ought to change the saying on your coinage from 'In God We Trust,' to 'It Ain't my fault,'" Paul said. Darren grinned. Paul continued. "I think you have too many psychologists and shrinks. Their worldview bears little resemblance to reality. They thrive on that little perverted view as though it was the essence of the universe. Those civilizations that have been around for thousands of years, like ours, as we see and hear such nonsense, we just cringe in sheer disbelief. I've often heard my countrymen exclaim, 'How can any race of people be so stupid?' You're too soft and, as such, many around the world are convinced history will eventually run you over."

Paul paused, heaved a big sigh and said, "Ah, Darren, listen to me. The ramblings of a man entering senility. I'm sorry to get so upset."

"It's okay. You and others who prophesy our demise may be right. We are certainly about to come face to face with our worse nightmare—ourselves. And you may be right about the psychologists and shrinks.

Paul nodded. "Yes, yes. Such a shame. Your people are anti-intellectual. Your politicians ridicule egg heads. You tease children about school. I've personally heard American parents say to their children, 'Too bad you've got to go to school today,' or 'I'll bet you'll be glad when vacation time comes.' You make fun of children who are studious. You call them bookworms, nerds, and so forth. Your people don't really think education is important except to get credentials. So your kids go through school very unhappy. I hear that most of them lie and cheat their way through school. That's why you get businessmen who lie and cheat. It's sad and the reverse of the way we Asians view schooling and education. That's why our students do so well. We revere education more than anything else."

"You certainly appreciate it more that we do, I'm afraid," Darren answered.

"Enough of this!" Paul sighed, sticking his arms in the air as if to surrender.

"What are your plans for tonight? he asked . "We can't solve your nation's social problems in one setting." Both men laughed.

"I think I'll stay in my room and get some paper work done," Darren said.

"I can understand that. Can I take you to dinner?"

"No, but thanks. I plan to saunter down Nathan Road for exercise, and then grab a light meal."

"And tomorrow?" Paul asked.

"I guess I'll be on the phone in the morning. What did you have in mind?"

"How about some golf?"

"Thought you'd never ask! This time I'll beat you."

HONG KONG
Monday, March 3

As Chapmann, White, Chudders, and others intensified the plot against the government, Ghaleb worked his shipping shell game, and Darren flew from Hong Kong to Bangkok via Thai Airways. The flight tracked across the South China Sea, over a narrow stretch of Vietnam and Laos, down the northern edge of Cambodia and into the new international airport at Bangkok.

Vasin Boonchanta, a university friend, pulled him out of the regular passport control line and led him through the back hallways of the airport to a waiting car. Vasin handed Darren's passport to an accompanying military officer, turned to Darren and said, "He'll return that to you at the hotel by breakfast time."

"Thanks."

As their car pulled away from the terminal, Vasin, with his brow furrowed in puzzlement, looked at Darren. "I've called Ann Jones' office many times. I've left many messages, but she never acknowledged a single one. Why not?"

"I don't know," Darren said . "But I'd like to find out. Can we go by the U.S. Embassy before checking in at the hotel?"

"Sure."

As they drove the crowded streets of Bangkok, Vasin said, "I've got us booked on a seven a.m. flight tomorrow to Chiang Mai. The hotel manager of the Sports Club is a friend of a friend. He'll have a car standing by at the airport to take us to the club. The staff knows we are coming and, according to him, they will be happy to tell us what they can about the group that stayed there back in January."

Darren and Vasin found the embassy closed for a local holiday. Darren showed his NSC credentials to the Marines at the entrance gate, and they connected him by private phone to Ambassador Dan Burck at a luncheon at the Royal Orchid Hotel. "Mr. Hopkins, I honestly do not know where Ms. Jones is. The intelligence group only tells me what they want me to know. Sometimes I think they run me, rather than the other way around." He chuckled. "Our CIA station chief is a fellow by the name of Charles Parks. He's fairly new. Have you met him?"

"No, I'm afraid not."

"I'll have Charles call you. Where are you staying?"

"I'll be at the Landmark on Sukhumvit Road."

"Okay. If Parks can't help you, I'm afraid I don't know what to tell you. Sorry."

"Thanks for your help, Mr. Ambassador. Sorry to have bothered you."

"Let me know what you find out. Ann's a great talent."

"She is that." Darren hung up, thanked the Marines and walked slowly back to Vasin's car.

"Well, what did you find out?" Vasin asked.

"I talked to the Ambassador by phone. I'm to talk to a Charles Parks." The car slowly threaded its way through the gaggle of motorbikes and tuk-tuks to the hotel.

Vasin followed Darren to the main desk and, once he had checked in, said, "Okay. Let's catch some lunch and prepare for tomorrow."

The next morning the two climbed aboard an airplane for the thirty-five minute flight to the northern city of Chiang Mai. Darren noticed a slightly built Asian man that seemed to be eyeing him in the departure lounge. He felt the hair stand up on the nape of his neck. He didn't say anything to Vasin.

A car and driver waited to take them to the Sports Club resort as they left the Chiang Mai terminal. After thirty minutes of driving through the verdant Thai landscape, they turned into a large iron gated entrance and down a winding, cobbled drive, protected by an acacia tree canopy laden with yellow flowers. The rambling lodge with its massive portico must have covered ten acres, Darren thought.

The manager, Mr. Keerikoolparn, met them at the entrance. Over breakfast, Mr. Keerikoolparn identified twelve staff members who remembered the men Darren was seeking. Vasin and Darren used a small conference room with comfortable chairs just off the hotel's kitchen for the interviews. Vasin handled the translations. Darren showed each some thumbnail size pictures of various extremists. When staffers agreed on a photo, Darren enlarged it to a full-screen view so they could make a positive identification. They finished the interview process at 1:30 p.m.

"Let's eat," Vasin said.

Over lunch they calculated that the staff had identified thirty-six of the attendees. A copy of the hotel registry for the January meeting allowed Darren to match pictures with real or assumed names. He knew the FBI had the capacity to match signatures and writing samples to their owners. He collected that data, but he had no way to identify the German skinheads, the Australians, Japanese, or half a dozen other nationalities in attendance.

Abu Nidal had his Lebanese chief there, as did the Democratic Front for the Liberation of Palestine (DFLP), HAMAS (a man from the Izz el-Din al-Qassam Forces wing of the group), Hizballah, Jamaat ul-Fuqra, Jihad Group, at least one member of Al-Qaida, and several others Darren could not identify. In addition, the Thai identifications revealed the presence of the Liberation Tigers of Tamil Eelam, a group attempting to set up an independent Tamil state. Also the Khmer Rouge, the Provisional Irish Republican Army and German's Red Army Faction. All sought weapons. The presence at the conference of John Chudders, Pete Petsch and Ron Chapmann did not surprise Darren. The staff also described some that did not appear in Darren's photo bank. He took as much descriptive detail as possible in hopes the FBI could identify these individuals when he returned to Washington. When they finished all interrogations, Darren and Vasin thanked the hotel manager and headed back to the airport. As they reached the main road to the airport, Darren spotted the man he had seen earlier in the Bangkok departure lounge sitting on a bench under a mimosa tree talking to a young woman. Darren recognized the woman as one of the Thai staff who helped identify the men attending the January conference. "Vasin, look at that guy!" Darren yelled.

"What guy?" Vasin asked, as he turned to look. The car stopped.

"He was over by that tree," Darren said, pointing. "See that gal over there? She's one of the waitresses who talked to us."

"Yeah, I recognize her, but I don't see any guy," Vasin answered. They both stared at the site for a few moments.

"Ahh, what the hell, let's go," Darren said. The car left the hotel grounds behind.

"Darren, I think you've been around those CIA guys too much!" Both men chuckled, but Darren's chuckle had a somber note.

Maybe he's right, Darren mused. Back in Bangkok, Vasin returned to his office, and Darren went to his room to call Washington and file his report. He included a brief description of the man who seemed to be tailing him and asked if there might be a way to identify him. As he turned out the light, he realized that he felt more than a little worried.

Darren arrived at the embassy at 9:00 a.m. sharp the next morning. He visited Marilyn Thompson, the only intelligence officer in the office. The CIA's Chief of Station, Charles Parks, who had not called Darren as per the Ambassador's promise, had not arrived. Marilyn took Darren in tow and they wandered from office to office, visiting a number of embassy staff who knew Ann and who might shed light on her whereabouts. No one knew anything or, if they did, they chose not to tell. He reported his findings at Chiang Mai to Marilyn and found that Langley had already briefed her. She said the embassy staff had expected his visit.

"How can an intelligence officer just disappear from the face of the earth?" Darren asked, showing his concern.

"You'll have to ask Charles Parks. I'm a low ranking member of this fraternity." She looked at her desk, rearranged some papers and blushed slightly. "I know it looks crazy. I'm sorry."

"It's all right," Darren said.

"As for these extremist characters," Marilyn said, "we certainly didn't know they had entered the country. We would have been all over them." Shehad barely finished the sentence when Charles Parks walked in.

After introductions, Parks said, "First, please accept my apology for not calling you earlier. I wasn't in a position to do so until now. Meanwhile, I understand you're chasing the identities of some guys that snuck into Thailand for a meeting with some Arab terrorists. Why don't we all move to a conference room where we'll be more comfortable."

He led the way to a modest conference room just off the main corridor and near the elevator. Once seated, a young Thai woman poured them a cup of coffee.

Darren then revealed his findings.

"Damn, wish we'd known," Parks said.

"Is there any way we could find out how these guys got into Thailand from Hong Kong? I've asked for the same help in Hong Kong but haven't heard anything as yet."

Parks scratched the back of his head as he thought, then said, "I'd venture a guess that the Iranians and Chinese set it up. They have plenty of financial and political clout with most of these terrorists. And, as I think about it, I'll wager the Chinese arranged a high speed launch to take them down the South China coast to Zhanjiang, then by air to a small air strip on the Thai border."

Parks rose and walked over to a large map on the wall. "They could have easily crossed the Thai border at a thousand sites, then bussed or trucked to Chiang Mai and returning the same route. That's an easy arrangement given the relatively cozy relations between those countries."

"I see," Darren said , as he studied the map. There was a moment of silence. Then Darren leaned over, looked Parks straight in the eyes and asked, "Charles, do you know where Ann Jones is? No one else seems to."

Parks looked startled as his eyes widened. "Darren, she left on assignment and disappeared. We have to wait for her. She'll contact us when she feels it's safe to do so."

"Well, that's the straightest answer I've been given over the weeks. Thank you for it. Let me hear from you if you come up with anything."

"Of course."

"Thanks a lot," Darren said "By the way," he added, glancing at his watch, "it's about lunchtime. I'm buying. How about joining me?"

"I promised some Thai generals I'd lecture a class of new intelligence agents this afternoon and I'm not prepared," Parks said. "Let me take a rain check."

"I can sure use something to eat," Marilyn said. "Some Thai friends of mine own a restaurant not too far from here. But you have to let me treat!"

"That's no problem."

"Doesn't matter. You're on my turf anyway. Let's go."

Arn Charnchainarong, the owner of the Mango Tree Restaurant at 37 Soi Anumarn Rachthon Surawongse Road greeted Marilyn with a big smile. The waiter escorted the pair to a table under one of the large mango trees in the garden of the classical one-hundred-year-old Thai house-turned-restaurant.

"The menu looks great," Darren remarked. "And it reads correctly. One time I noted that a Japanese restaurant advertised hot coke on their menu! A misspelling, thank goodness." Marilyn laughed. "Then, on a recent stop in Jakarta I went with some friends to a Vietnamese restaurant, and on their menu they offered pork with fresh garbage. And in Japan I've seen such menu items as buttered saucepans and fried hormones and one that read 'fried fishermen and Teppen Yaki—Before Your Cooked Right Eyes.'" They both laughed.

"Do you like the hot Thai food?" Darren asked.

"Yes, I do. I grew up in New Mexico where Mexican food is hot."

"Where in New Mexico?" a wide-eyed Darren asked.

"Deming. A small town on Interstate Ten in the southern part of the state."

"I know where that is. My dad graduated from high school at Silver City, just north of Deming about sixty miles or so."

"Small world, isn't it? Where did you grow up?"

"I was born in San Antonio but raised in Austin. My grandparents moved from New Mexico to Laredo before I was born. Needless to say, we ate a lot of Mexican food. I couldn't survive without it." Again they laughed.

Darren suddenly spotted a man at a window of the main dining room, the same man he had seen at the departure lounge on his way to Chiang Mai and again on the lawn of the Sports Club Resort Hotel.

Darren jumped up, with a brusque "excuse me" and hurried to the main dining room. The man had disappeared. He quickly headed out the front door and saw the man scrambling into a blue Mercedes-Benz.

Hoping to get the license number, he ran after the car but suddenly a man appeared from behind a van and caught him just behind the right ear with the butt of a revolver. He had seen it coming out of the corner of his right eye but couldn't dodge the blow. Blacking out, he hit the graveled parking lot like a sack of flour.

He regained consciousness a few minutes later to find Marilyn and a few others staring down at him. She applied a cold, damp cloth to the area where he had been hit. "Who in the hell was that?" he groaned softly.

"I don't know, but someone seems pretty anxious to get you," she replied. Darren slowly regained his feet in a few minutes.

"I'll never make a good spy!" he muttered. Marilyn looked concerned as they went back into the restaurant to find a distraught Arn Charnchainarong.

"What happened?" she cried, twisting the small apron around her waist with an anguished look.

"Darren just bumped his head chasing a guy in the parking lot," Marilyn explained. "Everything's all right. We're sorry to cause you any problems."

"Oh, no, please no worry. Shall we call doctor?"

"No. Everything's fine, thanks." Darren laughed, embarrassed to have created a public scene. Turning to Marilyn, he said, "Sorry for this. I don't understand any of it."

"Don't worry about it, Darren. Let's make sure you don't have any real damage to your head!"

"Oh, I'm sure I'm all right. Whoever hit me didn't get a solid blow."

Returning to their table Darren said, "Maybe my imagination is working overtime. But that guy keeps cropping up. Wish I had gotten the license number."

"Darren, believe me when I tell you that all of us in the intelligence community have our moments when it seems like everyone's watching us. We're all targets. I think it's good that whoever this man is, he is not very stealthy. You have seen him on three separate occasions. A good surveillance man would never let that happen."

"Do you have a de-bugging device I can use to sweep my hotel room?"

"In fact, we do. I'll get one of our people over there and have it done for you. It might be wise if they go through all your personal effects. Listening devices are so small that they can plant them under one of your buttons and you wouldn't know that it's there."

"Thanks. Any idea what else I should do to protect myself?"

"Not really. If they wanted you dead, I think you would be by this time. They've had plenty of opportunities. They may just want to know where you're going and to whom you want to talk to. Again, whoever 'they' are!"

"Yeah, whoever."

After a few moments, Marilyn asked, "How'd you meet Ann?"

"Back in grade school."

"You're kidding?"

"No, it's true. But let me tell you the crazy story of how we renewed that relationship."

"Yeah, this has got to be good."

"It involves one of the most embarrassing moments of my life. During a golf game at Singapore's Sentosa Island Country Club, I hit into the rough on the fourteenth fairway. I used a new utility wood and smacked that sucker as hard as I could. The ball hit a tree, ricocheted into the adjoining fairway, and hit Ann's cart! She thought someone had taken a shot at her. As I searched for my ball, she and three other agents seemed ready to jump me. One had his gun drawn! They scared me to death."

"That must have been scary."

"I thought one of those guys would beat me up just for the fun of it. One shouted, 'You idiot, can't you even stay in your own fairway?' Nice stuff like that. They even mixed in a few well-chosen curse words"

"Did Ann recognize you?"

"No. And I didn't recognize her. She moved from Austin just before we both started the sixth grade, so we hadn't seen each other for many years."

"What happened next?"

"Oh, she calmed down after I apologized. In fact, we all laughed about it, they let me buy lunch and we started talking about our personal backgrounds and both mentioned Austin. Then when she said she went to my elementary school, lights began to go on. I think we both remembered each other at the same moment."

"What'd she say?"

"She put her right had over her mouth, her eyes got big and she said, 'I don't believe it! My God, it's little Darren Hopkins."

"So you started dating?"

"Well, I found that we stayed at the same hotel, so we met for a late night drink and the rest is history, as they say."

"Unbelievable," Marilyn said, shacking her head.

"That it is," Darren said . He then looked at his watch. "What time do you need to be back?"

"We better go."

As Darren and the technical specialist entered his hotel room, they were startled to find his personal belongings strewn around the room. Even his toilet articles had been dumped on the floor of the bathroom.

"Well, hell!" Darren said.

"Boy, someone doesn't like you," the technician replied.

"Guess not. They sure made a mess."

"There are different ways to search a person's stuff. If one is just looking for important documents, then it's done surgically. No prints are left behind to alert the victim that anyone has been into his things. On the other hand, when a mess is made like this, they want you to know they have you in their sights. They're trying to intimidate."

"Thanks, I think."

Darren followed the man about as he scanned. He soon found a small microphone planted inside the seam of Darren's small, black phone book, one in the flower vase on the small round conference table, one under the lapel of his newly-cleaned, navy blue business suit and one under a seam of his carry-on garment bag. Darren watched in disbelief.

"How'd they get in here?

"Well," the technician said. "It's almost four o'clock. The hotel cleaners probably returned your suit in the last hour or so. Someone entered your room fairly recently. The bugs in your luggage and personal phone book could have been there for days. The one in the flowers is interesting. Pros don't do that anymore. They probably thought you wouldn't check such an obvious place. Although these computerized card keys now make it difficult to enter anyone's room, it's amazing what money will buy."

"Isn't it!" Darren said

The technician picked up the large floral arrangement from the large round table in the living room area, held it high and turned it around as he examined it. "It's likely they arranged the plants outside and had hotel staff bring them to your room. The flowers are changed when the room is getting its daily cleaning." He sat the flowers back on the table, and then walked over to Darren's newly cleaned suit hanging on the closet door, "Your suit came back from the cleaners in the middle of the afternoon. It's easy to pay a hotel staff member to plant these devices. Or let someone into your room. Ten or twenty dollars is a lot of money to people here."

Darren sat down stunned and emotionally drained.

After the technician left, Darren called General Burcks' secure phone line and reported the day's events. He gave a brief sketch of the man tailing him in hopes the intelligence network might know his identity. He also received a fax from Paul Yee in Hong Kong that read, "Need your presence. Our mutual friend believes you will be most interested in a golf game with him. Can you meet us in Singapore tomorrow?"

"Boy, can I," Darren said aloud as he read Paul's message. Darren arranged to be on the first flight out of Bangkok the next morning and faxed that information to Paul Yee.

Darren felt exhausted. He must be more alert and a lot smarter. He called Vasin and reported the latest events and his early morning departure. Vasin insisted that they meet with General Paitoon Sudasane as soon as possible.

Vasin picked him up at 5:30 p.m. for dinner. They met General Sudasane at a private club. After the introductory ritual, Darren explained his situation. "I need to get to Singapore without anyone knowing. Right now I have a reservation on the earliest flight in the morning. Can you help me?"

"I think so," Sudasane said very slowly, casually. He then turned away, raised his right hand and motioned for a waiter.

"What would you have, Mr. Hopkins?" Sudasane asked.

"Something light," Darren said. After they finished ordering, Sudasane said, "The man from the embassy debugged your room. I assume the phone you used to book your flight to Singapore is clean, but let's not take any chance. They probably don't know where you're going. They will follow you when you leave the hotel. We've got to keep them from knowing where you are and where you are going. What flight are you on?"

"Singapore four sixteen. It leaves at six fifteen a.m."

"Okay. You and Vasin go on with your evening and leave the rest to me." Sudasane then excused himself and left.

Darren then turned to Vasin. "Isn't he going to stay and eat his dinner?"

Vasin chuckled. "No, he told the waiter in Thai that he would leave his guests before the dinner, but to take good care of us. And he also signed the check, so everything's paid for."

Darren crawled into bed at two fifteen a.m. His head still ached from the blow, so he took a pain pill and went to sleep. Sometime during the night the phone rang. Darren awakened with a start and, eyes still closed, reached for the phone.

"Darren, I'm okay," a soft voice said. "But get the hell out of Dodge. Your life's...danger...love." Then he heard a dial tone. Ann's voice!

"Well, hell," he muttered aloud. Now he was awake. He watched TV but couldn't go back to sleep. At least she's alive and seemingly well, he thought. But maybe not.

At five in the morning, a gentle knock on the door sent shivers down his back. He staggered to the door, opened it slightly and found an elderly Thai woman who said General Sudasane sent her to get him ready to travel. She barged into the room.

"You call me Nel," she demanded. "We go to bathroom, I make you over so your mother not know you! Come!"

She applied makeup that added twenty years to his appearance. She even had different color contact lenses for him to wear. Once she installed a wig and Darren put on the old clothes she had brought, Darren didn't recognize himself.

There was a soft knock at the door and Darren watched through a crack in the door as a Thai man entered carrying an old suitcase. He and Nel quietly stuffed Darren's garment bag into the suitcase, and then the man left.

"Okay. You come now. Here, carry this bag," she commanded. She stood back, looking him over. "You follow me, but you walk more slow. Bend over, so you act like old man."

Nel quietly opened the door, poked her head out to scan the hallway, and then headed toward the elevators. A man in a black suit waited for them. Darren looked at his watch: six a.m.

"Where are we going?" he whispered.

"You shush...follow. Come. Hurry." She led Darren to the service elevator and down to the hotel basement. They wound their way through a maze of corridors and storage rooms until they reached the laundry room. An outside door opened onto a loading dock where a Ford van stood with its motor running. Two men were loading bundles of dirty sheets. As Nel and Darren come out the door, they motioned Darren into the rear of the van. He discovered a nice padded area in the middle and snuggled down.

Forty-five minutes later, the van slowed and stopped. He heard men talking in Thai and could hear the whine of aircraft engines. "Ahaa, the airport," Darren muttered. None too soon, he thought. Then the van drove on and after a few sharp turns, stopped again. The back doors opened, and hands began to unload the laundry bags.

Darren heard Vasin's voice before he saw him. General Sudasane and Vasin helped him out. "I'm glad to see you guys."

"Is that you, Darren?" a smiling Vasin asked. "Wow, she did a good job!" They all laughed. "Did we have you worried?"

"Did you ever!"

Sudasane said, "Step in here and put this Thai Airways coverall suit on."

Leaning against the van, Vasin said, "The men driving the van work for Thai Airways and do some odd jobs for Mr. Sudasane from time to time. You can trust these men." Then, pointing to a nearby seven-forty-seven Thai Airways plane, said, "You're going to take the tools they give you and take them to that plane. You will help load luggage onto the plane. You will be told to crawl up in the hold to arrange some packages. There you will meet a man who will show you the crawl space into the main cabin areas. You will find some of your clothes hanging in the first-class restroom. We thought it wise to change your flight at the last moment. Don't worry, this flight stops in Singapore. Get rid of that makeup and wig and clean your face before the crew comes aboard. You'll find your ticket and boarding pass inside your suit coat pocket hanging in the restroom. I believe you are upstairs in business class, seat five C. When you get to Singapore, a man named Ari will meet you as you come off the plane. Listen to him. He understands the problem and he'll cover your backside. Be careful!"

"Vasin, how can I ever thank you?"

The men shook hands and bid farewell. All went as planned.

# 10

**VERA CRUZ, MEXICO**

Sunday, March 2

While Darren worked to make a case against the terrorists in Asia, Mark Easton and FBI's explosive expert, Joe Morgan, were meeting CIA's top Mexican operative, Daniel Rodriguez, at the Hotel Villa Rica in Vera Cruz, Mexico. The little hotel at the north end of M. Avilo Comacho Boulevard had the best view of the harbor. They had to pay extra to encourage the young couple occupying the northeast, fourth-floor room to move. Unfortunately the room wasn't air-conditioned, but it had a ceiling fan.

Once settled into the hotel, Rodriguez and Morgan left Easton behind and drove to an old, seemingly abandoned building at the far north end of the city's airport. Two men waited by the building's heavily padlocked doors. Together they entered the warehouse, rolled open a large door and drove in. Then they carefully unloaded ten khaki-colored, Army surplus backpacks and a load of plastic explosives. Then Rodriquez and Morgan drove to a secluded beach site south of Vera Cruz where Morgan bundled the explosives and readied each for use.

After that the agents returned to the hotel to clean up. They joined Easton for dinner at the Gran Cafe El Postal, located at the corner of Independencia and Zamora off the Plaza de Armas. While Morgan and Easton finished their meal, Rodriguez drove to a truck stop south of town to meet a notorious Mexican outlaw commonly referred to as El Jefe. Rodriguez had used El Jefe's skills in the past. To El Jefe, Rodriguez was simply Señor Moran.

The two men greeted each other in a familiar manner and Rodriguez ordered each a cerveza. After asking about each other's general well being and each had been served, Rodriguez explained the job. Rodriguez emphasized that money would not be paid unless the explosion went off after all the crew had left for shore leave. Would El Jefe do the job under that condition?

El Jefe asked how much it paid.

"Ten thousand U.S. dollars," Rodriguez replied.

El Jefe's eyes widened. "How many ships you want blown up?" The men laughed and ordered another cerveza. After a few minutes of meaningless chitchat, El Jefe said softly, "I think, Señor, there is more to this than you say to me." Rodriquez stared him down for a moment. El Jefe finally laughed, threw up his arms, smiled big and said, "But it's okay, amigo!"

"Do you have the men and equipment to do the job?" Rodriguez asked.

"Si, of course," El Jefe said. "I have a good bomb man. But I must have a few days to get more explosives from the black market."

"Don't bother," Rodriguez said. "I'll give you all the plastic explosive devices you'll need. Once the job is finished you can keep what's left, but only if the ship and all its cargo is totally destroyed with no hope of salvage."

"Oh, yes, muy fácile," El Jefe said, again throwing his arms up as a sign of confidence. "When is ship to arrive?"

"We expect it any night now. "I'll call you when we know for sure."

"Okay," El Jefe said. "You call me!"

"Yes, as soon as I hear something," Rodriguez said. "And I'll give you the explosives now."

The two men departed the noisy and smoky dining facility for the parking lot. El Jefe motioned into the darkness and the lights of a fairly new, black GMC Suburban, pierced the night. The Suburban slowly followed the two men to Rodriguez's parked car. Once he got a nod from El Jefe indicating it was safe to do so, Rodriguez popped his car's trunk lid and revealed ten heavily loaded rucksacks. El Jefe then flicked his wrist toward the Suburban. Two men jumped out and rapidly loaded the sacks of plastic explosives into the back of the Suburban.

Rodriguez then handed El Jefe a manila envelope with twenty-five hundred U.S. dollars cash and pictures of the ship's layout. They agreed to meet when the ship arrived. If Jefe's men did the job as instructed, Rodriguez said he would pay the remaining seventy-five hundred dollars at the same parking lot one hour after the explosion. His mission accomplished, Rodriguez joined his colleagues at the Gran Cafe El Postal.

How'd it go?" Easton asked.

"Piece of cake. Once he saw that I had the explosives, he didn't argue over money. He would have probably done the job in return for the extra explosives," Rodriguez replied with a grin.

"Well, let's hope he's got the sense to let all those men get ashore!" Morgan said.

The others nodded agreement and sighed in resignation. After a few minutes, Rodriguez asked, "What if the Arabs pulled a switch? How do we know for certain that the weapons are on that particular vessel?"

"I watched those crates loaded at Odessa," Easton said, "then unloaded at Istanbul. I saw them re-loaded aboard The Golden Vessel." Easton then placed his arms on the edge of the table and stared down at his empty plate. Morgan sat staring out the large window at the thinning evening crowd.

Easton broke the lengthy silence, saying, "Oh Jeez, they might have pulled a switch if they thought someone knew about the equipment, but I don't think they did. Nothing indicated such."

"Could they have switched the cargo at sea?" Morgan asked.

"I don't know," Easton answered. "What can we do?"

"We might ask our local man to check the cargo before he blows the damn thing up," Morgan suggested.

"He'll do that," Rodriguez countered.

"Make sure your man checks the contents first," Easton said. Tell him we feel it's a wise thing to do in case there's anything in the holds that we may want to salvage later. He can be in on the split. Will he go for that?"

"Sure. I'll meet you back at the hotel in about two hours."

Rodriguez rushed out and used his car's cellular phone to call a line in Mexico City which patched through to a number in Vera Cruz.

A woman answered, "Bueno?"

"El Jefe, por favor."

"Momentito."

El Jefe came on the line huffing and puffing. Rodriguez apologized for bothering him, then presented the challenge of checking the cargo before blowing the ship. A long pause ensued as El Jefe considered the situation. Finally, he said, "Está bien, pero si you no blow ship after inspection, you still pay ten thousand dollars?"

"Yes, if we decide not to blow up the ship after your inspection, we will still pay the agreed upon sum," Rodriguez said. "And, we will give you special walkie-talkies to use in speaking with us during the inspection."

"Ahaa, very good!" El Jefe said.

"But, remember, do not set any explosives until we know what cargo the ship is carrying."

"Si, Señor."

Rodriguez met El Jefe back at the truck stop an hour later and delivered three small phones. They went over the strategy again to ensure that El Jefe understood Rodriguez's expectations. Back at the hotel, the agents got to bed at 2:00 a.m.

At noon on Thursday, CIA headquarters in Langley reported the ship off the coast of Mexico on a course for Vera Cruz and scheduled for arrival around 7:00 p.m. Rodriguez alerted El Jefe. As night fell, the agents took up surveillance positions. Morgan watched from the hotel room's fourth floor window. Easton moved to one of the jetties off Malecon Street, abutting the main pier. Rodriguez sat on the wall overlooking the harbor at the corner of Malecon and Insurgentes, several hundred yards north of Easton's position. All three had night vision binoculars and stayed in constant communication. Langley's report proved correct. A few minutes after 7:00 p.m., Morgan and Easton both, almost instantaneously, sighted the ship slipping quietly into the harbor.

The three American agents waited for the crew to disembark. Finally, at 10:00 p.m., they observed several launches approaching the ship. A few minutes later they could hear faint laughter echoing across the bay as the crew came off the ship. Finally, thirty minutes after the crew had left, the agents watched as a smaller launch pulled up alongside the ship and took the officers aboard. Two men who had been left behind began securing the ship. Rodriquez notified El Jefe, and they met on the docks overlooking the harbor. After pointing out the ship and going over the instructions again, they parted. It was now 10:52 p.m.

The agents waited for word from El Jefe. Finally, at 12:05 a.m., Rodriguez received the report. The Golden Vessel carried only fertilizer, scrap metal and junk. Rodriguez told El Jefe to abort their mission. He thanked him for all his efforts and assured him there would be future assignments.

The three agents huddled in their room until Rodriquez left to pay El Jefe as promised. Easton felt terrible. He immediately contacted Langley and asked them to contact agents in Istanbul to find out what other ships unloaded at the same time as The Golden Vessel. He reasoned that a ship headed for the Americas would have left within a few hours of The Golden Vessel's departure. It would take a day or two for their Turkish sources to get the information. The agents packed up and headed back to Washington.

SINGAPORE
Thursday, March 6

While Easton and the other agents were heading back to Washington, Darren arrived in Singapore without further incident. Ari met him as he deplaned and started down the tunnel toward passport control. After an introductory nod of his head, he grabbed Darren's right arm, swung him around and to the right, then gently pushed him down the employee stairs to a waiting car on the tarmac. The driver opened the back door and, as Darren stepped in, he glanced quickly to his left to see a Thai airport employee place his bag in the trunk. Neither Ari nor the driver said much as they drove Darren to the Conrad International hotel. He thanked them profusely as they unloaded his luggage. Then he turned and entered the hotel, assuming his guides had left. Not so.

As he started across the marble lobby, he found himself flanked by the two men. They ushered him all the way to the registration desk, constantly scanning the lobby. After registration, Darren again thanked the two men. They both nodded politely, and Darren followed the bellhop to the elevator. As he entered the elevator, so did his two shadows. The whole entourage got off at the eighth floor. The bellboy stared fixedly at the elevator's panel, but Darren suspected this show of force made the young man nervous. Upon arrival at the eighth floor, the bellboy motioned Darren and his shadows to leave first, then led the group down the corridor to room eight forty-one. As he opened the door and stood back for Darren to enter, General Sudasane's men rushed in, motioning for Darren to wait outside in the hallway as they checked his room. One man pulled an instrument from under his coat and scanned the room for any electronic devices. Great guns, Darren thought as he peered into the room to see what was happening, this is a little much. They finished, then nodded for Darren to enter. At the same time, they ushered the bellhop out and down the hall. They then shut the door as they left and Darren found himself alone, still stunned. "I guess they didn't find any bombs or bugs," he said aloud with a slight smile. He felt the tightness in his chest once again.

He needed to talk to a friend. Someone. Anyone. He had never felt so alone and vulnerable. He ached to talk to Ann. He didn't care what time it was back in Texas. He picked up the phone and called Mo.

A sleepy voice answered, "Yeah?"

"Mo, this is Darren. You awake enough to talk?"

"Darren, where the hell are you? I've been needin' to talk to you for days."

"I'm glad to hear that. What's up?"

"Oh man, you're not gonna believe this. I had dinner the other night with a separatist in San Antonio. He got pretty well plastered and talked his head off. He made me promise not to print any of his information, so I have to sit on it."

"Sit on what, Mo?"

"According to this guy they're smuggling millions of dollars worth of foreign weapons into the country, right under the noses of the feds!

"Mo, when is this taking place and where?"

"He didn't know. He's waiting for a phone call that's supposed to come any day."

"Any idea of where these guns are coming across?"

"No, he said they didn't tell him anything. He has to wait for instructions to pick up a load and haul them to Chudder's place."

"If you can find out any details we could surely use the information. Call General Burcks's office and leave a message."

"Okay, I will if I hear anything. I think the guy is going to wake up and realize he spilled the beans, and when he does I don't think I'll hear any more."

"Don't get yourself in trouble."

"Okay. You doin' all right?"

"It's been interesting." Darren explained what he had been through since his landing in Thailand.

"Wow, that's wild. You better get out of that business before you get killed. When are you coming back to the States?"

"In a few days. I'll call you when I get home."

"Okay. Keep your head down and don't vomit, man."

"I'm tryin'." After he hung up, Darren sat by the window, staring out over Singapore's South China Sea and tried to think through his dilemma. Talking with Mo made him feel connected with his friends once again. The lonesome feeling disappeared. In a few moments, the phone rang. He jumped. Vasin's familiar voice boomed across the distance.

"Darren, we're just checking to see if you arrived safely. Did the men meet you okay?"

"They sure did. They wouldn't even let me enter my room without checking for bugs. I can't thank you and General Sudasane enough!"

"He's happy to do it. He's my uncle, by the way." Darren could hear Vasin chuckling.

"Well, he's a good man. I owe both of you big time."

"Don't worry about it. He'll call you one of these days for a pay back."

"Whatever he wants, he can have," Darren answered, adding, "but I haven't got much."

"Darren, we don't want to worry you any more than you already are, but do you remember your original flight?"

"Yeah."

"It blew up as it taxied down the runway for take off."

"Oh, shit!?"

"Out of two hundred fifty-four passengers, they may have lost four. Fortunately, they took off late."

"It blew before the plane got in the air?"

"Yes. And they believe the bomb exploded in the front baggage compartment, under where you would have been sitting." Darren couldn't think of a thing to say. Vasin continued, "The fire did most of the damage, but the crew had it out and passengers evacuated in record time."

"Oh my God, I feel terrible." He felt a little dizzy. And the pain in his chest increased. I've got to get home and see a doctor, he thought.

He heard Vasin say, "We understand. Someone wants you pretty bad, even though they're pretty sloppy."

"Any chance they'll catch the guys who planted the bomb?"

"I don't know. My uncle's in the middle of the investigation. He won't say anything about you, but that knowledge helps his focus. I'll keep you informed."

"Please do, Vasin. Tell him to get in touch with Marilyn Thompson at the

U.S. Embassy. She can shed some light on this also. Again, so many thanks for your kindness and help."

"You would do the same for us. Just take care of yourself. When you call me do it on my cell phone. And don't use your real name. I recognize your voice so you don't have to use it. I don't want you to get caught up in this mess."

"Good thought. Talk with you later."

Darren looked at his watch as he stretched out on the bed. He had forty-five minutes before a late lunch with Singapore friends. He got up, soaked a washcloth with cold water, then returned to bed and applied the cloth to his forehead hoping it would help him relax. He had a hard time stemming the tears as he fought to overcome the grief that gripped him. He had been resting about five minutes when the muscles in his chest and stomach began to spasm. His breath stuck in his throat. It reminded him of being hit in the stomach as a kid. Maybe it's a heart attack, he thought. Or a physical reaction to the stress. The spasms soon stopped, his breathing returned to normal and the dizziness seemed to disappear.

By the time his friends called from the lobby, he felt fine. He washed his face, combed his hair and headed out the door. As he opened the door, he found one of his Thai bodyguards on duty. "Why are you still here?"

"Orders. Have orders. Must stay." Somewhat embarrassed, he realized he should have arranged security from the American Embassy. But, as a low-level, Johnny-come-lately in this government mess, his request would probably have been refused. He decided that he would never be able to convince his security guards to leave, so he had to adjust to their presence. In the light of the bombing in Bangkok, he found himself grateful. His new shadow followed him halfway to the elevator.

Darren stepped out of the elevator into the lobby and saw his two friends waiting. As he moved toward them the other bodyguard moved to his side. A third man, who seemed to be of Chinese origin, now joined him. Darren met his two friends, but before he could greet them properly, his bodyguards asked to see their personal identification. Darren stood helplessly by, somewhat embarrassed. The Thai guard turned to Darren and said, "Please, no worry. We check."

"Who's the other guy?" Darren asked.

"He's our man. You no worry. You be okay."

He noticed the shocked look on his friends' faces. The security men cleared his friends and moved off a brief distance while continuing to keep their eyes on others in the lobby.

"Boy, Darren, what's going on?" Y.C. Lin said. "Are you under house arrest?"

"No, no," Darren exclaimed. "Nothing like that. Just a precaution. I apologize for the inconvenience." They all chuckled over the situation.

After the meal, Darren escorted his two friends through the lobby to the hotel's front door. Mr. Lin leaned over before getting to his car and said, "Darren, I don't want to alarm you, but your security guards followed us all the way out here. I really believe you must have stolen the hotel's best silver." The men laughed.

His shadows followed him as he re-entered the lobby and stood by as he entered the elevator. When he stepped off on the eighth floor, sure enough, the guards met him and followed him down the hall to his room. I hate this, Darren thought. Just think what a confining life people of fame must live with. It must be hell. With those thoughts in mind, he sprawled out on the bed and fell into a deep sleep.

After a few hours, he woke up and lay in bed pondering the events of the past weeks, and then realized that General Burcks should be getting to the office. He rolled over and grabbed the phone.

"General. Darren here."

"Hey, we've been worried. Understand someone blew up your plane. Anything you want to tell me?"

"The answer to that depends on one's perspective. Given the situation, I would say I'm doing extremely well. And although I'm scared shitless, I'm getting madder than hell." Darren got up and walked over to the large window and stared out across the Singapore nightscape.

"Give me some details."

Burcks quietly listened as Darren chronicled events since landing in Thailand. He also relayed Mo's information about the arms smuggling across the border.

Burcks softly answered, "I'm not surprised. I'll check to see what we're doing to catch them. Are you ready to give it up?"

"Hell, no. They're not going to quit just because I chicken out and run for cover. I've got more resources in my present position than I would back in my former job. They'd get me for sure if I went back to my old job. Anyway, General

Sudasane has me well protected for the time being. I could use some help when I get to Japan, however." Darren sat down in a straight-backed chair at the small oval table next to the window, stretched out his legs and stared around the room as he listened.

"It'll be arranged. Meanwhile, you may want to stay away from your friends lest they get hurt too."

"Oh crap, I didn't even think about that." He got up and turned back to the window. He could see a few headlights traveling along the coastal highway.

"Think about it. And let me know your departure as soon as you can. Any news from Ann?"

"Nope. They seem to believe she'll check in when she can. And they don't seem to be worried."

"Of course. It's also true that one can't accept what other intelligence officers are telling you. Lying is a career specialty!"

"Yeah. I've thought about that. What's the latest in the political war with the super patriots?"

"We have members of the administration who want to declare war on anyone that's even associated with those groups."

"Just add the bunch to the Muslin terrorists?"

"Something like that," answered Burcks. "You keep your head down. Each morning and night I want to hear from you. Understand?"

"Yes, sir."

Paul Yee arrived at the hotel early the next morning and called Darren. As Darren prepared to leave his room, he peeked through the small security port in his door. He didn't want another heart stopper. A new security guard was on duty. As Darren opened the door, the man bowed respectfully and said, "Good morning." Then he scanned the corridor and lead Darren down the hallway to the elevator. Once again, two security agents waited as Darren stepped off the elevator into the lobby. They checked Paul's identity papers then respectfully distanced themselves as they followed them into the dining room.

"What's that all about?" Paul asked .

Darren explained the series of events. "Paul, it may not be safe to be in my company."

"Do you think they know where you are?"

"I hope not. But I suspect they'll find me sooner or later. I've got to move on as quickly as possible."

"I understand. Let's talk to my friend before you go."

"Oh, I'm sure Aung knows what he's doing. I've rented one of the hotel's cars, by the way." Within a few minutes Paul and Darren pulled up in front of the Raffles Country Club to find Mr. Aung waiting. The bodyguards pulled up in another car, got out and met Mr. Aung. They all bowed graciously and exchanged business cards. The guards seemed relieved to find Darren in the company of a Hong Kong police officer.

They entered the clubhouse, paid their green fees and rented carts. "Mr. Hopkins," began Mr. Aung, as they drove their golf cart to the first tee.

"Please, call me Darren."

"Okay. Darren, what's the protection for?"

Darren explained how a mysterious man had followed him in Bangkok, struck him in the head, bugged his hotel room, and how he had been smuggled out of the country.

Aung listened carefully. "It seems some of the men you listed have high political connections in Chinese government. I had to be careful. I discover that your Americans landed in Hong Kong in pairs, not as a group. That you said. They stayed at several hotels." Aung handed Darren a copy of the hotel bills for each American as they stopped at the first tee.

Darren and Aung then walked up to the tee box. Paul had set his tee and prepared to drive, so they stood quietly. The 186-yard fairway dipped slightly, and then rose sharply as it doglegged to the right. Paul, using a three wood, hit a high shot that landed on the left side of the fairway where the dogleg began. Aung moved to tee up his ball next.

While waiting, Darren admired the huge acacia and palm trees that lined the fairways, accented by flowering bushes of many varieties. The scent of flowers, mixed with that of fresh cut grass, invaded the senses. A harmony of bird songs echoed across the tropical hills.

Aung, using a four iron, hit a line drive that just barely stayed in bounds at the far right side of the dogleg. Darren stepped up and, using a five iron, drove his ball down the middle of the fairway to the dogleg junction. They all had nice chip shots to the green.

They got in their carts and headed down the fairway. As they did so, Aung leaned over toward Darren. "They gathered on a Chinese sampan late second night.

Once at safe distance, they went on a high-speed launch, as I suspected. The boat took them down China coast where they went ashore and flew safely to the Thai-Laotian border. I don't know where they land along coast, but probably near Zhanjiang. The Chinese central government looked the other way, as officials in Vietnam and Laos helped these men get to Thailand. The Chinese societies not involved after all. Someone paid big money to one smuggler gang to get this done. Or a political trade-off took place. That is all I find. What else can I do for you?"

"I thank you very much for all your effort. I hope you didn't put yourself at risk in this."

"No, I did not. When I told my superiors that some Americans slipped into our country in a strange manner, they told me how it happened. They also told me to forget about it."

The men chipped onto the first green, but differed in putting ability. Aung put his in for a birdie, Paul three-putted for par and Darren bogeyed the hole. As the men drove to the next tee, Darren asked, "Why do you think your government helped these guys?"

"Purely a response to powerful men in Mideast. Although Chinese government watches events in America carefully, I don't believe anyone views your patriots as anything other than criminals. To us, America is full of criminals running up and down the streets at night. This does not seem new to us." Aung enjoyed the jab at America, and Paul laughed. Darren just grimaced.

The men continued their golf game, though an extremely slow foursome in front often held them up. As they waited on the fifth tee, Darren leaned toward Aung and asked softly, "Any idea who might be trying to kill me?"

"Well, I will see." Aung and Paul laughed. Darren didn't.

They finished the first nine holes by lunch. Darren lost to Paul by two points. "Darren, I don't think your mind's on the game." Then after a slight pause, Paul smiled as he said, "So, let's play another nine holes!" The men laughed. Darren picked up the lunch tab, said his good-byes and returned to the hotel. The other men continued their game.

The Raffles Country Club's lush environment and serenity helped calm Darren's fears. Almost. After a refreshing shower back at the hotel, he called the airlines and worked out a circuitous route back to the States via Manila and Tokyo. They put him on the next day's early flight to Manila, giving him a four-hour layover in Manila before his Quantas flight to Tokyo. As soon as he hung up, the phone rang. He immediately recognized Agent Lenora Carlson's voice.

"Darren, Burcks called and gave us an update on your trip. How're you doin'?"

He sat down in a chair by the bed, crossed his legs and relaxed. "Right this moment I feel pretty good. It's not much fun having some unknown ass-hole trying to kill you!"

"Yeah, a nightmare. None of us can be too careful anymore. We are at war. How reliable is your Texas source on the weapons delivery?"

"He's tops. Take it to the bank!"

"Okay. It confirms our own intelligence. We didn't have the details your source does. Can he get us any specifics?"

"He may, but the guy that tipped him is probably too scared to say anything else. If my friend finds anything out I know he'll call. If he does, then I'll call you. Okay?"

"That's fine. We'll be waiting. When will you be back?"

"I'm coming back after a brief stopover in Tokyo."

"Okay, but you can't be too cautious."

"I'm trying to be careful. We've identified the key players at that January meeting in Chiang Mai and know how they got to and from Hong Kong. The only good I see coming out of this is the impact the media may have on public opinion." Darren got up and started pacing the floor as he talked.

"The more the public knows, the harder it is for these guys to recruit."

"True."

"The task force meets regularly now. And we are more and more frustrated. A lot of top administrators and congressmen are retiring. People fear for their lives and those of their family."

"I don't blame them. They've a lot to be nervous about," Darren said , as he walked over to the window and stared out at the city and the South China Sea. "I'm wondering if some of our crazies might try to light up the sky on or around April nineteenth! That's the anniversary of the Ruby Ridge affair. If the government conducts business as usual a lot of innocent people may get killed."

"I don't know about you," Lenora continued, "but if all this terrorism continues very long, I think I'll move to a secluded island in the South Pacific."

"Oh, you couldn't stand it. You'll be in the midst of the brawl until they turn out the lights."

Carlson laughed. "Yeah, but not by choice. By the way, we'll be looking for you at our task force meetings when you return."

"Okay. Thanks for calling." Darren sat quietly staring out over the South China Sea and pondered Lenora's call. The war against terrorism had led to a domestic nightmare, he solemnly mused. He felt like a fish out of water. His fear was turning to rage. Life was about to get even uglier for Darren and his colleagues.

A frightful noise shattered his sleep the next morning. He awakened and looked around in a stupor until he realized the phone ringing. He picked it up to hear Mo's voice.

"You awake? What time is it there?"

"Four thirty in the morning."

"Oh, I'm sorry. I never could remember time zones."

"What's this about?"

"You told me to call you if I heard anything more about the arms shipments."

"Have you heard any specifics?"

"It's not good. I hear they've muled that stuff across the border and stashed it in prearranged bunkers all over the place. A large batch has been unloaded in the Vancouver area."

"Oh, lord, that's bad. Would you mind calling General Burcks' office for me?"

"Darren, I decided that I can't do that. As I told you before, I will share information with you as long as it doesn't come back to bloody my reporter's nose. I cannot afford to be known as a government snitch."

"Okay. Not to worry. I appreciate all this very much."

"Okay. Talk to you later. Go back to sleep."

Instead, Darren called Burcks and reported Mo's information. Burcks was not happy.

# 11

**A WEST TEXAS HIGHWAY**
Saturday, March 8

"You boys wuz sure speedin'. Y'all goin' to a fire somewhere?" the Texas Highway Patrol officer asked, as he walked up to the driver's window. "I got'cha clocked at eighty-five, and seventy's the limit. Step out here and show me yer license." While the officer threw the beam from his flashlight into the back of the nineteen ninety Suburban, his partner verified the car's ownership and status through headquarters in Austin.

"I guess we wuz tired, lost in talkin' and jest weren't payin' 'tention," muttered the driver of the Suburban. "Sorry 'bout that. I promise I'll slow it down." The officer had retreated to the rear of the vehicle preparing to write a speeding ticket. The young driver handed the officer his driver's license. As the officer studied it, he looked up and said, "Gosh, boy, are you old Homer's son?"

"Yes, sir. I sure am."

The officer put the book down, studied the boy for a few moments, and then said, "Son, your daddy and me grew up together out in Van Horn back in the sixties. We played some mean football together. I was an end and he was a fast tailback. What'cha doin' over here around Sonora anyway? Head'n home?"

"Naw, sir. Me and my friend went down to San Antonio looking for work. Thought we'd make a few bucks hauling some spare parts to El Paso for a man."

"Yeah, noticed that van rode pretty low in the back." At that, the officer once again peered in the side window at the wooden crates stacked in the back. "Well, I'll let y'all go on this one because of your daddy, but if I catch ya out here speed'n ag'in I'm goin'a have to give ya a ticket, hear?"

"Yes, sir. Thank you. I'll slow it down," the young man said with a sigh of relief.

"Tell your daddy Jack Burleson said hi."

"Sure will." The young men, both in their early twenties, climbed back into the suburban and headed on down the highway. The passenger said, "Wow, that was close. Glad he knew yore daddy."

A HIGHWAY IN WESTERN CANADA
Sunday, March 9

Twenty miles east of Hope, British Columbia, at 4:00 a.m., a Canadian Highway Patrol parked off the highway under the canopy of an abandoned gas station watched as two eastbound pickup trucks shot by. The officers pursued the trucks and pulled them over a few miles down the highway. The Canadian Highway Patrol arrested George McKinley and James Wright for speeding and possession of contraband Russian weapons. The Canadian authorities impounded six crates of machine guns, mines and grenade launchers.

TOKYO, JAPAN
Monday, March 10

While the Russian guns were being smuggled into the U.S., one of Sudasanes' men flew with Darren to Manila and Tokyo. Both flights went well. The four-hour wait at the Manila airport went fast. Darren called a few Filipino friends and then browsed the kiosks as he walked the terminal hallways.

The Quantas flight from Sidney arrived and left on time. When Darren and his shadow arrived in Tokyo in the early evening, Fred Watson and several members of Japan's military intelligence staff whisked them off the plane. At this point, Darren's Thai shadow bowed respectfully and departed to catch a return flight to Bangkok. Darren again expressed his deep gratitude. Darren turned to Fred and asked, "Can he catch a flight at this hour?"

"Yes, it's already arranged. They're holding a Thai flight that arrived from the States earlier. He'll be aboard and on his way before we get to the express train."

Fred, an Afro-American friend with a long and distinguished career with U.S. Army Intelligence, had been posted in Japan for over twenty years. He knew the Japanese intelligence community as well as anyone. Darren wanted to know more about the Japanese Red Army—a.k.a. the Anti-Imperialist International Brigade—Aum Shinrikyo Doomsday sect, and others devoted to terrorism scattered around Asia. Fred would know or could find the answers. Darren was not disappointed.

On the long drive into Tokyo, Fred handed Darren an up-to-date report on the key Asian terrorist groups and their leaders. "No doubt about it, several of the men at Chiang Mai represented Aum Shinrikyo," stated Fred. "We're glad to know of the meeting. Evidently they're seeking arms and funds."

"I suspect they got both," Darren said.

"So do we. We've notified the Japanese authorities and they're going to pick these guys up as soon as they find them. They have some law on their books that makes characters like these, who have been repeatedly warned, subject to imprisonment for associating with other terrorists. They'll interpret the loosely-worded law as needed and put them away." Both men laughed.

"Our legal system should be so decisive!" Darren said.

"Yes, until you're looking down the barrel of that gun."

"Of course," Darren said. "Tell me about the Asian groups."

"The Filipino group focuses on drug dealers and corrupt government officials, now that the U.S. military has left the islands. The U.S. arrested several leaders of the Red Army while attempting to set explosives in the nineteen eighties. And you remember that Arum Shinrikyo's older leaders detonated poison gas in some Tokyo subways a few years ago and are in prison."

"Yes," Darren replied. "I remember. By the way, have you kept up with the rise of our super-duper patriots?"

"Somewhat. I try to keep up, but my workload makes it impossible to read every report coming in. How'd you get mixed up in all this?" Ted asked, with a smirk.

"I sure didn't plan to!" Darren said. "Have you ever found yourself going down a trail that seemed to open up willy-nilly?" Darren related the history of his recruitment by Burcks right when the super patriot movement dramatically escalated. He included his frustrations with leaks, the inability to recognize patriot supporters within government and law enforcement circles, and the various threats to his physical safety.

The men arrived at the Akasaka Tokyu Hotel. The hotel's twelve floors spread across several blocks, which, in Darren's mind, made it a safe haven against the daily earthquakes. Darren checked in, then put his clothes in their proper place as Fred and his men stood guard in the hall. They continued their visit over a dinner at a restaurant in the nearby Akasaka district.

CHAPMANN'S COMPOUND
OKANOGAN NATIONAL FOREST, WASHINGTON
Monday, March 10

As Darren went about his business in Tokyo, the Chapmanns were trying to monitor the incoming shipment of Russian arms from their Okanogan forest compound. Jill Chapmann poured her husband another cup of coffee as he spoke by short wave to a member of the Washington militia in Vancouver. "Jack, do you know if any of our trucks have gotten lost?" Ron asked.

"None but the two caught by the Canadian Highway Patrol. We've been lucky. Has any reached you?"

"Only one shipment. A truck brought twelve crates in here early this morning. I suspect others will be showing up shortly. I heard that some of these guys may unload the stuff in their garages and lay low for a few weeks."

"Yeah. Guess so. Hope no others get caught."

Chapmann leaned back in his chair, stretched out his legs and ran his hand through his hair as he thought about the situation. "Well, no matter how well you plan and how many times you give directions, there's always some idiot who's either not listening or doesn't care," he said. "Thank goodness those Canadian guys don't know anything or anyone. Maybe they'll keep their mouths shut about what they do know."

"Well, I hope the rest of the stuff gets to the right parties," Jack said.

"Keep monitoring the situation and if you hear anything call me immediately. Okay?"

"Yep. Talk with you later."

Chapmann monitored the arms deliveries over the next several days. At the end of the second day four trucks had failed to call in, but each warehouse manager claimed to be in touch with the drivers.

Finally Chapmann sent a coded email message to Gahlib through the Turkish Embassy in Washington, D.C., assuring him that the gifts had arrived safely. Everyone at the Chapmann compound spent the next several weeks working the phones and radios to get the arms distributed.

One of the New Mexico warehouses had problems. The rancher on whose property the facility had been built refused to distribute the weapons. It took White, Boorgers, Chapmann, Chudders, and half a dozen other influentials to persuade rancher Tom Ship that he had to share the goods.

"Good Lord, what an ass!" White exclaimed to Chapmann by phone after the dust settled. "No wonder the Feds have trouble with that sucker over grazing lands."

"Yeah, Jill thinks his family probably wants to kill him, too."

"He must be a real, honest-to-goodness sociopath. We better watch that guy or he'll get us all in trouble."

"Oh, I think he's too dumb for that," Chapmann said . "But we do need to sit down with him to prevent this from happening every time we get a load of weapons. The facility will be unusable!"

"Right. Besides, we raised the money for the construction of that warehouse. He didn't pay a dime!"

"True," Chapmann said .

"Well," White thought, "if we can't work with him, he may have to go."

"You mean go, as in period, Colonel?" asked Chapmann.

"Sure as hell."

"Well, okay. But that seems a little final to me," Chapmann said with a nervous laugh.

"These are final times," White said . "By the way, bring a complete report to the leadership council meeting Friday at Ship's ranch."

"Certainly. I'll be in there Thursday night."

"Excellent. Boorgers and me need to be out 'a there sometime Saturday afternoon or evening. None of us should be in one place very long."

"I understand. I'll get in touch with Petsch and the others and make sure they'll be there."

TOKYO

Tuesday, March 11

Back in Tokyo, Darren had gotten up early and was just stepping into the shower when the phone rang. He picked up to hear Fred's voice. "Turn on CNN right now. I'll be up soon."

Darren hung up and sat on the edge of the bed and clicked on CNN to see a visibly distraught reporter named Abby Smyth standing amid litter and smoke on a street in Washington, D.C. "The police have made us move because a wall of the building may fall."

Then Darren heard the anchor say, "Abby, we want you out of there now." He sat immobile as CNN reported on the bombing of the FBI Building, a number of the Congressional office buildings and dozens of military installations across the nation. Suddenly there was a soft knock on the door. He got up to let Fred in.

"Well, you felt in your gut this would happen, didn't you?" Fred asked.

"It was my worst nightmare."

"Maybe a splinter off the Al-Qaeda network did this?"

"That's not outside the realm of possibility," Darren replied. "But let's wait and see whose signature is found."

They watched the television coverage for another thirty minutes, and then Darren said, "Let's get some breakfast."

"Okay. What time's your flight?"

"Four-fifteen this afternoon." And then, after a slight pause, he said, "This will be a gloomy flight."

"This is such a damn shame," Fred said. "What in the hell does anyone hope to gain by doing all this?"

Darren shrugged his shoulders and shook his head. At breakfast Fred said, "I've got a brief meeting this morning, but as soon as it's over I'll be back. We've got a man keeping an eye on you, and we'll get you to the airport."

"Thanks, Fred."

After Fred left Darren read the two English language newspapers and worked the crossword puzzles while his security guard sat at a nearby table. When he had finished, Darren started to his room to finish packing, and then noticed a slightly built Asian man coming up the escalator—the same man who had shadowed him in Thailand. Darren yelled as he ran to the escalator, "Hey you son-of-a-bitch!" The man turned and raced back down, knocking several people out of the way as he did so.

Darren got to the top of the escalator in time to see the man race toward the main doors. Darren quickly raced down the escalator as fast as he could with his security man on his heels. By the time they had reached the main entrance the man had disappeared. "Did you see a man wearing a brown suit come out?" Darren asked the bellhop.

"Ah, yes." He pointed down the street. "He got in white Toyota." Darren could just barely see the car as it disappeared around a bend in the street.

Back in his hotel room, Darren finished packing, made some calls back to the States to check on family members, and then headed for the elevator. Fred was just getting off.

"Just in time. What's this I hear about you chasing some poor slob down the escalator?"

"News travels fast."

"Yeah. Was that the guy who's been following you?"

"He's the one."

"Okay, then. Let's go back to your room."

"What?" Darren asked with a strong note of disbelief in his voice.

"Just do as I say. This guy seems pretty good at getting information, so let's see if we can outwit him."

Back in Darren's room, Fred called Japan Airlines and arranged a new reservation back to the States for Darren, called Continental and canceled the original, and then had a lengthy conversation with his office. Finally, he led Darren down the back steps to the hotel's kitchen and out the back door to a waiting car.

"Pretty sneaky, Fred. You're not going to roll me in some old smelly rug, are you?"

"We thought about that, but decided you'd have problems getting through U.S. Customs," Fred replied with a smile. But we're not through yet."

Over the next two hours, Fred and several intelligence officers led Darren through a maze of Tokyo subways and alleyways until they finally arrived at Narita Airport. They led Darren through employee tunnels and hallways to an office overlooking the runway. After speaking with Narita officials, Fred turned to Darren and said, pointing to a JAL 747 sitting on the tarmac near the office, "That's the plane you're going to be on. We've checked your bag through on the old flight. The FBI wants to see who shows up to watch it."

"Okay," Darren said. "I guess we just wait?"

"That's right." At that moment a large Japanese man entered and greeted Fred in Japanese. Fred turned to Darren. "Darren, meet Mr. Kobayashi. He has to be in San Francisco anyway, so we've asked him to sit with you. Added protection."

"Thanks for the company." Kobayashi nodded without saying a word. Darren turned to Fred and extended his hand. "Thanks for all your help, Fred. I hope I can make it up to you one of these days."

"Well, you can by helping put an end to this crazy stuff."

SAN FRANCISCO
Tuesday, March 11

Darren's plane landed in San Francisco at seven thirty a.m. Pacific Standard Time, one hour early. He had eaten breakfast and shaved before landing. He had been able to sleep during most of the flight. An FBI agent was waiting as the plane's door opened. He escorted Darren and Kobayashi down the service stairs to a waiting car, stopping at the security center to clear Darren and Kobayashi's passports. Agent Kobayashi then left for his assignment in the San Francisco area, and Darren followed the FBI agent aboard a waiting helicopter.

That 'copter delivered him to a military plane waiting at Alameda's Nimitz Field destined for Washington. As the plane lifted off, Darren glanced at his watch and noted that it had only been twenty minutes since his flight from Tokyo touched down. "What about my luggage?" he asked the agent.

"It'll arrive in Washington on your regular flight, as planned."

"Hope they catch someone."

Darren arrived at his Washington apartment by mid-afternoon and his suitcase arrived later that night. The agent said he had been told that no one had shown any interest in the bag. Relieved, Darren unpacked. The clear sky and cool weather beckoned him outside, so he gathered his laundry and cleaning and walked down to drop them at the cleaners.

Later that evening he remembered that he had forgotten to check his answering machine. He stared at it for a few moments. Then, with a sigh, he punched the message button.

Several messages invited him to social events, but one got his full attention. "if you want Ann Jones...then...you...back off...or you're both dead...and we..." He couldn't understand all of the message, so he hit the save button, removed the tape and put it in an envelope to take it to the FBI lab. All of a sudden he wasn't sleepy. He read into the night, finally falling asleep around 2:00 a.m.

CNN NEWS
Wednesday, March 12

"Good morning, this is Ralph Combs, CNN News Central, Atlanta. The smoke has gradually cleared in the aftermath of a violent night. The country has not witnessed this much internal destruction and loss of life since the Civil War of the eighteen sixties. Authorities estimate that three hundred and eighty-six federal facilities took hits from bombs, mortars, grenades and various missiles during the night. The damage and loss of human life is huge. We go live to the White House, where Presidential Aide, Boyd Waggoner, is standing in for the President."

The camera switched to the small press corps room, filled to capacity with approximately four hundred reporters. The President's Chief of Staff, looking grim, strode to the lectern. Squinting into the spotlights, he said, "Thanks for coming ladies and gentlemen. I will read a prepared statement from the President, then take a few questions." Waggoner looked down and cleared his throat. "The last few days this country has suffered enormously at the hands of people purporting to be patriots. Three hundred and eighty-six federal facilities have been significantly damaged; approximately six thousand federal employees and innocent by-standers have been killed. Another twenty thousand have sustained injuries. The damage will run into the billions."

Waggoner looked up from the page, glanced at his audience, adjusted his glasses, and continued. "These are unconscionable acts and we will prosecute those responsible to the fullest extent of the law. As President of the United States, I have asked the Attorney General to draft legislation to be sent to Congress today for immediate action that makes any and all attacks on federal property and those resulting in the death of federal employees, acts of treason, punishable by death."

As he finished, Waggoner cleared his throat and said, "I'm willing to answer a few questions at this time."

As all shouted for attention, Waggoner pointed to the senior White House reporter from The New York Times seated on the first row, then smiled wanly. "Yes, I believe you're always first Elizabeth."

"Thank you," said an elderly, dumpily dressed lady who had covered the White House for decades. She took off her glasses and in New York accent asked, "Is the president going to call for martial law? And second, how sure are you that these domestic terrorists weren't acting with Muslin terrorists?"

"He's discussing the option of martial law," Waggoner said. "But we believe that state and local law enforcement will work closely with federal officials in bringing the perpetrators to justice. Second, all evidence points to domestic terrorists, but we are continuing our war against foreign terrorists throughout the world." There was a pause and he nodded at a CBS's reporter halfway back in the center section. "Sam!"

"I have two questions. First, we've had reports that some local law enforcement personnel are sympathetic to these people. How can you have faith in local officials to do the job? Second, have there been any arrests connected with last night's bombings?"

"We believe there are enough honest and professional law enforcement personnel out there to uphold the Constitution of the United States. We will help them get the job done. We don't want to step in and take over local law enforcement, but are prepared to do that if it becomes necessary. Second, at this point two hundred and twenty-four men and women were arrested across the nation during the night. You can pick up a copy at the door as you leave." Then pointing down to a woman on the third row to his left, he said, "Nancy, I believe you're next."

The representative from Reuters asked, "Do you know how many terrorists law enforcement personnel have killed?"

"Our latest report indicates forty-six died trying to place explosives," Waggoner replied. "There could have been others whose remains are yet to be found."

"Did these people get caught at the scene?" the reporter continued.

"Yes. And quite a few died at their own hands. Others were caught either driving an explosive-laden car or truck, firing mortars or grenades, or a combination of the two. And some, fortunately, were caught before they could plant and detonate those explosives. So, the answer to your question is yes."

As he paused, a loud, deep voice in the far-left corner of the room stood out above the others. "John Allen, Houston Chronicle."

"Yes, Mr. Allen."

"What have those caught used as their rationale for committing such violent acts?"

"Mr. Allen, the people who do such things share a belief that the government has betrayed them," Waggoner said. "It's the same line we've heard from extremists, right and left, for years."

Waggoner then pointed to a woman near the back. "Yes, ma'am."

"Pam Robertson, L.A. Times. I've got two questions. First, we understand that some of those arrested insisted on being treated as prisoners of war. Is that true?"

Laughter broke out and after the group quieted down, she continued, "Second, how soon before we can get a list of the government employees and innocent bystanders who have been killed and wounded?"

Waggoner cleared his throat. "Some of these terrorists do see themselves as members of a foreign nation. But that's fanciful thinking. They're traitors to their country, and they will be prosecuted as such. As to the names of those killed and wounded, I don't know. That will take some time. As you know, relatives must first be informed. I'll check on the status of this as soon as we've finished. Okay. That's it. Thanks for coming."

Waggoner then added, "Oh, the President did want me to mention that because you all cover federal affairs, be extremely careful. We wouldn't want to lose any of you."

CNN then returned to its Atlanta newsroom and Darren got up to pour another cup of coffee. "So there you have it," the anchor said. "We will take a station break and return in a few minutes with more about these catastrophic events."

Darren picked up the phone and called Mo Childs in Austin.

"Hey, glad you're home," Mo said. Have you had time to watch the news?"

"Yep. Terrible stuff."

"We knew it would happen, just didn't know when."

"What have you heard from your sources since we last talked?"

"They've all scurried into hiding. I've only found two of my patriot friends at home around the state. Some may have been killed."

"What did you get out of those two?"

"Not a heck of a lot. I think all these guys are scared."

"They should be. By the way, how are people reacting to the President's use of regular military?"

"Oh, most of the people our reporters have talked to think it's about time. Then there are those who believe the sky is falling. They think he's using this as a political ploy, a pretense to install a dictatorship. One guy wrote a letter to our editor suggesting that the terrorist movement had been mobilized by the President."

"Mo, I need to let you go. Keep digging and call me when you have any news."

ISTANBUL
Thursday, March 13

Unknown to Darren and others, Javad delighted in the knowledge that all except a few of the weapons reached their American destination and that they were being used. He spent most of the day phoning and faxing the good news to his colleagues throughout the Middle East and North Africa. Messages of congratulation came into his Turkish office from all over the world as the news spread. His own president wanted him to return immediately to be feted. Leaders from around the Arab world called to congratulate him. He had proven himself to be a smart operator and a new kind of architect in the war with the evil American Empire.

At the end of the day he arose from his desk and walked out on his apartment's balcony and looked down at the darkening street scenes as the sun sank in the west. How can we keep the American patriots at war with their own government? he asked himself.

# 12

## RESERVE, CATRON COUNTY, NEW MEXICO

Friday, March 14

As acts of domestic terrorism increased across America and the government's task force worked to get it under control, the self-appointed ad hoc leadership council for militias, separatist groups and assorted organizations of the radical patriotic movement gathered at the twenty-thousand-acre Tom Ship ranch in western New Mexico.

Two hundred members of the New Mexico and Arizona militia provided security. The militia had set up a military-style camp on a meadow not far from the ranch entrance off State Highway Twelve. Radar trucks monitored the sky from various hilltops adjacent to Ship's private landing strip.

As key leaders gathered by the fireplace in the guesthouse that first evening, they celebrated their victories.

"Damn, we snuck those guns in right under their noses!" Arlo White exclaimed, almost beside himself.

"Well, it shows the strength of the cause," Petsch said . "You know, I keep sayin' there's a lot of anger and resentment out there among the American people. Most will tell you they're fed up with a government that lets Arab camel jockeys continue to walk all over us. We should have gone in and wiped out all Arabs after we finished with the Afghans and Iraqis, but we didn't. No guts! And people don't mind helpin' the poor, and they don't mind some foreigners and people of color, but they've had it up to their eyeballs with a welfare system that jes' keeps a growin', national borders that leak like sieves, minorities who blame whites for everythin' from stomach aches to their lack of education, and an increasingly Godless society."

"Good grief," White cried. "That's a mouthful."

Boorgers added, "We've got to take advantage of that anger if we are to bring down this government."

"Ron," White said , "have you talked to Ship about the guns and his attitude?" The question sobered the group.

"Nope. Maybe we should confront him together. What do you fellas think about that?" They all nodded, but it was obvious that no one relished the task of confronting the rancher. His volatile temper was well known. "We'll wait until he's had time to get to know us and all the warm fuzzy feelings of camaraderie have done their work."

"Fine. Why don't we let General Boorgers handle the chore?" White said . "He can singe the whiskers off a buzzard at two-hundred yards."

"Good idea!" Chapmann said . "General, the job's yours!"

Boorgers looked at Chapmann with a smirk.

They continued visiting, waiting for lunch to be served. Finally, Tom Ship strode into the room. He introduced himself around and then said, "You better turn that TV on. All hell's brokin' loose!"

"What are you talking about?" Chapmann asked, eyes wide in wonder.

Tom Ship turned the satellite TV to CNN where a news anchor reported that bombs had exploded in federal buildings as workers arrived for work in Baltimore, Atlanta, Miami, Dallas, Houston, San Antonio, Kansas City, Omaha, Denver, Phoenix, Los Angeles, Seattle and other cities. Military installations across the nation had also been bombed. Air base hangars had been blown up, damaging F-16s, AWACS, B1 bombers and assorted aircraft. In addition, ground-to-air missiles brought down an A-10 Thunderbolt jet over southern Colorado. Search crews hunted for the wreckage.

Petsch had a huge grin on his face as he raised his fist in the air and shouted, "Hallelujah!"

The others looked at him, smiled, then turned their attention back to the TV as CNN News broke away from the field reports and switched to Washington. Cameramen ran toward the scene of an explosion at the front entrance to the FBI building at 10th and Pennsylvania Avenue. They showed flames and smoke engulfing the front and eastern walls.

A CNN reporter interviewed a bystander who witnessed the event. "This is Vernon Thompson, who works at the National Archives, just down the street. Mr. Thompson, tell us what you saw"

Looking dazed, Thompson said, "Well, it happened so fast that I'm not sure. But I was walking to work and looked up when I heard a lot of honking. The school bus seemed out of control. I first thought it had blown a tire. It just accelerated right through the wall around the FBI building and jumped up into the air, landing right up by the front doors."

"What did you do then?"

"Oh, I don't remember," he said, eyes squinting as he tried to recollect his next reaction. "Guess I just froze."

"Do you remember what happened next?"

"People around me started yelling. Most thought children had been trapped inside. Then the whole bus just exploded!

"Was there more than one explosion?"

"Oh, yeah," he said as he held out three fingers. "The concussion knocked me down. I landed against that fence."

"It must have been very scary."

"Oh my, yes. Dust and junk went everywhere. I remember throwing my hands up to protect my face from the blast." He bent over as he brushed his hair with his right hand, trying to knock off the dirt. Then he looked at the reporter and asked, "Do you know if the bus carried any children?"

Boorgers stared at the TV screen, passively smoking a cigar as the patriot leaders looked grim. Chapmann, head resting in his left hand, looked somewhat pale and stared at the floor. White stood up, arms crossed, as he watched the carnage on TV. Chudders had leaned back in his cushioned chair, shaking his head to stay awake. Petsch had leaned toward the TV screen, his arms resting on his upper legs, as if ready to jump and run for the door.

The TV interview continued. "No, we don't. Thank you for sharing that with us, Mr. Thompson. You probably need to get some medical care." The reporter, visibly shaken turned to interview another eyewitness. "What's your name ma'am?"

"Nancy Gilpatrick."

"Miss Gilpatrick, we understand you witnessed the bombing. Tell us what you saw."

Pointing at the southwest corner of 10th street and Pennsylvania Avenue, she said, "I was over there. Then, just as I started across the intersection, I seen this bus speedin' down Penn from the Capitol and crash into that building." She pointed at the FBI building. "That bus just swerved in front of all the traffic in the right lane, sped up and jumped over those barriers. Oh my God, I couldn't believe it! Then it exploded, and I ducked down and ran over by the IRS building."

"Wheweee!" shouted White as he turned from the TV. "I hope they annihilated that goddamn place." He headed for the kitchen, then stopped, and looked back. "Anyone want a beer?"

No one answered as all eyes were riveted to the television. The reporter asked the eyewitness, "Did you see any children in the bus?"

"No, I didn't. When it careened in front of traffic and jumped that curb I didn't see any children at the windows."

"Thanks for that report." Then, facing the camera, the reporter said, "In addition to the fire trucks, dozens of ambulances and Army troop carriers are arriving. Soldiers are taking up positions around the area. It looks like Al-Qaida continues to spread terror. This is Abby Smyth, CNN News, Washington, D.C."

"Al-Qaida?" Chapmann asked, as he peered quizzically at the others.

"Al-Qaida shits," White replied. "That's our folks, but let 'em blame the fuckin' Muslims."

"Man o' man, they really hit the Feds where it hurts," Chapmann responded. "I can't believe it."

"Believe it," Boorgers said "This is just the beginning." They all looked at Boorgers, but no one dared ask what he meant. "Let's listen."

The TV anchor's voice then came on. "Abby, don't go away. We've received reports that Andrews Air Force Base, southeast of Washington, D.C., has been hit by mortar, that the Air Force transmitter facility out east has been car bombed, and that. . ." CNN lost contact with the reporter. The anchor shouted, "Abby, are you there?"

White, having returned, stood by the window watching the screen. He stiffened when an explosion rattled the TV background and the camera lost transmission.

The TV monitor returned the viewer to the station, showing the anchor shifting in his chair and looking bewildered. He picked up some papers and tried to align them as he said, "We seem to have lost transmission with Abby. We will return when we've reestablished that link."

At that moment the connection returned and the reporter said, "Paul, can you hear me?"

"Yes Abby, we can hear you. Go ahead."

"Paul, people are running in all directions here. An explosion knocked our cameraman down. We're going to move up Pennsylvania Avenue to see if we can find the source of the bombs. When we do, we will get back to you."

The TV audience watched as the reporter and cameraman trotted down the sidewalk, the camera still running. As sirens blared and people shouted in the background, the viewers could see smoke and debris littering the street as people scurried in different directions.

The anchor's voice could be heard saying, "Abby, if you can still hear me you need to get out of there."

"We're okay, Paul. But we will. Oh, oh, the police are waving us away. We'll get back to you when we can."

The screen turned black, and then returned to the CNN anchor. "Those of us at CNN hope Abby and the other members of the CNN crew get to safety. This is Paul Pune, CNN, Atlanta."

Agent Lenora Carlson was reviewing Thursday night's communications in the task force's basement suite when the explosion occurred at the front entrance of the FBI building. Alarms echoed throughout the building. The staff moved quickly, calmly and efficiently to adjust to the emergency. All entrances to the building were immediately sealed. Computers and communications systems began running off auxiliary systems. Reports on the disaster came in from all over the country. Lenora called for more communications help. In thirty minutes, top staff transferred their activities to the underground operations, while support staff helped with damage assessment and clean up.

The terrorist task force room inadvertently became a beehive of activity. Addressing Deputy Director Wade, Agent Carlson said, "We should know the extent of the damage by nightfall. It looks pretty bad. They blind-sided us once again."

"And, once again, it was not foreign terrorists," Wade said, almost in a whisper.

Wade had large purple bags under his eyes and Carlson's red eyes betrayed her dried tears. Carlson looked intently at Wade, then quietly and calmly asked, "Where's the leak?

"Perhaps it's a coincidence," he said.

"Ummm, maybe. Maybe not. They moved those weapons right under our noses. And they may have known about the heavy security we planned for the nineteenth. There's too much coincidence."

"Aw, Carlson, don't go getting paranoid on me. These guys on the fringe don't have enough sense to come in out of the rain, for God's sake. Hell, I have a friend who is part of this extremist mush, but he's harmless. At Oklahoma State University, he played tailback on the football team. And every time he started to run out on the field, the coach would yell, 'Hey Bill, get your tail back on the bench.'"

Carlson mulled over Wade's punch line for a moment, then smiled weakly. In the midst of all the destruction, humor seemed hollow.

As reports continued to pour in, one agent on the phone with a colleague in Salt Lake City yelled for Carlson to click to channel three. A hush settled as all eyes focused on the TV.

"Here at Hill Air Force Base." The reporter stood near the entrance in Ogden, the home of the 388th Fighter Wing, as she reported damage to that facility. In the background agents could see smoking wreckage of F-16 fighters and hangar facilities. The network then switched to an anchor in New York.

"That's a report from Diane Sawbuck in Ogden, Utah. Are you still there?" The reporter reappeared on the TV screen, her long blonde hair blowing in the gusty winds.

"Yes, I am," she said tersely, eyes squinting.

"Tell us again how many are believed killed."

She looked down at her blowing notes. An aide whispered a number, and the reporter looked into the camera. "Forty-two officially, but many are still missing and assumed to be in the rubble. A final count is expected late tomorrow."

"What's happening now?"

"Well, Dan, they're still trying to put out fires and secure explosive armaments. It will be hours before they can even begin to sift through the debris."

"Thanks, Diane. We'll get back to you shortly." The anchor turned to face the camera, minus the smile that usually played on the edge of his mouth, and said, "Base authorities estimate that twenty-five planes, thirteen hangars and many other key buildings have been severely damaged by mortars and missiles. And this is only one of dozens of federal facilities around the country experiencing attacks during the morning hours. We go now to Keesler Air Force Base and Fred Deats."

The anchor faded from the screen, and the image of a reporter appeared standing outside the gate of an airbase. Palm trees swayed amidst blowing smoke. Some buildings still burned and building debris littered the grounds. Fully armed Air Force personnel stood guard at the entrance.

"Yes, Dan, this is Fred Deats at Keesler Air Force Base in Biloxi, Mississippi, the home of the eighty-first Training Wing and the Air Force Reserve Command. As you can see behind me, there has been a lot of damage here. Guards at the main gate report that a gray van sped through the gate at about eight o'clock this morning. Before pursuit could stop it, the van drove into hangar fifty-three. The maintenance crew that had just come on duty ran for cover. I have with me Corporal John Aspen from La Feria, Texas."

The reporter turned to the young airman, put the mike to his face and asked, "John, I understand you saw the van enter the hangar. Tell us what happened." The thin, pimply-faced, young man seemed high-schoolish as he nervously tried to button up his Air Force fatigues. He wiped the sweat from his face with a red mechanic's rag and listened to the reporter.

His eyes seemed focused on the ground as he said, "Well, we wuz standin' around under the wing of one of them B-fifty twos talkin' 'bout who wuz goin' a do what as we put the number four engine back together, when we heard a screechin' noise. We thought one a' our guys wuz hot-doggin' it. Any wheels on those painted floors squeal anyhow. Then we turned and here wuz some maniac drivin' a van into the hangar." The Airman's eyes seemed to fill with tears as he remembered the scene.

The reporter cut in. "That's okay, take your time."

"Yeah. Sorry. It wuz goin' fifty or sixty miles an hour! We just stood there with our mouths open." He stopped to wipe his eyes.

"Could you tell what the driver looked like and how many people were in the van with him?"

"Just one white guy. One scrawny little ole fart with a beard. He screeched to a stop in the middle of the hangar under the wing of one of our planes, jumped out and started runnin'."

"Did anyone try to stop him?"

"Not at first. We stood there like wooden statues! Then Master Sergeant Mike Glenn started after the guy. But he must not of taken two steps before the crazy guy started yellin', 'It's goin' to blow! It's goin' to blow! Take cover.'"

"What happened next?"

"Oh, we ran like hell to get out'a there. I had just gotten through the door when that whole place blew. The impact threw me twenty or thirty yards away." The airman held out his arms and pulled up his sleeves to show the cuts and abrasions he'd received.

"Did everyone get out?"

"I don't know. I think so. There wuz only about ten of us in there. Should 'a been forty to fifty of us. The rest wuz in a class over in Building Q." The camera moved to focus on the building behind as the young airman spoke. Smoke and flames still billowed forth from the building.

"Tell us more, what did you see when you got up from that fall?"

"Oh, the hangar wuz in flames."

"And the others?"

"I didn't see anyone behind me. Guess I wuz the last one out. If that little nut hadn't warned us we'd been cooked for sure!"

"Did you see what happened to him?"

The airman's face grew taught and his eyes narrowed with anger. "Nope. I hope he didn't get out! If we catch him he'll wish he had never been born."

"Thank you, Airman Aspen." Then, turning back to the cameras, the reporter continued, "In addition to the car bombing, we are told that mortar and missiles hit numerous facilities. When we get details, we'll report back to you, Dan. This is Fred Deats, reporting live from Keesler Air Force Base."

"Thanks, Fred." The anchor turned to face the cameras. "These have been but examples of the devastation our country has experienced this morning. We will take a short break and then continue with our report on these disastrous events."

Members of the terrorist task force sat stunned. After a few moments, someone yelled, "See what NBC's reporting, Sam." Agent Lockney clicked the TV to NBC, where a reporter stood outside the main gate of Falcon Air Force Base, Colorado.

Smoke billowed from burning buildings in the background as sirens and alarms pierced the air. The reporter, wearing a tan winter trench coat, cupped her right hand over the transmitter in her right ear so she could hear the anchor's questions. She shielded her eyes from the sun with a large notepad, ". . . and extensive damage to the main communications facility here at Falcon Air Force Base, Colorado."

The anchor broke in. "Cindy, how many people have been killed?"

"Authorities don't yet know. Right now they're busy trying to put out the fires and check electronic equipment to see what's operational."

"Okay, thanks a lot, Cindy. We will hear more from you later." The NBC anchor, wearing a crisp navy suit and looking fresh, said, "Falcon Air Force Base is part of a complex that includes Cheyenne Mountain and Peterson Air Force Base outside Colorado Springs." Pictures of the facility flashed on the screen as the anchor spoke.

"Falcon is the heart of our nation's defense system even though it doesn't have an airfield. It is not used for flight training. It is a three hundred-fifty-acre facility some fifteen miles east of Peterson and home to the Fiftieth Space Wing. They control the communications to our satellite and early warning security systems.

We will take a station break and return with continuing coverage of the latest disasters. This is Kathy Stevens, NBC news."

"Well," agent Wade sighed, "the crap has hit the fan. I hope the President and congress will finally take off the gloves and go after these guys."

Out in New Mexico the patriot's leadership continued to watch in awe as reports of the day's bombings continued coming in. CNN returned to Abby Smyth in Washington and the group watched her report.

Out-of-breath, hair disheveled, and with bits of debris clinging to her suit, the reporter said, "Paul, a number of explosions have taken place on Capitol Hill. We had to leave our van and go on foot because fire and law enforcement officials sealed the area. A firemen said a four-wheel-drive hummer drove up the front steps of the capitol and detonated." Abby took a shuddering breath, then went on. "The driver lost his life in that explosion. And I've been told that a delivery truck exploded at one of the quadrangles of the Rayburn Building. Damage is unknown at this time."

She paused and wiped tears from her eyes. CNN's anchor said, "Abby, we want you all out of there."

She glanced down at a yellow pad in her left hand and continued, "First let me tell you that we've been told bombs have gone off at the Cannon Building, the Russell Building, the Supreme Court, and numerous other sites. Paul, there has been so much damage and chaos that it will take time to sort it all out. The loss of life has already been staggering. The early morning explosion caught many people at work. We're all afraid that there are more bombs set to go off."

CNN's anchor cut away, saying, "Abby, you people get out of there now. We'll be back after this station break with more coverage of the day's events. CNN News, Atlanta."

Boorgers turned the TV sound off. "Mr. Ship," Boorgers said.

"Yes, sir."

"We've got a civil war on our hands. Do you understand that?"

"It looks that way," Ship said, smiling naively at the others.

"We want to make it clear that all armaments stored around this country belong to the movement. In other words, the arms stashed in the hills of your ranch are not your personal weapons. Do you understand me?"

"Well, I."

"Mr. Ship, do you understand?" Boorgers boomed as he fixed Ship with a steely look, his large body lurching forward threateningly.

"Yes, sir," he quietly replied.

"Fine. There'll be no more crap from you about where those arms go. We don't have time to coddle anyone. You're either a member of the team or you're the enemy. Understand that clearly."

"Yes, sir."

And so Boorgers hammered down the nail that had been sticking up. The group broke for a rest until dinner. A few hours later, Chapmann found himself on the patio with White and Boorgers.

"Holy smoke," Chapmann said. "I figured a lot of our phantom cells would act on or around April nineteenth, so today's activity really surprised me. Did you or Boorgers know about this?" No one said a thing, but Chapmann noticed that Boorgers and White looked furtively at each other. A slight smile crossed White's face, which seemed strange to Chapmann at the time.

"Undoubtedly we are seeing the result of extensive planning and communication between cells," he continued. "We've learned a lot from the al-Qaidians."

"By the way, General Boorgers," Petsch asked, "where did you get your information that the feds planned major security coverage of all federal facilities on the nineteenth?"

"Well, let's just say that I have friends in high places and let it go at that."

"There's something else we need to discuss," White said . "One of our men hijacked that A-Ten Warthog jet over southern Colorado. It's safely tucked away in a hangar on a private airfield near Alamosa, Colorado!"

"Great guns!" Chapmann exclaimed. "Who pulled that off?"

"A man called and said the armed bird would be available as needed," White said. "But he reserved the right to decide if the mission is risk-worthy."

General Boorgers chimed in, "Fellas, this may trigger a wholesale movement of troops to our cause."

"It may," Chapmann said softly. "Or it may trigger an onslaught by the feds."

Boorgers looked at Chapmann, then turned to the others. "Fellas, the feds will undoubtedly move on our weapons depots right away. Disperse the men guarding the ranch. Tell 'em to go home. There's no way in hell we want to fight their kind of war."

When Ron Chapmann walked in the back gate and headed up to the door of their home, Jill met him, saying, "Well, it looks like all hell has broken loose!"

"Yeah, are people blaming Al-Qaida?" Chapmann asked.

"There's been a few suspicions floated, but most of the evidence points to what they are calling super patriots," Jill said.

After a few moments of silence, Ron said, "I'm getting uneasy about all this." He stepped inside and took a seat at the small kitchen table. Seeing the puzzled look on Jill's face he said, "The more I'm with Boorgers and White, the more I get the feeling their organizational strategy has been to take control of the movement. They may be behind the ransacking of our home a while back."

Randy Chapmann, Ron Chapmann's brother, sat at the kitchen table and eavesdropped while he drank a cup of coffee. "Are you sure?" he asked.

"No. Just guessing," Ron answered. Leaning back and looking at Jill, he continued, "I guess I thought that all this weaponry would be to protect our families. It seems I didn't really think any of these guys was really serious about killing feds."

"It sure is easy to get caught up being against something," Jill said.

"Yeah," Ron agreed. "It certainly is that. And it's heady wine to be asked to speak to groups all over the nation and be treated as some type of super patriot. But, now we are going to reap the maelstrom of our own creation—a war that most people can accuse us of inciting. We can't win it, for God's sake. We've surely lost the support of the American people now that we've blown up all these facilities and killed a lot of innocent people. I can't believe all these guys that are doing these things have forgotten the effect on the nation of the World Trade Center attack."

"What do we do now?" Randy asked.

"Well, I really think we ought to get rid of all the weapons we have in storage and then stay right here until the dust settles," Ron said.

Looking at Jill, Ron said, "I worked in a statewide political campaign in my youth, and the manager had real smarts. He looked at me one day and said, 'Ron, you're very idealistic. But what you need to remember is that those you support today, you'll have to fight tomorrow.' How true. The oppressed seem to become the oppressors. This is happening to our movement before we even get off the ground."

# 13

**THE OVAL OFFICE**
Friday Evening, March 14

President Carl Evans strode into the Oval Office where members of the Cabinet, Joint Chiefs of Staff and the NSC waited. Some stared at their notepads, others off into space. On this particular evening, with so much death and destruction visited upon the nation once again, the President's tight-set jaw and quick pace reflected his anger.

He began by stating, "I've observed Washington from various windows on the top floor of the White House. My God, it's like a war zone! Smoke and fire are billowing up all over the place. There are explosions every few minutes. And the evidence continues to be that these are not Muslim terrorists but our own damn crazies."

Turning toward General Burcks and the Attorney General, he grimly stated, "Get the U.S. Marshals and National Guard units around sensitive federal sites immediately. I assume the order I signed earlier putting all National Guard units under federal control has been activated. Are the governors following through?"

Burcks replied, "To answer your second question first, some are, some aren't, Mr. President."

"Why aren't they all?" he said, his neck muscles bulging.

"Mr. President, as your National Security Council has reported on various occasions the last few months, these patriotic groups have neutralized many governors and National Guard units. We don't think you can rely on them even if they do take up defensive positions. Some would return fire, but many others would not. Some might even fire on our own troops." There was a moment of stunned silence.

"This means my only option is to mobilize our active military forces, is that right?"

"Yes, sir. That seems to be the case. In answer to the first question you asked, Mr. President, the fact that all these events are taking place earlier than the nineteenth of April, as we had assumed and planned, indicates we may have a leak."

The President stared at Burcks for several seconds, scanned the other members of his administration, and then in a steely, clipped voice said, "Damn! How did we get in this position? I've got to surround federal properties in every single damn state to protect them from our own citizens! Not from the Russians. Not from Mideast terrorists as we've recently had to do. No! Our own goddamn people. And you are telling me we can't even trust our National Guard units! And, as if that's not enough of a kick in the ass, you're saying that we have traitors in this administration. Ain't that a bucket of cold spit?" The President hammered the desk with his fist. "

"May I suggest, sir," an aide said, seemingly unmoved by the President's outburst, "that we move you and some key White House staff to the safety of the underground facilities?" Members of the cabinet nodded their agreement.

"Hell, no!" he shouted. Then, through clenched teeth, he droned, "I'll die here before I'll let those two-bit traitor-sons-of-bitches force the President of the United States to leave his office!" He glared at the group for a few moments, then turned, locked his hands behind his back and walked to a window overlooking the rose garden.

The Secretary of State whispered to the Secretary of Defense, "I think we better keep our mouths shut until he calms down." Finally, the President turned and slowly walked back to the table.

Calmly and softly he said, "Okay. How are we going to deal with this?"

The head of the FBI, Gordon Inglis, reported, "According to our terrorist task force, these people have not heretofore been organized. At least not in a conventional sense. One or two people carry out a bombing or an assassination and keep their activities to themselves."

"Just like Al-Qaida. Yet it's obvious that there's some coordination going on somewhere," the President said. "Who's the Osama in our backyard?"

"Mr. President," Burcks said , "We think there's a number of leaders. We know that some charismatic ex-military men have been traveling the country teaching phantom cell guerrilla warfare to militia and anyone else that will listen."

"Have we become another banana republic?" the astonished President asked, scanning the group and waiting for an answer, but none came. He then asked, "Didn't we learn anything from the Al-Qaida attacks? How can these people do this after living through the World Trade Center attack? I find it incredible that Americans can passionately laud democracy with one breath, and in the next, damn the political leadership whom they've elected. My God, has everyone gone insane?"

"And not all of these military participants are exes," Burcks said.

"What do you mean?"

"I know it sounds crazy, Mr. President, but there's a lot of support for this new patriotism among the rank and file of our military and law enforcement personnel. For example, we suspect that the Warthog we thought had been downed in Colorado is really stolen. It was an act of defection by a pilot working with the extremists."

Looking across the table at the Secretary of Defense, the President asked, "Is that right?"

"Yes, sir, I'm afraid so."

Looking toward the Secretary of Defense the President asked, "How long have this pilot's superiors known that he supported the extremists?"

"They didn't know, sir."

"Oh, hell! Why haven't we arrested any of these people for treason?" the President, asked, rubbing his forehead in anguish.

"Mr. President, what we know and what we can prove in a court of law are two different things," the Attorney General said. "We can't arrest people for expressing their opinions or owning guns. They have to do something illegal."

"Aw hell, I know that. But a number of these patriots have robbed banks and committed all sorts of crimes. Why aren't they in jail?"

The Attorney General continued, "While there are warrants for the arrest of some of these men, getting to them without drawing fire and risking the lives of others has proven difficult."

"Also," the Director of the FBI interjected, "the warrants are for tax evasion, driving without license plates or driver's licenses and other such acts. While we can probably get a conviction once we catch them, the general public has been sympathetic to their cause."

"So we now we let these nuts bomb and kill?" the President shouted, as his right arm swept out toward the windows toward and the city of Washington. "It's a damn shame they're not working for the country. Any group that can smuggle millions of dollars worth of Russian weapons into the United States without being caught and carry out this kind of destruction right under our noses has lots of moxie!"

Another period of silence fell over the group as the President again turned, locked his hands behind his back as though in deep contemplation and walked back to the windows. Finally, he turned to the group and in a calm voice said, "Okay. Let's go clean out any and all ammo depots, and let's move to take the leaders of this movement at all costs, even if we have to arrest them for loitering. Screw the public relations crap. Hopefully innocent people won't get hurt, but Goddamn it, this shit's going to stop." Turning and pointing at the Attorney General, he said, "Get your staff to prepare the legal stuff to support this immediately."

The Attorney General nodded.

Eyeing his chief -of-staff, the President said, "Get the White House staff working with members on Capitol Hill. They need to support this wholeheartedly. Then, let's get our message out to the American people. I mean, damn it, I want a barrage of information detailing every dastardly thing these people have done over the years. And wrap Al-Qaida's shroud around them from head to foot. Understood? Then let's get at it. I don't want to go down in history as the last American President of a free, democratic society."

NSC OFFICES, OLD EXECUTIVE OFFICE BUILDING
Saturday, March 15

Darren arrived at his office Saturday morning, along with the rest of the NSC staff. He found Jo Clark hard at work. "Darren, wow, you look shot! Oops! Excuse the expression."

"Yeah," he replied, as they both laughed.

"The General wants to see you. Go on in. He's got some other staff in there."

As Darren entered, he found him engaged in a conference call with the President, the Director of the FBI, the Major General in charge of military intelligence and the Director of the CIA on a speakerphone, as a few other NSC staffers listened.

Over the speaker phone Darren heard the President say, "Yes, I've ordered regular military units to each state to take control of reserve units. If any governor gets in the way, arrest the SOB. But I also want all other projects put on hold and everyone to focus on the problems we're facing with these terrorists. When's the task force meeting again?" Before anyone could answer, the President said, "I want that bunch meeting around the clock. I want further solutions to this nightmare. We can't afford to look back and say, 'Golly, gee-whiz, wish we had done this, or wish we had done that.' I want to wake up soon and find it all behind me! Understood?"

"Yes, sir," Burcks answered, and each of the others in their turn. The President hung up. Burcks, speaking to the other members involved in the conference call, said, "Well, fellas, we've got our marching orders."

"Fine," the others echoed.

Turning to Hopkins as the other filed out of his office, he said, "Darren, I want you to stick with that terrorist task force like ticks on a hound dog."

"Okay. Is there anything specifically I should watch for?"

"Just keep an eye on its general operation. See if action is carried out. All federal bureaucrats are subject to a disease called institutional numbness caused by career fear. And this numbness does not give birth to creative action. It's crippling."

"I understand," Darren replied. "How are you feeling?"

"Oh, crap. I feel like the lady with twelve kids who was asked what the very worst thing she could get on her twenty-fifth wedding anniversary and answered, 'Morning sickness.' I feel sick. Everyone I know is sick about all this. We've got to recover."

"Yes, sir. I got a disturbing phone call and thought you ought to know about it." Darren reported what he knew and played the tape from his answering machine.

The General listened intently. "Yeah, take that over to the Bureau next time you go and see what they can figure out." There was a pause as the two men considered further action. Burcks broke the silence by saying, "You know these crazies are probably just playing with your mind. They love to intimidate and scare people."

"That's what I've been thinking. How would they even know about Ann? It had to leak from someone we know in the administration. How else?"

"That's certainly true. Of course, they could have tapped into your phone conversations over the months."

"That's possible. Well, I'll get this to some people who might be able to tell us something. And I'll call Bangkok again tonight."

Darren left Burcks' office and joined the task force in their basement suite, entering at the rear of the building due to the destruction of the main entrance. Security had been extremely tight since the attack. The room had a floor-to-ceiling-size computerized map of the U.S. lit up like a Christmas tree. Huge TV screens dotted the rest of the walls. He soon learned that the system could handle live satellite images, TV, videos or computer images.

Agent Lenora Carlson waved Darren over. He nodding greetings to those he had met in other meetings, shook hands with those he had not met, then located a vacant chair. "Darren, glad you could make a meeting!" Agent Lenora Carlson said.

"Do I have time to look around?" he asked.

"Sure. We'll get started in about ten minutes. There's coffee and water at the back table."

Darren made his way to the large electronic map encircling a fourth of the room.

"Hi. I'll be glad to help you interpret the map, if you'd like," a young staff member said.

"Yes, I'd like that very much," Darren responded.

"First, the red glows on the big board indicate federal facilities attacked and damaged. The numbers represent the nature of the facility. One is for a federal office building. You can see the ones in red sites in Dallas, Atlanta, Sacramento, Denver and so forth. The twos represent Air Force bases. Again, note the twos in red at Tinker AFB, Oklahoma City, Hector AFB, Fargo, North Dakota, Hill AFB, Ogden, Utah, Holloman AFB, Alamogordo, New Mexico, Duke AFB, in Florida, and so forth."

"Good Lord," Darren said . "I didn't know we sustained this much damage. How many planes did they take out?"

The Defense Department's General Craft heard Darren's question. "Darren, I'm Lewis Craft. We met last month. I may be able to help with that if the young lady doesn't mind."

"No, sir, please go ahead," she said.

"We received extensive damage to over five hundred and sixty-four aircraft. That means they're no longer air-worthy. Of those, we estimate that eighty-six can't be repaired. The majority of the others will only need minor repairs."

"What received the most damage?"

"No doubt our AWACS, JStars and rivet joint aircraft," he said, as he used a laser pointer to indicate the bases housing those facilities. "These are most vulnerable because they're too large to hangar but too delicate to be left on the field. Most of our AWACs are kept at Tinker AFB in Oklahoma City, and they've been badly damaged. Because of the complicated electronics in these planes, a fifty-caliber rifle can do extensive damage. It only takes one well-placed shot to the fuel tank and boom, a fifty- or ninety-million dollar plane is up in smoke."

"It's sad that these people had the capability to do this much damage," Darren said, shaking his head. "Is there any evidence of Mideast terrorist's fingerprints in any of this?"

"Nope, this is all homegrown. And everything's well planned. It took some good military minds to pull it off. No, no. All this has not been accidental or a game played by a bunch of stooges. No, sir. The people who planned this are familiar with our military capability and strategy."

"U.S. military or foreign?" Darren asked.

"I suppose some of both. Reports indicate they used U.S. and Russian weaponry."

At that moment, Agent Wade, the FBI's Assistant Director, called the meeting to order. Darren and the general returned to their seats. Lenora turned the meeting over to the director of the FBI, Gordon Inglis, who said, "I have no intention of co-opting the management of this task force. You all have done a fine job, and unfortunately, the nation will never pin medals on you for it. I've mentioned to the President and to others that over the months, we have not had one complaint of agency bias in your behavior. That is an exceptional feat!" Laughter rippled around the room.

"Keep up the good work. We must quell this violence and do it quickly. The rest of the world is watching us, so we must do it in a masterful way. We want to show them how a democratic system can handle this without resorting to dictatorial conditions. Okay? Fine. Get on with it."

Agent Wade took control of the group and thanked the Director for his comments. "Yes, sir. We appreciate your words and your presence. Let's review where we are and where we're going. General Craft, would you bring us up to date on the military movements?"

"Yes, sir. As members of the group can see from the big board, the green colored flag icons represent military deployments." All eyes turned toward the large, electronic U.S. wall map. "Each flag carries the unit's number and branch. The AFB flag icons indicate planes that are air-ready around the clock. Depending on the base commander's intelligence, any number of these planes are in the air at all times."

"Doing what?" an agent asked.

"Some are supporting ground troops and law enforcement working in a specific areas; others are monitoring an area, and others are flying in ready status."

"We assume, then, that surveillance is being conducted by AWACs and similar equipment?" Wade asked.

"That's correct. Every AWAC plane that can still fly is in the air."

"I hate to be a spoil-sport, but do you think it wise to continue this full alert more than a few days?" Agent Lockney asked.

"What do you mean?" CIA's Henry Washington exclaimed.

"The damage has been done—carried out by a bunch of marginalized people from the back of trucks and vans. They used what they had been given, and then ran for cover. They're back at their jobs, whether plowing the north forty, checking on herds, minding the store, or whatever. Just like most of the Iraqi soldiers did during that war."

A strange silence fell over the group.

"And? Craft asked.

Lockney continued, somewhat uneasy at going against the grain of prevailing wisdom among these elite government bureaucrats. "I'm not taking issue with the mobilization as an initial thrust. The country needed that. But, the point's been made. If we continue a full scale mobilization, we'll lose our advantage."

Another agent asked, "We've brought a modicum of peace to the landscape. What happens if we fold our tents and disappear?"

Lockney looked at the agent, nodded his understanding, and then continued. "Look, the bulk of the American people are now solidly behind their government. The rebels, or whatever you want to call them, have split their britches. Those who thought them harmless cranks are now wide-awake, and they're frightened and angry. But if we continue to maintain such a tight security blanket, people will get further stressed. The American people, while not remembering where the sentiment came from, share Julius Caesar's view, and I quote,

"Beware the leader who bangs the drums of war in order to whip the citizenry into a patriotic fervor, for patriotism is indeed a double-edged sword. It both emboldens the blood, just as it narrows the mind. And when the drums of war have reached a fever pitch and the blood boils with hate and the mind has closed, the leader will have no need in seizing the rights of the citizenry. Rather, the citizenry, infused with fear and blinded by patriotism, will offer up all of their rights unto the leader and gladly so. How do I know? For this is what I have done. And I am Caesar.'"

During the ensuing silence, some leaned back in their chairs and stared at the ceiling. Others stared at the table in anticipation of a rip-roaring debate.

Finally, Wade said, "Lockney might be right." The group discussed the issue for fifteen to twenty minutes in a calm manner. The anticipated angry debate didn't materialize.

Lucretia Martin, the FBI's lead investigator of extremist groups east of the Mississippi, asked, "Won't a stand-down be interpreted as being soft?" This led to a further lengthy discussion of what makes a policy, or strategy, soft and what doesn't. Finally, the group decided to go back to their respective agencies and research the question.

Then the representative from ATF brought the group up short by asking, "I thought our task revolved around developing strategy, not advocating policy?"

All eyes focused on the FBI Director, who said, "Right now the door's wide open. Nothing's out of bounds." The members of the group looked at each other, then a number of private conversations broke out.

Wade, realizing that they had little time to bring the topic to a conclusion, brought the group back together by saying, "Okay. We'll table this until later. Meanwhile, General Craft, why don't you have your people draft a step-down time table we can recommend if we decide to so recommend?" A ripple of laughter broke out.

"Yes, sir," Craft said, smiling at Wade's Yogi Berra-like statement.

Still addressing Craft, Wade asked, "Could you summarize our surveillance of the last few weeks. We have a few newcomers."

"Yes, Sir." Approaching the wall map, he said, "There's been intense construction and renovation activity taking place in the White Mountains outside Bishop, California." He pointed to the area, then continued to point out the other areas as he said, "And more near Olney, Montana, at a large farm outside Bemidji, Minnesota, on an island in the Saint Lawrence River, at a farm outside Georgia Center, Vermont, a warehouse facility in Gloucester, Connecticut, a farm northwest of Old Saybrook, Connecticut, a warehouse in New Orleans, a large ranch near Laredo, Texas, and a large excavation is still going on at a ranch near Reserve, New Mexico."

Agent Lockney asked, "But there have always been groups digging bomb shelters or stockpiling weapons for fear the Russians are coming. What's different now?"

Agent Wade said, "Sam, maybe nothing. But these are large arms depots that far exceed a casual fear of bombs or foreign invaders. Nodding to General Craft, Agent Wade said, "Please continue." Craft continued to spot newly developed arms depots around the nation as Darren took notes.

Finally, Craft said, "In addition, there's an underground storage facility being constructed on a ranch near Elgin, Arizona." He turned back to the group, tapped the floor with his pointer and said, "We calculate that once all these storage facilities are finished, if that's what they are intended to be, they can warehouse enough arms to make life miserable for a whole lot of people for decades to come. Remember, these are new facilities. The extremists already had underground caches at Ron Chapmann's and John Chudders' properties. There are hundreds of small arms caches stored in militia members' garages all over this nation."

A hush fell over the room. A few continued staring at their scratch pads as if in a trance. Others looked at their colleagues in amazement.

"What are we doing to neutralize the rebels' arms depots?" an agent asked.

"We are quietly taking possession of those that have little loss of life risk," Craft said. "Sorry that we didn't alert you to the anticipated action. The President felt it in the best interest to just quietly go do it. The operations have gone well. We are now using Cobra helicopters to drop Special Forces teams in to neutralize an area and seize the arms. the weapons are taken to the nearest army depot for sorting, cataloging, filming and heavy security storage."

"What about Davis Mountains and the other big ones?" another asked.

"We've got each under scrutiny," Agent Carlson said.

"Is there a special task force set up to take them?" Agent Martin asked.

"We assumed we'd use the same military force that has been taking the others." Then, looking from Wade to Craft, she asked, "Isn't that right?" Wade affirmed her assumption by nodding.

"A lot more lives will be lost if we bomb the hell out of some of these places like we did in Afghanistan, especially the fortress that old preacher man in the Davis Mountains has built," Agent Martin said. "There are a lot of women and children in some of those places."

Wade looked at Martin and said, "Put your thoughts on paper."

The meeting then disbanded and Darren sat quietly as others gradually filtered out. He stared around the room, looking past the glass partitions at the huge electronic boards, maps, TV monitors, and staff hard at work. He suddenly realized how surreal all this felt. As he walked out of the underground complex, he felt as if in a time warp. He had no training in all this.

When he returned to his office, he found Burcks standing there, hands on hips. "What happened at the meeting?" Darren briefed him as they walked to the elevator.

"Darren, get in touch with Colonel Tillman at the Marine Commandant's office. He's got some teams that are tops. See if he'd be willing to use them," Burcks offered, as he started into the elevator.

"Will do," said Darren. "And, by the way, they're expecting to see a plan from Agent Martin by eight in the morning."

Burcks' voice faintly echoed down the hall, "Tell Tillman that. Tell him also that the President of the United States says this is a priority."

Darren quickly called Agent Carlson to see what she thought of Burcks' plan.

"Let's go see Tillman," Carlson said.

Tillman dropped everything to meet Darren and Carlson at his Pentagon office. Tillman's chief aides attended. After the preliminary social amenities and a briefing by Carlson, the group quickly sketched an assault plan. Tillman instructed the attack teams to report the next morning for preparation. They would be ready if and when the task force and the President signed on. Tillman's efficiency stunned Darren and Carlson, who returned to their respective offices around 6:00 p.m.

As Darren walked into Jo Clark's office to check his messages, he heard the beeping sound of the fax machine. He usually ignored incoming faxes, but his adrenaline still raced from the excitement of Tillman's meeting. He snatched the fax as soon as he saw it was from Watson in Tokyo. It read:

"Darren, your shadow is Chinese. A mercenary trained by the Chinese. We captured his girlfriend and she sang like a canary. She said he picked you up in Hong Kong and followed you to Thailand. He studied you well. Knew your Asian haunts, friends and hotels. He flew into L.A. via United Airlines that landed one hour before the flight you were supposed to be on. When he couldn't find you, he got lost in the city. His girlfriend didn't know who hired him, except they were ex-military out of California. Sound familiar? Your friend, Ted Watson."

# 14

**WASHINGTON, D.C.**
Tuesday, March 18

An alarm shattered the early morning quiet. Under blankets on the sofa, the hulk stretched and exuded a few ohhhs as he painfully greeted the morning. Darren peered out from under the blanket, opened one eye, looked at his watch, shook his head in an attempt to clear the cobwebs, and then stumbled toward the basement facilities of the Old Executive Office Building to shower, shave and put on a clean shirt. It dawned on him that Ted hadn't called back during the night. "Must be some problems," Darren muttered to himself.

George Burcks arrived at 7:00 a.m., just as Darren returned from his morning ritual. "Good grief, Hopkins, don't you ever sleep in your apartment? We would have saved money just renting you a closet here in the building!"

"Yeah, but no one told me I'd be working twenty-four hour days!" Darren replied. As Darren prepared the coffee, he said, "Got a fax from my friend in Japan last night." He paused, squinted and gazed around. "Or was it early this morning?" He shrugged and went back to preparing the coffee. "Anyway, I put it on your desk. The nut that's been trying to kill me is a Chinese agent turned mercenary."

As he walked into Burcks' office with two hot, steaming cups of fresh coffee, the General was standing at the window reading the fax and looking at the photo Watson had sent. "I'm sure the Chinese government doesn't want their role in this to get out. They probably recommended the guy."

"I suppose. By the way, I'm headed to the task force meeting. One of the agents recommended what you military guys call a step down to the high profile military activity. He claims that if we don't, many will be calling this a police state."

General Burcks's listened as Darren went on. "He thinks our bomb throwers have melted back into their common, daily routine. What do you think?"

"I think," Burcks said, "that as soon as we drop our guard they'll hit us. Just like the Al-Qaida. We can't afford to be lax in our security."

Darren slouched back in his chair and rested his head on the chair's upper cushion. "Of course, you're right. But, with all due respect, I don't think our super patriotic movement has the manpower or the will to sustain the kind of violence we've seen of late. Most are good, well-meaning citizens who believed the government had over-extended itself. They're not revolutionaries. They never have been and probably never will be."

As Darren spoke, he could see Burcks's shoulders relax and the taut look on his face disappeared. "I suppose so," Burcks interjected, "but we'll always have some crazies in our midst!"

After a few minutes of silence, Darren asked, "Is there a way to be militarily ready without flaunting it publicly?"

"Of course, but there are those who will argue that a show of force is a deterrent. And they are extremely vocal. Geez, there's some guys in the White House who want to just put everyone in prison camps."

Darren rose and walked over to the window. Gazing out toward the White House, he said, "I understand. As you know, I'm not a warrior. But the administration seems to have the American people on its side now. All this senseless destruction and killing is so reminiscent of the Muslim attacks that the vast majority of the people are turned off by the super patriots' cause. I suspect many of the movement leaders thought the American people shared their views of the state and federal government, or hoped that once the attacks began they would all jump on the bandwagon. It didn't happen. It isn't going to happen."

"Yeah, that seems to be true." Burcks moved to the window near Darren, arms crossed behind his back. "But we still have all those leaderless phantom cells. We've got to have better security for government employees and facilities. You're right about public opinion. The President's worried about that also. He'd love to reduce the military presence if, and only if, we can balance it with increased security. I've never seen him so mad."

Darren slowly walked back to his chair and sat down. "Certainly we know enough to secure the nation to some degree. But, as you pointed out, we will always have people who can rationalize violence, especially if they can cloak it with the kingdom of God a la scriptures. If Congress passes that bill to make attacks on federal property subject to the penalties meted out for treason, it'll put the brakes on a lot of extremists, right or left."

"Maybe," said Burcks, as he continued staring out the window. "But we still have some congressmen and women who are highly sympathetic to these super patriots. I think they'll water down the bill so it means little."

"That's unfortunate," Darren answered. "They not only fear for their lives but are defenseless against the religious framework so many of these patriots invoke. Just like the Klan."

"Yeah," Burcks said, nodding. "It's a shame the mainline churches are so silent. They weren't during the Civil Rights Movement or the Vietnam war. Where are they now?"

"I suspect that most who took the lead in those early movements have either left the ministry or are too old to get involved."

"What can we do to mobilize the mainline churches against these super patriotic evangelists?" Burcks asked.

"I'm not sure we can. Most people, and especially those in the media, are fairly ignorant theologically."

"Hmmm, Burcks said . "Come on, do you believe that one religious view is better than another?"

"No, but some are more dangerous. If you listen carefully to what these TV evangelists say you will find that it is, for the most part, pop psychology mixed with a hundred worn out clichés and various texts slopped up from the Bible. As you know, the KKK and the Nazis have been able to use scripture in this fashion to rationalize their agenda."

"Good Lord, Darren, I'm constantly amazed at the breadth of your thought," Burcks said. There was a moment of silence. Finally, pursing his lips in thought, Burcks walked back to his desk. "Did you take Agent Carlson and talk with Tillman and his team?"

Darren went over the plan to take Boorgers's, Chapmann's and Tom Ship's arms caches. Then, he looked Burcks in the eye and asked with a slight grin, "By the way, working with Tillman was too easy. You knew Tillman already had plans for such an action, didn't you?"

Burcks sat down at his desk, smiled slightly, but admitted nothing. "Tell Agent Carlson that I'll take this to the President first thing this morning. Tell her there's no go on this until he's given his approval. He's listening to those who want to bomb the hell out of those sites. Okay?"

"Yes, sir." Suddenly, a loud explosion caused both men to rush to the window and look down Pennsylvania Avenue. A city truck hauling tree branches had backfired and smoke streamed from its exhaust. "Oh shit," Darren said, as he headed for the door. He thought about telling Burcks of his plan to go along on some of the raids, but decided to wait until after the fact and take his licking.

TASK FORCE HEADQUARTERS
Wednesday, March 19

Darren arrived at 8:20 a.m. to find the meeting well underway. As he threaded his way around the room to an empty chair, he noticed that most looked as if they had slept little the past twenty-four hours.

As Darren took a seat Lockney nodded from across the table. An agent from the CIA had the floor, speaking of the need to maintain satellite surveillance of foreign targets critical to national security. Darren glanced over at Agent McCall, who had his head down on the table. After listening a few moments, it became apparent to Darren that some members of the task force wanted satellite coverage for domestic use, creating a dilemma for international surveillance.

"Why not make a priority list of key sites and work on those we can agree on?" Agent Carlson suggested.

"Sounds reasonable to me," a CIA agent said. "There are dozens of sites and hundreds of people on the extremist list. Let's rank them." The group devoted the next few hours to ranking the various groups and people known to be associated with the recent acts of domestic terrorism.

"Let me play devil's advocate and ask what legal charges we have against each that will stick in a court of law," agent Martin interjected, as she popped the lid off a soda can.

Carlson replied, "You'll find a list of the people and charges filed against them in the packet in front of you. Our legal staff, in conjunction with the U.S. Attorney General's staff, updated this during the night. They wouldn't provide a list of the witnesses for us but assured us that hundreds of people have been coming forward since the bombings to support the case against these people. We have enough evidence to convict seventy percent of the people who actually planned, set and/or projected bombs and missiles this week."

Darren received an urgent call from George Burcks at ten thirty. He took the call in a private office just off the main conference room.

"Hopkins, is McCall in that meeting?"

"Yes, sir."

"We have every reason to suspect he may be a main leak in the operation. The CIA Director will be calling him back to the Agency in a few minutes, at which time he will be removed from active service until the investigation can determine his culpability one way or another."

"What led to McCall?"

"The Agency has been quietly checking staff background, and it seems he's had a lot of contact with some key players within the patriot's movement. Until we know for certain, it's best he be removed from any connection to the task force."

"Okay." When Darren returned to the meeting, McCall had disappeared. He turned to the agent sitting next to him and asked, "Where'd McCall go?"

"He left. Evidently had an emergency," the young man answered.

Darren waited until the group took a break, then approached Agents Wade and Carlson. "What's up?" Carlson asked. Darren relayed the information he'd received about McCall.

Both Carlson and Wade looked stunned. Carlson slumped against the wall. Wade's body slackened, then he took a deep breath. "Damn!"

After a few moments, Carlson said, "Well, we've said all along there had to be a leak! Everything we've planned has backfired. But McCall? I've known him and his family for many years."

Darren said, "General Burcks said we may want to allocate pursuit strategies to various teams and let them submit the details to the President's desk directly, rather than coming back through the task force in case there are any other leaks."

"Well, shit. How are we to explain this to the rest of the task force?" Wade asked.

"We can explain it as a time and staff efficiency move," Carlson offered.

"Yes," Darren said, "and all plans have to be cleared with Agency chiefs before it goes to the President, doesn't it?"

"Sure," Wade said. "Instead of wondering about some thirty or more task force members, we would only have the one or two persons putting the project together, plus their boss. If a mission fails and it looks like a leak, then we've narrowed the search for other leaks."

"By the way," Darren said, "Did Carlson tell you about the plan to take Chudders's, Chapmann's and Ship's arms caches?

"Yeah. And it looks good," Wade said.

"I suspect General Burcks has already sent it over to the President for review," Darren said. If there's a lot of negative criticism about this, I know General Burcks will back off."

Wade nodded as he said, "Oh, I don't think any members of the task force will have problems with the plan. It looks good. Besides, no one really enjoys putting his own troops in harm's way."

They returned to the task force meeting and talked about ways to locate and arrest Arlo White, Ernst Boorgers and dozens of militia leaders who had actively pursued and trained recruits. Wade mentioned the use of Tillman's Forces to confiscate the remaining armament supplies.

"How soon can we expect the President to sign off on this?" Lockney asked.

"I guess that's something we have no control over, Sam," Wade responded.

However, Burcks called Darren at 11:52 a.m. to tell him that the President had given the green light for the Special Forces mission. Darren stood by as Carlson called Tillman and relayed the news to the task force members, then rushed back to his apartment to pack his bag and grab a flight to Austin.

YAHWEH CITY, DAVIS MOUNTAINS, WEST TEXAS
Wednesday, March 19

The citizens of Yahweh City finished their somber dinner without the usual cheerIness. John and Sara Chudders planned to send their tribe into Mexico for hiding. The oldest son, Philip, would be in charge of the fleeing group. John Chudders had prepared for this moment years ago when he had the group build another retreat on the lip of the Barranca de Cobre Canyon southwest of Chihuahua City, Mexico, some twenty kilometers from the village of La Bufa.

"Philip, everyone ready to go?"

"Yes, sir."

"It'll be dark soon and you need to get'um moving. I jest know them feds will be all over us like fleas on a hound's back any day now."

"But, John," Sara said, "we didn't have anything to do with all those bombings!"

"Momma, ya don't understan'. We handed out all those weapons and gave hundreds of those boys sanctuary and trainin'. Uh-uh, they's a comin'. I guarantee it. Don't want none'a these young'uns caught up in this. Best they git while the git'ins good. I'll join 'um in a month or so, or bring 'um back, whichever looks best."

As John Chudders ate and talked, a young man of about fourteen delivered a fax message to him. It read, "Desperate need to come and talk with you. Urgent. Regards, Darren Hopkins (friend of Mo Childs')."

"Uh oh. Looks like troubles," Chudders muttered to his wife. Then he turned to the young man and said, "Ask him when he's comin'." The young man raced away.

"It's interesting that we ain't heard nuthin' from all those big talkers!" A tone of disgust laced Sara's voice.

"Well, Momma, that's life. I suspect they's in hidin'!"

The young man returned with another message from Darren Hopkins. It read: "Can be there Thursday morning. Rgds/ Darren Hopkins."

"Radio the young'un back and tell him it's okay," John Chudders said. "Ask him if he's comin' 'lone. I know about that 'un now. Guess it's time to talk." The bulk of John Chudders' community dribbled out into the West Texas desert during the night after a community worship service. Two vans, or a van and a truck, pulled out every thirty minutes on their way to the Mexican border. Mexican friends met them and ferried them across the Rio Grande River. Visas had already been prepared for each member. Each year they made a mission trip to Mexico, which the children viewed as a vacation. In this case, no one advised them otherwise.

### OKANOGAN NATIONAL FOREST, WASHINGTON
Wednesday, March 19

The Chapmanns sat by their large picture window looking out over the south meadow as the sun set. Deer grazed in the distance. Intermittent sleet and rain had fallen for several days, but the sky cleared in mid-afternoon. Still, the cold weather kept them inside.

"Do you think the feds will show up?" Jill softly asked.

"Oh, yeah!" he sighed. "All that death and destruction turned the American people against us, and we probably lost most of our own people. Have you noticed how silent our communications have been?"

"Chudders called yesterday morning."

"Oh, hell, I don't want any more to do with that old fart. I think he really believes he's the incarnation of Jesus Christ. What a wacko." The thought of Chudders caused Ron to get out of his chair and stare at Jill with a wide-eyed expression of exasperation. "I don't know why we let ourselves get caught up in all this in the first place. We came up here to be left alone."

Finally, after a period of silence, Jill sighed and said, "It just did. Too many people egging us on."

Boy, what a fool I've been," Ron muttered.

"Well, we didn't know," Jill said. Then, as Ron relit his pipe, she asked, "Ron, what will they do to us?"

Ron looked at Jill. She wiped tears from her eyes with one hand and reached for a Kleenex with the other. "Hon, I don't know. I hope they try me for income tax evasion. I can fight that issue. I certainly don't want to be picked up as a participant in all these bombings and killings. I may be kooky, as some in the press say. But I am not a killer of innocent people."

"Will they find out you helped get all those Russian weapons?"

"My God, I hope not." There was a moment of silence, then Ron said,. "Randy and Hardy should have distributed all those weapons by now. We better check and make sure they did."

"Why don't I just call them?" Jill asked.

"No. You know all our communications are tapped. Let's go down and check. I think it's time to disarm those booby traps around the perimeter before someone really gets hurt or killed. Drive down and get Hardy and Rod to help, would you?"

YAHWEH CITY, DAVIS MOUNTAINS, WEST TEXAS
Saturday, March 22

Darren and Mo reached the flat turn around at the main entrance to Yahweh City just as the sun peeped up in the east. "No one's here to meet us like last time," Mo said. "Shall we just push the gate open and head on up? I don't want to get shot!"

Just then John Chudders came down the road in a Jeep, pulled up, waved an arm and yelled, "Open the gate and follow me. Coffee's on!"

"Whew, I'm glad to see the old guy," Mo said softly.

"You know, when I pull out my credentials, he's going to be mad as hell at you for bringing me up here under false pretenses last time."

"If he does get mad, I'm gonna maintain our original story. You came along to go rafting down the Rio Grande and that's a fact, Jack."

They reached the lower limits of the enclave and parked in the same lot adjacent to the little church. Nothing had changed since their last visit. The silence echoed off the canyon walls. They followed John Chudders into the little office behind the church. Then they noticed that pictures had been removed from the walls and the few bookcases emptied. Darren and Mo looked at each other knowingly.

Chudders wore a beat up leather World War II flight jacket with a furry collar over his overalls. His bloodshot eyes with their large blue-black sacs hanging slightly over his ruddy cheeks indicated that he hadn't slept much and he seemed nervous and preoccupied.

After the usual greetings, Chudders poured each a cup of coffee and Darren asked, "Where is everybody? It's quiet."

"Oh, they're on a mission trip."

"You're all alone up here?" Mo asked.

"Oh, some of our Mexican friends are with me. So what can I do for you boys?" Chudders took a drink of coffee and fidgeted with paper clips on his desk.

Mo pulled out his note pad and pencil as he asked, "I'd like to get your reaction to all the bombings a few days ago. Did you expect it to happen?"

"No, sir, I didn't," Chudders said, turning around slowly. He punched the air with his coffee cup as he said, "Had nuth'in to do with any of it. We don't believe in killin'." Coffee spilled on the floor as he talked and soaked into the carpet.

"You know a lot of the people that did the killing, don't you?" Mo continued.

"Oh, not really. They's all kind'a people come aroun' up here." Chudders opened his desk drawer, shuffled a few things, and then shut it. He would alternately scratch himself, then rub his eyes and forehead.

"Mr. Chudders," Darren said, "I came up with Mo for his interview a month or so ago so we could take some time to go rafting. But I also came because I had heard about your community and wanted to meet you. We didn't see any reason to tell you that I worked for the government and spook you unnecessarily." Darren pulled out his National Security Council credentials and placed them on the desk in front of Chudders.

"Oh, yeah, I figured ya wuz. Now what?"

Darren leaned back in his chair, crossed his legs, put his arms on his chair and said softly, "I'm not in law enforcement." He let Chudders think about that for a few seconds. "My role is strictly advisory." Then, in a slow and deliberate tone, punctuating each word, he said, "You should know that your activities with the patriot organizations are well documented." Chudders took another swig of coffee and looked down at some keys on his desk as he stroked his long white beard.

Darren continued, "They know you went to Thailand in early January and met with leaders of Mideast terrorist organizations and that they supplied your various groups with Russian weapons. This puts you right in the same league as the infamous Osama bin Laden." At this Chudders looked up, his eyes widened, then narrowed and he turned pale.

Darren continued. "Further, they have satellite pictures that reveal the weapons you have stored in caves." At this, Chudders broke out in a sweat. He took out his handkerchief and wiped his face, then buried his face in his hands.

Finally, he looked up and said, "We don't have no more guns. People come and took 'em."

"We know that," Darren said "And we know that some of those people used them last Thursday to kill a lot of innocent people. You are an accessory to these crimes."

"I didn't access nuth'in," Chudders said irritably. His face turned red as sweat continued to pop out on his face.

"Look," Mo said quietly. "Darren's not here to arrest you. He doesn't have the authority. He's trying to tell you that trouble is eventually goin' to come up that road and it's comin' swiftly and with great force. The American people are mad as hell about all those bombings and deaths. They see you guys as pawns of Arab terrorist groups. Heads are going to roll, and we would rather yours not be one of 'em." There was a period of silence and Chudders walked to the window, hands in his hip pockets.

Darren finally said, "Have you sent your people into hiding?"

Chudders turned slowly, eyed Darren, then Mo, and said, "Yep, you boys is right." He shook his head and sighed heavily. He slowly walked back to his desk and sat down. Without looking up, he said, "Gosh, we jest wanted to be left alone up here."

"Tell us how all this came about," Darren said. Chudders then outlined the events that led to the various disgruntled citizens using his hideaway. Mo taped the entire session as Chudders told of the meetings with Chapmann, White, Petsch, Boorgers, and all the other extremists of national fame, of the meeting in Thailand to secure Russian arms, and all the rest. But he vowed that he had no knowledge of any bombings, assassinations or other killings.

"Are you willing to testify against White, Boorgers, and all these others in a court of law?" Darren asked.

"I'll think on it. Ain't ya got 'nough? I'm not part of the United States," Chudders insisted with a tone of anger in his voice. "It's an evil empire and I won't bow down to it."

"Well, there are thousands of people in that evil empire that just lost their lives in part because of your actions over the years," Darren noted. "Doesn't that bother you any?"

"Not a whole lot. That's God's vengeance upon them for their wicked ways."

"Why don't you come with us and talk to the authorities. I'll bet they will cut you some slack," Darren said.

"Oh, boys, I'm an old man. It doesn't make any difference what happens to me. I've lived a good life. But I'll think about your offer."

"Mr. Chudders, you don't have a lot of time," Darren said.

"Well, maybe that's right. But I'm not goin' to rush into this. Anything else I can do for you?"

"Yes, sir, there is," Darren added. "I'd like for you to take us to those caves and let us assure ourselves that there are no concealed weapons. If we can, then the troops won't rush in here ready to shoot anything that moves."

"Aw heck, I guess you can see the caves. Let's go." The tour lasted nearly an hour. As they left the mountain compound and walked down the path toward the church parking lot, they told Chudders they would return early the next morning to get his decision. The old man nodded.

The next morning, Darren and Mo were waiting at the entrance gate to Yahweh City in the early morning dark as federal agents and Tillman's men arrived. John Chudders had flown the coop. The terror was not over.

# 15

## DAVIS MOUNTAINS, WEST TEXAS

Thursday, March 2

The high arid desert of West Texas seemed cooler than usual as Darren and Mo returned to Austin after witnessing the destruction of Chudders' caves and the confiscation of numerous arms caches throughout West Texas and southern New Mexico. Federal and state agents raided hundreds more across the nation. Although not complete, the count of those arrested ran into the thousands. Darren felt a sense of sad relief. Maybe some of this craziness would end.

But did the nation's leaders learn anything as they watched thousands of ordinary Americans become so angry that they willingly laid their lives on the line for their vision of patriotism? Social events of such major proportions don't happen without a reason. Such dramatic rebellions only occur when a nation's institutions no longer serve its citizens well. Darren mulled these issues as he prepared to head back to Washington.

The sun had almost appeared above the horizon as Darren and Mo climbed aboard the old Ford Bronco in El Paso and headed east toward Austin. Mo's exclusive report on the raids and Chudders' confession delighted him. His stories had captured the world's attention. As they chugged down the interstate, Darren tuned the radio to a Del Rio station. They reminisced about days passed when self-styled ministers hawked Christian mementos to the gullible over radio waves beamed from Del Rio and Clint, Texas.

"Those were the days," Mo sighed, with a big smile, "when some jackass on the radio ranted and raved in the name of Jesus." He raised his voice to a high pitch and mimicked the nasal tone of the old time radio preachers as he said, "Brothers and sisters, if yaaa'll jes' send us two dolla's, we'll send you an autographed picture of Jeeezzzz-Us. Hallelujah!"

"Yeah," Darren said, "or a piece of the old rugged cross!" Both laughed and shook their heads in disbelief. After a pause, he added, "Their ancestors have polished the approach for TV audiences"

When the station faded, Darren searched the airwaves for another. He finally picked up music on KGNZ-FM out of Abilene. They had settled back to enjoy the West Texas scenery when the station interrupted with a news bulletin.

"A report just in to KGNZ-FM. The nation awakened to sounds of further violence this morning." Shocked, Darren and Mo looked at each other without saying a word. Mo's jaw dropped, Darren felt his chest tighten.

The announcer continued, "Explosions greeted federal employees as they reported to work along the East Coast. Bombs reportedly ripped through federal courthouse buildings and offices in Albany, New York, Philadelphia, Baltimore, Pittsburgh, Charlotte, Tampa and numerous other cities."

"My God," Darren uttered, as he bent over and slammed his fists into the Bronco's dashboard.

"Federal agents, reportedly U.S. Marshals on their way to work this morning, have been gunned down in Washington and Philadelphia." The radio went silent.

"Damn it," Darren said.

The same announcer's voice, steady and unemotional, continued, "And this wire just in. Several missiles have hit the White House."

"Holy shit!" Mo cried. Darren put his hand to his head in disbelief as the news continued.

"President Evans fortunately had not left Camp David as originally planned. Numerous White House staff have been killed. We will have more news for you as the day's events unfold. This is Arnold Demster, KGNZ News."

"Mo, pull up at the nearest pay phone and let me call the office."

"Why not use the cellular?"

"I tried it earlier. There's no service out here." They reached Ozona in about fifteen minutes, whipped off the Interstate at exit 365 and found a phone booth at a Texaco station on the northeast corner of the intersection. Darren called his office while Mo filled the Bronco with gas.

"Jo, Darren here. I just heard the news. How bad is it?"

"I don't know. General Burcks is at the White House now. He heard the explosions and ran right over. Ambulances, fire trucks, police and military forces are all over the place. Streets are blocked off in all directions. From here it looks like the damage is confined to the West Wing office area. They've carried out a lot of body bags."

"Tell General Burcks I'm on my way back to D.C. as soon as I can get to an airport. Would you get me a plane reservation out of San Antonio? I should be able to catch one around noon."

"Okay. But I wouldn't hurry. There's nothing but chaos here."

Mo drove his old Ford Bronco down Interstate 10 as fast as it would go. "Darren, if I get a ticket I'm expecting you to get it fixed!"

"What are you talking about? This ole jalopy wouldn't go past seventy if your life depended on it. That Abilene station faded on us. Let's see if we can pick up WOAI in San Antonio." The station came in clear.

A woman's voice said, "...and the men in the green van just opened up the side doors and started shooting at that other car."

"What happened then?" the reporter asked.

"The van just headed west on Market Street. I thought they'd hit one of those other cars, but they wove their way in and out."

"Thanks, Melissa. This is Paula Fernandez at the site of a drive-by shooting at Main Plaza, in San Antonio."

"Thanks, Paula. To recap, police report a number of drive-by shootings this morning, and there are unconfirmed explosions at Randolph and Kelley Air Force bases. As soon as we learn more, we'll report back to you. Now back to music on WOAI."

Mo dropped Darren off at the terminal, and headed to Austin as fast as the old Bronco would go. Darren checked in for his flight, moved to the departure lounge, and called Agent Lenora Carlson's office.

"Lenora, Hopkins here. I'm in San Antonio and catching a flight back to D.C. right away. How bad is it?"

"Let's put it this way: It ain't good! All evidence suggests our super patriots are at it again."

"What's the extent of the damage?" Darren asked.

"As of mid-day, we've confirmed twenty-four buildings hit. But there have been dozens and dozens of drive-by shootings of federal employees. We watched this activity spread west across the country as people went to work in the different time zones. We've minimized the potential damage because a lot of the people watching the early news from the east stayed home."

"They've shifted from an attack on facilities to federal agents."

"Looks that way. The President has asked all federal employees to be cautious going to and from work. Some are talking about arranging armored buses to pick up workers."

"When's the next task force meeting?"

"Tonight. Seven o'clock. We met briefly this morning, then all hell broke loose, so everyone rushed out in different directions."

"Who did we lose at the White House?"

"Five domestic employees, three reporters and thirteen White House staff members. There's an additional thirty-six injured, as far as we know at this moment."

"Where did the missiles come from, and why couldn't they be detected coming in?"

"Alarms did sound, but people say they didn't have enough time to do more than crawl under desks or hide in closets. Some got to underground shelters. Someone launched missiles from mobile trucks. One man said he saw a guy pop up through the roof of an old school bus and shoot a rocket while driving down Constitution Avenue. Police caught the bus, but the occupants opened fire and ended up being killed by the police."

"Okay, got to run. They're loading my plane."

TASK FORCE HQ, WASHINGTON, D.C.
Thursday, March 27

The big board on the wall in the task force's situation room had a totally new set of colored splotches. Florescent orange highlighted the day's damage. Two new sets of computerized windows tracked the numbers killed and injured. One showed three hundred and thirty-six dead. The injured count changed as he watched.

The large room had been redesigned since Darren's last visit. The west end now had a glass wall and sliding glass doors that partitioned off a second, and smaller, meeting room. Darren noticed the somber mood hanging over the group. No one exchanged smiles or greetings.

Agent Wade shut the glass doors, sat down, then after a few moments said, "You'll find in front of you a list of those facilities and federal employees killed and injured as of six p.m. This list grows by the hour, especially the injured list. Jeff, a lot of your marshals and ATF personnel got killed and injured. We're all very sorry."

"Thanks. It's been devastating. Calls started coming in to my office at eight-thirty this morning. I only hope our enemies don't find out how much damage they've done."

Agent Lockney said, "Let's put the correct information out and get on with it and hope the media doesn't beat this dog to death like it does every other event." He put his head down on the desk in resignation.

And agent sitting across from Lockney chimed in, saying, "Boy, I agree with that."

"I wish someone would do a study to show how many wars and violent events the media is responsible for starting or maintaining for the story's sake," another said, with a tinge of bitterness in his voice.

"Okay folks," Carlson said, as she rapped on the table, "There's nothing we can do or say to the press that's going to alter their institutional mind set, so let's get on with our tasks."

"From what John Chudders said in Texas it seems that the super patriots have tapped into most, if not all, federal electronics communication systems," Darren said. "They seem to know everything your agencies are planning."

"I'm not surprised," McKinny sighed, throwing his pen down on the table. It slid across and landed near Lockney, who picked it up and slid it back with a smile.

Darren took this opportunity to report on his visit with John Chudders. He walked over and handed the tape of their conversation to Agent Carlson.

"And, for everyone's information," Agent Wade added, "now that Chudders' compound's cleaned out, that pretty well sanitizes Texas. At least the most visible elements."

"How many of today's bombers have we caught?" Mullins asked. Everyone looked to Wade and Carlson.

"This is a list of those killed or apprehended during today's activities," Carlson said, as she handed out a Justice Department memo. "Note that among those apprehended, we have several dozen in the category of 'serious suspects.' I don't have the details of all those killed. Identification of the bodies will take some time. The authorities we've talked to swear that each had numerous opportunities to surrender. There's not one case of indiscriminate firing by our people. In fact, a number of federal and state law enforcement people would still be alive if they hadn't been lenient."

Lockney asked, "Where are Boorgers, White, and their associates?"

"We haven't found them." Carlson turned toward Deputy Director Wade and whispered an aside.

He turned to the group, and leaned over as he said, "I've been asked to inform you that Bob McCall has disappeared." The task force members looked stunned as they looked around the table at their colleagues. Lewis dropped his head.

"Disappeared?" General Craft asked. "As in abducted?"

"No," Wade said. "If you remember, the Agency Director called him out of this meeting last week. He never reached the agency."

"Then that's abduction," argued Craft.

"I hate to tell you, but the Director had him return to the office to face charges that he had been passing information to some of the extremist leaders. His friendship with General Boorgers surfaced. They went through Marine boot together. They served in Nam together. Since he disappeared, we've also learned that he kept company with Arlo White and other extremists on numerous occasions. All of his bank accounts have been emptied. Closed. Most unfortunate." Silence hung over the group for some time, each wondering who else could be an informant.

Carlson said, "Meanwhile, let's be aware that every member of this task force is targeted." Agent Carlson warned, "Check every car you get into for explosives. Joe, help us here."

Agent Morgan said, "These birds know their explosives. Today's bombings resulted from Semtex plastic explosives with micro-timers placed in lunch boxes, office supply deliveries, telephones and so forth. They're also carrying up-to-date Uzi machine guns and have night vision goggles, mines, booby-traps and electronic devices as sophisticated as any we have."

"Who is the enemy?" Agent Carlson sighed softly.

"Yeah, makes one yearn for the good ole days when the only worry seemed to be the Russians, doesn't it," General Craft said, as he rose and walked out.

"When is Tillman's group going after Ship and Chapmann?" Lockney asked, looking around the table.

"It's scheduled for tomorrow night," Carlson replied.

"Meanwhile, we've got to do something about this electronic eavesdropping," Wade said. "Each of you get in touch with your computer people and let's see if we can do something about it. That should be a number-one priority immediately! It's bad enough to have these yokels killing and bombing with seeming impunity, but to let them beat us technologically is unforgivable."

"Is it possible to get the computer experts together and coordinate this effort?" Lewis asked. "Given the number of computer geeks in our agencies, they surely ought to be able to block this stuff. And I would think that IBM, Microsoft and some of the other companies would send some of their top people to help."

"Good idea." Looking at her boss, she continued, "Christine Woods is the senior member of our computer team and would represent it well. Surely it's not that difficult for each branch of the task force to identify their top computer gurus and get them to meet together. I'll contact IBM and the others." Wade nodded and the others agreed.

No sooner had this item been concluded than in walked President Carl Evans, the Deputy Director of the FBI, General George Burcks, several presidential aides and a Secret Service escort. Everyone stared in amazement, then respectfully rose.

"Good morning, ladies and gentlemen. They told me at the White House that Presidents don't go to agency meetings. I told them I'll damn well go where I please." Everyone laughed and a few applauded. "So, they tell me this is the heart and soul of the task force. I wanted to come over and tell you personally how sorry I am that you have lost so many colleagues and to congratulate you on doing a great job."

He paused to let his condolence sink in, then continued. "You know better than anyone what a tough task we're facing." He made eye contact with each member as he spoke, then, motioning with his arms, said, "Sit back down and tell me where we are and what else we ought to be doing to stop this insanity."

Wade and Carlson had moved down the round table to make their chairs available to the President, his aides, and the Deputy Director of the FBI. Then Wade and Carlson led a brief summary of the day's hits, arrests and deaths. Members of the group had straightened their ties and those who had taken their suit coats off now put them back on. All sat erect as the President spoke. The President listened carefully as they discussed the various explosions. He asked questions designed to add to his understanding and responded thoughtfully to each member's views.

Finally, he asked, "Are there merits to the charges made by these people?" No one responded. The members looked around the table at their colleagues to see who would dare broach the subject. Finally, he said, "Aw, forget all this bureaucratic crap. It's time for honest people to speak honestly. What we say stays in this room!" He emphasized the last statement by turning to Deputy Director of the FBI Wade, General Burcks, and other agency bigwigs who had slipped in to witness this unique session.

Darren said, "Mr. President, I've talked to a number of our home-grown extremists and find most to be well-meaning citizens. While they believe that the government had become too large and was intruding unnecessarily in their lives, they would never actively participate in such atrocious acts. Those who have been doing the bombings and killings were people who can't cope with life in general. They are social misfits. While Darren spoke, Burcks whispered something in the President's ear.

The President looked at Darren and said, "I understand you work for General Burcks and are fearless in expressing your point of view. Good for you."

"Not really. I'm just naïve," said Darren .

The President smiled and then looked around the room and asked, "Others?" That broke the ice. The members of the group undoubtedly told the President more than he wanted to hear.

Finally, the President stood. "Well, thank you very much. You really unloaded. And, by the way, I don't know if any of you realize it or not, but I didn't detect anyone's rank, agency jargon or party line."

Some of the group smiled, while others nodded. Then, pointing to General Craft, the President said, "Obviously Craft's uniform tells us he's a General." People smiled. "Yet, you all talked as equals. I like that. My God, we need to have more exchanges like this in government. We must get to the truth, regardless of the consequences. Most of us thought that once we had rooted out the Muslin terrorists we could get back into a peace mode. Unfortunately, we were wrong. I've learned to never say never, but a return to the peaceful eras prior to the World Trade Building bombings is highly unlikely. Now we face a major internal struggle. After we came together so solidly to go after Al-Qaida and Saddam, who would have believed we'd be fighting our own people. Our nation has a new terror in its belly. What you do in the days, weeks and months ahead will largely determine our nation's destiny. Keep up the good work." He turned and swiftly walked out the door as everyone stood respectfully.

"Wow," exclaimed Carlson as she turned to Wade and several others standing near. "That's a first."

"That's for sure," Lockney said. "What a gutsy thing to do."

# 16

## LUKE AFB, PHOENIX, ARIZONA

Friday, March 28

Darren caught a mid-morning flight from Washington to Phoenix, arriving at Luke Air Force Base as the crews of the six new stealth helicopters rehearsed the night's assignment. A two-man crew and a human payload of eight filled each helicopter. Colonel Tillman had cleared for Mo to come along as a representative reporter. After the assault, Mo would share information with a reporter pool. Darren found Mo and several local reporters already there and taking copious notes.

The team, comprised of forty elite Special Forces agents, six FBI agents—all formerly Special Forces members—Darren and Mo prepare to assault the Ship ranch in Catron County, New Mexico, one hundred twenty-five miles east of Phoenix. All but Hopkins and Childs had spent the last twenty-four hours studying details of the ranch and planning the assault strategy.

The ranch contained twenty thousand acres, six miles north of Reserve, New Mexico, on State Highway 12, in the middle of the U.S. Government's Gila National Forest. Ornate adobe brick columns highlighted the ranch's main entrance on the west side of the highway. A twelve-foot wide arched, adobe roof, covered by red, Spanish clay tiles, joined each column. An electronic gate discouraged guests. The ranch house was located six miles from the entrance. The large valley gradually faded as one followed the ranch road southwest into the rugged piñon pine and juniper-covered rolling hills.

The sprawling Spanish-style home included six bedrooms, six baths, a large kitchen, a spacious dining room, a playroom, and two large living rooms. Only adobe brick and native logs were used in the construction. A three-foot-high decorative fence, also of adobe and native wood, encircled the house. Four horse barns and a bunkhouse sat west of the main house.

The teams had aerial maps of the ranch, which also included the location of numerous claymore mines (a fan-shaped set of c-4 explosives that shoot pellets in a semi-circular pattern) and other booby-traps installed around the facilities. A laser detection system had to be neutralized without awakening the occupants. Anyone tampering with the front gate or coming up the main road off Highway 12 triggered the laser-controlled alarm at the bunkhouse and main house. The security system included sirens and a system of spotlights, which lit a large area of the compound. Regardless of one's assault direction, dogs and horses had to be quieted.

Tillman assigned Colonel J. C. "Ace" Cole, age 38, of Gotebo, Oklahoma, to command the expedition. Cole had acquired the nickname "Ace" because of his golf game. He met Darren upon his arrival at the ready room, next to one of the large hangers. "Mr. Hopkins, good to see you again."

"Same here. Looks like you guys moved right out on this."

"Hey, yes, sir. What can I say? That's our job."

"I'm impressed with how efficiently you did it. I see you've met Mo!" Darren grinned.

"Yes, sir. He's fittin' in real well. Grab a chair over there and let me know if you need anything. There's coffee and drinks at the back wall."

"Thanks, I'm fine. Do what you've got to do." Darren got a cup of coffee and joined team members who had crowded around a large table near the front of the room. A scaled, three-dimensional geographic mock-up of the Ship ranch filled the table. Teams were using the ranch model to review their particular tasks.

Finally, Cole moved to the front of the room. "Listen up!" he shouted. "You've all met our reporter, Mo Childs. He's representing a reporter's pool and will be taking pictures and talkin' to you as we go. If he gets in the way, just gently shove him aside." Laughter echoed around the room. Mo blushed and lowered his head. "Now I'd like you to meet Darren Hopkins of the President's National Security Council." Cole pointed at Darren, and Darren waved in return. "He's part of the group that arranged this party. So if anything goes wrong, just point a finger at him!" Again the troops laughed. "But make sure he doesn't get killed. We don't want to answer to the White House. And we sure want someone like him to take the blame in case anything goes wrong!" The group laughed and cheered. "As for reporters, hell they're a dime a dozen. You'll probably get a medal." Everyone roared as Mo started for the door. Cole yelled, "Just kiddin!"

"Okay. It's now twenty hundred hours. We jump off in one hour, sharp. Finish your prep, check each other's equipment, and be loaded by twenty fifty hours. All clear?"

"Yes, sir!" they shouted in unison.

Cole turned his attention to Hopkins and Childs. "Although you are non-combatants, both of you still need to get into special gear for your own protection. As you see around you, we wear black knitties, as the ladies in the group like to call them. Black pants and black shirts. And smudge your face with our special black grease, find a pair of black sneakers that will fit you in that cabinet in the far corner, and put on one of those black stocking caps from the pile on the table. They've all been laundered, by the way."

Then, pointing to a young man standing next to him, he said, "Sergeant Bonilla will see that you're properly outfitted. Once you're dressed, the sergeant will brief you one last time on what we're planning so you'll know what to expect. We hope we can seize the advantage and get these guys without giving them a chance to fire back, but there are no guarantees. According to instructions from the Pentagon, we are not responsible if either of you gets hit. I understand that you both have signed notarized documents releasing us from any and all liabilities. Is that correct?" Both men answered in the affirmative and followed the sergeant to get into proper combat dress, minus the weapons.

Sergeant Bonilla saw that Darren and Mo were outfitted, then took them back to the ready room where they moved from group to group and discussed the final assault instructions with the troops. Then Bonilla led them to the scaled geographic table-model of the Ship ranch and went through the planned execution.

Darren pointed down at the three bunkhouses that had been chosen for the assault and asked, "I notice that there are eight bunkhouses scattered around the ranch, so why were these three chosen for assault?"

Bonilla said, "We've observed continuous activity at those three houses for several days. Especially the largest facility below Red Butte."

"Okay."

"Each site will be assaulted by one team," Bonilla continued, as he pointed out the various sites on the model. Mo furiously took notes.

Continuing, Bonilla said, "If a unit's site is clean, that unit will immediately proceed to join the back-up units in preparation for an assault on the main ranch house. There are backup teams for each of the three main assault teams. Until we know what we've got at these three cabins, we will not proceed to the main ranch house."

"You know where people are sleeping in each cabin?" Darren asked in disbelief.

"Yes, sir." The Sergeant pointed out the bedrooms at the main house and the number of occupants their latest photos revealed to be occupying the facilities.

"I understand that if the men we're seeking are in one of these facilities, there will be no assault on the big house. Is that correct?" continued Darren, as he reached over and pointed to the various bunkhouses.

"Yes sir, those are our instructions." There was silence as the three men stood staring at the model.

Darren took his handkerchief out of his back pocket, wiped his forehead, and asked, "What about the weapons storage facility reportedly built on the ranch? Where is it on this model?"

"We have evidence of recent truck and dozer activity up Juniper Canyon, north of Red Butte." The sergeant pointed to the canyon on the scaled size table model of the ranch. "They cut a cave into the side of the canyon. A series of photos taken over several months shows a gradual build-up of dirt and rock back down the canyon, which greatly improved the road. The area at the mouth of the cave has been expanded, along with an area back at Jerkins River. We assume the construction is for helicopter use. That's what we plan to use it for."

"Great."

Then Mo asked, "How y'all goin' to get the weapons out'a there if you find them?"

"Sir, two Chinook C-forty seven cargo helicopters are standing by in a field near Lyman's Lake, just across the Arizona border." Bonilla pointed to Lyman's Lake on the table model. "Those Chinooks will handle all cargo found on the ranch." Mo nodded his understanding while writing notes.

Darren pointed again to the model. "Okay. Show us how the main ranch house is to be taken."

The Sergeant carefully briefed Darren and Mo on the attack plan. "What about booby traps and mines?" asked Mo.

Looking at Mo, Bonilla said, "Those are planted around the perimeter of the ranch house. We bypass those coming in vertically with the helicopters. Evidently the Ships didn't want explosives close to the house for fear they would be accidentally triggered by wild animals, small children or their pets," the sergeant explained. "Lucky for us."

"Yeah, lucky for us," Mo uttered quietly to Darren.

Sergeant Bonilla stood patiently waiting, arms now folded behind his back. Darren glanced up and noticed the sergeant looking across the room at Colonel Cole.

Then, the sergeant looked at Darren and said, "If you're worried about Ms. Ship, their children and grandchildren, rest assured they're all in Albuquerque. That's one reason there's a hurry up and go status placed on this operation."

Cole interrupted the briefing. "Mr. Hopkins, you and Mr. Childs will go with Major Peters in our command bird. Follow Major Peters and load up."

The two men climbed aboard the black, sleek helicopter. Six troops joined them. Once all were secured, helmets on and special gear stored, the door silently closed. The only light in the cabin came from the front instrument panel's soft glow of orange and small greenish glows on either side of the large side door. The helmets of the three crewmen had built-in imaging capability.

Once his eyes adjusted to the darkness, Darren looked around the small, cramped cabin at his colleagues. Several had begun to doze. Others stared out the windows. Everyone seemed relaxed, except Darren and Mo. A small vibration shook the craft as the motor started, and then there was silence as the plane began its slow climb into the starry Arizona sky. They departed to the west, then veered north, climbing to what Darren felt must have been about one thousand feet. He glanced out the window behind him, but he could only see a series of green and red running lights from the lead craft. They continued climbing as they flew due north out of the Phoenix metropolitan area. Darren guessed they had climbed to three thousand feet before leveling out. Then they veered sharply east. After thirty-five minutes at that altitude, they gradually descended to about a thousand feet. Colonel Cole followed valleys and canyons as he led the others east toward Catron County, New Mexico.

Darren and Mo looked at each other in astonishment. "Wow!" Mo whispered.

"That's why they call this helicopter a stealth," Darren said. "I never would have believed it." They could not hear the rotors. In fact, one's own breathing and a slight cough from one of the crew contributed the only noise. Then Darren realized that the small, soft green lights marking the entrance had gone out. The darkness felt scary. He looked out the small windows and could not see any of the other helicopters. An occasional house or yard light flashed by, indicating their high speed and low altitude.

A voice spoke softly in his headgear, "Mr. Hopkins, this is Colonel Cole.

This is a marvel of technology, isn't it?"

"I'm speechless!" Darren said. "Are we all connected by the communications systems in our head gear?"

"Yes. You can turn it off by pushing a little red button on the side of your helmet, but the commander of each ship has a master switch so he can immediately activate everyone's unit. Right now, for example, every member of this assault force whose headphones are open can hear our conversation. You haven't heard any talk until now because we don't waste a lot of time talking up here."

"I can appreciate that. Sorry to have broken the silence."

"Oh, no, I expected it. Our ground speed is three hundred forty-five knots. And that's not full throttle. We're on a course east and a bit north, which will take us just south of Springerville, Arizona. We'll turn a few degrees south and enter New Mexico in three minutes. We'll be over the ranch as soon as we cross the state line. We'll track to the valleys south of Jim Smith Peak until we pick up the Jerkins River Valley. At a certain point west of Red Butte, there's an old gravel road. We'll quietly sit down there while the three teams responsible for the outlying targets take care of 'em. No one as close as ten feet will ever hear us or know we were by this way. Although they may feel us. I guarantee that none of the people at any of the ranch facilities will know we're there until we blow our way in. Once we see the results of the raids on these three smaller houses, we'll probe for the weapons cache and either return to base or take out the main target."

"Sounds good to me," whispered Darren. Silence descended once again upon the assault teams. A few minutes later, Cole said, "Lead bird just crossed state line. Bus stop in three minutes. Get your luggage ready."

Darren could see the shadowy trees zip by his left side window as the 'copter shot down the river valley. They couldn't have been flying more than six feet above the surface of the small river. He looked out the window on the right hand side and felt he could reach out and touch the canyon walls. Whew, if we clip something, we're dead! he thought. He looked over at Mo and their eyes communicated mutual understanding and astonishment. As the 'copter wound its way down the valley, Darren made a hand gesture to Mo, indicating that he could now stand on his head! Mo nodded his understanding. They laughed quietly.

The helicopter slowed and came to rest on a grassy area next to the county's gravel road. No one moved. Three other units settled within twenty yards of Cole's. The others fanned out in different directions as they focused on their respective targets. The only sound came from Cole saying, "Good hunting." Again, dead silence.

Finally, after what seemed like an eternity the door quietly swung open and the cool mountain air rushed in. It felt great. The others motioned for Darren and Mo to follow. Once outside, Darren faintly made out the silhouette of the two other helicopters and their crews stretching their legs in the night air. Several took off their helmets to enjoy the refreshing cool mountain air. A few whispered to each another but quickly put their helmets back on so they could hear the next command. They had to be ready to back up the three main teams.

Darren kept an eye on his watch. Fifteen minutes elapsed before the first report came in. "Momma Bird, this is Gamma. Three aliens secure. Moving to support Sigma."

Again, silence descended upon the units. Colonel Cole passed a written message to Darren saying, "That's the line shack up northeast of Apache Mountain. We didn't expect our targets to be there. Alien is code for ranch hands."

Another five minutes elapsed, then Lieutenant Rob Parker, commander of Zeta team, said, "Momma Bird, Zeta reports all secure. Two sleepy-eyed pigeons netted. Await orders. Over."

"Momma Bird here. Move to support Sigma and Gamma," commanded Cole.

He no sooner finished the sentence than Captain Fred Cutter, commander of Sigma team, said, "Five non-English speaking aliens ran for the hills. We didn't want to shoot. It took time, but we have them. Returning to Momma Bird. Over."

"Ten-four. Good work." In a few minutes the three helicopters settled down next to the other three. Darren and Mo would not have known of their arrival if not for the sudden increase in the wind. "What happens to the innocent cowboys?" Darren asked Cole.

"They're sedated. They'll awaken in six or eight hours with a stiff headache and blame this nightmare on too much of their own cooking. I suspect they'll head south as fast as their legs will carry them."

"May I ask Lieutenant Parker about the two pigeons?"

"Sure, but when we get back. Right now we've got to finish our mission." At those few swift words, Cole gave the command to move out in a low voice. "Let's go." The teams immediately climbed back into their respective helicopters and the rotors turned as the doors shut silently. "Time is now twenty-one eighteen hours. Mark," said Cole. He lifted his craft swiftly and silently into the night sky.

The six helicopters snaked along the Jerkins River for approximately six miles. Then they cut sharply south for a few miles, then a mile east before turning to a northerly heading that would bring them in over the rocky escarpments south of the ranch house. The bedrooms were in the back, or northwest corner, of the house. Ship and his fellow patriots shared a common belief that a legitimate attack would come from the open meadow to the north. His people wagered that the feds would come roaring up from the main gate on Highway 12 with sirens screaming and all kinds of lights flashing. If they come at all.

Wrong! The helicopters moved into place, hovering noiselessly some forty feet above their respective targets. The three teams not involved with the earlier assault on the three line cabins took the lead. One, carrying the Blue Team, hovered a few feet above the door to the room housing the electronic surveillance system. Two crewmembers lowered Special Forces Officer Lieutenant Eileen Marks in a sling to the booby-trapped door. She used a device that decoded and shut off the door's defense, then opened it. She entered and within ten seconds disarmed the whole security system and set plastic explosives to go off in fifteen minutes. They had to move quickly.

Meanwhile, the Orange Team led by Major Pam Dixon descended upon the peripheral buildings. Four agents entered the log house used by seasonal ranch hands, situated thirty yards beyond the last stable. The front and back doors had not been locked. The assault team quickly tranquilized the six sleeping cowhands. While a team took the bunkhouse, other troops sedated the animals in the stables and barns. A few hens flew from their perches in one barn but soon quieted. The brief racket didn't seem to awaken anyone in the main house.

They hoisted Lieutenant Marks back to her helicopter and moved to assault the main kitchen entrance. The second helicopter, Colonel Cole's command unit, carrying Darren and Mo, moved to assault the front of the main house.

Pam Dixon's Orange Team set up over the northwest corner of the house—the location of the master bedroom. Only enough explosives to blow a six-foot by six-foot entrance through the north wall had to be affixed to the adobe siding. Satellite imaging had revealed a bed against the far wall, approximately eighteen feet from the point of explosion.

The other three assault teams hovered in line to follow on the heels of the first wave. The lead helicopters hovered for what seemed an eternity to Darren as the Colonel waited for everyone to be in position. In fact, only two minutes had elapsed. Finally, Colonel Cole said quietly, "Hopkins, you and Childs are the last ones out. There's a clump of junipers about twenty yards to our rear. You guys get in that cover as soon as you hit the ground and stay there until we secure this house."

"Yes, sir." But a chill rippled through Darren's body as the moment of truth approached.

Three seconds later, Cole uttered the word they'd all been waiting for, "Go!" As the helicopters swiftly dropped to ground level each disgorged its troops in what seemed like one large heave. Each team member ran to his assigned position as Darren and Mo ran for the junipers. Within a few seconds the helicopters lifted off and assumed assault positions, their rockets and fifty millimeter cannons aimed at the house. The explosives set in the room housing the ranch's electronics system exploded with a series of dull thumps. Five seconds later three explosive charges detonated simultaneously. It sounded like one muffled ba-room! The troops followed the blast through the cavities before the dust had settled. Darren and Mo heard a few shouts, some sporadic machine gun fire, and then silence.

Darren watched as three shaken men with their hands up, dressed only in their underwear, stumbled out the front door coughing with two members of the Special Forces team ushering them along. They were forced to lie face down in the grass. The hovering helicopters now illuminated the house and surrounding grounds with bright spotlights. Darren could hear Mo's camera clicking.

A few moments later troops escorted six more men out the kitchen door, their hands also high in the air. These men had their pants and shirts on, but no shoes. Last, seven more stumbled out the front door, coughing and spitting with Colonel Cole and his team on their heels. The captives were lined up and cuffed, and then Agent McGuire read them their rights.

Other members of the assault team immediately fanned out for a more thorough search of the premises. A pile developed as Russian-made AK-47s, assorted U.S. military issue machine guns and thumpers, also known as grenade launchers, surfaced from closets, behind doors and out of attic niches. Agents recorded each weapon for later identification and Mo photographed each in turn. They soon found more weapons stashed in the barns.

Mo moved freely throughout the premises with his camera while Darren watched FBI officials take down names and other information from those who had been arrested. Armed guards accompanied each captive back into the house to retrieve sufficient clothing to stay warm.

A fairly small, wiry man in his late sixties, at the far end of the line, drew Darren and Cole's attention. His cussin' and fussin' could be heard for miles. "What goddam right ya got coming on my ranch, you sorry bastards? Look at all the damage ya caused! I'm go'in to sue the pants off you sons-a-bitches! I will, by God! You wait and see."

Colonel Cole walked over to him, introduced himself as the commander of the assault team under orders from the Joint Chiefs of Staff. "You must be Tom Ship."

"I goddam well am," Ship yelled.

In a calm voice, Cole said, "Sir, we have a warrant for your arrest. Once you're booked, we'll be more than happy to assist you in reaching your damned attorney." Cole then leaned to within a few inches of Ship's face as he yelled, "Meanwhile, shut your mouth or we'll shut it for you!"

This quieted the old man down, but the fire in his eyes continued to burn. They made him sit cross-legged on the ground, hands cuffed behind his back. Later, Cole casually returned to Ship, knelt down and whispered, "You're a lucky man. Did ya know that?"

"Why?" asked a mystified Ship in a voice still vibrating with anger.

"Cuz you're being arrested in America. Hell, I've been in countries where they blow sobs like you away without so much as a howdy-do. In fact, you've got another reason to thank God tonight that you're taken by a team of FBI agents and solid American boys and girls doing their country's duty. Cuz, if they'd let me come in here alone like I wanted to in the first place, I'd-a killed every damn one of ya with one well placed missile from my 'copter!" Cole abruptly stood up and walked away, leaving rancher Tom Ship with his jaw hanging halfway down to his belly button. Darren overheard the exchange and turned away to hide his laughter.

"Hopkins!" Cole shouted.

"Yes, sir."

"Know any of these guys?"

"Oh, I think I can identify a few," Darren replied. "The man third from the right is Bob Wildman, former aide to one of our esteemed Presidents."

"Is that right? He sure doesn't look very important right now, does he? Who else?"

"The man on the end is Jeb Fulamore, big time wheeler-dealer with a whole bunch of extremists. We understand he spends most of his time raising money for the killing and bombing that's been going on. Third, the skinny guy down near Tom is Pete Winters, a self-styled preacher who hates Jews, African-Americans, and everyone else you can think of. He and the fat one in the middle with all the tattoos, Ron Flukke, are members of the KKK and the Nazi skinheads. The rest of these guys are wannabes. I suspect we'll find they're related to the more violent strain of militia and super patriot organizations."

"Good. I want my guys to know what they've accomplished," the Colonel said. He paused to scan the western sky, then said, "Any minute now two big Chinooks should arrive. One will load up the prisoners and the FBI, stop by that bunkhouse and pick up those other two nuts, then haul'em on back to Luke AFB for processing. The others will follow us to that canyon and see if we can find any weapons to haul back to Luke." Cole immediately called for Gamma team's captain, J.C. Enfield.

"Yes, sir," Enfield replied, rushing up.

"Get your crew on up to Juniper Canyon." Enfield's crew quickly jumped aboard their helicopter and were off.

Darren watched they vanished into the night sky without a sound. Walking over to Cole, he said, "Colonel, I'd like to call in and report to General Burcks if you don't mind."

"Of course. Dixon!" Pam Dixon quickly appeared. "Assist Mr. Hopkins in getting through to General Burcks."

"Yes, sir." Dixon dialed the number and handed the phone to Darren.

Darren put the phone to his ear. Finally a sleepy voice answered, "Hello."

Darren apologized for getting the general out of bed, and then reported on the night's activities.

"Yeah, Tillman told me you went on that assault. Sometimes I think you're crazy, Hopkins!" Burcks said

"You're probably right," answered Darren.

"Anyway, I admire your willingness to put your life on the line. Tell the troops how pleased I am. I'll call the President immediately. He'll be able to have a fairly sound sleep for a change. By the way, any sign of Boorgers or White?"

"None, sir. No sign of General Boorgers or Colonel White. Maybe some of these guys will talk, but I don't know. They're a sullen bunch."

"Oh, I'd be surprised if any of them do much talking. They're a macho bunch and they've wrapped their cause with such religious garbage that they probably believe they're martyrs for Jesus. We ought to just load all these idiots up and dump them in Afghanistan!"

"That would probably make a lot of people happy."

"Yeah. And by the way, do not use the titles General or Colonel when referring to Boorgers and White. They're traitors and I refuse to acknowledge their military rank. Anything else?"

"No, sir."

"Then I'm goin' back to sleep."

Darren handed the phone back to Dixon, then returned to the crowd as the large Chinook helicopters began arriving. One loaded all the human baggage, then Cole gave the order to evacuate the premises and motioned Darren and Mo aboard the command craft.

As the returning helicopters reached the site where Juniper Canyon spills into the small Jerkins River Valley, four of the stealth copters sat down near Captain Enfield's plane. The sixth helicopter continued flying escort for the Chinook carrying the prisoners back to Luke AFB.

Once on the ground next to Enfield's plane, they moved up the small canyon road until they found two of Enfield's men guarding the entrance to a fairly large cave. The entrance stood six feet wide and ten feet high. After traversing a fifteen-foot corridor, Cole and his troops entered an oval-shaped room of approximately one thousand square feet packed with U.S. and Russian armaments.

"My God," Cole exclaimed. "Hopkins!" Darren rushed into the room. "Yep. We got'em! Hot damn. Look at this shit. There's enough stuff here to fight World War II all over again! Don't anyone touch anything until the FBI gives directions. Finish getting portable lighting in here. Hopkins, when they give the okay, we'd appreciate you and Mo helping load this stuff in the Chinook so we can get out'a here."

"Yes, sir. Whew, what smells in here?" Darren asked as he wrinkled up his nose and covered it with his hands.

They all turned to look at him and one said, pointing to the back of the cave, "There's a dead coyote behind some crates over there."

"Geez, that smells terrible," said Mo. "Don't you guys carry some spray deodorant?" Everyone laughed.

The FBI agents immediately went to work. Several took fingerprints. Others organized the troops and explained the inventory procedure. Mo photographed everything. The whole process took about an hour. It took another thirty-five minutes to load the arms. By 3:40 a.m., exhaustion had set in.

Darren, wiping sweat from his forehead with his handkerchief and breathing pretty hard, approached Colonel Cole and asked, "Are you planning to blow this cavern?"

"Yes, sir. The explosives should be almost in place." They watched as the men loaded the last few crates. "Okay, let's get out'a here." Darren, Mo and all the troops returned to the helicopters except for two demolition experts who finished setting the explosives. They soon reported to the command copter.

"Sir, it's ready to blow."

"Good. Load'em up. Let's go home." The helicopters lifted off, circled the area and climbed into the cool, starry sky to about two thousand feet. Colonel Cole turned to Darren and Mo and motioned with his thumb to look down. They peered out the left side window. As they gazed into the blackness, a sudden white flash lit the sky.

Cole's voice came over the telecom system, "Let's go home and get some sleep."

# 17

**PHOENIX**
Saturday, March 29

Returning to Luke Air Force Base, Mo shared information with the reporter pool. Mo had to return to Austin, but Darren stayed.

The stealth units now with three fresh crews, prepared to depart at nightfall to neutralize the Chapmann compound in Washington. While waiting for departure, Darren tried to stay informed of the FBI's interrogation of the Ship ranch prisoners.

Only Bob Wildman cooperated. A Federal District Judge in Phoenix arraigned all the men and refused bail in each case. Wildman ended up in a Washington, D.C., safe house. Over the next few weeks, he provided several hundred pages of testimony. The prosecutors from the U.S. Attorney General's office believed they had evidence to convict Arlo White, Ernst Boorgers and dozens of other self-styled leaders of trying to overthrow the United States Government. The Attorney General's office issued warrants for the arrest of those at large.

Meanwhile, as night fell, the three stealth units departed for Fairchild AFB outside Spokane. They arrived at ten that evening and began final preparation for the early morning assault on Chapmann's place in the Okanogan National Forest. A foggy cold mist greeted the group as they deplaned. They headed for hangar 77 which had plenty of room to house the helicopters and still provide warm quarters for the assault personnel.

Darren deplaned last, and as he entered the large hangar, he turned back to gaze across the misty field. Multi-colored lights created an eerie effect, but the cold air smelled fresh. Feeling the damp air penetrate his light shirt, he turned and shut the door behind. A team of local airmen had started to service the helicopters to the far right of the hangar.

Cole was watching Darren from a comfortable perch at the rear of the large room. After a few moments he got up and walked over to Darren. "You okay? I know that you don't have to do this."

"Yes, I'm fine. I'm enjoying the local scenery."

"Sandwiches and drinks are on the table over there," he said, pointing to the far wall. "By the way, we all think it's gutsy of you to come along on these missions. I wish more Washington bureaucrats would risk their asses."

About that time one of the men responsible for Rod Chapmann's place showed Darren what they were walking into on a map. "Sir, up this narrow, unpaved forest service road, this man's home is hidden among the pines to the left." Then, pointing to the left of the residence, he said, "And there's a heavy-duty gate at the drive's entrance. It's about fifty yards from the gate to the house." He looked to make sure Darren understood, then continued. "This gate is about one-quarter mile from another, more heavily fortified gate that marks the entrance to the whole Chapmann enclave."

"I can see that," Darren said.

"We're concerned about the two little boys, six and nine."

"Yeah, we certainly don't want them hurt," Darren said.

The young man nodded. "Meanwhile, Mr. West's home sits one-half mile farther north and several hundred yards east of the road, and they have a four-year-old girl."

"Besides the children, what other problems do you foresee?" Darren asked

"Rod Chapmann's and Hardy West's homes are hidden among the pines, so we prefer not to access them from the air. Ron Chapmann's home, on the other hand, sits on the north end of a nice open meadow and invites an air assault," he said, as he pointed out the map sites once again. Cole walked up at this point.

"Is everything falling into place, Darren?" Cole asked.

"I can see this may be difficult."

"It certainly is if we don't want any peripheral damage."

"No, certainly not. What do you know about the families' routines?" Darren asked.

"We've been watching them for about a week. Rod Chapmann and Hardy West both have horses and other animals that have to be cared for each morning. Rod has boys old enough to do this, but he often helps. Hardy West does the chores each morning by himself."

"What about dogs?" Darren asked.

"According to reports, there's only one dog at each house. Both are kept indoors most of the time. I don't think the dogs will be a problem. The real issue is isolating the men." Darren nodded.

Cole then went to the front of the room and asked for quiet. A hush fell over the room. "Okay, we plan to take out Ron Chapmann first. Once that's accomplished, we'll move on the other two houses. It's a short flight, so let's plan to load at 0 two hundred hours. Get some sleep while you can."

Some walked outside for a smoke; others found a quiet and comfortable niche for a nap.

Darren climbed up and nestled down in a comfortable crevice only to awaken several hours later when a voice blared, "Rise and shine, let's load up!"

The three helicopters flew almost directly northwest to Washington State's Okanogan Forest. A meadow near Patmar Lake served as the initial landing point prior to their moving into position at the Chapmann enclave. As Darren hopped out of the plane he noticed that, although the rain had stopped, it seemed colder.

The teams huddled and again rehearsed every detail of their respective plans, then lifted off for the assault. Cole's lead team took up its position above Ron Chapmann's house. The other two helicopters positioned themselves to support Cole's team by quietly hovering fifty yards at either side on an east-west axis.

Ron and Jill never heard the intruders. They awakened to find three heavily armed soldiers standing over their bed, pistols drawn and aimed directly at them. An FBI agent informed them of their arrest and read them their rights. The Chapmanns dressed, then sat on the living room coach. Two members of the assault team stood guard as Darren prepared and served coffee and tried to engage the Chapmanns in conversation, but they refused to respond. Several troops were posted outside in case of unexpected visitors. A small table lamp provided the room's only light.

Darren sat in a small padded lounge chair adjacent to the couch as he addressed the Chapmanns "You must be chilly. Can I turn up the heat a bit?" Getting no response Darren got up and found the thermostat in the hallway. He turned the heat up, then returned to his seat.

After a few moments of silence, he said, "I know how you must feel. I'm sorry it's come down to this." The Chapmanns refused to even look at Darren when he spoke. Finally, after a lengthy silence, Darren leaned over and looked Ron

Chapmann in the eyes. "It would help your case if you could help us find Boorgers and White."

Ron looked at Darren for a few moments, eyes narrowed with anger, then said, "We know nothin' about those damn guys."

Meanwhile, other members of the assault crew scoured the Chapmann premises for weapons. They found six rifles and two pistols in the main bedroom closet. Cole came in from helping search the grounds and ordered two men to search the underground chamber and pack up all they find. Darren noticed that Ron Chapmann jumped slightly, then glanced at his wife when he heard Colonel Cole give the order. Jill's eyes widened. They didn't think the feds knew about the underground facility.

In the underground chambers, the team found a few weapons and a large map showing the sites of booby-traps. In addition, they found a few files detailing the extremist movement's membership, plans and activities over the past five years.

Once Cole's team secured Ron Chapmann's place, the other two helicopters lifted off and took their assigned positions near the other homes. The team responsible for the raid on Ron's brother Rod's house sat down on the little road outside the gate leading to the house. The team crept close to the house and, using heat-sensing devices and night vision goggles, determined that all the occupants were asleep. The dog slept in a small-enclosed porch off the back kitchen. Two men moved in to disconnect the security system while the other two sedated the two ponies housed in a barn, sixty yards west of the house. Three men waited for Rod's early morning visit to feed the horses, while the rest found secure positions at the front of the house.

The third team, responsible for apprehending Hardy West, faced a somewhat more difficult challenge. They also had to land on the road several hundred yards east of the house. Colonel Cole left Ron Chapmann's place and flew down to join those encircling the West home. They knew a great deal about the security system surrounding the property. The team moved to their respective positions at the edge of the forest surrounding the West home.

As the sky began to lighten, the men to moved closer. One crept in from the west and one from the east. A few minutes later all hell broke loose. Lights went on, land mines exploded and a siren screamed a staccato warning that echoed out across the pine forest. The other members of the assault team rushed the house. Booby-traps exploded in every direction. Only two Special Forces men reached the house. One immediately kicked open the front door and stepped back in time to miss a hailstorm of bullets.

The other kicked open the back door and met a similar barrage. The Wests had awakened and, heavily armed, were prepared to meet the assault. The soldiers retreated to the protection of the forest.

"Stay down," Cole uttered. "Damn! Let's get our wounded out'a here." Of the five hit by mine fragments, three managed to crawl to the safety of the forest. Two remained in the yard, but Cole couldn't tell much about the condition of either. Several crawled out to their fallen comrades to find them both unconscious and seriously injured. They had almost reached the safety of the forest with the first injured colleague when powerful yard lights came on and bullets began ricocheting around them.

"Knock out those lights," Cole yelled. Good lord, he thought. I sure didn't want this to happen. We've got to secure the area and back off before more get hurt. Finally, they managed to knock out the lights. "Okay, let's get our wounded out'a here." Three had fragments in their backs and arms, but the damage did not appear serious. A medic patched them up and they returned to help with the assault. Two seemed seriously hurt. The medic told Cole, "We've got to get'em out'a here. They need more than we can give them."

"Okay," Cole said. "Get'em to Fairchild quick. And have Fairchild dispatch some backup units. Our cover's blown."

The lights came on in Rod Chapmann's house as the siren blasts from Hardy West's home echoed across the forest. The assault team stayed hidden and waited. They could see people peeking out from behind window blinds. Finally, the yard lights came on and someone opened the back door to let the family dog out. The dog ran around the yard sniffing and barking. He finally squatted down, urinated, ran some more and then headed back to the house to be let in. Rod opened the door, then walked out on the back porch. He carried a rifle and scanned the area. As he went back into the house he said to his wife, "Maybe that siren went off accidentally. I told Hardy the damn thing would be a menace." Then he shut the door.

"Wow, he must not have heard those gun shots over the noise of the sirens," one of Cole's men said.

"Unbelievable!" another said softly.

In about thirty minutes, Rod Chapmann came back outside, still carrying his rifle, and headed for the barn. He clicked on a large flashlight, opened the barn door and stepped inside. Immediately the agents grabbed him, threw him to the ground and cuffed him. While an FBI agent read him his rights, the Special Forces members quietly moved to secure the house. Several entered through the back door and found Doris Chapmann at the kitchen table leisurely drinking a cup of coffee and listening to the radio. She looked up in shock.

"Please don't hurt my boys," she cried softly.

"Where are they?" one of the team members asked.

"They're still sleeping."

"Can we trust you to quietly wake them and get them dressed?"

"Yes," she said, fighting back the tears.

"We only have a warrant for your husband. Be thinking of where we can take you and the boys so you'll be taken care of."

"Well, I've got a sister in Boise. Can we go there?"

"Sure."

Cole then had Rod Chapmann flown to Fairchild AFB at Spokane and placed under light security until the Bureau could determine his future. Doris Chapmann was taken to Boise. The Ron Chapmanns also went to Fairchild, but were placed in a more secure facility.

Darren had not been able to get Ron Chapmann to talk. One of the FBI agents even offered a lighter sentence in exchange for his testimony against other movement leaders. No deal. Ron refused to even confirm his own name. Jill Chapmann followed suit. Chapmann turned to Darren as the FBI agents led him away. "I hope you find White and Boorgers. They're responsible for all the killing that's gone on over the months."

Darren nodded. "That's well and good, but it would help a great deal if you would give us details of their responsibility."

Ron did not reply.

Meanwhile, a standoff continued at Hardy West's place. The assault team encountered some unexpected booby-traps but the Wests couldn't get away.

In addition to a medical team, Cole had requested a tank with a specially constructed dragline system for clearing minefields. A large Chinook helicopter flew in from Nevada with the proper equipment and sat it down on the road outside the West home by late morning. The three-man team accompanying the rig got an aerial view of the premises, then studied the grounds from the cover of the pine forest.

"Well, what's the verdict?" Cole asked.

"Colonel, that doesn't seem to be a large field," the Sergeant in charge of the operation responded. "Quite honestly, we can't figure out why in the world a guy would create a monster like that when he's got a little four-year old girl who might stumble into it. How'd your guys miss all that?"

"I'm not sure. It didn't show up on any of our scanners. Let's clean it up. I don't want anyone else hurt."

"We'll have it done in about thirty minutes," the Sergeant said.

"How are you going to get in there to drag that thing?" Cole asked.

"Oh, just watch." The bulldozer-like machine headed up the little driveway to West's house. It tore down a number of trees as it bulldozed a wider path. Assault team members watching heard a number of muffled pops and booms as the tank made four large loops around the house detonating the rest of the mines. The largest concentration seemed to be in a twelve-yard swath some twenty yards from the house. A later count revealed sixteen holes. The tank then rumbled back down the road about one hundred yards and the sergeant came back to Cole and asked, "Anything else we can do for you, Colonel? We'll be happy to drive right into that ole house."

"Yeah, I know you would. But we've got a small girl and her mother in there and we don't want them hurt."

"Good luck, Colonel. We'll head back."

"You bet. And thanks!"

"Our pleasure. We aim to please!" The two men laughed and parted. In a few minutes Cole could see the large Chinook heading out over the forest with its load dangling below. He took a battery-operated speaker and addressed the West house.

"Mr. and Mrs. West. This is Colonel Cole of the U.S. Special Forces. The FBI is with us and we have a warrant for Hardy West. We don't want to harm anyone. Why don't you put down your weapons and come out before anyone else gets hurt? We have Ron and Rod Chapmann in custody. It's over. Nothing good will come from postponing the inevitable." There was no response from the house.

"Where's Hopkins?" Cole called.

"He went back to Fairchild with the Chapmanns."

"Well, get me the head of the FBI team. This seems like his cup of tea." Within an hour, a helicopter delivered an agent on the road adjacent to the West's property.

The agent approached Cole on the run. Cole looked at him, then said, "We've got a problem here. They're not even answering fire now, and some of the troops could have been hit if West had wanted to do that. As the agent in charge here, I thought you might want to appeal to his sense of importance and get him to talk. What do you think?"

"I'm willing to give it a shot. Do you have a white flag?"

"Oh, surely we've got a white tee-shirt we can put on a stick that'll serve that purpose," Cole said. One of Cole's men got a white cloth from the medic and affixed it to a branch cut from a tree. As the agent took the flag, Cole said, "Here, study this layout of the house and, goddamn it, get a flak jacket under that shirt."

The agent then crept as close to the house as possible under cover of the forest, then raised his white flag and called out, "Mr. and Mrs. West, this is FBI. I'm coming up to talk and I don't have any weapons." He rose from his hiding place, hands high in the air and screamed, "I'm unarmed!" He waved the white flag and slowly walked toward the front door.

The agent arrived at the porch, took off the bullhorn attached to a thong around his neck and gently set it down on the edge of the porch. Then he removed his handkerchief from his back left pocket and wiped the beads of sweat from his face. Facing the front door he yelled his message again. Still no answer. He banged on the front door while keeping his body to the side as he had been taught, praying all the time that high-powered bullets would not come zinging through the timber siding. He was also aware that the door could be booby-trapped. No answer. He peeked inside the door's small window. No one. He reached down and turned the doorknob gently. The door opened. Using his right foot, he shoved it completely open and yelled again. No answer. "I'm coming in. Don't shoot. I'm unarmed. I just want to talk."

The agent held his hands high while waving the white flag gently and declaring his mission as he walked across the living room floor toward the dining room. He peered in carefully. Empty. He let out a deep sigh and noticed for the first time how fast his heart pumped. Sweat dripped down his eyebrows even though the outside temperature was in the low thirties.

He leaned against the doorsill of the dining room, then called out again. Nothing but silence greeted his pleas.

He eased around a door and into the kitchen. The floorboards squeaked. He jumped. Empty cartridges littered the vinyl kitchen floor. Once in the kitchen he strode across to the back door window. He could see into the small utility porch and out into the back yard where three Special Forces troops were standing at the tree line. He then cautiously crept down a hallway to the bedrooms and bath on his left, continuing to call out as he worked his way slowly and carefully through all the bedrooms and the bath.

He even checked the closets, noticed that a number of drawers looked pretty messy. Then he went to the front door and waved at Colonel Cole. "Come on in, it's empty!"

The assault teams quietly converged on the small three-bedroom house. "Where'd they go?" Cole asked. "Check the attic and watch for trap doors in the floors. They may have an escape tunnel."

Soon one of the men called Cole and the others to the bathroom. "Colonel, look at this." The portable linen closet slid away to reveal a four by four-foot hole in the floor. Cole sent for flashlights and several volunteers took on the task of pursuing the tunnel to its end.

"Why didn't this tunnel show up on the satellite's imaging?" Cole asked.

One of the technical guys answered. "It wouldn't unless there's someone or something emitting heat from within or the tunnel had something in it of a different density."

The handheld radio soon came alive. "Colonel, we've found the tunnel exit. It's about three hundred yards straight north of the house. There's a crude set of steps up and into an old hallowed-out stump. The stump has been fitted with a wooden lid and made to look natural. I don't believe we would have found it wandering around out here."

"Any signs of the Wests?"

"No, sir."

"Stay and keep an eye on it. Look around in a systematic fashion and see if you can pick up their trail. Look for tire tracks. They might have kept some type of old vehicle there for just this type of an emergency."

"Yes, sir."

"Well, we blew that. And we got some injured. If we lose any of those people I'll have that West guy's hide on my wall before I die," Cole declared. "Let's get the clean up crew in here to go over everything. Then let's seal the house. Blow that tunnel once you have enough pictures. The FBI can chase the Wests. Our job's done here."

# 18

**WASHINGTON, D.C.**
Monday, March 31

The sun streamed in Darren's bedroom window. He rolled over, painfully peeking at the clock. It read eight thirty a.m. The flight from Phoenix had landed in Washington just after midnight. Exhausted and sore, he felt like he could sleep for a week. He sat on the edge of the bed for a few minutes, yawning, scratching his head and stretching. "Oh, Lord," he said.

He clicked on the bedroom's portable TV and heard the newscaster saying, "how many have been killed, Andrea?"

"Ralph, Fairchild's command says an assessment is currently taking place. Rumors suggest extensive damage to buildings, planes and other equipment."

"Andrea, we'll come back to you "

At that moment Darren heard an explosion in the background and saw the reporter cringe as the blast knocked her from view. Then the network lost the transmission. The news anchor reappeared, and said, "This is Ralph O'Conner at CNN, Atlanta. We don't know what caused the loss of contact with Andrea in Spokane. Now we go live to Pete Williams in San Diego. Pete, what's happened there?"

Darren, watching fires billowing in the distance as the camera panned the area, realized that his whole body had tensed, and he had been holding his breath. As he exhaled, he could feel his heart race. He sat on the edge of the bed as he continued to watch flashing lights of fire trucks and ambulances dance in the distance, their sirens, horns and screams blaring.

The San Diego reporter raised his voice to be heard over the din and said, "Ralph, it's five-forty in the morning here. Missiles started raining down on the

Naval Base about an hour ago. Bombs exploded in buildings and on ships. Chaos, utter chaos, is the only way to summarize the conditions"

Darren turned the TV off, sat in silence for a few moments, then shook his head in disbelief as a slight nausea washed over him.

Upon arrival at the office, Darren found Burcks with an office full of National Security staff, FBI, U.S. Marshals, CIA, watching two television sets. Burcks' popularity with other Washington bureaucrats had not escaped Darren's attention over the months. He seemed to be the Papa Bear to whom most came for advice and help. Burcks saw Darren at the door. He yelled, "Darren, come on in. Bring a chair from another office. Looks like your buddies are still at it."

Darren got a wicker chair from his window table and returned to Burcks's office, sitting just inside the door. He noticed Lenora Carlson nearby and nodded a greeting. A somber, almost funereal pall pervaded the room. No one had smiled at Burcks's attempted humor. Leaning toward Lenora he asked in a whispered voice, "What's the count so far?"

"Sixteen western facilities, twenty-eight in the Midwest, nine in the south and twelve in the Northeast," then sighing, Carlson said, "and it's only nine fifty a.m. But the good news is we've been able to stop over one hundred other acts of violence."

"That's great," Darren said

She continued as she referred to her notes. "Across the country we've caught thirty-six vehicles carrying explosives and apprehended fourteen assassination teams before they could carry out their tasks. The other incidents represent explosives found before they could detonate."

"Our nation's worst nightmare," Burcks said, as he looked toward Darren. "My God, how vulnerable we are! We've got every available law enforcement officer at county, state and federal levels on duty. And our own citizens try to shoot us down in the streets like dogs."

"Well-trained and armed citizens," a CIA agent said. "And all the pundits kept saying the war against the Al-Qaida terrorists unified the nation. So much for wishful thinking."

The ensuing silence was broken by Burcks asking, "What have you guys at the Agency done to cut off those Russian weapons sources?"

"We've made a little headway," said the agent, with a smirk. "A few days ago a number of Russian arms warehouses and factories went up in smoke." He snapped his fingers on both hands and motioned upward. "The Russian government is blaming Muslim separatists." One of the CIA agents threw a clenched fist in the air as a sign of victory.

"Damn good," Burcks said.

"How unfortunate," Darrren murmured, not expecting to be heard. "There is a God, after all." But the noise of other chatter had ceased unexpectedly, but Darren's words echoed throughout the room. The others glanced in his direction and smiled.

The CIA agent looked at Darren. "Yeah, let's leave it at that."

Darren took the hint. This CIA activity fell into the category of plausible denial.

"And then," the agent continued, "a few weeks ago, one of the Russian's key weapons brokers, a guy named Yuri Tavanovich living in Marseilles, contacted our Paris office and asked for asylum in return for information on the sale of weapons to the Arab terrorists."

"What did he give us?" Carlson asked.

"Oh, he detailed his contact with an Arab guy living in Turkey named Ghaleb and described their meeting in Tunisia and the whole nine yards."

Another silence fell over the group, broken again by Burcks as he looked back at Darren. "We've picked up most of the extremists' top leadership to date. Some are television evangelists, and they're screaming like banshees. But we've got enough evidence to put'em away for life. They'll probably set up television studios in prison and continue to bilk the American public out of millions of dollars. But, dad-gum-it, we haven't caught White or Boorgers. Is that right, Agent Carlson?"

"Right," Carlson picked up. "Latest reports indicate that White and Boorgers floated around the extremist underground for a few days, but when we closed in, poof, they disappeared."

"Uh-oh," Lockney muttered, "shades of Osama bin Laden!"

Carlson continued. "We believe they've left the country."

"Where would they go?" National Security Council Attorney, Russ McDonald, asked.

"They could find sanctuary in the Mideast," Darren offered.

"Certainly could," the CIA agent said. "The Arabs have a lot invested in White and Boorgers. They might want to protect them until they can find a way to inject them back into our system."

Burcks said, "I don't think so. Those guys hate the Arabs. They wanted the arms bad enough to meet with them, but the idea of having to live among those guys wouldn't appeal to 'em. Naw, they'd go in another direction."

Turning to NSC's Ron Cox, the man responsible for coordinating media activity out of the White House, Darren asked, "How's the administration doing on the public relations front?" Every eye turned on Cox.

"Six staff members are doing nothing but cranking out news of terrorist activities and the government's response across the nation. The media darlings use most of the data but still tend to put their own spin on it. I must say, however, that the White House reporters are doing a fine job. They just don't like to feel they're being manipulated. We do a live news conference every few days. Polls show ninety-two percent of the people are appalled by all the violence. They can't figure out what's triggered this fanatical activity. We have people calling and writing who want us to line up the culprits and shoot them. No trials."

Jo Clark stepped into the room at that comment, "Darren you have an urgent phone call. It's your friend in Austin."

Darren glanced at Burcks, who nodded. "I'll take it in my office." He stepped across the hall. "Mo, what's up?"

"One of my sources says that White and Boorgers have been orchestrating the attacks from Nuevo Laredo, Mexico."

"How're they doing that?" Darren quickly reached for the pad on his desk and began taking notes.

"From what I understand they drive across the border to Laredo and use a public phone to call three or four of those phantom cells. In turn, each cell calls ten or twelve more and so forth and so on. A ripple effect. The message is coded and also goes out on the Internet."

"Do you know what Internet site or sites?"

"No. Neither did this guy. I asked him to find out, but since he's not computer literate, they may suspect something if he starts asking too many questions."

"That's for sure, but we need to know. Do what you can. What about the telephone message code? Can he get any handle on that?"

"He'll try, but I doubt it."

"Does he know where these guys are hiding in Nuevo Laredo? Hell, we'll pay the guy for more information."

"No, don't get into this. All this guy knows is that he's helping me with a story. If he thinks I'm passing info on to you, he'll bolt for the South Seas! He's still one of them."

"Okay. Still, see if you can get more details. I'll pass the info on to the right folks here."

"He also said they planned to shut down the nation's computers on April nineteenth. Some new kind of virus. And the next attacks are planned for April twenty first. I think that's it."

"That's great information, Mo. Thanks. We couldn't do without your sources. I suppose you're going to want the President to dedicate a building in your name or build a monument to you next to Jefferson or something."

"Well, now that you've mentioned it."

"Ah, birds, go stand on your head in the corner!" Both men laughed.

Darren imparted Mo's information to the group gathered in Burcks' office. "We'll get a team in Nuevo Laredo immediately," Carlson said, as she raced from Burcks's office.

"Do it quietly!" Darren yelled. "Let's not get my friend in trouble with his contact."

"Will do!" Lenora shouted from down the hall. "Carrasco and McKinney can head this up. McKinney speaks fluent Spanish."

"Who's the key to the computer people?" Burcks asked, glancing at the agents sitting around the room.

Darren looked at Lockney. "I guess that would be Chris Otwell at Justice."

Burcks then said to Lockney, "Sam, call Deputy Director Wade and tell him what Darren's heard and see how he wants to handle the process."

"I'll do that." Lockney started for the door. The others gradually filtered out.

Darren turned to Burcks, "What about preparations for the assaults on the twenty first?"

Burcks had walked to the window and seemed to be lost in thought. It took a few moments, but he turned his head toward Darren and said, "Oh, yeah, the twenty first. I'll talk to the President about a quiet move toward high alert." He turned back to the window. "I could swear we've been hearing explosions over the last hour. The floor trembled. Did you hear or feel anything?"

"No, sir."

"Maybe I've developed a case of paranoia. Maybe old soldiers reach a point where the past gets mixed up with the present. It faintly reminded me of heavy artillery." Then he turned, shook his head as if to clear it, rubbed his forehead and returned to his desk and a stack of papers.

Darren smiled, and started toward his office, only to be stopped by Jo Clark, who motioned him back as she headed for Burcks's office.

"General, I think you'll want to turn your TV on. The Supreme Court Building has just been hit."

"Oh, crap!" he said. Through the jostling, blurry screen, he could see a camera crew running toward the front entrance to the Supreme Court. The audio picked up hard breathing and frantic directions given by someone in the background. Rocks and other litter filled the area in front of the building on First Street. Smoke and fire billowed from doors and windows. The roof seemed blown off. Finally, the crew set up across 1st Street, a few yards south of Maryland Avenue. A young woman, wind blown and out of breath, stepped in front of the camera with her back to the burning building.

"This is Marilyn Randel. We have been told that explosives ripped through the Supreme Court Building just a few minutes ago." She smoothed her hair as she continued to talk. "Fortunately, the Court did not meet today, and most of the justices had not come in to their offices. However, a large number of staff is feared killed in the blast. Firemen on the scene believe most of the building will be gutted before they can put out the resulting blaze."

Burcks said, "My God, that's what I've been hearing and feeling!"

Darren blurted out, "The whole building's ablaze!" Burcks sat in silence. Jo Clark stood by the door, both hands to her face. Tears running down her cheeks as she turned and left.

The CNN report continued. "D.C.'s Fire Chief, Archie Bohannon, agreed to speak to us for a brief moment. Chief, how bad is it?"

Soot already covered the fire chief's white bunker coat and helmet. He removed his glasses to clean them, as he said, "Oh, it's bad. We'll be lucky to save much, if anything."

"Any idea how it started?"

"Well, it took an enormous amount of explosives to do this much damage. We talked with some people who reported hearing deep explosions about fifteen minutes ago, but thought they came from trucks or cars backfiring. The fire spread quickly and, coincidentally, fairly broadly, which suggests that explosive charges had been set deep within the basement of the building."

Darren and Burcks went to the office windows and could see the black smoke billowing in the distance. In the background they heard the TV reporter saying, "Thank you, Mr. Bohannon. We'll let you get back to work. And now, we are going to talk to Alice Stevens, a secretary for Representative John Foster of Wyoming. She was running an errand for her boss and had just come out of the Library of Congress across the street when the explosions took place. Ms. Stevens, tell us what you saw."

Trembling, she said, "I just came out of the library when I heard this dull thudding sound and the ground shook. I first thought of the underground trains, but the shaking was just too violent." The camera backed away to show Ms. Stevens extending her arms and rapidly shaking her fists to demonstrate the shaking ground. Darren and Burcks could see people running in the background.

"What happened then?" the reporter asked.

The camera zoomed in to catch Ms. Stevens's face as she said, "I glanced toward the noise and saw the Supreme Court Building lifting off its foundation." The camera panned the area, showing the Supreme Court Building engulfed in flames and smoke. Ms. Stevens continued, "It settled back down, and dust, rock and smoke just spewed everywhere. Just like the World Trade Center."

The camera returned to Ms. Stevens. She looked down at her clothing and tried to remove pieces of debris from her hair. "Oh, God, I look a mess."

The reporter asked, "Did you see anyone leave the building prior to the explosion?"

"No, I didn't even look over there. I seem to remember seeing some people at the bottom of the steps when I first glanced in that direction. But I'm not sure. If I did, I don't know what happened to them. I just couldn't believe it! Oh, my Lord, who would do such a thing? And where's all the security we supposedly put in place after the World Trade Center mess?"

"Thank you, Ms. Stevens." Turning back toward the camera, the reporter said, "Gordon, needless to say, this is a mess. Another sordid chapter in what has, unfortunately, become a way of life in America."

Darren and Burcks stood immobile as they watched the coverage. Finally, Burcks said, "It's time the President asked Congress for some special powers."

"What'd you have in mind?" Darren asked.

"I'm not sure, but, for one thing, it's obvious that one of the most revered targets for these nuts is the U.S. Capitol. Our security isn't working against an unseen internal enemy. We've got to do something differently. No one gets in or out of the central federal district, as yet to be defined, without a pass."

"How do we know we can trust all the Federal employees?" Darren asked. "Whoever set the explosives to the Supreme Court Building knew what to do."

"We don't. We have to rely on justice to ferret out the traitors in our midst without turning it into a McCarthy-type side show."

Just then Jo Clark stuck her head in Burcks' door. "Darren, Agent Carlson for you. She says it's important."

Darren returned to his office and picked up the phone.

"Darren, Ron Chapmann wants to talk to you."

"Why me?"

"Seems as though he trusts you. He liked your style during the assault on his hide-away."

After jotting down the number, Darren asked, "You sound depressed, is everything all right on your side?"

"Well, we win some, we lose some. You know how that is."

"Unfortunately," Darren answered. He moved over to his window and looked out at the traffic as he spoke. "It's strange isn't it? We're engaged in a war that's never going away. The world, and even our own nation, is full of people who hate and want to kill. Many are even willing to die in the process of killing others."

"True," Carlson responded.

"Yet," Darren continued. "I'm looking out my window at the traffic. People are going about their normal routines as if everything's fine. Last night I noticed people shopping and dining as though nothing had happened."

"Yes, it's surreal, isn't it?" Carlson answered. "Wars don't arrive as they used to. They sneak up on a people and eat away, like a huge nest of termites. It happened to Lebanon and Vietnam. Now here. The enemy could be your neighbor—or anyone you run into on the streets or at the mall. A bomb can go off in one's office, a ball game, busy street, or anywhere else. It's crazy."

"Yeah, I've noticed that too. In a way, I hope they are sleepless and tired. Misery loves company! Speaking of sleepless, I've got to go. Talk with you later."

Darren then asked Jo Clark to get Chapmann on the line. Thirty minutes later Darren's phone rang. "Darren, Mr. Chapmann's on the line.

"Mr. Hopkins, I've got some information that might be helpful. But I want something in return."

"What's that?" Darren asked.

"If I give testimony against White, Boorgers and all their Washington cronies, what will the Attorney General or President do for my family?"

"I'm not sure. All I can promise is that I'll agree to give that information to my boss, General Burcks. He'll take it to the President with a recommendation. I'm just a flunky aide."

"That may be. But I'm gambling they value your advice."

"I see. Well, I guess I'll be gambling on the usefulness of your information. If it isn't, then I lose credibility. And you'll have a difficult time getting anyone's attention in the future. We both have a stake in this."

"I understand that," Chapmann said.

"Then let's quit wasting time," Darren urged. "Tell me what you've got, and I'll do the best I can for you."

"First, promise that my wife and I will be protected during our confinement."

"That shouldn't be a problem."

"Promise me that," Chapmann demanded.

"I promise to do what I can." Darren could hear Chapmann's irritable sigh. "What's the big secret?"

Chapmann's voice dropped to a whisper. "Boorgers, White and all those guys you picked up at the Ship Ranch in New Mexico are part of a large group across this nation dedicated to bringing down the federal government."

"We know that," Darren responded.

Chapmann continued, "Boorgers and White got phone calls from Washington at the conclusion of every task force meeting, every White House staff meeting, every FBI and CIA staff meeting and on and on. Those guys have friends in every federal agency who keep them informed of everything. This is also true at the state level."

"Do you have any names?"

"Go back over the last month's phone calls out of the top dogs of each federal agency and see who's talking to Boorgers, White and the others. Look specifically at the following phone numbers." Chapmann gave Darren a dozen phone numbers, then said, "You better figure out how to investigate without using the usual bureaucratic process. Boorgers and his friends will block any investigation that gets close to them or their supporters in the federal government."

"Okay," Darren answered.

Chapmann continued, "When any of us wanted White, Boorgers and the others, these are the numbers we called. Look at the President's top aides. See whom they called on a daily basis. Look at their bank accounts. See where the money's going. The network will astound you."

"Do you want to name names?"

"No. I want to be able to deny giving you any names. You have everything you need. Just do the research. Let's just say that you'll find key players in the different agencies I mentioned earlier. And don't ignore members of the U.S. Supreme Court, as well as some of your most powerful members of Congress. In addition, look at the wealthiest people in Dallas, Denver, Houston, Kansas City and Atlanta. They heavily bankrolled all the activities."

"Mr. Chapmann, we don't want to get into witch hunting. We had one of those back in the early nineteen fifties, and we don't want to go down that path again."

Chapmann's voice became steely. "Shit, you won't have to. Put the network together. Follow the phone records and money. You'll have all the evidence you need."

"Okay," Darren said. "We'll do it." There was a pause as if Chapmann had reached the end of his story. Darren then asked, "Do you know where Boorgers and White are hiding?"

"I honestly don't know. You may not believe this, but these guys used me. Most of the people I associated with hated government of any kind and just wanted to defend themselves. These ex-military are the ones that pushed the proactive war."

"Anything else you want to tell me?" Darren asked.

"Nope, that's it. Now you fulfill your part of the bargain."

NUEVO LARDO, MEXICO
Wednesday, April 2

Dr. Carlos Hernandez Espinoza DeLeon, one of the finest plastic surgeons in Mexico, shook hands with his two patients as they left his private medical clinic on Hidalgo Street in the suburbs of Nuevo Laredo. "Your surgery went well. The redness will disappear over time. Keep the salve on for at least two more weeks. If there are any problems, you have my phone numbers. Good luck to both of you." The two men thanked him and the larger of the two men handed the doctor an envelope containing a cashier's check for one hundred thousand dollars.

As Ryan B. Boorgers, alias Roy Horton, and William J. White, alias John

Vinton, climbed into the car sent to take them back across the border to the United States, the driver handed each a manila envelope. "Here are your new passports, credit cards, driver's licenses, business cards, check books, plane tickets and new biographies. You are each to commit your new biography to memory."

Boorgers had lost seventeen pounds since entering the Nuevo Laredo clinic to become Roy Horton. His original thinning brown hair had been dyed coal black, which matched his bushy black eyebrows. "Getting used to a totally new identity is going to take some time," he murmured to his colleague.

"Sure is," White responded. "I think our wives and children will have an even tougher time getting used to our new names."

"That's if we get to see them again," Boorgers said.

"I certainly intend to see my family again!"

"Of course. But our own mothers wouldn't recognize us now. I hope it's all worth it."

The men rode through the streets of Nuevo Laredo in silence, each lost in his own thoughts as they studied their new identity papers. White had also lost weight. His six foot, two-inch frame looked thin. He felt thin. His usual burr-cut silver hair, now dark brown, had grown out. Both now wore glasses. They could have been mistaken for academics, or government agents in their new navy suits.

They crossed the border without difficulty. The driver dropped them at the Laredo airport where Roy Horton and John Vinton caught a flight to the Dallas-Fort Worth airport and disappeared in the crowds.

WASHINGTON, D.C.
Thursday, April 3

While Boorgers and White returned to the American landscape, Federal computer programmers worked to prevent extremist hackers from shutting down the system. Darren arrived at the task force meeting late. A computer specialist was explaining the nation's systems.

"Lenora, what's happening?" Darren whispered.

"The new firewall systems our computer folks put in place seem to work. We had a report this morning that several Western military installations crashed, but our computer people discovered that they had ignored the recent directives and had not applied the patches. Some Pentagon staff flew out and spent the night making the corrections. They're also investigating the officer in charge out there. It's four fifteen p.m. We think we've beat'em."

"I suspect the patriots will continue to find ways to break in and shut things down. Don't you?" Darren asked.

"Yeah. But we think we can beat them at that game. We'll keep our best computer people on this."

The next morning George Burcks leaned back in his chair and listened as Darren reported on his visit with Chapmann and the status of the computer systems. As Darren finished, he handed a copy of the Chapmann interview tape to Burcks, then moved to the window overlooking the White House. Several minutes passed, but finally Burcks said, "We'll keep this business of traitors within the administration between us until I visit with the President. Don't write me any memos, don't take any notes, and don't breathe a word of Chapmann's tips to anyone under any circumstances." He turned, crossed his arms over his chest, stared at Darren and said, "Frankly, I knew this might be the case, but I didn't think it would prove as extensive as Chapmann claims. And he's right about our attempts to find traitors in our midst. All attempts have led nowhere. We've got to figure out how to investigate without alerting them."

"I'm probably speaking out of turn, but do you think you can convince the President not to share this information with anyone on his staff until we can find out who's a traitor? I sense from Chapmann that there are problems with the White House staff."

"I don't know. That'll be touchy. Some of those people have been with him since he first decided to run for office. As they say, they brung him to the dance."

"How can I help?" Darren asked.

"Well, we need to get our hands on the financial records of White House staff without alerting anyone," said Burcks. "Do you think you can trust Carlson?"

"I think so," Darren replied. "At least I hope so. She seems totally professional. As far as I can tell, there's not a political aspiration in her body. She's certainly not part of the 'good ole boy' network for which the bureau is infamous."

"See if you can work with her. From what you've told me she is a by the book person, so she may not be able to help you gather information that isn't cleared up the line. Make sure you have a clear understanding of that before you use her, or we'll both be in the soup."

"Yes, sir."

"As to phone records, we can handle that," Burcks muttered. "Call Patricia Axtell at the phone company. Ms. Clark has her phone number. Tell her I need them. She'll understand."

"Won't we need to get authorization from the Justice Department for such an investigation?"

"No. I'll take the risk."

"Okay." Then, sensing that the meeting had ended, Darren lowered his head and walked out.

Darren asked Jo Clark to help prepare a list of high-level bureaucrats, then called Ms. Axtell and arranged to meet at her office to discuss the project. He found her a willing partner in the search. She volunteered to run an analytical computer scan for each of the people Darren submitted. Her system would rank calls by number and frequency and indicate the name of those receiving the calls. Darren felt like he had hit a gold mine. Her staff could produce results on one hundred names within a few minutes. The fact that President Evans had reduced his White House staff made the task easier.

He returned to help Jo Clark finish the list and waited for Burcks to return from a meeting at the State Department. Burcks needed to review the list before he delivered it to the phone company. Since Burcks would not get to review the list until late in the day, Darren decided to use the intervening time to meet with Agent Lenora Carlson. He arranged to meet her at the Willard Hotel coffee shop at three thirty.

Darren and Lenora took a corner table and discussed the task force. Finally, sensing that Darren had something on his mind, Lenora said, "What's up? You look troubled."

After a pause that demonstrated his discomfort, Darren looked around to make sure no one could overhear their conversation, then leaned forward, arms on the table. "I've know you've been concerned about security leaks. Every time an operation failed, you raised this issue and it got shoved aside. No one seemed willing to deal with it. Now, how strong are your feelings?"

"Pretty strong," Lenora said, as she narrowed her eyes and rose, back straight as though ready to throw a punch.

"How willing are you to stick your neck out?" Darren asked.

"There's no need to play games. Tell me what you have in mind, and I'll give you my word that if I can't participate, for whatever reason, I'll forget this conversation took place."

"Fair enough." Darren then reported his conversations with Ron Chapmann and General Burcks.

"Well, I'm not surprised. There's been a high level of frustration within the group all along. Nothing we did had much effect until we moved to small units of operation. But, let me ask you how trustworthy are members of the NSC?"

"That's fair. Fortunately, Burcks is a straight shooter. Loyal as they come. That doesn't mean all members of the NSC are. We've got to do our homework and find out precisely who the key players really are. Until then, I've been ordered to keep this activity secret. Burcks gave me permission to talk to you. Want to help?"

"I'd like to, but before I commit, let's be clear about what 'help' means." They spent some time discussing strategies. Carlson finally agreed to participate, but with the understanding that her name never be used in any communication. Further, they agreed to minimize their contact with each other lest it draw attention. No tracks. Both felt that task force meetings provided enough time to share information. Paper records were to be kept in Burcks's office under lock and key. Since Darren had already arranged the analysis of phone records, Lenora agreed to seek bank records of White House personnel and other key government figures. Most of that, she admitted, existed in the Bureau's data bank. She had to figure out how to access the data without calling attention to her activity.

Meanwhile, Burcks worked at seeing the President of the United States. He finally caught him ten minutes before he had to meet a bi-partisan Senate committee studying the renewal of the People's Republic of China's most favored nation status. He didn't waste time as he reported the sum and substance of Darren's visit with Chapmann and noted the high incidence of assumed security leakage in all efforts to curb the super patriot's activities. "Mr. President, we need to meet when you have more time to review personnel and agree upon a means of smoking these traitors out."

The President got up from his desk, walked to the window looking out over the White House lawn, crossed his arms on his chest and said nothing for several minutes. Burcks rose from his chair at the same time. Finally, President Evans turned to Burcks and said, "I use to wonder what kind of dummies ran this country. After several years in office, I believe I've got it narrowed down but can't decide. Are they smart imbeciles or dumb geniuses?" Burcks smiled. The President pushed the button that summoned his secretary.

"Ms. Baker, General Burcks and I will have breakfast tomorrow in my office at six thirty. It takes priority over any other time conflict. We will be through by seven thirty. I don't want us to be interrupted by anyone. Period." He looked sternly at her for emphasis.

"Yes sir."

"Thanks for coming General, see you in the morning."

"Yes, sir."

Burcks immediately called Darren. "Prepare a briefing paper setting forth the aborted attempts by the task force to circumscribe the domestic terrorists. Second, bullet the key points of the Chapmann interview. Then set forth a strategy for identifying those within the administration and federal agencies actively supporting the terrorists. I've got to be prepared to report to the President first thing in the morning."

Meanwhile, Darren felt a sense of relief in the knowledge that he had been preparing such a report since his Chapmann interview.

# 19

**WASHINGTON, D.C.**
**OFFICE OF THE PRESIDENT**
Friday, April 4

Burcks arrived at the White House at precisely 6:30 a.m. When ushered into the Oval Office, the President was reading a morning newspaper at a small dining table set for breakfast in front of his desk. "Good morning. Please sit down," the President said.

Burcks took a seat and handed the President a copy of Darren's report. "Please order some breakfast as I look at this," the President said.

The President sipped his coffee as he studied the documents, shaking his head from time to time.

Looking over at Burcks, he said, "Not a pretty picture, is it? When will you have the phone and bank records?"

"Should have them today," Burcks replied .

"Let's see what they tell us before we rush to judgment. My first concern is the Attorney General. I've known Matt Dial since grade school. If he's in on this conspiracy, I'll fold my tent and slink away into the night. If I've learned anything during my brief sojourn in politics, it's that power can corrupt the best of people. You have to constantly watch your backside. Socrates rightly noted that 'the shifts of Fortune test the reliability of friends.'"

"Mr. President, I don't think the Attorney General's involved," Burcks said. "I certainly hope not. We'll need his cooperation rooting out all the skunks in the hen house."

"We'll see. Meantime, let's keep the list of those actively involved in the search as short as possible. Who do you have working on this?"

"Only my chief aide, Darren Hopkins. He's attentive to detail and can be trusted."

"If anyone else is added I'll make the decision."

"Mr. President, there's one FBI agent we need on our team. Darren's worked with her on the terrorism task force. Agent Lenora Carlson saw the leaks early and has been very vocal about them."

"What do you know about her?"

Burcks whipped out Carlson's bio from a manila file folder. The President scanned it then handed it back. "Okay. But keep an eye on her in case she breaks. Tell her she has my support if her superiors get wind of her involvement and give her trouble."

"Yes, sir."

"General, we've only got a short time to clean this mess up." As the President spoke, he rang for his secretary. "Ms. Baker, give General Burcks' calls top priority. When he or a Darren Hopkins need to talk with me, put them on my calendar immediately. They'll only ask if the matter's extremely urgent."

"Yes, sir," she replied, handing him the President's private phone number.

"Okay, General. Get back to me with a report on the results of the phone and bank records as quickly as possible. And, by the way," his voice fell in volume, "don't leave any paper or messages with Ms. Baker. She's loyal, but you never know who's looking over her shoulder from time to time. And I don't want a paper trail of any kind. These incessant congressional investigations can take a Father's Day card from your daughter and turn it into a criminal offense." Burcks smiled. "So, memorize that private phone number"

Burcks returned to his office and had Darren rush the list to Ms. Axtell at the phone company. She glanced through the list and whistled. "Wow!" She looked at Darren. "This will be ready in thirty minutes or so. Do you want to pick it up, or shall I send it to you?"

"Oh, I'll pick it up."

As Darren turned to leave, Ms. Axtell added, "And tell the General that I have no idea what's in here, and no one else will see it."

Darren returned to his office and waded through the stack of accumulated mail. Ms. Axtell called in thirty minutes. Darren darted out the door. "Elevator's too slow," he muttered, as he scrambled down the steps. He rushed out the massive front doors and stopped a cab going north on 18th Street. "Take me to the phone company building just off Thomas Circle on fourteenth street."

When they arrived in front of the building, he had the cab wait as he ran into the building, picked up the package and returned to his office. The entire episode took forty minutes.

Once back at his office, Darren shut the door and carefully opened the package. Atop a ten-inch stack of printouts, he found the promised summary—six pages. As he studied the report, he could feel his heart beating rapidly. He knew he held a smoking gun because he could smell the gunpowder. Finally, he went to Jo Clark's office and asked to see the General.

"Darren, General Burcks went to a Pentagon meeting and I don't expect him back until after lunch."

"If he calls, please tell him I desperately need to see him."

Darren returned to his office and called Carlson. She was also in meetings. He left his name and phone number. Where are people when you need them?

Lenora called at 11:30 a.m. "What's up?" she asked.

"I've got the phone records report, and it's dynamite. When will you have the banking records?"

"I've been in meetings all morning. Let me check and call you back.

As he hung up he turned to find Burcks standing at the door." Thought you would be tied up 'till after lunch?"

"Ah, hell, I couldn't stomach another luncheon, so I excused myself. What did the phone analysis find?" Burcks walked over to Darren's worktable by the windows and sat down.

As Darren handed him the report, he said, "It's powerful stuff." Darren stood up and stared out the window as Burcks read the report.

Burcks scanned Darren's one-page summary and the six-page analysis, then looked up at Darren as he stuffed the material in his briefcase. "You're right. Don't breathe a word of this to anyone. Not even Agent Carlson."

"Yes, sir."

"When will she have the banking records available?"

"I'm waiting for her call now."

"Let's wait and see how her data supports the phone records and vice versa before setting it in front of the President."

Carlson called after lunch to say the report would be ready mid-afternoon. She added, "We're closing in on White and Boorgers. They've undergone reconstructive plastic surgery and received new identities in Nuevo Laredo, Mexico. We hope to know their new identities soon."

At four p.m., Carlson stopped by Darren's office. She handed him a manila envelope with the next day's task force agenda and associated reports. Then she pulled a floppy disk wrapped in tissue paper from her purse and handed it to him, saying, "The information you want is compressed on this disk. I've made sure my fingerprints are not on it. I didn't look at it, so I have nothing to tell. If caught I'll find myself assigned to Dilley, Texas."

"That wouldn't be bad duty. At least you could eat all the watermelon you want."

"Thanks a lot. I'm gone."

Darren slid the disk in his computer and opened the file. It contained information on deposits, withdrawals and checks written by White House staffers and three hundred of the government's top administrators. He used his computer's sort program to organize the data in a variety of ways. A number of top government officials had socked away big chunks of money. While some accounts reflected what seemed to be normal investment returns, a number had received funds from think tanks known to be supporters of the most violent strain of super patriots. He looked at his watch as he started printing out various reports.

At that moment Burcks peered in again and said, "Haven't you had enough for one day?" Startled, Darren almost fell out of his chair.

"You scared me to death. I didn't hear you come in."

"You're not the only one who works late. Did she deliver? What's the verdict?"

"Beyond a doubt, the President's Chief Domestic Advisor is up to his ass in alligators. There's a whole gaggle of others. I'll have the printouts in a few minutes. Shall I bring them to your office?"

"Yeah, do that."

Thirty minutes later Darren placed the reports in front of Burcks. When finished going over them, he frowned, pursed his lips, and then carefully put them in his briefcase—all without saying a word. He put the briefcase in his office vault and locked it. Then he turned to Darren, smiled grimly as he shook his head and said, "Are you ready to get out'a here, or are you going to sleep in the office again?"

"No, I'm ready. I'll walk down with you."

They entered the dimly lit underground garage to find it almost empty. The musty smell always bothered Darren. They walked toward Burcks's car without either saying a word.

"I'll see you tomorrow," Darren said ass they reached Burcks's car.

Suddenly a shot rang out and Darren felt like someone had hit him in the upper arm with a two-by-four board. Burcks wheeled around to see Darren duck behind a pillar. "Stay put, Darren, I'll get the son-of-a-bitch," he yelled. He jerked his car door open, grabbed a revolver from under the front seat and crept over to Darren. "You okay?"

"Yeah, got me in the arm." Darren had dropped to a sitting position and was holding his right hand over the wound. "It feels numb."

"Just a graze. But it's nasty. It sure ruined a good suit. Did you see where it came from?"

"Not at all. It must have come from near the entrance."

Burcks scurried from one pillar to another as he made his way toward the entrance, scanning the shadows as he moved. He heard footsteps and spotted two policemen, revolvers drawn, entering the garage on the run. They ducked behind a Ford Explorer near the entrance.

Burcks stuck his gun in his belt behind his back and stepped slightly out from behind the pillar, hands in the air. "Hey, over here. We've a man down." The police took aim at Burcks as they came toward him.

"Darren, move into the open where they can see you."

Darren, using the pillar as a prop, stood up, then stepped out into the light, still holding his left arm. The police rushed up and searched them both. Darren and Burcks showed their NSC credentials and explained the shooting to the officers.

While one officer took notes, the other went back to the garage entrance and found an empty 38-caliber cartridge behind the right rear wheel of the Explorer. At that moment two Capitol police cars barreled down the driveway, lights flashing, radios blaring. A few minutes later an emergency medical unit arrived. The parking garage quickly turned into what Darren later characterized as a police convention.

The EMTs treated Darren's gunshot wound and released him. The chief technician said, "It's a flesh wound and not serious, but get your doctor to look at this in a few days. You don't want an infection to set in. It'll be sore for four or five days. Tomorrow morning you'll think a mule kicked you, and the upper arm will start turning black and blue."

After all the questions had been asked and answered to everyone's satisfaction, the police escorted each of the men home. Darren crawled into bed at 1:30 a.m. He fell asleep painfully aware that someone was trying to kill him or Burcks, or both. Meanwhile, Burcks arranged police protection for himself and Darren before crawling into bed himself.

A call awakened Darren a few minutes after six the next morning. He picked up the phone to hear a reporter for the Washington Post ask, "I understand you got ambushed in the garage at the Old Executive Office Building during the night. Do you know who did this?"

"No, I don't know who did it. Probably some kid looking for some easy money. There's no news here. Just another street thing."

The reporter realized he would not get a juicy, bloody story from Darren, so he hung up. Darren still felt sleepy, but he got up, took a painkiller, sat and watched the early news for a few minutes, and then got dressed.

Just then the phone rang. Darren listened without answering. One came from the police department. He took the caller's name and phone number to call later. Others followed, most were news hounds better left alone.

Just as he reached over to pour himself a cup of coffee, the phone rang again and a woman's voice said, "We missed you last night, but we'll get you next time." Great, he thought. They know where I live.

He suddenly realized it was a Saturday, but he needed to finish a few projects, so he dressed casually and headed for breakfast and the office. As he left his apartment, Darren noticed two men in a blue Ford Taurus following him. He called Burcks from his cell phone.

"Hoped you wouldn't notice," Burcks said. "I took the liberty of arranging some coverage for you. I also called the President this morning and told him what happened. He approved the coverage, so don't worry."

"Thanks," Darren said. "But I suspect they were after you. I'm only a low-level functionary in all this."

"Aren't we all?" Burcks asked.

He soon pulled into the underground garage at the OEB and parked. He watched as the men following him pulled in and parked next to him. He got out, locked the doors and found himself drawn to the spot where he had been hit. The agents joined him. After introducing themselves, one asked, "This where it happened?"

"Yeah." Then pointing toward the entrance, he said, "The shot came from up there."

"Here are our cards. Call and let us know when you're leaving your office. We'll make sure the area is clear. How long will you be working?"

"A few hours. I'll be through by eleven thirty."

"Just keep us informed of your plans. We can cover you best if we know your moves." They followed Darren to his office floor, then disappeared.

He found a message that Burcks's family doctor would see him at 3:00 p.m. Darren noted this on his desk calendar, answered his remaining mail, cleared a few reports, made some phone calls, and left promptly at 11:30. He, agent Sam Lockney, and another agent named Robertson had planned to attend the University of Virginia football game. Sunday, he planned to stay home and rest. Despite all the chaos and tragedy, life did go on.

He got to the elevator and remembered the doctor's appointment. Burcks had gone out of his way to arrange a Saturday appointment, so Darren didn't want to ignore it. He called Lockney and told him to go without him. Darren's shadows met him as he stepped off the elevator in the parking garage and followed him home. He told them of his doctor's appointment.

The phone awakened Darren from his late Saturday afternoon nap.

"Darren, Lockney here."

"Hey, is the game over? How did it come out?"

"Yeah, it's over. Truth of the matter, it was over before it started. It didn't last more than three minutes of the first quarter."

"Why?" Darren asked, as he sat upright in bed.

"A bomb went off under the stadium. Two west side bleachers came down."

"Oh, my Lord. "Where were you guys sitting?"

"On the east side, but it could have been our side just as easily."

"I'm so sorry."

"We just wanted you to know what a great event you missed," Lockney said, with a touch of sarcasm in his voice.

"Glad I missed it," Darren said. "It's not safe in public anymore, is it?"

"Not very."

"Thanks for telling me, Sam."

"Yeah, see ya Monday."

Monday morning, Darren called and gave Jo Clark his itinerary, then went directly to the FBI building for a task force meeting. Only about half of the members were there. As Darren walked into the room Lockney called out, "How's the arm?"

"Good grief, how'd you know about that?" Darren asked.

"It's all over town," Lockney said with a smile. "One whisper after another spreads information faster than a prairie fire in this town. Haven't you ever wondered why Burcks keeps you so close?" Lockney grinned broadly.

"You're probably right about that," Darren said with a smile, although it looked feigned. "Undoubtedly some kid panicked. That's all. It could happen to anyone at any time of the day or night around here. You all know that."

"Of course," Lockney said.

With that exchange, the task force went about its business. The meeting only lasted for forty-five minutes. They heard that forty-two people were killed at the University of Virginia football game. No one knows who set off the bomb. Six hundred forty-four people were arrested in connection to the previous weeks' bombings and awaited disposition. None were foreign terrorists. Trials had started in most cities across the nation, adding an increased burden to an already overloaded judicial system. Retired judges had been called to active service to help handle the load. And the twenty-first of March had come and gone without the anticipated attacks. Agent Carlson reported Boorgers's and White's new identities, distributed pictures of the reconstructed faces and asked all agencies to aid in the search for the two men.

Agent Martin asked, "Won't these guys get word that we've got their new number and run?"

"We hope so," Lenora replied. "We want them running. They'll eventually make a mistake or be seen by someone."

Darren returned to his office and worked back over the bank records Lenora had delivered the previous Friday. He got to Ted Roberts's account, the President's Advisor on Domestic Affairs, and as he stared at the report, he noted that Roberts had written an inordinate number of checks to the Capitol Travel Agency. Why? The White House had its own in-house travel agent. And a number of deposits from some Western think tanks to cover various travel expenses looked strange. He took this to Burcks.

"Isn't this unnatural?" Darren asked, as he handed the red penciled items to the General. Burcks studied the items as Darren continued, "How can we get Ted Roberts's records from this Capitol Travel without drawing anyone's attention?" Again, Burcks didn't answer. "Do you know anything about these particular think tanks?" Darren asked.

Burcks looked up, chewed on the eraser of his pencil and said, "Uhmm. They don't register." He looked back down for a few minutes, then said, "Darren, leave this to me for the time being."

Darren left, realizing Burcks handled some matters in his own special way.

On Tuesday morning, Burcks called Darren to his office. "Roberts certainly made a lot of trips to Denver, New Orleans and Dallas. And on his own time," he said, showing Darren Robert's travel schedule. I've got a friend in private practice investigating. Let's see whom he visited. Meanwhile, check these dates and see if any of those top-level crazies happened to be in those cities on those particular dates. I've also asked for information on those think tanks he's been visiting out there."

"Do you mind if I ask Agent Carlson to run a check through their computer? They have software that makes correlations within seconds."

"Make sure she will do that without asking any questions or reporting it to the Director."

Darren immediately called Carlson and gave her the dates and cities.

She called back in ten minutes. "I'm going to download the information to your computer."

He saved the data and printed a copy for Burcks. Darren got a nod of approval from Jo as he walked up to Burcks' office.

He knocked softly at the open door and Burcks looked up, leaned his chair back with his arms over his head, and said, "Come in. What'cha got now?"

Burcks looked startled with the report. He quickly got up and said, "That got done in a hurry. How can we get that software over here?"

"I think the Bureau's computer wizards have developed that system for their own use. You might ask the Director."

"Uhmm. There seems to be a gathering of patriots everywhere Roberts goes. Call our friend Morgan at the Secret Service Office and see what else we know about these particular meetings. I'd like to know who attended, for starters. If we get enough evidence to put him away for a long time, he'll rat on the others. He's always been a chicken-livered weasel." Burcks got up and walked to the window, arms folded behind his back as he thought about Roberts. "The son-of-a-bitch is only interested in feathering his own nest. Hell, he hasn't got the balls to take the full rap. Especially if we threaten him with a firing squad."

"When do you plan to see the President about this?"

"When we get enough to put Roberts away for several lifetimes. The President called me at home at five-thirty this morning to see when we would finish. I said we needed a few more days to build a solid case. We can't afford to misfire. We not only have to put these bastards out of business, but the evidence must also be so overwhelmingly convincing that the whole damn American Bar Association can't screw it around." Then, after a pause, he muttered, "Never have liked that ass-hole."

"The patriots have been very quiet of late. Maybe they've run out of ammo and anger," Darren said.

"You wish!" Burcks exclaimed, looking up with an expression of incredulity. "As long as White and Boorgers and their buddies are still out there, we've got problems. I'm just relieved that Arab terrorist haven't gotten involved."

"You're right. Just wishful thinking on my part."

At that moment Jo came to the door. "General, you're due for a meeting." Burcks rose as Jo held his coat. As he put it on, he turned toward Darren. "Don't forget, you're to attend the Senate hearing investigating domestic terrorism this afternoon."

"Sure took them long enough to get started," Darren said.

As he trudged out, he called back over his shoulder, "Yeah, that's the way things are done in this great city. Congressmen and women wait until they see they can politically benefit before they act. They're not often motivated by truth, justice and the American way. We'll get copies of the transcriptions, so don't waste time taking notes. Get the list of attendees. Watch eye movement and interaction between participants. Those tell us more than the spoken words, which are political conundrums."

"Any possibility we can get a copy of someone's videotape of the event to study carefully?" Darren asked.

"Yeah, good idea. Call and ask the President's secretary to arrange that. Just have her ask that the tape be sent to her office. We'll pick it up there."

Darren arrived at the Senate hearing room early and, after looking around, chose a seat on the far right, opposite the entrance so he could rest against the wall and watch who came and went. Few liked to get locked in during these lengthy hearings.

The large hall could seat several hundred. The committee members sat on a dais some two feet above the floor in cushy chairs. The chairperson occupied the center seat and members of the two main political parties sat on either side. Dozens of aides sat along the wall behind the committee members.

The committee members finally arrived. But the chairman, Republican Senator Ron Rule of Alabama, was nowhere to be seen. Darren glanced at his watch. "Two o'clock, the meeting should start, he thought to himself. At five minutes after the hour, a young woman entered with one of the security guards in tow, strode swiftly to the dais, and whispered a message in the ear of Vice-Chairwoman Eleanor Johns, democrat from California. She picked up the gavel, struck the board twice and called for order.

"Ladies and gentlemen, we've just had word that Senator Rule has been shot."

Gasps echoed throughout the room as people headed for the door. Amidst the uproar Senator Johns announced that the hearing would be suspended until further notice.

Darren quickly made his way through the crowd and followed Senator Rule's aide back to her office for further details but found the corridor blocked by police and Secret Service agents. Darren noticed an FBI agent whom he recognized. "What happened?" he asked.

The agent said, "I've been told that a Capitol security guard shot and killed the Senator with a single shot to the back of the head as he came off the elevator, heading for his office."

Darren immediately returned to his office where he found Jo Clark in tears.

"Darren, have you heard what's happened?" she sobbed.

"Senator Rule has been shot. Is there something else?"

"No one has a complete count, but eighteen senators, twenty-two representatives and two Supreme Court justices were shot within the last hour. I just got off the phone with the U.S. Attorney General's secretary. She said someone also tried to kill the Attorney General and the Director of the FBI. The attempts failed, thank goodness!"

Darren slumped down in a chair by Jo's desk, stunned. "Did they catch any of the shooters?"

"They killed those who shot at the Attorney General and the FBI Director. I haven't heard of any others. It's still unfolding over there."

Darren, feeling like the wind had been kicked out of him, watched the news with Jo on her office television. The killing had extended far beyond Washington. Reports poured in from around the nation. Hundreds of top-level state and federal politicians, judges, and career bureaucrats had been shot during the early afternoon hours.

# 20

## CIMARRON, NEW MEXICO

Friday, April 11

Ernest Boorgers and Arlo White, each with a glass of scotch in hand, relaxed surrounded by patriot colleagues on the patio of Jim Hicks's ranch home eight miles southeast of Cimarron, New Mexico. Several followers of the new Christians Reconstructing America Party were barbecuing brisket over a large pit in the distance and others strolled casually across the vast grounds surrounding the opulent ranch house. They stopped to watch a herd of elk grazing in the distance as the sun dipped below the mountains to the west. The cool breeze carried the sweet smell of fresh-cut alfalfa from nearby fields. Light jackets helped ward off the cool evening temperatures.

Several hundred uniformed and armed young men provided security throughout the ranch. Three helicopters, two F-16 fighters, and four executive jets, all fitted with rockets and machine guns, peered menacingly from camouflaged hangars adjacent to the ranch's landing strip.

Hicks, addressing Boorgers and White, said, "I wouldn't have recognized you guys. How long before the bruise marks disappear?"

"Another few days, I suppose," Boorgers said .

"How'd your families react to your new looks?"

"My wife thought I looked cute!" White snorted, with a sneer. The men laughed. "After a few days she got used to it and said it felt like being married to a new man." More laughter.

"My daughter and son-in-law laughed about it, but my grandchildren didn't much care for it," Boorgers said glumly, as he spread his legs and leaned over to stare at the patio's adobe-tiled floor. "It scared them for a few days. I'm not sure they really felt comfortable with me during this visit."

"How old are they?" asked another member of the revolutionary council and chairman of the board of one of the nation's largest retail firms. He was perched atop the three-foot adobe wall that separated the patio from the expansive yard.

"Three to eight. My son's thirty-five. One daughter's thirty and the other's twenty-seven."

"Oh, they'll come around," Boyden, a high-tech guru from Boston, said as he swished the ice cubes in his drink. "Time will take care of that."

"I hope so," Boorgers replied, as he looked up. "I'm not sure how much time I have left for my grandchildren."

"By the way, General, how confident are you that the feds don't know of our meeting?" asked Hicks, standing, arms crossed over his abundant stomach.

"Oh, hard to tell. My old colleagues will make sure nothing gets out of hand." And then, after a few seconds he muttered, "At least I hope so."

A period of silence fell over the group as each quietly reflected on the General's words. Finally, the cooks finished their work and hauled large pans of hot brisket to the picnic tables on the patio.

"Come and get it!" Hicks yelled.

As the men lined up, White tapped one of the glasses with a dinner knife to get their attention. "Gentlemen, let's ask Bobby Joe Armstrong to lead us in grace."

All bowed their heads as Armstrong delivered the prayer. "Oh Lord, our God, your disciples ask for your guidance as we gather to continue to lead this nation back to you. Grant us the strength to fulfill the task you have set before us and bless this food for the nourishment of our bodies. Amen."

Armstrong, a nationally prominent television evangelist and colleague of Petsch, sported a luxurious lifestyle, thanks to millions of gullible disciples across the nation and the continual coverage of his comments on national and international affairs by CNN and the Fox News. He owned a forty-room mansion in Hollywood, an ocean front hideaway in Santa Barbara (reportedly worth six and a half million), a golf course townhouse in Palm Springs, California, and a huge home in Palm Beach, Florida. Rumors said he'd recently purchased a large chateau in the Swiss Alps. Hollywood stars and starlets found his showmanship and Disney-esque brand of Christianity seductive. Simply put, the showbiz Jesus represented by his spectacular media shows had been transformed into an Anglo-American, capitalistic and politically ultra-ultra-conservative savior. Armstrong hawked wealth and national prominence as signs of God's approval. Getting right with God meant one would acquire wealth and fame. Armstrong labeled any idea, organization or institution that did not agree with him as demonic. Not surprisingly, the Federal government fit that image. His passionate hate of the government far surpassed that held by most of his super patriot colleagues. He owed millions in back taxes and constantly fought the IRS in court. Many believed he would have been jailed years ago if not for his ministerial cloak, wealth and national following.

After the men finished dinner, they made their way to a large den on the second floor of the ranch house. Darkness gradually descended on the rolling New Mexico hills and mountains, and the panoramic second floor view acted as a magnet. A fire crackled in the fireplace.

The men seated themselves around an expansive round table set up near the fireplace. "Gentlemen," Boorgers said, "let's review our present status, then take a look at our plans for the future. Fred, give us a treasurer's report."

"We're doing very well," Fred gloated, as he distributed a simple financial statement to each. "We have thirteen point five million on deposit at a number of banks around the nation. We've distributed twelve million to two-hundred and eighty-six groups over the last two months." Each man studied the financial statement silently.

Finally, White asked, "It looks as though our recent activities cost us some financial support. But not much. We lost two point three million monthly, but picked up some deeper pockets. They've promised a total of four point six million monthly. And some of our foreign sources say they'll make up any shortfall we have. All we have to do is ask."

"Where did this one contribution of ten million come from?" Jim Hicks asked.

"Let's just say it came from abroad and leave it like that," Boorgers stated firmly, with a sweep of his hand. No one dared pursue the matter further. "Hand your report back to Fred. We don't want any of this stuff floating around." Once Fred collected all copies, he casually walked to the fireplace and tossed them in the fire. He stood and watched the financial reports burn.

"Arlo, how are the troops?" the General asked.

"Most are fine. Some, as predicted, dropped out. As you're all aware, we've had a real impact on the nation. People take us seriously for the first time.

Politicians at all levels are terrified of our retribution, so they're beginning to seek our counsel before voting on issues."

"How many men have we lost?" Armstrong asked.

"Forget it!" Boorgers shouted, as he glared at Armstrong. "Put the sacrifices out of your mind. There'll come a time to remember and grieve, but this isn't it."

White continued, "While we've lost a number of highly active groups, we've gained others. Training is currently being conducted at thirty-six sites for approximately twenty-four thousand people." The men smiled more confidently. "The feds can kill some of us, but thousands more will step up to take the place of the fallen ones in the name of Jesus Christ's America."

"Amen!" Armstrong shouted, waving his right fist in the air. Then, after a few moments of silence he continued, "I don't mind telling you fellas that the support from all those heathen foreigners bothers me greatly." He gazed first at Boorgers, then at the high-tech Bostonian.

General Boorgers, in a voice that had a paternal edge to it, looked at Armstrong like a father to a wayward son and said, "Please don't worry about that, Reverend. Once we're in control of the country, we'll immediately withdraw from the United Nations and cut off all association with the trouble makers."

"They won't like that," Armstrong replied with a huge grin. After a moment realization lit and a shocked look came over his face. "What's to prevent them from continuing to carry out terrorism against us?"

"We'll nuke 'um," stated White, in a steely, emphatic voice, eyes narrowed and fist clenched for emphasis. "As we've said many times, there will be no more Vietnams. There will be no more political molly-coddling of those who take our money with one hand and burn our flag with the other. We'll wipe 'um out, by God!"

Deathly silence settled over the group. Most smiled at Boorgers's tough posture, others nodded their heads in support. Then, in an audible whisper, Armstrong said, "Yeah, kill them ungodly sons-of-bitches!"

Boorgers studied each man's face as White laid out the new party's simple foreign policy for a new America. After he finished and the men had time to absorb White's statements, the General, with narrowed eyes, jaw set tight and a voice that dared the listener to disagree again, asked, "Any questions about that?"

"Although the Muslim terrorists will continue to be a problem, that Chinese bunch will be sooner or later," Fred Box said, stretching out in his chair, arms folded across his chest, eyes closed and head shaking violently from side to side.

"We'll move immediately to destroy anyone's ability to do damage," White said quietly but emphatically. "We have satellite maps showing where every Chinese missile is planted, every arms factory is located and every arms storage depot is hidden. At the right moment we'll take them out. Those that remain will be hit with missiles." He leaned back in his chair as he let these words sink in. He stared hard at Fred Box.

After a few moments he continued, "Rest assured, China will be disabled and kept that way. Any saber rattling, no matter from what country, will be met with immediate force. And we will nuke any Arab county that even twitches more terrorism."

"That's a strategy long overdue!" Jim Hicks cried in a voice tinged with anger as he came up out of his chair and started clapping. Tears welled up in his eyes. A few others joined him in the emotional display.

After the group quieted, Boyden asked, "How we doin' with weapons?"

"We have a few depots around the country, but nothing extravagant," White said . "The feds confiscated the last of the large arms caches we had at Ship's ranch." He wiped his brow with his left hand.

Boorgers, shaking his head in disgust, spat out, "We tried to tell Ship to disperse those weapons, but he felt like he owned them, the stupid idiot. He got what he deserved."

White leaned back and stretched as though bored as he said, "There's enough weaponry out there now. We may need to borrow some missiles and other materials from time to time, but our boys have done a good job of getting U.S. military issue from local sources. In fact, if the truth could be known, I suspect we probably control a majority of the fed's hardware." White smiled broadly as the other men laughed.

THE WHITE HOUSE
Late Tuesday Evening, April 15

Admiral Chris Bent, chairman of the Joint Chiefs of Staff, sitting rigid and formal in his battle-ribbon-bedecked white naval uniform, opened the meeting. "Mr. President, we believe our struggle against the people trying to overthrow the country is in its last gasp. And to date we've heard nothing from any Muslim terrorists that might still be lurking in the wood pile."

The President, sitting at his desk in the Oval Office, leaned back calmly as the Admiral and other staff reported on troop deployment at all government, communication, banking and airline facilities across the nation. He rested his left elbow on the arm of his chair. From time to time his left hand doubled up as a fist as he silently pounded the arm of his chair.

"Admiral," the President said, "the Arab terrorists don't have to do anything. Our own people are doing the job for them. We've got eight governors and thousands of citizens under lock and key, awaiting trial on charges ranging from murder to sedition. What jury's going to convict these people?" As the President's words sank in, a heavy silence overcame the group. The President leaned forward, placed his arms on the table with hands clasped together and waited.

He continued, "We're almost paralyzed. People are afraid to go to work. They're afraid of their neighbors and afraid to testify against the people who've been bombing and killing indiscriminately. The Attorney General reports that local law enforcement officials have turned thousands of known killers loose because they fear for their lives and the lives of their family. These so-called patriots are crazy. What are they calling themselves now?"

"Christians Restoring America Party, Mr. President," the Commandant of the Marine Corps said.

"Well, whatever. For your information, the acronym for that's CRAP! Do you think all those people introduce themselves as members of CRAP?" Everyone smiled, while still maintaining a rigidly formal posture. Heads either looked at the President or down at their note pads.

The Secretary of Defense, looking across the table at the President, said, "Mr. President, our allies around the world are starting to believe that our preoccupation with internal affairs will keep us from honoring our global commitments. How do we dissuade them?"

After a few seconds, the President said, as he eyeballed each member of the committee, "I don't want what I am about to say to leave this room. Our allies are right. We don't have the resources to help anyone else right now." Again, he pounded a fist into the arm of his chair. "We're devastated. This is the greatest domestic crisis we've faced since the Civil War of 1861."

He eased back in his chair. Approximately twenty seconds passed as the President sat quietly looking down at his hands. He then said, "Yet, somehow we've got to present a more confident posture abroad." He raised his right hand and waved it in reference to all nations beyond U.S. borders as he said, "And we've got to keep foreign governments from knowing the true extent of our predicament. If we don't, our troubles will be compounded. There are still a number of bully boys around the world who would love nothing more than to dance on our grave." He smiled wanly, then looked back down at his hands interlocked in his lap. "If they believe we are weak, they'll pounce." He shook his head for emphasis. Then he sighed as he said, "I just don't know how much longer we can maintain the pretext of global strength."

"We've got enough historical capital to carry us for awhile, Mr. President," the Secretary of Defense responded. Others nodded their confirmation.

The President thought about this for a moment, nodded slightly as he looked around, then got up and walked toward the window. He stared out for a few moments then turned to the group. "When we were boys, we'd whistle as we walked by the cemetery at night." He crossed his hands behind his back as he walked back to the table, and surveyed his staff. "I've been doing a lot of whistling lately."

When a White House network correspondent reported the late night meeting on the Wednesday morning news, she stated that "members departed the late night meeting with the President in a somber mood."

While the President met with his military Joint Chiefs of Staff, Burcks had Darren and Agent Carlson in his office. They reviewed the accumulated evidence against top administration officials. After several hours, Burcks leaned back in his chair, clasped his hands behind his head and said, "I'd rather not go to the President with this until we have enough evidence to connect and convict all these people. If we go public with Roberts, the others will run for cover. We don't want that. It's best if they're picked up at the same time. What do you think Agent Carlson?"

Carlson leaned forward in her chair, reached up with her left hand and ran her fingers through her hair. Finally she said, "Well, you're certainly right. The Bureau staff is currently running a computer correlation on the suspect list using known phone numbers, locations and associated data pinpoints of top leaders of the patriot movement. It's searching tons of data, so we thought we'd let it run during the night to minimize attracting attention. Let's wait and see the results."

"Good!" Burcks exclaimed. "How soon do you think that will be?"

"If the system doesn't go down during the night it should be ready when I get to the office in the morning."

"What time?"

"To be safe, let's say seven thirty."

Burcks looked directly at Lenora, "So be it. But, take it directly to the President at the Oval Office. Mark it for his eyes only. You will not have to clear it with any of your superiors."

Wednesday, April 16

Darren arrived at the office at 7:00 a.m. At 8:00 the phone rang, and as Darren reached for the phone, he noticed Jo Clark pass his door on the way to her office.

"Darren, this is Lenora. I'm leaving to deliver the report to the President. Is the General in yet?"

"I haven't seen him. I'll call and give him your message. Go ahead and deliver the report." Darren hung up and called the General's car phone, but received no answer. He called the house.

Mildred Burcks answered.

"Ms. Burcks, this is Darren. Has the General left yet?"

"No, Darren. He never came home last night. I thought he might still be at the office. You know I can't keep up with him."

"I'm just checking. I'm sure he'll show up soon." Darren suddenly felt alarmed.

After hanging up, he called Lenora Carlson's pager. In a few seconds she returned his call from her car.

"Well, it seems the General didn't get home last night."

"Oh, Lord! Okay, I'll alert the Bureau."

Darren, frightened, felt a tightening in his chest as he ignored the office elevators and ran down the stairs. He slowed down to ease the pain. He reached the White House and waited for Carlson. The pain in his chest gradually subsided. When Lenora arrived, they had to wait for President Evans's secretary to get out of a staff meeting. Lenora sat on the sofa while Darren paced the floor.

Finally, the secretary rushed in. "Sorry, I couldn't get out of that meeting." Then she turned to Darren, "Mr. Hopkins, good morning. How can I help?"

He introduced Agent Carlson, who handed the packet of material to her, saying, "General Burcks told us to deliver this material to the President first thing this morning. We understood he had an appointment with the President."

The secretary took the packet and then looked at her appointment book. "I don't see anything down here. Wait just a minute and let me check with the President."

"I don't think that will be necessary," Darren said. "General Burcks hasn't come in yet and the rest of the material is locked up in his safe. The President needs the complete file."

"That's true," Carlson said.

"Why don't I give the President this packet and you bring the rest as soon as you can. Will that be all right?" she asked.

"That's fine," Darren said, as he and Lenora left.

"I'm sure he got derailed somewhere," Jo Clark muttered, trying to mask her fear as she looked down at her desk.

"Jo," Darren said, "I called the house and talked with his wife. He didn't come home last night!"

"Oh, Lord." Jo sat down, clasping her hands.

Jo, Agent Carlson and I just left some sensitive material with the President's secretary, but the rest of the report is locked in the General's safe. He wanted to take the whole report to the President this morning."

"I'll get it for you," she said as she regained her composure.

Darren, for the first time, used the President's private phone line. An unidentified female voice answered, "Yes?"

"This is Darren Hopkins, General Burcks' aide at NSC. I need to get a message to the President." A pause ensued until the President came on the line.

"This is President Evans."

"Mr. President, this is Darren Hopkins, General Burcks aide. Agent Carlson and I have retrieved the rest of the investigative report from General Burcks's safe and would like to bring it right over. Agent Carlson delivered a set of disks and a printed report to your secretary a few minutes ago. Quite frankly, General Burcks didn't get home last night and he hasn't shown up this morning. He made us promise to meet him as soon as Agent Carlson got the computer analysis. I'm afraid something's happened to him. I don't want to maintain possession of this material any longer. May we bring it over?"

"I understand. Come right over."

President Evans's secretary met them as they entered the building and escorted them directly to the Oval Office.

As they entered, Darren said, "Good morning, Mr. President. I'm Darren Hopkins. This is Agent Lenora Carlson."

The President, wore a light gray suit, white shirt and maroon tie with blue and yellow stripes. He shook hands with Lenora and Darren, saying, "Yes, I remember both of you from my visit to the task force meeting. Good to see you again." Then, motioning toward a round worktable near the window overlooking the Rose Garden, he said, "Please sit down."

Darren handed the President the remainder of the material. "Let's see what you have," the President said.

"We believe this gives you overwhelming evidence of those in the administration who are involved in the conspiracy to overthrow the government," Darren said.

The President studied the report and without looking up asked, "You say General Burcks never showed up this morning?"

"That's correct, sir."

"That's strange." The President never took his eyes off the reports as he reached under his desk. His secretary came in. "Ms. Baker, get in touch with the Attorney General and the directors of FBI and CIA and have them in my office in one hour. Cancel everything else."

The President put the report down on his desk and stood up. "Thanks to both of you. I'll be in touch soon. Meanwhile, let me know when General Burcks shows up."

Once outside, Lenora said, "I'm heading back to the office. Let me know about the General."

"I certainly will. And again, thanks for all your help on this."

"I hope it proves useful. And I especially appreciated meeting the President," she said, with a broad smile.

"Yeah, me too. I'm glad you came along. It gave the report credibility."

"We'll see about that. Meanwhile, I see two possible outcomes of this report. One's good and one's bad."

"Well, let me have the good first."

"He'll have all those people arrested."

"And the bad?"

A slight smile flickered across her face. "We'll both show up missing!"

"Yeah, I know," Darren said softly.

The President met with the Attorney General and directors of the FBI and CIA and presented the report implicating three hundred and forty-six top-level Federal employees in the terrorist activities and the plot to overthrow the United States government. The list included a number of his own White House staff, a U.S. Supreme Court Justice, fourteen Federal judges, twenty-six members of Congress and various members of the federal bureaucracy—justice, state, the FBI, and other departments. The President ordered the Attorney General to have all arrested immediately under a war powers executive order, to be supported by the FBI and CIA.

Jo Clark was standing at her office window as Darren returned from meeting with the President.

"What is it, Jo?" Darren asked, cold chills shooting through his body.

"They. . . ," her voice choked.

Darren put his arm around her." Take your time."

"They found his body washed up on one of the Three Sister's Islands in the Potomac." She burst into tears. He could feel tears welling up in his own eyes. He had lost a great friend. "I thought he had security with him at all times?"

"Aw, you know him. He worried about you and others, but he didn't pay any attention to his own safety."

Darren sat down feeling totally drained. Finally, he wiped his eyes with the back of his hand. "Has anyone notified Ms. Burcks?"

"The police notified the White House just as you left the President's office. Annie Parrish, one of the President's aides and an old friend of the General's, called Mildred's minister. She'll go with the minister to see Mildred. You've met Annie, haven't you?"

"Yes, one time. She seemed to be a fine lady."

Darren, lost in thought, moved to the window as the phone rang.

Jo picked it up." Just send the material to my attention."

Darren took a few deep breaths. "You okay?"

"Sure," she said as she wiped her eyes.

"Why don't you go on home? I'll take care of things here."

"No, I couldn't stand that. It's best I stay and answer the phone. I need time to adjust to this."

Staff members from other offices in the Old Executive Building started trickling in, so Darren stepped out.

He walked numbly to his office and called Annie Parrish. "Oh, Darren. Such terrible news. Everyone's so sorry"

"Does the President know?" Darren asked.

"Yes. Ms. Baker walked in and gave it to him. She should be calling you soon."

"Why me?"

"I don't know. She just said she had to call Darren Hopkins."

At that moment Jo Clark came in and motioned that he had an important phone call waiting.

"This is Darren Hopkins."

"Darren, this is Margie Baker, the President's secretary."

"Yes, ma'am."

"The President wanted you to know that he's deeply grieved over General Burcks' death. He asked that you please continue your work and report directly to him for the time being. He will have a replacement for General Burcks soon. Oh, here's the President now. He wants a word with you."

"Darren, I know what a shock and loss this is to you. I can't even begin to tell you what a loss this is to me, given the state of the nation at this time. You and George Burcks made a great team. Of all his staff, he depended on you."

"That's kind of you to say, Mr. President. I had great respect for the General."

"Unfortunately, and I know this is going to sound callous, but we don't have a lot of time to grieve. We must do as much as we can as fast as we can to preserve the nation. I need you to continue as if General Burcks still ran that office. You know his thinking, so you continue on. Ms. Baker will contact Ms. Clark and have her continue to cut your travel and expense vouchers. She can send them to Ms. Baker for authorization."

"Thank you, sir."

"What else do you need?" the President asked.

"I can't think of anything right now, Mr. President. But thank you."

"Call Ms. Baker when you need anything. Give me some time to consider who is going to be left on my staff that I can trust to work with you. I'll get back to you later about that."

# 21

**ALISO VIEJO, CALIFORNIA**
Wednesday, April 30

Back at his California town house, Darren threw his golf clubs into the back of his Jeep Wrangler. Burcks's funeral had been a big affair, and Darren sorely missed him. This trip to California had been Darren's first vacation in months.

As he climbed into the Jeep, his cell phone rang. His heart sank and he slumped over the steering wheel, eyes closed in exasperation. Caught in a tug of war with his conscience, he sat in the Jeep for a few moments, looked at his watch and calculated that it would be ten in the morning in Washington.

He picked up. Agent Lockney's voice echoed loud and clear. "Darren, sorry to bother you on vacation, but you should know we've located Boorgers and White."

"Where are they?"

"Boorgers entered Indonesia a few days ago. White is somewhere in Central America. He crossed into Guatemala from Mexico three days ago. Agent Carlson thought you might want to go to Indonesia and make sure we get old Boorgers to the U.S. in one piece. You know a lot of people down there."

"Obviously I'd like to go, but what would the pros in charge down there think."

"Hey, let them do their work and you do yours. Flex your White House credentials!"

"Well, I appreciate those nice words, Sam. By the way, who's in charge of the Indonesian chase?"

"The Indonesians," Sam laughed. "They let us know right up front that we would not be allowed to run our own operation in their country. But they've agreed to let us participate as observers. I hear our CIA station chief will be present at all times. Lenora knows the female CIA chief down there and asked her if we could send some observers. She said she'd be happy to have some. Lenora mentioned your name."

"Why is everyone trying to get me killed?" Darren asked. He could hear Sam chuckling.

"Anyway, I've got to go. Call Carlson. She only asked me to chase you down and give you the info. She's coordinating arrangements."

"When would I need to leave?"

"As quickly as possible. But, again, talk to Carlson. Here, I'll transfer you."

A few seconds later Carlson came on the line. "Darren. I assume Sam filled you in. Want to go to Indonesia?"

"Yeah, as long as I don't have to go to Timor."

Lenora laughed, and then said, "I don't think Boorgers will be going there either."

"Just kidding. I'll call Jo Clark and have her arrange my flights and paper work. She knows how to do that."

"That's fine. Have her call me. Talk to you later."

"Wait, what about White?"

"We're on his tail with a vengeance."

"I sure would like to know what happens," Darren said.

"I'll call you when we get him."

Darren phoned Jo Clark at home, and she informed him with a steely voice he rarely heard, that she expected him to inform her of his every movement. He realized that until someone replaced General Burcks, Jo planned to manage him. God knows, he thought, I need all the managing I can get. He also knew that as soon as Lockney mentioned going to Indonesia, he had to try and contact Ann Jones again. His heart skipped a few beats. Were his motives pure about wanting to be in on the kill? He wondered.

Darren then called Mo. A sleepy voice answered.

"Mo, Darren here. You still sleeping?"

"Yeah, what time do you have?"

"Almost eight here!" Darren said.

"Well, I didn't get in until almost four this morning."

"Why so late?"

"My editor had me chasing a story in the Hill Country, and I got to talking to guys up there and lost track of time. What's going on?"

"Well, the CIA located White in Guatemala and Boorgers in Indonesia."

"Great, give me the details."

Darren explained what little he knew and promised to call Mo from Indonesia as the chase unfolded. "But you can't submit the story until you get an okay from me."

Mo agreed and as Darren prepared to hang up, Mo asked, "Are you planning to check on Ann Jones?"

"That's been worrying me off and on for some time. I'd like to. I asked Jo Clark to inform Army Intelligence in Bangkok of my travel plans in case they've heard anything from Ann. I'll let you know."

So much for the golf game.

SINGAPORE
Friday, May 2

As Darren stumbled, groggy-eyed, off the plane in Singapore and headed down the wide and spacious halls decorated with earth tone drapes and a deep carpet on his way toward immigration, a figure gradually sidled up on his right. Startled, he ducked and covered his face as the person reached for his right arm. He stopped dead in his tracks and stared in disbelief—Ann Jones, in the flesh!

"Heyyyyy!" Darren yelled. "You scared me to death!" he said, holding his hand over his heart. "Where the hell have you been?"

Before she could answer, he pulled her over to the wall, into his arms, whispering, "I can't believe this. I had about given up on you."

"Sorry, I got caught in a mission that took longer than expected and I couldn't communicate with anyone."

Darren fought to maintain his composure "Oh, my God, you're crying!" she said, gently stroking the back of his neck and shoulders. "That's sweet of you."

"Sorry, I'm very tired," Darren said. "And after all these months—the fear that you were dead or a hostage—Burcks's death—all the tension of these months. And then you just pop up in such a remote place."

"Sorry, Darren." Holding hands, they started down the concourse. Ann suddenly noticed his red face, put her arm around his waist and pulled him close. "Oh, are you embarrassed?"

"Just a little."

"You men hate to show your emotions, don't you?"

"Yeah, it's tough. A macho thing we learn, unfortunately."

"I got back yesterday and heard you had been asking about me. I called your apartment in D.C., but no one answered. Then I called your secretary who told me you had left for Indonesia. She wouldn't tell me about your assignment, but my boss received notice of the search for Boorgers in Indonesia and your name was on the list, so he said, "Get down to Indonesia and monitor that situation."

"Great," Darren said. "Can you tell me anything about where you've been?"

"Not for the time being."

"I figured as much." Darren said, "Let's get something to eat."

Darren couldn't keep his eyes off Ann as they ate. Blue eyes and black, naturally curly hair, highlighted her 5' 6" lithe frame. She was one of those people who turned heads. "Did you call and leave me a message to get out of Dodge when I visited Bangkok last year?"

Ann, with her fork in a pancake, looked up, shook her head and said, "No, I didn't. In fact, Marilyn told me about that. I believe you also had a message from me at your Washington apartment. Right?"

"Yeah, he said, looking puzzled. "Was that you?"

"No, it wasn't."

"My mind must have been working overtime. It sounded exactly like you." He pushed his chair back, crossed his legs and sipped his coffee.

"Did my voice have a mechanical, staccato quality? Hear a lot of static?"

"Yes, it did. Why?"

"Someone must have gotten a recording of my voice, then electronically cut and spliced it to create the messages they wanted you to hear."

"That's interesting," Darren said. "My God, who would go to that much trouble?"

"Who knows the twisted minds of terrorists? Somehow they thought this might scare you, or at least cause you to lose your grip on things. We don't know. We've got records of dozens of people getting such messages."

"Well, they did scare me. But I'm sure glad you're okay."

"Come on, let's get our luggage and get out of here. I've also booked a room at the Pan Pacific, and I'm confirmed on your flight for Jakarta at seven fifty tomorrow morning. We've got a lot of catching up to do!"

After checking into separate rooms at the hotel, they headed for the mall attached to the Pan Pacific.

"We get some information about domestic issues over here, but certainly not detailed," Ann said.

"Tell me what you can about your work," Darren asked.

"It's pretty routine investigative stuff, for the most part. As you know, Southeast Asia has its share of political movements. And sometimes these groups are fighting oppressive political machines," Ann said. "We have to do our homework and often walk a thin and treacherous path of involvement."

"I can imagine," Darren said. "Asian regimes always seem to rule with a heavy fist."

"True. It's difficult for Americans."

"How did your assignment go?" Darren asked.

"I guess it went well. There were some who welcomed us with open arms and there were some who didn't."

"That's always the case, isn't it?" Darren asked. "But why couldn't we contact each other?"

"Once we got on the ground someone in the Philippine government decided that it would be wise to shut down all communications in order to ensure secrecy," Ann said.

"Yeah, but why didn't someone in Bangkok tell me that?"

"When I said that all communication was shut down, I meant exactly that. All communication was cut off. I couldn't even keep in touch with my office. And we don't share information with any other agencies."

"Why?" Darren asked. "That's been one of our key problems over the years."

"True. But bureaucracies are like that. Everyone is afraid to say anything for fear it will be misunderstood or misused. And then bad things happen to good people."

"That's most unfortunate. At least I could see that they were concerned about your safety." Darren responded.

"That's putting it mildly." Then, passing a Chinese restaurant, she said, "Let's stop in here and have something to eat. I'm buying."

During dinner, Darren leaned back in his chair and said, "If your group was concerned about the inability to communicate with you in the Philippines, then why did it continue? I don't understand any of this."

"The Philippinos held firm. My boss told them there would be no more sending staff if this was going to be the way they operated."

Leaning across the table, Darren said, "These months you were away have been terrifying. I really missed talking to you."

"That's sweet. I really did miss you, Darren."

After dinner they walked slowly through the mall hand in hand, watching the mob of shoppers and clusters of teenagers. They finally returned to the hotel for drinks at the lobby bar.

"Darren, we've both experienced a great deal of stress over the past few years," Ann said. "but I'd like to see if we can't pick up where we left off."

Darren leaned over, looked Ann in the eyes, "I really want to give our relationship a try, but promise me you'll not let them send you on any more of those damn blind assignments."

JAKARTA, INDONESIA
Sunday, May 4

Upon landing at Jakarta's Soekarno-Hattei International Airport two days later, Ann and Darren checked in at the Hilton Hotel. After putting away their personal items, they took a taxi to the U.S. Embassy on Jalan Merdeka Selatan, #4-5.

They signed in, passed security and followed an aide down a flight of stairs to a conference room lit only by florescent lights. Ebony wainscots defined the walls, and a light native wood created swirley patterns in the floor. A dark conference table and fifteen chairs comprised the only furniture in the dank room. White floor-to-ceiling drapes absorbed the sounds that otherwise would have ricocheted around the room, and a dark green chalkboard covered the southern wall. A slide projector had been set up, street maps of Jakarta and Bandung hung on the east wall, and packets of material lay in front of eight chairs at the northern end of the large conference table. Two U.S. Marines guarded the door.

By ten o'clock the whole team had assembled. Darren, Ann, the CIA station chief, Mary Lynn Knight, and agents Bob Williams and Morris Bratton comprised the U.S. group. The Indonesian team leader, General Idris Aziz and his aide, Bambang Sudiro, took charge of the briefing.

Mary Knight introduced the various members of the group to the Indonesians and said, "General Aziz, the briefing papers indicate Boorgers is in Bandung, but I believe you have updated that information. Why don't you fill us in."

The General stood and walked to the head of the table. He picked up a long pointer lying in the chalkboard's tray and turned to address the group. "Yes. He entered Indonesia with two young men named Leonard Janez and Paul Hardesy. They had forged passports, so they will be arrested and sent back to the States. I am told they are fugitives from your country also, but that's your problem."

"I thought Boorgers had a new identity," Darren said.

"Yes, he uses the name of a Ryan B. Dyson. Unfortunately, he had already entered when your people notified us of the false passport. We found him by looking in our records for his old friends. He moved into a house on Jalan Bartimbang, Kebayoran Baru, with an Indonesian woman in her late fifties. I understand she had been his mistress when he worked in Southeast Asia in the nineteen seventies." Aziz looked around to see if the group had any more questions, then proceeded.

Using the pointer, the General located the house site on a large map of Jakarta that had been hung on one of walls, then said, "We put the house under surveillance immediately. After a few days, Boorgers and his lady moved to a small white cottage on the outskirts of Bandung, a city in the mountains southeast of Jakarta." Again he pointed to Bandung on the map.

Then, tapping his left hand with the pointer, Aziz said, "And yesterday he moved to a country home about an hour from Jakarta in a mountain region we call Cisarua." The General turned to his aide and nodded.

The aide showed a slide picture of the house as the General located Cisarua on the wall map. He continued to tap his left hand with the pointer nervously as he turned back to the group and said, "They left that house early this morning and have not come back. One of our men tried to follow them but lost them because a car accident blocked his way."

The aide projected images on the screen of the streets and terrain around Cisarua. The members of the group groaned in unison at the sight of the mountainous terrain. One picture showed the large, single story home, with its stucco, red-tiled roof, perched in a cut on a steep mountain slope. Gorges framed the sides of the house and left about forty yards of solid ground along the sides. A well-manicured lawn flowed for several hundred yards down the front.

"Wow," Williams said, as he looked at the expansive estate. "If you try to approach the rear or western side of the house by coming down the mountain, you've got to hack your way through all those native bramble bushes."

"He certainly found a hideaway that's easy to protect!" Agent Bratton said.

"Given his background, I'm not surprised," Aziz said. As the aide projected aerial and ground pictures of the house from each angle, he continued, "I offer you more bad news."

The aide showed pictures of the servants' quarters as Aziz said, "There are at least fifteen gardeners and watchmen coming and going around the house each day. One couple lives in the servants' quarters at the rear." After letting these images sink in, the General sat down. "Bambang, you take over," he said to his aide.

The slides continued as Bambang provided more information in his broken English. "Watchmen visit house every hour during night. When finish, different pair makes rounds. This go every hour." He pointed out the usual night watchman's route on an aerial view. "As team reach home and find it safe, one hit bell hanging on pole in yard. That ring echoes across valley telling everything okay. If bell not ring right time, all people run to help."

"Don't the bells wake up the people in the house?" Ann asked.

"I think no. People sleep through ringing."

"How often do the watchmen appear around the house where Boorgers is staying?" Williams asked.

"Every hour. They ring bell every hour, on hour."

"That suggests several options," Ann said. "We can position people somewhere near the house and hope they will not be seen and move in between the local watch segments. Or we can wait to see if he moves again in a few days. Or we can fabricate a ruse to go in there, or get him to come out." Aziz looked at Ann and nodded his head several times, but no one else spoke.

"Who does the grocery shopping for the household?" Bratton asked.

"That lady he with," Bambang said.

After a pause, Aziz said, "We can go through the local police, but he and his friends probably paid some of them for protection. If he did, they will alert him. Besides, the home belongs to a wealthy and respected family. Their relation with Boorgers goes back a long time. I think he feels secure there. I don't think he will want to leave unless he really has to."

"What do you suggest?" Knight asked.

Aziz thought a minute, then said, "Well, if you really want to take him back to America, then we should replace the grounds keepers and night-watchmen with our own." He threw a transparency on the screen that detailed the plan. The Americans all looked at each other and exchanged smiles. Aziz reflects the usual Indonesian social graces that make us Americans come across as over-bearing, thought Darren. Aziz didn't hit his American colleagues over the head with his knowledge of his own backyard. He let the difficulties of the task sink in and then offered a well-thought-out plan of his own.

Agent Knight said, "You said 'if we really want to take him back to America.' What did you mean?"

"Oh, we would not hesitate to kill such a man."

"Okay. We understand that," Knight said, as she looked around the table with a smile. Aziz continued with his plan, which relied on a fairly large Indonesian military contingent.

Afterwards Bratton asked, "What's the downside?"

"We'll lose a man or two. There's no way a man of Boorgers's background will be unarmed. We have yet to detect anyone else staying with them other than his mistress and the maid's family. The maid and her husband probably won't help him. But someone will probably get hurt unless we are very careful."

"Are there alternatives?" Ann asked. "Is there mail delivery or any other visitors to the house?"

"Yes, we thought of that, thank you. But one man cannot be expected to take a man Boorgers' size without killing him outright."

"We're back to the gardeners," Ann replied. "Can we buy these guys off?" She looked at Williams, who picked up on the cue.

"Yeah, why not. What would that cost us, and how much confusion would it cause in the neighborhood to see all these guys suddenly replaced by new faces?"

"We thought of that but didn't know if you would pay the bill." Then Aziz, using his fingers to count off the problem points, said, "Besides, that will take longer. One of the gardeners could say something to a friend and rumors would fly, or Boorgers could sneak out while we are setting the trap. Boorgers will run if he senses any change in routine." Then he drawled, "Anyyyy change."

Williams asked, "Do you think he already knows the faces of the gardeners?"

"Well," shrugged Aziz, "he's your war hero. What do you think?"

Knight said, "Yeah, he's no fool. He studied every aspect of that environment before he moved there."

"You're right," Bratton said, shaking his head. The others nodded their agreement. Aziz smiled.

After a few moments of silence, Mary Knight said, "General Aziz, can we take a ten minute break?" He nodded, laid his pointer in the chalk tray, looked at his watch, nodded at his aide and left the room. Bambang quickly followed.

Knight turned to her American colleagues and said, "Okay, let's have your thoughts on this."

They reached a consensus before Aziz reentered the room. "General, we've been discussing this and would rather see a plan that will maximize efforts to take General Boorgers alive."

Smiling, Aziz said, "I thought you would. Who's going to sign off on the bill?" All eyes looked at Darren, who shrugged and said, "Don't look at me. I'm just an observer."

Then all turned to Mary Knight who said, "Okay, I'll sign off," she said, as Darren smiled. Knight cupped her mouth and whispered across the table to Darren, "You better help me get the funds."

"Okay," he whispered back.

The group decided to replace the yardmen and security people without alarming Boorgers. Each of those displaced would be offered payment for the inconvenience. Members of Indonesia's Secret Service would escort each worker to his or her home to get family members and then take them to an undisclosed destination where they would be told of the danger back in Cisarua, then fed, given new clothing and funds to take a trip of their choice.

Aziz looked around at each American, narrowed his eyes, pulled himself into a military posture, hands clasped behind his back, as he said through taut lips, "Regardless of what happens, I must remind you that this is Indonesia. If this man pulls a weapon or gives us any trouble, we'll kill him without a moment's hesitation. We don't, how do you say? Coddle such people in our country. Is this understood?"

Knight answered, "General, we understand. Do what you have to do." Knight looked around the room as she made this comment, but no one dissented.

"Thank you, but with all due respect, we need your President to send our President a note to that effect," Aziz said matter-of-factly.

Knight's eyes widened as this statement caught her somewhat off guard, but she kept her composure and said, "General, I will ask my director to handle that chore." Aziz nodded and bowed appreciatively.

The group spent the next hour watching the Indonesians develop the mission's details, and then General Aziz's men began their implementation. The President of Indonesia received President Evans's approval the next morning.

Monday night eight assault teams met in a meadow four blocks from Boorgers hideaway to rehearse the plan set to begin at 2:00 a.m., Wednesday morning. Darren planned to follow the team moving directly up the mountain toward the front door, while Agent Knight assigned Ann the task of monitoring the team approaching from the east road. As they left the meeting, Ann, with Darren in tow, went up to Aziz and said, "Well, General Aziz, your men have moved in a very efficient manner."

"Wait until your government gets the bill!" the General said with a big smile. "Since your country is paying the bills in U.S. dollars, I have put my men on U.S. wages. They are very, very happy."

Darren did not sleep. Following his assigned team as they crept up the hill, he felt as tense as a man without formal military training could under these conditions, but he felt an odd need to observe as closely as possible. Adrenaline flowed, his throat felt dry, his heart beat like a trip hammer, and sweat trickled uncomfortably down his face and the back of his neck.

Activity soon overrode anxiety. The Indonesian soldiers' use of animal sounds to identify each other amazed him. They sounded natural, since the sound of dogs barking, cats fighting, and donkeys braying always laced the Indonesian night. The team masquerading as Boorgers's night watchmen rang the bell outside Boorgers's house precisely at 1:00 a.m. They slowly sauntered over to the road that ran along the east side of the house. Once outside the wall that separated the property from the road, they ducked down in the darkness, pulled their weapons from their native knapsacks and waited. Agent Bratton's unit cut the power to the house.

Darren watched as members of his unit inched their way up the hill to the front porch where they waited. Darren stayed back some thirty yards near a flowerbed. All used night vision goggles. At 1:55 a.m., Darren heard voices as the next group, emulating the night watchmen, approached the house. This time they exploded through the door and into the kitchen. Immediately, the other units attacked their assigned positions. Darren heard the sounds of crashing, tearing and grunting as he crouched by the flowerbed. The Indonesians in his group had darted forward and thrown their bodies against the front door, knocking it off its hinges! He heard shots and immediately lay flat on the ground.

A few moments later he heard an Indonesian soldier call out, "Put gun down and come out!" Darren heard nothing for a moment, and then several bursts of automatic rifle fire shattered the air.

Trucks equipped with spotlights had surrounded the house and lit up the whole area. Dozens of Indonesian troops emerged out of the thickets and ravines surrounding the house. Several helicopters appeared and started sweeping the surrounding terrain with their spotlights.

Darren spotted Ann kneeling against the wall to his left. Aziz stood next to her and shouted an order in Indonesian. Tear gas canisters immediately soared through windows as the troops bailed out of the house. Smoke filled the house and billowed out of the openings, while everyone waited for Boorgers' exit.

After ten or fifteen seconds, a woman could be heard choking. She cried out in Indonesian, then stumbled through the kitchen door. As she exited a soldier grabbed her, checked her for weapons, then took her to a medical truck where she was treated for smoke inhalation and a minor bullet wound. No other sound came from the house.

Agent Knight, seeing the house totally consumed by tear gas and crawling with well-protected and heavily-armed Indonesian soldiers that would just as soon shoot to kill, finally yelled, "General Boorgers, the area is totally surrounded. Come on out for God's sake." No one answered.

Aziz again snapped an order and weapons blazed inside the house. O Lord, thought Darren, they're going to kill the guy yet. Soon, the noise stopped. Aziz again barked an order. Almost immediately, the soldiers that had invaded the house started dribbling back out. An emerging soldier looked at Aziz, shook his head and said, "No one."

This comment had no sooner passed the soldier's lips than they heard the noise of loose tiles on the roof. The troops immediately scrambled for the yard with Aziz yelling orders. Bratton and Williams, hiding near a rear wall, watched as soldiers poured out the back door.

Crouching low, Darren ran for the west wall that formed the compound and followed others toward the rear of the house. He heard automatic fire as he ran. He noticed Ann, Knight and Aziz kneeing behind a truck equipped with powerful spotlights.

As he knelt, Ann turned to him and pointed toward the house. "He created an escape route over the roof and evidently scampered to the brambles up the mountain under the cover of all that smoke."

"Oh crap, he'll probably get away," Darren said.

Aziz heard Darren and turned slightly as he said, "Mr. Hopkins, my men grew up in these brambles. General Boorgers couldn't have made a worse mistake." Aziz turned back as he calmly monitored and directed his troops.

The Americans gathered around Aziz to watch the chase. Bratton and Williams spoke Indonesian well enough to keep Darren and Ann up to date on the hunt's progress as they listened to Aziz's communication. Bratton turned to the others. "They have him in sight and keep shooting at him, but he's evidently become well-acquainted with the thicket."

"Yes, my men are surprised that he does so well in the brambles," Aziz said.

"I'm not surprised," Darren said. "Do you think he will get out of that mess?"

"We have the area sealed off. We'll get him." About that time, gunshots echoed across the mountains. Aziz spoke by phone with one of his officers. When he finished, he turned to Agent Knight and the others and said, "We got him. Sorry, but I'm afraid he may be dead."

In about ten minutes, a team of four dirty, sweaty soldiers emerged from the briar patch carrying Boorgers's body in what looked to Darren like a large rain poncho. They placed the body down in front of Aziz and the Americans.

"Let's get him to a hospital," Knight said. General Aziz turned to Bambang and gave a crisp order. Soon a helicopter landed and loaded Boorgers aboard. Darren and the rest of the American contingent climbed into the craft and joined General Aziz. An Indonesian medic stopped Boorgers' bleeding and started a blood transfusion. After a few minutes, he opened his eyes and looked around.

"Where are they taking me?" he asked.

"To a hospital in Jakarta, then home to the States where you will stand trial for treason against your country," Agent Knight answered.

No one said anything for a few moments. Then, looking around again, Boorgers said, "We almost pulled off a coup."

"Not by a long shot," Darren said. "Not by a long shot."

"If you think you've nipped the revolution in the bud by taking me, you're dead wrong," Boorgers spat back.

"Maybe. But I think we've rounded up most of the leadership and stopped most of the money flow."

"Son, you got a big surprise coming!" Boorgers coughed in pain, then closed his eyes.

Ann looked at Darren, but neither said a word. The medic shook his head. Boorgers was dead.

After a few days of filing reports, being interviewed by U.S. State Department personnel regarding the details of the Cisarua incident, and thanking all those who helped with the capture, Darren and Ann found themselves sitting alone in the Hilton Hotel's dining room.

"Well, what now?" Ann asked.

"I'm not sure. I keep worrying about what Boorgers meant about a big surprise."

"I just hope he intended the threat to be his last angry breath."

"Me, too, but I'm afraid that's not so."

"What's bothering you?" Ann asked.

"For one, the prevailing Washington view is that Islamic terrorism is a political strategy, albeit a barbaric one."

"And so"

"I think that case can be supported in the Palestinian struggle for land and self-determination against Israel, but the real impulse fueling the fire in the bellies of religious terrorists is the fear of modernity," Darren said.

"Why are they afraid of modernity?" Ann asked.

"Because the modern worldview is scientific and spawns secularism, all of which undermines religious worldviews."

"Yeah, that's why the Islamic Imams and Ayatollahs are so threatened," said Ann.

"Exactly. As are Christian fundamentalist preachers and Sikh elites. In fact, science is a threat to any religious worldview. This is why such people go to incredible lengths to denigrate evolution."

Ann stared into the distance. "This is also the reason they try to control people's thinking by banning books."

"Exactly. Give religious fundamentalists control in any society and you'll see a repressive state like Iran or Saudi Arabia." After a short silence, Darren added, "Well, I know I'm very, very tired." Then, shaking his head and smiling slightly he said, "Boy, how naive I've been all my life!"

"Haven't we all?" Ann said.

"I guess. This may be a good time for me to leave. I never asked to get mixed up in all this anyway."

At that moment the restaurant's maitre d' came to the table. "You have a phone call, Mr. Hopkins."

Darren went to the house phone and picked up the receiver.

"Mr. Hopkins, my name is Larry Heacock. I worked for President Evans before he became President. He's asked me to join his White House staff a few weeks ago. I need to talk with you over a more secure line. Could you go to the Embassy in the next hour or so and give me a call?

"Ann Jones will be with me. She's with Army intelligence stationed in Bangkok."

As Darren and Ann stepped out of the taxi at the U.S. Embassy's gate, two U.S. Marines escorted them directly to the communications center. The room had no windows and only one heavily reinforced steel door. Air conditioners and dehumidifiers kept the room cool and dry.

The ranking Marine showed Darren and Ann to a large desk that jutted out into the room across from the entrance. Darren helped pull up two chairs as the lone Indonesian technician manning the facility seemed preoccupied with several computer screens and four printers pouring forth text and pictures. The technician finished his task and walked over to Darren and Ann.

"We're to call a Larry Heacock at this number," Darren said, as he handed the number to the young man. He motioned to the phone on the desk in front of Darren and Ann, then turned and walked to the far end of the room.

"Boy, he's a talkative sort!" Darren whispered to Ann.

The phone rang, the young man turned and nodded. Darren picked up the phone.

"Thanks for calling me back and sorry to put you through that travel across town," Heacock said.

"What's this all about?" Darren leaned back in the old wooden recliner chair.

"First, the President wanted you to know how much he appreciated all you've done in the Boorgers case."

"Thanks, but I didn't do anything. Mary Knight, Ann Jones and the Indonesian soldiers did all the planning and took all the risks. I just watched. You know the guy died before we could get him to the hospital, don't you?"

"Yes, we have a copy of Knight's report. Most unfortunate."

"That's certainly true," Darren said. He heard a slight chuckle from Heacock, then continued by asking, "Larry, would you call Mo Childs who's with the American-Statesman in Austin, Texas? Tell him we talked and that you would like him to run the White House press release on Boorger's death. He'll run the story without embarrassing us."

"I'll be glad to call him, but he needs to cite you as his source so we don't get in trouble with the Press Corps here."

"He'll be happy to accommodate, just tell him what to do. I promised him, so please give him the story."

"Consider it done. Now, I've got a second item of business. Agent Carlson told me to tell you that they caught Arlo White in Guatemala."

"That's great!" Darren exclaimed Darren as he smiled broadly. He covered the phone with his left hand and whispered, "They got Arlo White!" Ann smiled, then leaned back in her chair.

Heacock continued. "Yeah. He gave up without a whimper. They found him staying at a small hotel in Panajachel, Guatemala, a small village on the north shore of Lake Atitlan, just sitting on a wharf fishing. Two Guatemalan intelligence officers and our man walked calmly over, introduced themselves and arrested him for treason against the United States. He looked at them, put his fishing pole down and said, 'Okay. Let's go.' End of story."

"That's great. I wish Boorgers would have been so agreeable," Darren said.

"You never know, I guess."

"Thanks for letting me know."

"Well, now for the bad news. Since you've been gone all hell's broken loose back here. We've arrested Ms. Baker, the President's secretary."

"What?" Darren said, sitting straight in his chair and his eyes narrowing.

"Our investigation within the federal government uncovered a network of over two hundred secretaries and office clerks. Ms. Baker managed the network. Jo Clark may have been compromised, but we don't know yet. White House phone records show they talked almost daily."

"Aw, shit!" Darren said. "I guess nothing should surprise me anymore, but this certainly does," Darren said.

"While we sort this out, we need you to work with Ms. Cindy Carmona, who works for former Senator John Burton, in Room two fifteen, just below you. She'll move up to your suite when you return."

"But, Larry, I'm willing to wager that Jo Clark knew nothing about all that. If she gave any critical information away, she didn't do so consciously."

"We certainly hope so. Sorry about all this."

"No apologies needed. By the way, tell Ms. Carmona I'm going to take a few weeks off."

"I'll take care of everything. Let us know where you are at all times and how we can reach you."

"I'll call in each day. Am I to assume that I should report to you from now on?"

"That's correct for the time being. There's a lot of change going on around here."

"I can well imagine," Darren said. "Any other surprises?"

"Not really, but since so many White House staff have either been arrested, killed or let go, you're now the pivotal person at NSC."

"Good grief, the country really is in trouble now," Darren said. He could hear a chuckle on the line. "Unfortunately, if you're seeking counsel from me you'll be in deep trouble."

"That's not what I hear around here."

"Okay. Thanks for that and all the information." Darren turned to look into Ann's eyes.

"So the President's secretary is a super patriot mole?" Ann asked.

"Yeah. But Jo Clark . . . General Burcks' death . . . my own assault in the parking garage . . . and what must be thousands of deaths due to leaked information to the patriot's . . .

The phone rang at 6:00 a.m. Darren had just finished showering.

"Darren, this is Carlson. Hope I didn't wake you."

"Unfortunately, you didn't. Where are you?" He watched as Ann headed toward the bathroom.

"I'm still at the office, but before I left I thought I would call and see if the President's new chief aide called you last night."

"Yeah, he did. Told me about the President's secretary and the rest of the group."

"Tragic, isn't it? It seems she was deeply committed to a fundamentalist church. And those churches had developed a network of congregations that financially and politically supported this whole super patriotic movement."

"We were just discussing these people. Lenora, I know Jo Clark would never participate in any such plot."

"I hope not, but you must know that our investigation knows no boundaries. We look at everyone. Quite honestly, I didn't know the extent of the inquiry myself."

"I talked with Jo after Heacock called, and she's devastated."

"I can imagine," Lenora said. "What do you think?"

"I believe her. I would be happy to endorse her innocence."

"Good, because the agent in charge of the investigation wants to talk to you when you return."

Ann came out of the bathroom in a pastel blue dress with splashes of aqua and purple flowers. Darren stood transfixed.

"Wow, you look stunning!"

DENPASAR, ISLAND OF BALI
Friday, May 9

Darren and Ann had finished breakfast on the terrace of their beachfront cabana at the Sheraton Nusa Indah Hotel. They had an unfettered view across the expansive South Pacific.

"There doesn't seem to be as many tourists as usual," Ann said.

"The Aussie economy is at a low ebb," Darren said.

"Yeah, this is their winter and they usually take over the South Pacific Islands during these months." They sipped their coffee in silence as they listened to the blue waves washing over the white sandy beach in front of their cabana.

"I don't think I've spent a more restful period in years," Darren said

"We've both slept most of the time."

Darren smiled at Ann. "And, it's just dawned on me that we've been able to put the violence out of our minds for a while." They watched as several sand crabs brazenly entered their terrace scavenging for food.

"What'll we do today, besides sleep and read?" Ann asked.

"How about another drive around the island?"

At that moment a hotel employee came charging around the corner.

"Oh, God," Darren said, "What now?"

"We think you have phone problem. May I check, please?"

"No problem. I disconnected the phone on purpose."

"Sorry. Some calls come, but cannot reach you. Please see our manager as soon as possible."

Darren returned with a hand full papers in his hand. "What's all that?" she asked.

"Messages. All of them frantic."

"From?"

"You name it. Mo, Larry Heacock, Lenora Carlson, my new secretary, Mary Knight at the Embassy in Jakarta."

"Call Mary Knight," Ann said.

"Darren, there's more trouble in the U.S.," Knight said, "and Ann Jones is wanted back in Bangkok. Larry Heacock called us from the White House and asked that you return immediately."

"What's happened?"

"More killings. Initial reports out of Washington indicate that a light private plane loaded with explosives crashed into Disneyland in California. Then, thirty minutes later two hit the Sears building in Chicago. But these were acts of Islamic terrorists, not our own kind souls."

"When did all this happen?" Darren asked.

"About two hours ago and we don't know if there's more to come. The White House is asking everyone to report to work."

"We'll pack it up. Thanks for the info Mary." Darren slowly put the phone down and turned to Ann. "Unfortunately, the Islamic terrorists have stepped into the void."

"Let's get the hell out of here before local Muslim radicals get the word and start killing westerners!" Ann said.

Darren walked out onto the patio and stared blankly at the sea. It didn't look as beautiful as it did a few minutes ago. After a few moments of silence, he said, "I think I'll go back to Bangkok with you and connect with Washington from there. I can sort out options better there."

"That's probably wise," Ann said. It's important to know what you're going to go home to. And I've got to get my marching orders. And we've got to remember that Knight's info may not have been entirely accurate."

"Yes," I certainly hope that's true." After a few moments Darren added,

"If we get our nation back together I think we ought to amend the constitution to the effect that no males can hold public office. Only females."

"Why?" asked Ann.

"Too damn much testosterone loose in the world."

Darren reached out for Ann. She laid her head on his shoulder as he pulled her to him. "Ann, I love you." He felt her body gently shake as she quietly sobbed.

After a few moments she lifted her head and Darren gently wiped the tears from her cheeks. "And I love you, Darren." She paused. "It's going to be hard to sustain a love relationship in the midst of all this mess."

"Yeah, I know, but I'm willing to try if you are."

"Let's go see how we can serve our country."

www.ingramcontent.com/pod-product-compliance
Lightning Source LLC
Chambersburg PA
CBHW030825310726
48980CB00006B/637/J

* 9 7 8 0 8 6 5 3 4 4 6 4 8 *